Acclaim for the  of REX

"Rex Stout is one of the half-dozen major figures in the development of the American detective novel."
  —*Ross Macdonald*

"Splendid."
  —*Agatha Christie*

"[Stout] raised detective fiction to the level of art. He gave us genius of at least two kinds, and a strong realist voice that was shot through with hope."
  —*Walter Mosley*

"Those of us who reread Rex Stout do it for…pure joy."
  —*Lawrence Block*

"The story has everything that a good detective story should have—mystery, suspense, action—and…the author's racy narrative style makes it a pleasure to read."
  —*New York Times*

"One of the most prolific and successful American writers of the 20th century…The writing crackles."
  —*Washington Post*

"Practically everything the seasoned addict demands in the way of characters and action."
  —*The New Yorker*

"One of the master creations."
  —*James M. Cain*

At the sound of the door closing behind Martha she suddenly turned over and sat up. The dizziness was all gone. It was all quite clear; it would be the simplest thing in the world. Her father's loaded revolver was of course in the drawer of the desk in his bedroom, where it had been kept as long as she could remember; as a child she had often opened the drawer a crack and shudderingly peeked at it, not daring to touch it. To get it now, unseen, would be easy, with Martha and her mother both downstairs. Then under her pillow. In the evening he would come to her room as usual, right after dinner. Maybe he wouldn't. Tomorrow evening then, or the next, or the next; he would come; she could wait. The revolver held six bullets, and all it needed was to pull the trigger. She would wait till he was quite close, the closer the better, even so she could touch him with it...

SEED on the WIND

by **Rex Stout**

A HARD CASE CRIME NOVEL

A HARD CASE CRIME BOOK
(HCC-161)
First Hard Case Crime edition: November 2023

Published by

Titan Books
A division of Titan Publishing Group Ltd
144 Southwark Street
London SE1 0UP

in collaboration with Winterfall LLC

Print edition ISBN 978-1-80336-484-1
E-book ISBN 978-1-80336-485-8

Design direction by Max Phillips
www.signalfoundry.com

Typeset by Swordsmith Productions

The name "Hard Case Crime" and the Hard Case Crime logo
are trademarks of Winterfall LLC. Hard Case Crime books
are selected and edited by Charles Ardai.

Printed in the United States of America

Visit us on the web at www.HardCaseCrime.com

SEED ON THE WIND

1

What startled her was the sight of the green coupé turning into the driveway. Through the window she watched it lurch, down and up, across the ditch at the edge of the sidewalk, then roll smoothly along the gravel, past the forsythia and peonies, to the bare rectangle splotched with oil in front of the little garage at the rear of the house. She frowned; this was Thursday, wasn't it? Was the man crazy? Manhattan must have exploded into fragments; or—she smiled to herself—was this a wild leap in pursuit of the extension of privileges? She stepped forward to get a better view through the dining-room window, and her amber-grey eyes filled with astonishment as she saw not one man, but two, descend from the coupé. Lewis Kane precisely and efficiently issued from the door on the left, from the driver's side, while from the other tumbled out a hatless man with a bony white face and a tangled mass of brown hair. Lora's head shot forward and her neck stretched out for a swift incredulous glance, then instantly she turned and made for the front hall and the door at the other side into the living room.

The three children in the room looked up indifferently as she entered; two small boys, five and seven, from a mountain of apparatus in the far corner, and a girl, a little older but scarcely larger, from the book under her chin as she lay on a long yellow cushion directly before the window. Their involuntary glances were indifferent, through ease of habituation and the absence of any petty chronic filial fear; but something in their mother's face and her pose, as she stopped in the middle of the room, held their gaze and quickened it; the elder boy got to his feet and the girl turned over and half raised herself.

Lora looked at the girl. "Where's Roy?"

"He went upstairs to get—"

"All right. Quick! Listen."

She spoke swiftly, three or four brief sentences, and the girl's intelligent black eyes answered them as they were spoken. As she ended, "You understand?" Lora had already moved across to the other door, leading to the smaller room in the rear where books and toys were kept, and disappeared through it and closed it behind her before the girl's nod was finished.

They would come in at the back, through the kitchen, she reflected; Lewis always did; doubtless it was more convenient, with the car parked in the yard, but his face would say plainly, as he entered the dining room through the swinging door, another triumph of prudence. At that rate he must average something like a dozen triumphs a day. But that could wait, time enough for that; it was not with amusement or resentment at Lewis's psychological costume that she was quivering and standing, drawn tight, close to the door she had shut behind her. That the other man should appear at all was impossible; that after twelve years he should suddenly and unexpectedly emerge from Lewis Kane's coupé was simply silly. He had been killed in the war; if not that, he had dissolved into some remote and alien atmosphere; at the very least, he had died lingeringly in a distant jungle. But there he was! What about Panther, who had not been trained to lie, except to people she knew? Would this gaunt ghost disconcert her? Poor child, her task would be complicated by the fact that Lewis would inevitably stop in the kitchen to ask Lillian, "Is your mistress in?" An hour earlier Lillian would have been upstairs....

She heard a low murmur of voices, then footsteps, then from the other side of the door Lewis's unnaturally loud greeting to the children; even in her suspended expectation of another voice she permitted herself her accustomed smile at his careful loyalty to the theory that children like you in proportion to the amount of noise you make. The other voice was not heard. "How's *my* boy?" came Lewis's booming tones, with the usual unconscious emphasis on the pronoun, and then the sound of Julian's little feet shuffling dutifully toward the paternal kiss. Then, "Where's your mother?"

She strained her ears to catch Panther's reply, but the door was too thick for those low quiet tones. The tone, though, was enough; she smiled at herself for having doubted.

An exclamation from Lewis; then, with a degree of concern remarkable for him, "When will she be back?"

An uneasy thought struck her: what if he decided to telephone; the instrument was in the room where she was standing, on the table not ten feet away. But no, he wouldn't want the children to hear, nor would he send them off; and suddenly she was grateful to a standard which to her meant nothing, a standard which would also keep him from confronting Panther with a contradiction from the maid. She felt secure as to that, though the tone of Lewis's questions, punctuated by the quiet murmur of Panther's voice, sounded more and more irritated and harassed; indeed he almost shouted; at length she heard, "Well, I've got to see her tonight. Do you know Mrs. Seaver's address? Out on Long Island, isn't it? Funny she didn't take the car."

Still the voice of the other man was not heard; perhaps he had remained outside? No, there had plainly been his footsteps. She needed to hear his voice, to make sure, as if the sight of that wild white face and that loose careless body was not enough! After all…the shock of that first glance had made her stupid. Why should she dodge? It was like her to make up her mind and act on it like a flash, only this time her mind had been made up wrong. Her shoulders straightened and her fingers touched the knob of the door—bah, ask him what he wants, maybe he forgot his suspenders—oh, only time is vulgar—but for Panther's sake the knob did not turn. A moment later Lewis's goodbyes were heard, and then his retreating steps, accompanied as before; the kitchen door opened and closed, after an interval—poor Lillian!—and the sound of the starting and roaring engine came through the window at the rear.

By the watch on her wrist it was ten minutes she waited before opening the door. She passed through. The boys were kneeling in their corner, fastening bits of iron together, not speaking; the girl sat cross-legged, looking straight at the door, her book face-down on the cushion at her side.

"They went right off," said Panther.

Lora nodded, moving across the room toward the hall door.

"I thought I could hear you breathing," the girl added.

"That man has legs like a wolf," exclaimed Morris from the corner, scrambling to his feet.

"He's my papa," said little Julian gravely.

"Gee, I don't mean your papa. Your papa's ears stick out."

"Say Lewis," came from Panther.

Morris grinned. "Aw, well…Lewis's ears stick out."

Lora, in the hall, was calling upstairs, "Roy! Oh, Roy!"

After a moment a door opened and closed, deliberately, somewhere above, there were footsteps, and at the head of the stairs appeared a boy, eleven or twelve, with a strong dark face, deep dark eyes, and bushy dark hair. He stood at the top, looking down.

"Yes, Mother?"

"Come down here a minute."

As they entered the living room Morris was sing-songing, apparently to the mounted globe beside the table:

"Mister Kane, that's his name, Mister Kane, that's his name.

Julian has to say Papa and I have to say Lewis. His ears stick out right out of his head." But he stopped as his mother began to speak to Roy, and stood staring at them with an impertinent speculative gaze.

"If the telephone rings you answer it," said Lora. "No matter who it is, I'm not here, I'm at Mrs. Seaver's on Long Island to spend the night and you don't know when I'll be back. No matter if they've telephoned Anne, no matter what they say, that's all you know."

Without replying, the boy kept his dark eyes on her face, taking in her words, then suddenly he said, "What if it's Mrs. Seaver?"

"Say Anne," Panther corrected.

"Mister Kane, that's his name," came softly from Morris.

"It won't be," said Lora.

"It might be," he insisted.

"All right, if it is I'll talk to her. There was a man I don't want to see...Panther will tell you...I must ask Lillian...."

In the kitchen, Lillian, distressed, was also indignant. It was bad enough for Mr. Kane himself to come bursting in through the back door without hauling a stranger in too. And to have been thus finally trapped by him! "Is your mistress in?" She should at least be permitted time to go and make the inquiry and return with an answer, decently and properly, but no, barely pausing on his way to the dining room he would direct the swift question at her with a darting immediacy that brought a "Yes, sir" popping out of her like a cork out of a bottle. Lora had heard all this before; what she wanted to know now was what Mr. Kane had said on his way out. Nothing much, the maid reported; merely that when her mistress returned or telephoned she should be told that Mr. Kane wished to see her without delay.

"I'm sorry I didn't know, ma'am," said Lillian.

"It doesn't matter," said Lora. She started out, but turned at the door. "That other man, if he comes back tomorrow, either alone, or with Mr. Kane, I'll see him," she added.

On her way to the stairs she paused in the dining room to draw the curtains and turn on the light. Outside was the early October dusk, and the brass knob at the end of the curtain-cord was warm from the steam radiator against which it hung. Her hands felt chilly and she closed one of them tightly around the warm knob and then released it again and turned to go. She loathed disquiet, particularly a suspended unreasonable disquiet such as now, unprecedented, filled her breast. With irritation she told herself that she had acted stupidly, but at the same time something within her was saying, oh, no you haven't, no indeed, you know what you're doing all right. Ridiculous. She would lie down; no, but she would go to her room and be alone, until dinner. After all, everyone has memories, god help them; given occasion to consider, she would have known that an unexpected sight of Pete Halliday would inevitably arouse an echo of the pain of that old disaster. Damn this silly uneasiness! She should have seen him and let him speak to her....

As she started up the stairs she heard little Julian's thin voice from the living room, trying to speak slowly so as to get all the words in: "If you say my papa's ears stick out your nose will fall off and I'll walk on it with my iron shoes."

In her room she sat in the chair by the window, with no light turned on, her back straight and her head upright, her hands folded in her lap.

II

Lewis Kane meant money to her. She sometimes idly wondered, without anxiety, what her life would have been like the past six years but for him. She couldn't have gone on forever selling the jewelry Max Kadish had given her. That was funny about the life insurance; someone had diddled her, no doubt of that, probably Max's mother and her lawyer. There was a curious thought for you: Max had meant money to her too, but how differently from Lewis! The money Max gave her wasn't money, it was merely a handy tool, like the needle and thread she used to sew on his buttons. Whereas with Lewis—ha, that was different, Lewis was the tool himself, poor dear.

Pete Halliday had had no money. Long before. She had worked day after day, nine long hours a day. Nothing disastrous about that, nor even about his leaving; but shift the scene a bit, to another bed, another man, another day....

Her thought shied off, darted like a frightened humming-bird around the years, and searching for ease settled again on Lewis Kane.

Her first knowledge of him was lost somewhere in the distant past; she had seen him a dozen times, here and there, of no account, before that day six years ago when a telephone call had unexpectedly come from him to the flat on Seventy-first Street. He had given his name, so clearly and precisely that she understood it the first time, unexpected as it was, and without preamble had asked her to dine with him.

"No, I can't do that."

"You mean you don't care to."

"No, really I can't. I never go out to dinner. I have three children to put to bed."

"But surely there is a maid...."

"Can't afford one. I never leave them alone except to go to the pawnshop."

To either the pathos or the humor there might be in that he gave no pause. He said at once:

"I could find a woman somewhere, a trustworthy woman...."

"No, really I'd rather not."

A week later he phoned again. In the meantime she had remembered things about him, his calm sensible face, his wealth, his air of assured propriety, and she had given some thought to the probabilities and her present situation. She was not bored, she was far from unhappy, but something was stirring within her. The practical difficulty with which she had put him off did not as a matter of fact exist; she had friends, especially she had Leah, Max's sister. Indeed, she had too much of Leah, who was orthodox, very short and fat, and talked constantly and disconsolately of her dead brother.

Yes, something was stirring within her. Unhappy or not, she wanted something she didn't have; that was as definite as she could make it. In Central Park of an afternoon, with Helen (not yet Panther) and the infant Morris both asleep in the carriage, and Roy dodging in and out among the moving trees that were pedestrians' legs, she would wonder idly which of the passersby were free, entirely free, of the unrest of desire. It would be simple enough, she told herself, if you knew exactly what it was. Say she wanted a new dress, or a home in the country, or a husband. How simple! How simple, probably, no matter what it was. She could think of no object that appeared to be beyond the scope of her powers, nor could she think of any that seemed to be worth their exertion. Did she want—she shifted about on the park bench, she looked in her purse to see if her keys were there, she called Roy to her and straightened his cap and pulled up his stockings—but at length, ignoring the interruptions, the thought completed itself: did she want another baby? Involuntarily she pressed her legs together, tight, and closed her eyes; then opened them again, and watched her hand carefully smoothing out the folds of her soft dark red skirt. Suddenly she smiled. Hardly. Hardly! Three were enough. Indeed, with those three she would soon be wanting something much more modest than a country home, unless something happened. A husband, perhaps. That was not as unthinkable as you might expect, but she would rather not. The perfect husband. Not any.

No. No more babies, thank you.

When Leah came, as usual, in the late afternoon of the day after the second phone call, and Lora asked her if she would stay with the children the following evening, she did not look up, and remained silent, bending over Morris's crib with her back turned. There must have been something in the tone of the question that startled her. Finally, still without turning, she said with quiet fury:

"You're going to do it again."

Lora, setting the table for two, paused with the knives and forks in her hand.

"Do it?"

"Yes, you are."

"I don't know what you mean."

"Yes you do. Tomorrow night you're not going to any movies with your friends. I won't come. I won't ever come again, and God will punish you."

"I never said I was," Lora protested. "I'm going to eat dinner properly with a middle-aged man."

"God will punish you. I told Maxie a hundred times there was a devil in your womb. I told him a hundred times."

Still she did not turn, and Lora, crossing over and standing behind her, leaned down and put her hands on the other's fat shoulders and patted them gently. "I know," she said. "Max told me; he shouldn't have made fun of you. I don't mind—perhaps I can get Anne to come."

At this Leah straightened up, glared at her, and shouted, "If you ask that woman to tend Maxie's baby I will never come here once more!"

"Well…if you won't…"

"Don't be a fool," said Leah, and bent over the crib again.

The first dinner with Lewis Kane was dull, undistinguished, and interminable. It also appeared to be purposeless. Tall, correct, smoothly strong, a little short of fifty, with a firm discreet mouth and steady grey eyes, he sat and ordered an excellent dinner and with obvious difficulty hunted for something to talk about. Lora, amused, refused to help him. He didn't matter anyway; she was being admirably warmed by her own fire. There was the mirror on the restaurant wall not ten feet away; and the green dress, though nearly a year old—Max had given it to her soon after Morris was born—was more becoming than ever. Any observer, on a guess, would have subtracted at least three or four years from her twenty-eight, and wouldn't have guessed the children at all. The mirror showed the fine brown hair, almost red, red in the glancing light, the smooth white skin stretched delicately tight and sure over the cheek's faint curve and the chin's rounded promontory, and even the amber threads and dots in the brightness of the large grey eyes. The mirror showed this to her; as for Lewis, he had long ago said correctly, "You are more charming than ever," and then, to outward appearance, had forgotten all about it. It puzzled her. What did he want? There was no gleam in his eyes, no invitation in his words; he sat and demolished a supreme of guinea hen calmly, leaving a clean bone and no fragments. The observer, invited to guess again, might have hazarded a lawyer with a not too important client or an uncle with a familiar niece, all talked out. After the dessert there were a couple of cigarettes, then an uneventful ride, soft and warm among the cushions of his big town car, back to Seventy-first Street, where he left her at the door.

The puzzle continued for weeks. His invitations became more frequent, always to the same little restaurant not far from Madison Square, and the dinners remained innocuous, never a theatre afterward, always the pleasant digestive ride uptown and the parting at the door. Once or twice he arranged to come early and they drove through the park or along the river for an hour or so with the windows open to the March breezes, he with the collar of his black overcoat buttoned tightly around his scarf, she with her throat open to the swift chill gusts. "He means something deep," she thought, "or he'd take me to a show or something. Probably he's going to offer me a job in his office as a filing-clerk; it's just his thoroughness. Anyway, the dinners are good and Leah loves being left alone with the children."

He talked correctly and unexcitingly of books, of dogs (Doberman pinschers particularly), of the superiority of Turkish cigarettes, of corruption in politics, of food and music and pictures and English tailors; never of himself or of her. But one evening late in April, as soon as they were seated at their usual corner table and the order had been given, he said suddenly, without warning, without any change of expression:

"You know I'm married."

Ha, she thought, this is the big moment, he is going to ask me to go to the flea circus. She nodded, laid her gloves on the table, folded her hands under her chin, and watched his face.

"I was married in nineteen-three, twenty years ago," he went on. "I was twenty-seven, she was a year younger. We have two children: George, sixteen, and Julia, fourteen. They are charming. Two years ago I discovered that I am not their father. Their father is a baritone who sings in a church, and I believe he now also has engagements on the radio."

He stopped to lean back from the waiter's arm with the soup, arranged the dish precisely in front of himself, with its edge exactly even with the edge of the table, and picked up his spoon. Lora, saying nothing, poised her own spoon ready for the plunge.

"You probably think I am leading up to a complaint against my wife," he resumed. "Not at all. Macaulay was wrong when he assailed the common judgment that Charles was an excellent man though an execrable king. Mrs. Kane is an excellent woman, an excellent wife, an excellent mother, but an execrable moralist. She thinks well of her generosity in permitting me to believe that I am the father of two charming and intelligent children."

He took another spoonful of soup and broke off a piece of bread; Lora, for punctuation, observed:

"She doesn't know that you know."

"No."

"Maybe you don't."

"Oh, yes, perfectly. I have the most exact proof; if I had not been blind I should have known long ago. Next month it will be two years since I found out."

"Well," said Lora, "maybe it isn't so bad. And maybe your proof isn't as perfect as you think it is. It's a rather hard thing to prove sometimes, there's only one way really, and since she thinks you have no suspicion...."

That was putting it delicately, she thought; Pete would probably have said, you never know what you're getting when you eat hash. But Lewis Kane wasn't listening; he looked at her in silence a moment and then said:

"I want to be a father, Miss Winter."

In order not to laugh she bent her head and took a spoon of soup. Ingenuous, direct, the words pleading but all the heart's yearning crushed precisely to the last drop out of the dull even tone, he went on, "I want to have a son. My wife's daughter, Julia, was named after my mother. I want to have a son and name him Julian."

"Well...that should be possible."

"Yes. You've been very patient with me, Miss Winter. No doubt you've been dreadfully bored these past two months; I couldn't help it; I had to make sure you were the sort of person I could trust. You have behaved admirably."

"I? I've eaten your excellent dinners."

He waved that aside. "I have found nothing that is not extremely creditable. Your conduct since Kadish's death—I knew him, you know—your general manner of living, your care of your children—by the way, what about Albert Scher? Do you see Scher often?"

This is delightful, thought Lora. What a man! What an incredible man! There was no telling; it might easily prove in the end that all he wanted was a wet nurse or a midwife. She was silent while the waiter removed the soup plates and replaced them with others, but Lewis Kane, not waiting, went on with a faint note of something like apology:

"I've missed out on Scher. My reports are very vague about him."

She suddenly remembered something, and looked at him aghast.

"That man in the brown suit who keeps walking up and down in the park!"

"Perhaps. Does he always wear a brown suit?"

"Great heavens!" said Lora, and began to laugh.

"When I want to find out anything," said Lewis Kane, "I take the most direct and efficient means at hand. I'm glad you aren't annoyed."

"Oh, I'm flattered! Terribly flattered! It would have been so amusing to know he was a detective.—But he seems to have fallen down on Albert. That wasn't very efficient, was it?"

He frowned and regarded her silently. "Bah, Scher doesn't matter," he said finally. "It is apparent, I think, that you are no longer interested in him. But one evening in February, the eleventh, I believe, he went to your apartment and remained till after midnight. I wonder—I would appreciate it if you would tell me what he was there for. Obviously I am not suspicious, or I wouldn't ask you."

Lora, almost annoyed, decided to go on with it. "I really am glad you're not suspicious, Mr. Kane," she said gravely; and then stopped suddenly at sight of something in the steady grey eyes that was incredibly like a gleam of humor—a swift infinitesimal flash, not believable, like a single distant firefly in a grey evening dusk.

"You think I'm making a fool of myself," he said. "Not at all. I've arrived at a very important decision. I'm attempting to provide every possible safeguard. I'm perfectly satisfied on every point but one. I must ask you again, what is the purpose of Albert Scher's visits to your apartment?"

She smiled. "Really it's none of your business, is it?"

"Yes. I think so."

"Really—"

"Yes. I think it is. Of course, Miss Winter, you are far too intelligent not to know what I'm driving at. Perhaps I'm not going about it properly; with women I have always been— somewhat—at a loss. Certainly it is obvious that what I wish to propose is that you should be the mother of my son. Six months after I learned that I was not George's father—by the way, he was named after his real paternal grandfather, which was an unnecessary impertinence—I decided that I should have a son. It took me six months more, of careful consideration and elimination, to decide on you, tentatively at least. I was just about ready to consult you when Kadish died, an unexpected complication. In a way I wasn't sorry, since the delay made possible a more complete inquiry. I waited a year, a full year, surely all that any standard of decency might require."

That was that, apparently, for he picked up his knife and fork, parted a chop neatly from its bone, cut a triangular morsel from one corner, and conveyed it to his mouth; following it, after a moment, with bread and butter and two swallows of milk. Lora, fascinated, wondered how many days, weeks even, had passed since he had determined to have lamb chops for dinner on this particular Thursday evening. She decided she must say something.

"In the first place, Mr. Kane, I won't pretend to resent your insult to my womanhood."

"Yes. Of course. It isn't necessary." The second bite of chop went in.

"But to speak of nothing else, the practical difficulties—for instance, it would be hardly possible to guarantee a son—"

"I told you I am not making a fool of myself, Miss Winter."

"And do you really mean—would you really have made this proposal to me while Max was alive?"

"I am making it to you today, and Scher and Stephen Adams are alive."

She caught her breath. "That's rude, and malicious. What do you know of Stephen Adams? How do you even know he's alive? I don't.—Besides, it's illogical."

"It is," he admitted. "The analogy is imperfect. But it was plausible to suppose that Kadish's fate would resemble that of his predecessors. I was willing to wait."

"I see. Six months to decide on a son, six more to pick out a mother, and a year to investigate her. These last two months—these dinners—I suppose their purpose was to make me fall in love with you? You were making love to me?"

"Good heavens, no!" His fork wavered in the air, was replaced on the table, then composedly he picked it up again, and resumed, "I selected you for a dozen reasons. You are healthy, and your children are healthy. Your education is sufficient. Your tastes are sound and not extravagant. You are young and handsome. There is no sentimental nonsense in your head. You have lived with three men, been faithful to each, and devoted to none. You never go to church. As for the past two months, there are certain personal inclinations that are discoverable only by intimate and frequent observation. Table manners. Cleanliness. Nervous habits—little nervous habits that escape the ordinary observer. If I thought I could make you love me I might try, though for my present purpose it would probably be inadvisable. My wife has told the father of her children—the letters have been destroyed, but I preserve them in code—that if I were left alone in the world with a million women the race would perish. She is a wit. You must understand one thing, the arrangement between us will be one of complete mutual trust. I do my investigating before, not after. I shall not annoy you. Your income, an adequate one, will begin at once. The details are here."

Lora, overwhelmed, took the blue folded paper which he drew from his pocket and handed to her; it consisted of four closely typewritten sheets; opening it at random, she saw near the middle of the third page:

17. In the event of an irreconcilable disagreement between A and B regarding education after the tenth year, the person named in paragraph 9 shall be consulted and his decision accepted as final.

She refolded the paper and handed it back to him. Of course, a joke. No, actually, it wasn't. She felt she must laugh, but she knew it was impossible. Poor man. She could laugh later. Somewhere behind the elaborate ridiculous façade, beneath the thick crust of efficient calculations and crisp phrases, even between the lines of the preposterous typewritten sheets, his harassed soul was squealing and trying to wriggle out of its trap. She could laugh later.

"So you haven't been making love to me," she said.

"No."

"Of course I'm flattered by your list of my virtues. But a little skeptical. It's too much to expect, even of myself. And I would die of anxiety for fear it might be a girl."

"Even there your record is good. Two to one"

"True," she smiled. "But no. I won't crowd my luck."

"There's no hurry. Here." He placed the paper back on the table beside her plate. "Take that home and read it. Take all the time you want. My mind's set on this, but there's no hurry. Let's talk of something else. Did you see those pictures I spoke of—the moderns at Knoedler's? If you like the one next to the end on the right as you go in, the red and blue things on a raft or something in the ocean, you can have it."

He turned and called to the waiter, who hurried over.

"Take these away and bring the salad."

III

Leah, her bulging form tightly encased in a shiny pink silk dress, the integrity of its seams a desperate tribute to the stubborn heroism of thread, sat in a straight-backed chair by the dining-room window looking vaguely down into the summer lethargy of Seventy-first Street. Suddenly, for the twentieth time within an hour, imagining she heard a noise from the next room, she went to the door and softly opened it, fastened her black Asiatic eyes on Morris sound asleep in his crib, closed the door again and returned to her chair. She was furiously angry. On Sunday afternoons she was permitted—*"permitted,* my God" —to take the baby, alone, into the park. Outside was July sunshine and a pleasant breeze, not at all hot; and merely because that fool of a doctor didn't like the baby's breathing here she was, helpless, sitting in a chair listening to that stupid man with yellow hair talking to that little baby girl—well—he was a bigger fool than the doctor. There was nothing wrong with Morris anyway; tomorrow she would come back and take him out into the sun, and let them try to stop her!

"Here's another one with a donkey," the man with yellow hair was saying. "Look, Helen. See the way his tail hangs down. See the lines of the branches on the cypress trees, they hang down the same way. That's pretty nice. Don't you think that's a nice one?"

He was seated across the room near the large table, with Helen on his knee and a portfolio of lithographs propped up so she could see. Five-year-old Roy, silent and looking a little bored, stood at his other side.

"What do the words say?" demanded the girl.

The man frowned. "There aren't any. Look, can't you see? There aren't any words. Pictures are one thing, and words are another thing; I've told you that a hundred times. I suppose you'd better say it yourself, repeat it....No, that won't do, that won't do, don't say it. You must feel it. You *must* feel it. See, here are these lovely trees and this lovely donkey, all these lovely lines—what do you want with words?"

The little girl's face, with its features, soft and delicate as they were, yet bearing an unmistakable resemblance to his own, was tilted mischievously upwards, full upon him. She liked this familiar game they were playing. She glanced across the room to where Leah sat silently fuming, then placed her finger on her lips and said softly, "She shows me nice pictures in the paper with words all over."

"Damn!" exploded the man, half turning, so that the portfolio nearly tumbled to the floor.

There came a laugh from the other side of the table, from Lora, who was passing through on her way from the kitchen to her bedroom.

"Still at it?" Lora observed. "You know perfectly well it's no use, Albert. You can't train a child in two hours a month. Anyway, she thinks you're playing a game."

"It would work if you'd help me instead of laughing," he grunted. "By god, it's got to work."

No use arguing, thought Lora, as she proceeded to the bedroom.

"By god by god," put in Roy, helpfully.

"Oh, be quiet!" the man exclaimed. "Here, hold this end. Look, Helen, look here, see the panther? With the grass all around him? These pictures were made by a man in Africa—wait, get your geography, Roy—no, no matter, no matter—see the panther, Helen? Isn't he lovely? Wouldn't you like to be a panther and lie in the grass? That would be a good name for you—Panther. I'm sick of Helen anyway. I think we'll have to call you Panther. Lora!" He raised his voice to carry to the bedroom. "Lora, we're going to call Helen Panther! What do you think of that?"

He felt a hard grasp on his arm and turned to find Leah there, her black eyes flashing menace. "It don't matter you think if you wake up a sick baby," she spat. "You should care if Maxie's baby dies."

"Oh, I forgot. I'm sorry. Really." He turned another page of the portfolio.

Roy was making faces at Helen and repeating over and over, "Panther, Panther, Panther...."

Leah shrugged her shoulders, tiptoed across, and silently opened the door into the room where Morris lay.

Lora, in her own room with the door shut, was lying on the bed, on her back, her eyes closed. She was tired, not painfully tired, but she needed to rest, and to get away from the people out there. It was amazing how complete an annoyance Albert Scher could be—mild enough, nothing desperate, but completely an annoyance; and as for Leah—oh, well, it didn't matter. All that did matter was inside her, in her womb. She loved the word, though she never spoke it. Now she repeated it aloud to herself, "Womb, womb." Heavens, what a word! No man ever thought of it, a woman did that. Within her own was a warm comfortable feeling, full and pleasant. That's ridiculous, she thought, it's too soon to feel that way. I just imagine it. She placed the palm of her hand flat on her abdomen, but the dress was too thick to feel properly, so she unhooked it at the side and pulled up the underwear and got her hand against the warm bare skin and rubbed it, gently back and forth, up and down, from right to left and back again, then let it lie there, still. Ridiculous, she thought, I just imagine it.

Yes, she was tired; she had been going since early morning. Doctor Hardy had been a nuisance, fussing around; that baby was perfectly all right, he breathed like a top. A top doesn't breathe. All right, all right. If Leah loved him so much, why didn't she wash out his diapers once in a while? But that was unfair; Leah was really a big help. Only there was that to be done, and feeding the others, and getting her own breakfast and lunch—squeezing ten oranges and straining the juice took half an hour. She would have to stop nursing the baby, that was too bad; anyway, it would take more time to attend to his bottles, and heat the milk, and mix that stuff in it....Leah was so tragic about everything, could she be trusted to do it right?

Even with Leah coming in nearly every afternoon, and the colored girl for three hours each morning except Sunday, there was too much to do. She wanted time to read a little, to get her stockings and dresses fixed up, to get a manicure and a shampoo with Nouveautone....Why then did she not accept Lewis Kane's offer and let him furnish the money for a nurse and a full-time maid, the rent for a larger apartment, a car to go around in? She made a face at the ceiling. Damn his money. Damn everybody's money. Not that she had any neat conviction of superiority to it, or any harassed spirit of personal independence against a world of threatening and malevolent impingements; she was merely irritated at its elusiveness. Apparently, she thought, there was no hole deep enough to give it, buried, the peace of security; those who had it seemed to be compelled to hold on with finger-muscles strained even more frantically than those who were still grabbing for it. She had had to grab for it too, but never with any great degree of violence; she had been lucky. "I've been lucky all right," she said aloud to the ceiling.

Then suddenly she shivered and closed her eyes, and her hand, still inside her clothing next to the skin, was pressed tight and tighter against her firm round belly. "I've been lucky about money," she said.

Nevertheless Lewis's offer must be accepted, soon. Soon it would be a necessity. And why not? Was she not carrying his son? Daughter? No. He was determined it should be a son. What if there should be five daughters one after another? Ten. Twenty. A thousand; an endless sequence of daughters, all in a row, the most recent an infant at the breast, the earliest a towering giantess with her head bumping the moon. Or even if it were just a thousand, that would be nine thousand months, nearly a thousand years—more than seven hundred anyway.... Maybe some of the old Jewish women in the Bible actually did it....

She stirred, rolled over and sat up on the edge of the bed, and tossed back her head to get the reddish-brown hair out of her eyes. Then she lay down again, on her side with her cheek resting on her upturned palm.

Child of love. She smiled with good-humored contempt; that, she thought, was a masterpiece among the meaningless phrases men have devised regarding children born out of wedlock. Look at that, you had to use another one to tell what you were talking about!

The man who invented "child of love" should have seen Lewis Kane that night two months ago. Whether he had for some time maintained bachelor quarters separately from his home, or whether the apartment had been prepared especially for this occasion, she had not known. It had not looked new; the furniture, clean and comfortably worn, had a settled air not to be found in a transient atmosphere. Lent by a friend, perhaps, she had thought, though that didn't seem like Lewis.

They had driven straight there after a late dinner; Lewis, after sending the chauffeur off with the car, had carried her little bag to the elevator, and on the twelfth floor to the door at the far end of the wide hall. Inside, he had turned on the lights, hung his hat and stick in the foyer, carried her bag to the bedroom and placed it on a chair, and returning to the large sitting room had lit a cigarette for her and started one himself, though he usually preferred a cigar.

"There's no one about," he said. "I thought you would be more comfortable."

She nodded her thanks. "You're a much more thoughtful person than you pretend to be."

He waved it aside. "It's merely a matter of common sense."

"And sensitive. You're really quite sensitive."

"I don't know. I think not. At the present moment I am in a situation popularly supposed to be emotional. If I am sensitive why am I so calm about it? Not that you are not charming; very charming. Chiefly I am concerned about our purpose; it doesn't matter what I feel or don't feel so long as I don't flunk it when it comes to the point. I confess that I have been restless all day, for these things are beyond our control. In that respect you are fortunate; you have no responsibility. Doubtless you have noticed my uneasiness?"

"I—really—I—" She gave it up and threw back her head and laughed, a little louder and longer than need be, for she was on edge herself, not embarrassed exactly, but shaky a little, even a little indignant. She thought, he's really an ass, the only thing he has forgotten is a pamphlet on hygiene.

An hour later she was in the room in front, in bed, with the covers turned down expectantly on the other side. A lovely, disturbing sight: her hair, almost black in the dim light, in sharp contrast to the white skin and the flimsy white gown, brushed smooth and glistening, seemed to whisper an invitation to urgent ravishing fingers; her bare arm curved across the coverlet; her half-exposed breast, large with milk, was at once shameless and a denial of shame. She was looking up and sidewise at Lewis Kane, who stood beside the bed wearing tan silk pajamas with enormous purple stripes, the corner of a white handkerchief sticking out of the breast pocket. He was standing up straight, and she thought to herself that he looked big and powerful and quite determined. And rather silly. She wanted to laugh again, as she had laughed in the other room.

"Do you want a drink of water, Miss Winter?" he asked. "No? I drank two glasses; I always do. I suppose I'd better turn out the lights. Do you want them all out?"

She said yes, and watched him go to the wall and press the switch, and then heard him return, more slowly but without hesitation, through the darkness. He got into bed, pulled up the covers, and lay on his side facing her and began at once to talk.

"It sounds pretty awkward, that Miss Winter. I think I shall have to call you Lora. You might call me Lewis, I suppose. These things seem unimportant, but we live so much by words and formulas that I imagine their effect is considerable—like the recoil of a shotgun. By the way, my uneasiness is over, thank heaven. One of us is to be congratulated—gallantry would say you."

Lora, embarrassed at last, lay on her back without replying, her eyes closed. Why should she help him? It was he who wanted a son. If he thought he could get one by talking…. But suddenly she felt his hands firmly and surely grasping her shoulders, the pressure gradually increasing, and she let her eyelids open—the barest slit—and smiled.

She awoke because something heavy was on her chest and it

was hard to breathe. Struggling painfully out of sleep, she gasped for air and with an effort pushed out her upper ribs against the weight that restricted them. What could it be? There was pain too, a real pain…then as sleep left, memory came and she sat up in bed and cupped her hands under her breasts. They seemed to weigh a ton. The milk, of course. She hadn't intended to go to sleep at all. What time could it be? Lewis's deep breathing came regularly from the other pillow. She got to the floor, groped around in the dark for her clothing, dropped a stocking and found it again, and made her way down the hall to the sitting room and turned on the light. A clock ticking on the mantel said a quarter-past two. She yawned, rubbed her eyes, and smiled at the neat pile of Lewis's clothing at one end of the long narrow table.

Half an hour later she was seated in the dining room at home, with Leah, who obviously had not slept at all, standing and glaring at her, while the baby industriously tried to make up for lost time. Lora was smiling and thinking to herself, "Certainly he needn't have been so uneasy. It's all a fake, his not feeling anything. His wife gave him a scare, that's all." She never saw the apartment again. A week later, at dinner with Lewis, at the same inconspicuous little restaurant, he expressed his belief that another effort might not be necessary; and in another fortnight she was able to announce the probability that he was correct. "Splendid, splendid!" he exclaimed as he dished the broccoli. She wasn't surprised, she explained, she was that way, she needed no more than a hint. Lewis went on to say that he supposed she was up on all the modern technique, he felt that he could safely leave all that to her, but did she have a good doctor? No, she admitted, as a matter of fact she didn't, Doctor Hardy was competent but too fussy; whereupon he produced from his pocket a card containing a name and address

and telephone number, saying that he had made careful inquiries
and that no better was to be had.

It was on the afternoon that Albert Scher came to visit his
daughter and gave her another lesson in the esthetic necessity
of removing the art of line from all contact with literature, that
Lora first noticed a look of suspicion in Leah's sharp black eyes.
Of course Leah was always chronically suspicious, but this look
was specific and direct. Bah, Lora thought, Leah had from the
first been annoyed by Albert's visits, infrequent and exclusively
paternal though they were, and on this day the annoyance was
increased to the point of rage by the doctor's insistence that
Morris be kept in the house. Nevertheless, sooner or later
Leah would know, and there would be the devil to pay. A good
thing she wasn't Italian instead of Jewish; give that stuttering
passion of hers a few drops of blood from the toe of the boot
and the problem would be serious. But, thought Lora, that
could wait; there were other more pressing problems. Should
she begin taking money from Lewis? Bah, he wouldn't be the
first, why not? Was this the way women who were married felt
about it? But she was much too realistic to let herself be confused
by that quibble, she knew that had nothing to do with it; married
or unmarried, the question is at bottom purely personal, each
case unique. It was because Lewis was so damned direct, "For
one male baby," he said in substance, "delivered in good condition, complete, I'll pay a thousand weekly installments of two
hundred dollars each. Here's the contract; look me up in Brad-
street's." Like that he would buy a baby. Oh, no, he wouldn't;
not her baby, not the baby she already imagined she was beginning to feel. But there was the rub; he really was going to pay
adequately, more than adequately according to the current
market. What, in fact, would be a fair and reasonable price for
an A Number One baby, guaranteed pure and unadulterated?

One-tenth of one percent benzoate of— Oh, piffle! His money was no different from any other money; what's the use, why make so much fuss?

She got up and crossed to the dressing-table and sat there brushing her hair; from the next room she could hear Albert's rumbling bass, the leaves of the portfolio turning, and now and then an exclamation from Helen or Roy; no doubt Albert would say at a fresh discovery of the esthetic delight of the pure line.

The following day even Doctor Hardy admitted that Morris's breathing was above suspicion, and when Leah came in the afternoon she was allowed to bundle him into the carriage and take him to the park. Lora, leaning from a window, watched them safely across Central Park West; you could never tell when Leah's contempt for an alien civilization might explode into a calamitous disregard of the physical properties of a speeding taxicab.

The rest of July and most of August were hot. The sun blazed down from above, and New York's pavements took the heat, mixed it with a thousand odors, increased it by some secret process to the temperature of a blast furnace, and hurled it up into the gasping faces of its citizens. Lora stuck it out. It was far from pleasant, what with the irritability of the children, a two weeks' indisposition of Helen's, Leah's torrents of perspiration, and the morning nausea, but though Lewis suggested an Adirondack hilltop or a place at the seashore, Lora decided that it wasn't worth the vast complication of the journey. She took off her clothes and lay on the floor somnolent in the heat, or went to the park with Helen and Roy and sat gasping on the grass while they tumbled around oblivious to thermometers. At home the new Swedish maid, paid out of the proceeds of Lewis's first checks, was sweating over the vacuum cleaner or the washtub.

Lewis had not insisted on the seashore; he had suggested it, enumerated its advantages, and then quietly accepted her decision not to go. A few days later he had departed for Canada, headed for a little chateau in the Saguenay country where there was golf and trout-fishing, leaving behind him a card with the address typewritten on it and an invitation to wire him if any difficulty arose.

"Difficulty?" said Lora. "What difficulty could there be?"

"I don't know. I'm quite ignorant," he replied. "Don't bother to write."

So every few days she sent him a line or two to say that the union of chromosomes (this, long previously, from Albert) was proceeding without hindrance. There was no word from him, but each week an envelope came from his downtown office— Kane, Hildebrandt & Powers—containing a check neatly folded into a crisp blank letterhead. Surely less than impeccably discreet, she thought, but doubtless the intricate machinery of the legal factory of which he was the head somehow incorporated this weekly disbursement with an ambient indistinguishable vapor that would defy all analysis. The checks were generous and made many things possible. She bought Roy a velocipede and Helen a doll that walked three steps, and new clothing for all of them; she repaid Leah several hundred dollars which she had borrowed the preceding winter; she rescued from the pawnshop the necklace with platinum links and clasp which Max had given her the day after Morris was born; and one Sunday afternoon early in September she told Albert Scher, who was making his first paternal visit since July, that he need no longer bother about his monthly contribution to her household purse. Albert, seated on the floor trying to make Helen's new doll go without falling over, looked up at her and blinked.

"What's that, what's that?" he demanded. Then he whistled in surprise and scrambled to his feet. "Let's go into the bedroom," he said; and then to Helen, "You try to make it go." On his way past his foot clumsily knocked the doll on its head, but the child's cries of protest went unregarded.

After she had righted the doll and followed him into the bedroom he closed the door and turned to her: "What's up? What are you talking about?"

"What I said, that's all," she replied. "I won't need any more money. There's nothing mysterious about it."

"I'm not being mysterious. There's no occasion to discuss it in front of Panther."

"But we don't need to discuss it, and children know everything anyway. It doesn't matter, that's all there is to it."

He stared at her, and blinked again. "Has anything happened? I don't get it. Has Roy's father turned out to be a bootlegger?"

Lora laughed. "Albert darling, listen. I'll need no more of your hard-earned money. Isn't that enough?"

"By god, you're going to get married," he exclaimed.

"No."

"Of course it's none of my business—"

"No," she agreed.

"But you can't do this. I mean, Panther is my daughter and I have a right to furnish her support—as well as I can. By the way, why won't you call her Panther? Helen doesn't mean anything; there are a million girls named Helen. Panther gives her individuality. A panther is itself a thing of beauty, of flowing living lines; the psychological effect should be tremendous. Think what your attitude toward yourself and art would be like if your name were Toad or Ichthyosaurus or Warthog. Gradually but inevitably you would come to hate all nature; you would be blind to everything but ugliness; you would probably even give up bathing—"

"You named her Helen."

"Then I was wrong. Not that Helen is bad; it's merely nega-
tive. But Panther! Don't you feel it? Panther!"

"I have no objection; Panther it shall be," agreed Lora. "Then
it's understood about the money."

"By no means. I am her father and I should contribute to her
support."

"But it isn't necessary. Honestly I don't need it any more."
She put her hand on his shoulder and patted it. "You are a dear,
Albert, but I don't suppose the magazines pay any better than
they ever did, and I know there are things you would like to
have...."

He frowned. "Last month, *Art of Today* handed me a hundred and fifty for the article on Van Gogh. Only four thousand
words."

"Yes, I know. It was worth three times that."

"And what about my experiment? If I contribute nothing I
could not expect you to let me see her, to promote the forma-
tion of her mind by a natural process, to keep constant watch
against the obscene vulgarities—"

"You've been here, I think, seven times in the past year. Not
so constant. But heavens, you can come as often as you want to.
You didn't think you were paying for it? It's just that I don't
need the money. Come whenever you like. Come every day."

"I'm frightfully busy—"

"All right. Whenever you like."

He shook his head. "I can't resign my share of the burden.
You shouldn't ask me to. It's not decent. I should feel restricted,
fenced out...."

"All right." Again she patted his shoulder. "If you insist on it.
But just think, fifty dollars a month. Put it away in a sock. Six hundred a year. In two years that would mean a winter in Europe—"

"You're tempting me, you slut. Get out of here." He grinned, and suddenly broke into a loud roar of laughter. "If you could see the holes in my socks! Get out of here."

He opened the door and out he went, back into the living room where Helen, from this day Panther, kneeled over the prostrate doll trying to pour water down its nose.

The next day Lora got out some old dresses, the two thin woolen ones and the grey tweed she had worn when carrying Morris, and even an old favorite from Roy's time, a beige silk which she had made herself; and tried them on in front of the long mirror on the bedroom door. The silk was far too long, and all of them hung like distorted bags. Surely all that fullness would not be needed! Why is a baby's outward show so out of proportion to its tiny and fragile frame? At any rate, she thought, nothing could be done now, thank goodness the moths had been kept out—though for that matter she would this time be able to get as many new ones as she wanted. It was fortunate that it would be a winter baby, like Helen and Morris, for otherwise an entire new wardrobe would have been required. Wouldn't it be amusing if it should happen to hit Helen's very day. Only she must say Panther. Certainly it would be the same month; Morris had been some weeks earlier. It was nicer in the winter, everything seemed so warm and the warmth was so pleasant. Those suffocating July days with the first one—good god, no, not the first....

As she bent over the bed folding up the dresses to go back into the box she became aware of a presence and, looking up, saw Leah watching her from the door.

"There's only two bottles," said Leah.

"Yes," said Lora. "Roy broke one. Two is enough. I'll get more when I go out."

IV

On a day in September which brought the first faint whiff of autumn a telephone call came from Lewis Kane. He had returned that morning, he said, was extremely busy with the accumulation at his office and would be for a week or more. Was everything all right? Perfectly, Lora reported; all departments of the factory were running smoothly. Splendid, he said, he would call again.

Throughout the fall months they met every week or so for a pleasant and unexciting dinner. Lora, expecting every moment to be bored, found to her surprise, that his invitations were always welcome, tried to account for it by various theories all of which turned out to be unsatisfactory, and ended by accepting it with an indifferent shrug. Certainly he was unfailingly courteous and good-tempered, and never intolerably inquisitive. Immediately upon his return he placed a car at her disposal, and a little later got her one of her own, a little dark-blue sedan. She wanted to drive it herself, but he begged her earnestly not to take the risk.

"A pregnant woman is too much of a fatalist to drive a car," he declared. "The doctrine of absolute determinism is essentially a feminine philosophy, based on the uncontrollable nature of conception. That isn't original. I've been investigating the matter. To tell the truth, Jameson, the specialist at Presbyterian, an old friend of mine, was with me in Canada. He used the word fatalist."

"A pregnant woman is like any other woman."

"Nonsense. You don't believe that at all. Do you now?"

"No."

"Admirable, I don't pretend to any right to command, but I do most earnestly entreat you—"

"All right, I won't."

So around the park or shopping—sometimes into the country —she went comfortably cushioned on the back seat, with Panther beside her and Morris occasionally on her lap, more often on that of Leah in the other corner, and Roy in front with the chauffeur. Roy, supposed to begin kindergarten this fall, had talked himself out of it by announcing at the end of the third day, not with any bitterness, that the teacher had reprimanded him for putting a paper cow's tail on the front end instead of the hind one.

"Then she's a pedant," said Lora. "There's nothing sacred about the position of a cow's tail. Do you want to go back?"

"No. She blows her nose like this." Roy pulled out his hand-kerchief, covered most of his face with it, and squealed like a mouse in a trap.

"Do it again," said Panther, waddling over and looking up at him admiringly. That exhibition, Lora figured, cost at least an extra month in Panther's education in the technique of nose-blowing.

Lewis Kane was never a member of the family motor excursions; indeed, he had never once entered the little apartment on Seventy-first Street. Lora mildly wondered why. Discretion, perhaps; but he had been to the door fifty times; he always got out of the car when he brought her home from dinner, handed her out, and escorted her to the vestibule. Was he waiting for an invitation? Improbable, for once when she had suggested that he might like to see the children enjoying the toys which his generosity had made possible he had passed it off with a reference to his unfortunate ineptitude with youngsters. She had never repeated the hint, thinking it just as well; he would be sufficiently a nuisance after Julian came. She had accepted the Julian with the same indifference with which she had greeted Helen's transformation into Panther. If it were a daughter, presumably it would be Julia; but maybe not, since he already had one; at least his wife had.

One cold snowy afternoon in December, with Panther beside her in the blue sedan and Roy in front, she gave the chauffeur Anne Seaver's address in Brooklyn. Leah, with Morris and his bottles and other paraphernalia, remained behind. The beige silk from Roy's time, recalled to service two months back, and now covered by a warm fur coat, comfortably encircled her daily expanding rotundity. The ample fullness which had in September made it hang like an ill-made bag was now barely adequate; a seam might yet have to be altered if it kept up at this rate.

She wore the beige silk purposely, in ironic memory of a day five years earlier under circumstances which differed violently from the present in all respects but one—that one being the phenomenon which made the beige silk necessary. Anne had then hated her, with the hatred of the guilty for the innocent victim, but Lora had never hated Anne. Her present ironic gesture was friendly in its intent, and she knew it would not be resented. She had not seen Anne for many months, not since the days following Max's death; and for one thing she thought that the sight of Roy might give her pleasure.

Anne was not at home. I should have telephoned, thought Lora; anyway it was a nice ride through the falling snow. But, the maid added, Mrs. Seaver was expected back at any moment, she had gone out for lunch and had said she would return at three. Lora took off the children's wraps and her own, helped the maid with them to the hall, and entered the living room just in time to drag Roy out of the fireplace. When Anne came not long after she found them all seated on the rug in front of the fire; Roy was explaining to Panther why it made a fire go better to spit on it; Lora, unheeding, smiled at the flames.

"What a picture!" Anne exclaimed, advancing on them. She was tall and slender, not quite filled out anywhere, with long straight legs and arms, a thin neck that showed the tendons, a good forehead and nose and chin but everything a little too sharp; twenty pounds tastefully distributed would have done wonders.

"I'm too comfortable to get up," said Lora. "Roy, you remember Anne Seaver, don't you? Of course you do. Anne, dear, you look younger and more virginal every day. Now that I'm here I wonder why I stayed away so long. Roy, don't you remember Anne Seaver?"

Roy ducked his head and mumbled, "Hello."

"Of course you do," said Anne. "Don't you remember, a long time ago, I gave you the red engine with a whistle on it?"

"It's broke."

"Yes, it would be. We must get another. Heavens, how you've grown! And Helen too—Lora, she's as beautiful as a dream. Albert's nose and mouth, obviously, don't you think? But where's the baby?"

Spiteful nervous woman, thought Lora; but no, probably it was envy, not spite, and certainly she had been helpful and sympathetic about Max, more really than had been required. Anne sat beside her on the rug, and they gazed into the fire together and answered each other's questions, while Panther nodded drowsily and finally slept and Roy tiptoed from room to room in search of a cat which he had seen gliding shadowlike from underneath a sofa. Lora learned that Mr. Seaver, Anne's husband, had been made vice-president of something or other and had subscribed to the opera; furthermore, that they had definitely decided on a trip to Europe the coming summer.

"I don't suppose you'll go to China," Lora remarked.

Anne gave her a sharp glance, then said quietly, "That's nasty, isn't it?"

"I suppose it is," Lora agreed. "But surely, after five years, you don't mean to say you're still tender about him?"

After a long silence Anne said to the fire: "It really wasn't at all nasty. You probably know there's no one else on earth I can talk to about Steve Adams. Though why I should want to talk about him.... Yes, I'm still tender. But I always was tender, and you were always tough. Tougher than him even. Today when I came in and heard you were here I thought at first you had heard from him and my heart stopped still; I stood at the door for ten seconds with my heart as dead as a rock. As soon as I saw your face I knew you hadn't. You haven't?"

Lora shook her head. "You didn't notice that I'm wearing the dress I had on the day he told me to go to hell?"

"Yes, and I was surprised, I thought you'd forgotten it...."

"It's a symbol. Thumbing my nose. Not at poor Steve particularly, just anyone. At the father of my new baby, perhaps. You hadn't noticed?"

Anne laughed, a laugh without warmth that began abruptly, showed for a moment her perfect gleaming teeth, and ended more abruptly still.

"My dear, you might as well have it on a signboard. I thought perhaps it wasn't being discussed. You certainly waste no time?"

"Due in a month," Lora announced. "It is to be a boy."

"Are you married?"

"Of course not. There is a father though."

Anne looked at her, shivered a little, and looked again at the fire. "I wouldn't be surprised if it were my own husband," she said. "Honestly I wouldn't; you know he wants children. I wouldn't put anything in the world above you or beneath you. You never did love Steve, did you? But you have his son. When I looked at Roy today, and thought, that is Steve's son, it made me feel empty and sick inside. I hated you; I do hate you I think; you never loved Steve; you don't even love Roy, you look at him as if he were a chair or something, something you'd gone out and bought somewhere—"

She stopped abruptly, still looking into the fire. I shouldn't have come, thought Lora, I shouldn't have brought him, poor Anne.

"I shouldn't have brought him," she said. "I'm sorry."

"No. You shouldn't have brought him. I'm miserable, Lo, just completely miserable. That was what he called you, wasn't it?"

A cat's frightful howl came from the hall. "Roy!" called Lora instantly, as quick as a reflex. Panther, startled out of her sleep, sat up with wide eyes. Anne was on her feet at once, calling out, "Siesta, Siesta darling!" and off she went.

Roy met her at the door. "I didn't hurt it any," he declared. "It wouldn't come out."

"You little devil." Anne brushed past him into the hall. "Siesta darling, where are you?"

"Come here," said Lora. He walked over to her, calmly and with poise.

"Let me see your hands. Did the cat scratch you?"

He shook his head. "It couldn't. It was behind that thing in the hall."

"Did you pull its tail?"

"It don't hurt a cat to pull its tail," he said. "It uses it to hang on trees with."

"It's too bad she didn't scratch you, then you'd know why you shouldn't pull her tail."

Anne returned, in her arms a big yellowish brown cat which nestled against her shoulder with its tail moving in little jerks and its eyes closed. She walked over to Roy and stood looking down at him with a bitter intensity. "You *are* a little devil," she said, "Now you can pat her nicely and beg her pardon." But at the scent of the hostile hand the cat scrambled loose, leapt to the floor and disappeared into the hall.

"Don't get ideas," said Lora. "All boys pull cats' tails, it's practically compulsory. They get over it."

"Not all of them."

"Roy will. Come here, dear." The boy was instantly at her side. "This is manners. You have hurt Anne's feelings. If you are sorry you will tell her so. Go on."

Promptly he walked over to Anne and held out his hand, and when she had taken it he smiled at her and said, "I am sorry I pulled your cat's tail."

"All right," she smiled back at him. "But you're a little devil anyway."

They left soon after. Anne insisted that they stay for tea, but Lora said no, the children must be got home and fed and put to bed; outside, it was already night, what with the winter solstice so close at hand and the curtain of clouds that had all day obscured the sun and sent the snow down. The snow was still falling as they made their way out to the curb and climbed into the car, Lora with short careful steps to avoid a fall on the slippery pavement.

"I'll come to see you at the hospital," called Anne from the door.

During the ride home Lora sat looking idly at the lighted windows and passing cars, her mind on Anne Seaver. It was pathetic and exasperating, she thought, that after four years Anne should still cherish the memory of Steve Adams. Not only the memory, apparently, even a hope—a vague amorphous hope, unfounded and desperate, plainly idiotic. What a waste of passion! A passion that Lora could not begin to understand. Passion was made for action; there was the object, here the purpose, the ultimate reason for both being quite obscure perhaps, but the present intention manifest. But a miserable purposeless passion, with its object so remote and inaccessible that in effect it did not exist at all, was utterly incomprehensible to her. You do not love Roy, Anne had said. Bah, that just didn't mean anything. She might as well say, you do not love your arm, or your right leg, or your big toe. You love the things you've got to have, that's all. Certainly Anne didn't have to have Steve Adams; if she did she wouldn't have lived four years without him—four years of dressing and undressing, of carefully prepared meals, of all the intricate politics, psychic and physical, of a social animal. That wasn't love, it was a disease, a perversion, a sick clinging to a necessity that did not exist.

Nevertheless Anne was suffering, no pretense about that. Damn Steve Adams. No, that was silly; it wasn't his fault. Maybe not, but damn him anyway, for it was painful to see Anne suffer. Her husband was an awful clod. Why didn't he stick a pin in her or something?

In Manhattan the traffic was more than usually congested and moved by almost imperceptible jerks; by the time they reached Seventy-first Street Lora was restless and impatient, for it was past six o'clock and she hated to have the children's routine disturbed. When they finally arrived and the chauffeur opened the car door Roy tumbled out and fell in the snow, but came up laughing; Panther scrambled out backwards; Lora followed with slow deliberation.

Upstairs there was no light except in the kitchen. The maid came hurrying out when she heard them enter and pressed the switches in the dining room and hall, then helped them with their wraps, shaking off the few snowflakes that had caught them crossing the sidewalk.

"Where's Miss Kadish?" Lora asked.

"She went out."

"That's funny." Lora pulled Panther's dress down and brushed back Roy's hair with her hand. "When did she go?"

"I don't know. She sent me out for some soap and things and when I came back she was gone."

"When was that?"

"It was three o'clock, ma'am."

The woman stood there, not doing anything, not returning to the kitchen. Lora looked at her face, then hurried into the living room, to the little bedroom beyond, and from that into the further one; then through the bath she went to her own room. When she got back to the dining room, having completed the circuit, the maid was there spreading the tablecloth.

"She took the baby with her," said Lora.

"Yes, ma'am."

"Did she say where she was going?"

"She didn't say anything."

Lora looked at her a moment in silence. "Feed the children," she said abruptly, and returned to the living room, to the little stand in the corner which held the telephone and directory.

When she got the number a woman's voice answered. No, she said, Leah was not at home; no, she had been away all afternoon. She might be back for dinner and she might not. Where was she? Nobody could tell that, she might be anywhere.

"I understand. This is Mrs. Kadish, isn't it? This is Lora Winter. This afternoon I went—"

"You know I will not talk to you, Miss Winter. I ring off."

"Please! It's about Leah. Wait, please!"

"You have killed her, too, maybe."

"Please, Mrs. Kadish! This afternoon I went out with the children and left Leah at home with the baby. When I got—"

"Leah should not go there. She is a bad girl. I tell you I ring off."

A click ended it. Lora stood a moment with the receiver in her hand, then replaced it on the hook.

"The damn old fool," she said quietly.

She had never telephoned the police before and didn't know how to go about it. It was quite simple, she discovered. The voice at the other end, rough and casual and disillusioned, told her that no accident to any baby or woman of Leah's description had been reported; yes, he would see that the patrolmen in the neighborhood were notified; the baby was in a carriage, did she say? Lora asked him to hold the wire and she hurried to the hall and back again.

"No, not in a carriage, she was carrying him."

"They'll turn up, ma'am, they always do." He took her phone number and said he would let her know of any report.

Not in the carriage, that settles it, thought Lora. She picked up the telephone again, then put it down and made her way back to the little corner bedroom. There, in the closet in the corner, she found two empty shelves. Everything was gone, caps, dresses, shirts, stockings, not a diaper to be seen; even the spare rubber blanket was missing. She turned to the crib. It apparently had not been disturbed; the little silk quilt lay neatly folded at one end, and it was there on top of the quilt, in a sealed envelope, that she found the note. The envelope was addressed in pencil, *Miss Lora Winter*. She tore it open; written on a sheet of her own stationery, also in pencil, were the words, *Look in the drawer where you keep the postage stamps.*

"Thank god," said Lora aloud, and on her way to her own

room she sat for a moment on Roy's bed to rest, pressing the palms of her hands against her belly. There was a faint movement there, like the fluttering of a grasshopper imprisoned in cupped hands. She smiled. I'll have to eat my dinner, she thought, and got up and went to her room and opened the top right-hand drawer of the bureau, where postage stamps were kept. There lay a roll of bills, a few fives and tens and several ones. Ha, she thought, so Leah's buying a baby, too! But no, this was, of course, to pay for the clothing and diapers. She counted it: eighty-seven dollars. Possibly all she had had, but more likely the result of a detailed appraisal and calculation. Lora folded the bills together and placed them in her purse.

In the dining room Roy and Panther were finishing their mush and milk, with crackers and a raw custard. Lora called out, "You may bring my plate, Hilda," and sat down across from them. Roy looked over at her solemnly.

"Your face looks funny," he said. "Where's Morris?"

"I don't feel like talking," said Lora. "Eat your dinner." After a moment he spoke again: "I'm glad Morris is gone so I can yell all I want to."

"Be quiet," Panther said severely,

Lora thought of telephoning the chauffeur to get the car from the garage, but decided against the delay; a taxi would be quicker. Should she have help? Probably it would be better, Albert, the police, Lewis Kane? Albert was no good. Certainly not the police, from what she had heard of them. Lewis Kane perhaps. But he was a lawyer. No, all that would mean complication and delay....

She finished her dinner, with the maid's help got the children to bed, and had been in the house altogether less than an hour when she stood again at the door with coat and hat on, woolen gloves and lined galoshes.

"Be careful, ma'am," Hilda admonished her.

"Yes. You stay till I get back."

The snow was deep in the street but had stopped falling, and it was turning colder; a crust was beginning to form on top. After a long wait on Central Park West she got a taxi and gave the driver the address, on Manhattan Avenue a few blocks beyond the end of the park. The taxi was not heated, and she pulled the fur coat close. I should have changed my dress, she thought. At One Hundred and First Street the taxi went across to Manhattan Avenue and then headed north again.

She had not seen the place for nearly two years, since the day she had stopped in front of it to wait for Max to go in for his camera, and his mother, leaning from a window above, had seen her and cursed her in Yiddish. It had sounded rather terrifying, and Max, saying not a word, had hustled her off around the corner. The building looked different, it seemed smaller, but there was the number above the door. In the outer vestibule were five buttons on each side with names above them; the middle one on the left said Kadish, and she pressed it, with her other hand against the door waiting for the answering click. It did not come, and she pressed the button again. Still no click. She pushed the button down and held it there, and then jabbed it again and again, viciously. Then she gave it up and went out to the sidewalk and looked up; the windows on the third floor were dark.

Those are just the front rooms, she thought; she must be there, she couldn't be anywhere else. She returned to the vestibule and pressed the button many times, time and time again, but the door did not open. Half an hour had passed, and she began to feel cold and weary and for the first time a little fearful. If her theory was wrong—but no, she knew Leah Kadish, she knew what was back of those wet black eyes. But where the

devil was she? Had they gone off like gypsies? Nomad blood
that from the Asiatic sands…for a hundred centuries….Bosh.
She knew Leah all right. It was getting colder every minute.

She had been there a full hour and was about to ring another
bell to get inside when a man suddenly turned into the vestibule
from the sidewalk, opened the door with a key, scarcely giving
Lora a glance, and bounced in out of the cold and up the stairs.
Her toe on the sill kept the door from reaching its catch, and
when a minute or two had passed she pushed it open and
entered. The hall was warm and pleasant, and she stood by the
radiator and rubbed her numbed fingers a moment before
going upstairs, two flights, to where a door at the front was
marked Kadish. Here she repeated the performance of the
vestibule; over and over she rang the bell, and could hear its
faint jingle from inside, but without result. She kept it up.
Finally a door across the hall suddenly opened and a woman's
head appeared. "They're not at home," the woman snapped.
"Thanks," said Lora, "do you know where they went?"

"No."

"All right, I'll wait."

The woman looked at her suspiciously and shut the door with
a bang. Lora went and sat on the top step of the stairs, opening
her coat and taking off her gloves. Her watch said nine o'clock.

She sat there two hours. Now and then she would get up and
go to the door and ring the bell and then go back and sit down
again. Several times, on the stairs and in the hall below, she
heard people entering or leaving; twice she straightened, expec-
tant, when the footsteps continued up the second flight, but
the first time it was a man with a dog and the second a woman
and a little girl; she sat close to the wall to let them pass on the
narrow stairs. Others passed her on their way down from the
flats above; once two young couples, laughing and talking, who
seemed not even to see her, and one of the young men stepped

on the edge of her coat, though she had pulled it as far out of the way as possible. The hall was hot and her head ached, but her feet felt cold. She was thirsty. She had just looked at her watch for the hundredth time—it was a little after eleven—and decided to ring the bell across the hall and ask for a drink of water, when they came. There was the now familiar sound of the vestibule door opening and closing from below, and footsteps, but no voices, on the stairs. They rounded the first landing and continued slowly up. Lora wanted to look over the rail, but instead sat still, her chin up, scarcely breathing. They came around the second turn and there they were in front of her, without seeing her, their eyes on the steps they were climbing. Mrs. Kadish, short, solid, bundled in a thick brown fur coat, was in front. Lora got to her feet, and Mrs. Kadish stopped with a jerk and looked up at her. Behind was Leah, the baby in her arms wrapped in an embroidered wool blanket which Lora had never seen before.

"Don't you know it's after eleven o'clock?" Lora snapped. "You ought to be ashamed of yourselves. Have you fed him?"

The two women stood looking up at her, apparently too dumbfounded to reply. Slowly Mrs. Kadish turned to look at her daughter. "It's her, is it Leah?" she asked. Then she looked up again. "Get out of my house!" she said; the words rattled out of her like pebbles.

"You old fool," said Lora. "Come, Leah, give him to me."

Leah pushed up, shoving her mother from behind, and they ascended the few remaining steps to the landing, while Lora stepped back to give them room, stopping with her back against their door. With an effort she kept back, and kept her hands down; she didn't like the look in Leah's eyes.

"Give him to me," she repeated.

Leah, her arms folded tightly around the bundle, seemed to speak without moving her lips,

"This is not your baby. Your baby is at home."

"That's a lie. Don't be silly. Give him to me."

"I will not. This is not your baby. You are a whore and there is a devil in your womb. Maxie told me that; he said, she is a whore, Leah, and my baby must go to you, my sister, and my mother. Now we have been to the rabbi and he is our baby; you can't have him. If you try to take him you'll see."

"Max never said that," Lora declared quietly. "Everything you say is a lie." Plainly, she thought, they were both crazy; she should have brought someone, if only Albert Scher or the taxi-driver. Then she clenched her fists as she saw the bundle twisting around in Leah's arms; from it came a whimper, then a louder one, then an open-mouthed yell.

"Get out of here, get away from our door," said Mrs. Kadish. She took a step forward, so that scarcely a foot separated them, but fell back again, startled by a sudden blaze in Lora's eyes. Leah too retreated; Lora's tone was furious and threatening:

"So that's it! You had him circumcised, did you! When you said rabbi I didn't think—of course that's it! Letting a dirty old man cut him with his filthy hands—I'll have you arrested—you'll go to prison, both of you—my god, you took him to a rabbi to be circumcised—here, Morris darling, baby darling, here you are, I'll bet it hurts, of course it hurts, doesn't it? All right, it's Mother, darling."

The baby, still yelling, was in Lora's arms, without anyone knowing precisely how it had got there. Leah, whose face a moment before had seemed darkly and dangerously menacing, now looked merely foolish; her mother spoke in a confused tor-rent of indignation and dismay, shouting above the yells from the baby:

"That is not so! When you say the rabbi's hands are filthy it is not so and God will punish you! Anyway if a thousand rabbis' hands was filthy who would that send to prison? I ask you, in

this country do they put you in prison for dirty hands? It was
the truth Leah spoke, my Maxie said it, you are a whore, Miss
Winter!"

"Sh-sh-sh, all right, darling, all right, sh-sh-sh!"

The yells became again a whimper, then that too ceased.

"Be quiet, Momma," Leah was saying. "She wouldn't have
us arrested, be quiet. Listen, Miss Winter." She put her hand
on Lora's arm and her voice trembled. "Let us have him. You
don't care, you don't love him. I thought you wouldn't care.
You've got two more and soon you've got another one. Momma
and me, we haven't got anything since Maxie died. Please let
us have him." Two big tears came out of the corners of her eyes
and zig-zagged down her cheeks, more followed, and she
wiped them off with her hand, leaving wide marks clear to her
ears. "For God's sake, Miss Winter, please let us have him."
More tears came, and her voice broke. She got out, "Maxie
didn't call you a whore," and then buried her face in her hands.

"I'm sorry," Lora said. She moved to the head of the stairs,
around Mrs. Kadish, who didn't budge, and the baby whim-
pered a little. "Sh-sh-sh, all right, darling. I'm sorry. I'll send
the blanket back tomorrow, I need it now to keep him warm.
You hurt him, damn it. If there's an infection or anything I will
have you arrested, both of you, and the rabbi too, so you'd
better tell him to pray."

Halfway down the first flight she called up, "I'm sorry, Leah.
Goodbye."

There was no reply; but when she got to the lower hall Mrs.
Kadish's voice, indignant, suddenly came from above:

"Wait a minute! Miss Winter! What about the money? The
money Leah left—eighty-seven dollars—"

She shouted up, "Send the clothes back and I'll send the
money."

"Wait a minute! You can take—"

The banging door ended it. Lora, in the outer vestibule, got her coat buttoned and her gloves on. The air was so cold it pinched her nose. She had to go to Eighth Avenue to find a taxi, and then it stopped so far from the curb that she slipped and nearly fell making the step.

"I'm sorry," said the driver, "I didn't see you had a baby."

"You're half blind as it is, I've got two," she laughed.

"Nuts," he said cheerfully, putting in the gear.

It was well past midnight when she got home and found Hilda seated at the dining-table with her head pillowed on her arm, sound asleep, an enormous piece of brown Swedish bread with a thick layer of butter clutched tightly in her hand.

That was the twelfth of December. On January sixteenth, missing Panther's anniversary by just three days, she had Lewis Kane's son, de luxe, in a commodious corner room of the Poole Hospital, with two special nurses and nine vases of flowers. She counted them many times in between the pains. The nurse in charge of vital statistics was somewhat bewildered; the information given did not seem to fit the mother's competent and business-like assumption of her position and its responsibilities. What were things coming to, she wondered indignantly, if the unmarried ones were going to act like veterans, without shame and without remorse? She couldn't help admiring Lora, but didn't like her at all.

Lewis Kane did not come to the hospital. His first sight of his son Julian was at the age of ten days, in the apartment on Seventy-first Street. The new crib was in Lora's bedroom, against the wall where the bureau had been; she sat in an easy chair by the window wearing a pale green negligee, a book in her lap and a tea-tray on a little table at her side.

"You know," said Lewis, touching the tiny sleeping infant with a fearful and reluctant finger, "I believe that with George and Julia I felt unconsciously, even at the time, that they were not mine. Perhaps I imagine it, but this one does seem different. I suppose you are right to stay on here for the present; May should not be too early for the country, that will be only three months. I'm glad your milk is adequate; you don't overlook anything, do you? The whole thing is very satisfactory, very."

He turned and approached her.

"I believe I will have a cup of tea after all."

V

That spring she wrote a letter to her father and mother, the first in two years.

I haven't a husband yet, but I have another baby. A boy, and the best yet, I believe. That makes four in case you've lost count. He looks a little like you, Dad, with his eyes wide apart and his nose as straight as a rifle barrel. Of course his own father thinks he looks like him, but he really doesn't at all. He was born on January 16th, so he's nearly three months old. By the way, Morris's father, Max, you remember I told you, the Jewish jewelry salesman, is dead. He got pneumonia and his heart was weak the doctor said a year ago last March. Morris is over two years old now and has the funniest little nose, I wish Max could see him. I wish you could see all of them—maybe some day we'll pay you a visit.

When it was finished she read it through twice, slowly, her brows drawn together and her lips closed tight. They'll read it all right, she thought; they'll leave it lying around for a day or two unopened and she'll finally open it and read it and then he'll read it too. Before sealing the envelope she went through a drawer of snapshots and enclosed a dozen or more. Several were of Leah, with Morris—on her lap, in her arms, held perched on her shoulder—and Lora shook her head at them. It's too bad, but I can't help it, she thought.

Leah had come to the apartment twice, once the day before Christmas and once in February, and on both occasions had been refused admittance. The first time Lora, lying big on her bed, had not even seen her; the second time she had gone to the door and told her firmly that she might as well stop coming, it was impossible to trust her. Leah pled and threatened and wept, tried to kiss Lora's hand, declared she would kill herself, asseverated once again that Maxie had not called his son's mother a whore. At the end, feeling her cause hopeless, she stated categorically that Morris was not Maxie's son anyway.

"Ha," said Lora, "you're right, he isn't." And at the new fury that blazed in the other's eyes she hastily and forcibly closed the door against her and locked it.

It was hard to believe that Max had been Leah's brother. Possibly he wasn't; the faith in paternity is always more religious than scientific. He had been placid, agnostic and Occidental, with questionable traits from beyond the Aegean showing but rarely; as for instance when at their third meeting he had asked her to marry him and she had said no nor anyone, he had at once proceeded to try the other road. He had said immediately in his agreeable modest tones:

"You're probably right; neither Yahveh nor Christ nor civil blessing could make it more agreeable to kiss your hand. Nor brighten the glory of your hair. I have never seen such beautiful hair. You're right not to have it cut; I want to see it down over your shoulders."

That had been on a September day in Union Square; Albert Scher had taken Roy, then a little more than three years old, to the Bronx Zoo, and Lora had as usual been six times around Union Square, with Helen, still in her first year, in the carriage with the broken wheel. Only a week had passed since Albert had brought Max to the diminutive flat on Eleventh Street at the dinner hour, having found him in a Fifth Avenue gallery examining with a magnifying glass a blue necklace on a Hals portrait. At that time Albert, big and booming and blond,

midway between thirty and forty, was still doing galleries and
exhibitions for the *Star;* Max, nearly ten years his junior, was
beside him remarkably compact and swarthy.

"My friend, Max Kadish," Albert announced from the threshold,
"is going to grace our table. This, my boy, is Lora the Lorelei.
Miss Lora Winter, permit me, engaged, as you see, in the miraculous process of turning beef stew into milk entirely without divine
assistance."

Lora, seated with Helen at her breast, unembarrassed and
unruffled, looked up at them and smiled. "Not tonight he isn't,
there isn't enough," she said. "How do you do, Mr. Kadish;
another time. You two go out and eat, there's only enough here
for me. You know I wasn't expecting you, Albert."

"Hell, we want an evening at home," Albert protested.

Max spoke, diffidently. "If you would permit me, I am a very
good cook, it would be a great pleasure—a big dish of scallopini
for instance, and chicory with oil dressing...."

"It's a lot of trouble," said Lora.

"Grand idea!" Albert declared. "And a bottle of wine. We can
do it in ten minutes. I'll help."

Out they dashed, and soon were back again, Albert with olives
and wine and bread, Max with a package of meat and cans of
mushrooms, string beans, tomato sauce, pimiento and olive oil.
Lora had got Helen into her crib in the little back room, where
Roy was already sound asleep.

"The door's shut," she said, "but for heaven's sake be quiet
anyway. I'll set the table. Albert, you'd better go in front and
look at pictures or something."

"Do you realize," Albert demanded, "that olive oil comes from
olives? It's incredible. Good god, think of the olives it must take."

The scallopini was excellent, the salad delicious, the wine
sour but possible. They sat on the wooden chairs in the kitchen

and drank coffee for two hours, then Albert and Max washed the dishes while Lora went in front to feed the baby again.

"We have a swell maid," Albert explained, "a wench from Alabama that looks like Aida except she's cross-eyed, but she only comes four hours a day and if we don't do these now we'll have nothing to eat breakfast on. So Lora would say. I demur. The Romans used no dishes. Today, in a belt within twenty degrees of the equator north and south, precisely on the earth's belly, there are half a billion people eating without dishes. In our decadence—"

The platter that had held the scallopini, now soapy and dripping, slipped from his fingers onto the floor, taking a carom off the garbage pail in its flight, and was shattered into a dozen pieces. Albert knelt, scooped the pieces together, and dumped them into the pail.

"In our decadence," he repeated, "we make gods of bread-and-butter plates."

A week later, the day they met in Union Square, Max told Lora that thanks to Albert he was already acquainted with a workable outline of her history. He had been told, he said, that she was twenty-six years old, had never been married, was intellectually and esthetically an infant, and was totally devoid of the vices of ambition, greed and curiosity. Lora merely smiled and let him hold her hand as they sat on the bench near the middle of the Square, though it was broad day and passersby were nudging each other and grinning at them. She didn't notice; she was wondering about Albert. For one thing, he was becoming impossibly careless about money. Presumably he still had seventy dollars a week from the *Star*, reinforced by an occasional check for an extra piece, but the proportion that got to her had gradually decreased until now it was touch and go even with such essential items as the rent and the grocer's bill and the maid's modest wages. That Albert had ceased to be amusing was not intolerable, that had always been only a sideshow; but that he was apparently no longer amused threatened danger. She did not feel herself in competition with the rich young widow from West End Avenue who was suddenly finding Albert's constant advice essential in her search for bargain Seurats and Gauguins, nor with the little blond art student, whose name she did not know, who was apparently a successful candidate for a solider and less subtle seduction; merely they were menaces to the sternest of all her necessities; and if they could not be removed must be evaded. The difficulty about money, she knew, came from pure inadvertence; Albert got his pay on Tuesday, and on Thursday or Friday, when he got around to consideration of the responsibilities of a father and the head of a household, no one was more astonished and irritated than he to discover himself once again plunged into insolvency. "Nobody will ever succeed in persuading me," he declared, "that the tendency of money to evaporate is controllable by human forces. So help me god, Lora mia, I had five tens in that very pocket yesterday morning."

She would not, or could not, compete with the widow and the art student. The expedient of dragooning Albert on Tuesday evening, before the process of evaporation had set in, did not even occur to her. Just as her body was always her body, and Roy and Helen always her babies, so was Albert's seventy dollars his money. It might by good fortune or the exigencies of existence become the grocer's or the landlord's or the maid's, but never was any part of it hers.

She liked Max Kadish. Often that autumn he came early in the afternoon to the apartment on Eleventh Street, helped her get the baby in the carriage and Roy ready for the street, and walked with her to Union Square or Washington Square and sat with her on a bench while Helen slept and Roy chased his ball or bruised pedestrians' shins with his scooter. When she protested that he must be neglecting his business he explained that in his line hours didn't matter, the point was contacts. Yesterday, he said, to give an illustration, he had bought for his employers, a big and highly respectable firm, for the sum of twelve hundred dollars, a ring which they had sold two weeks ago for four thousand. His commission, as usual in such trans- actions, had been twenty percent of the gross profit. This par- ticular ring was an uncommonly fine one; his firm had sold it no less than four times in the past year. Contrary to the popular belief, he said, it wasn't always millionaires who bought nor chorus girls who sold; one of his best contacts was a woman who lived with her husband in a quiet little apartment on Lexington Avenue and gave teas at the Mayfair.

"It's ugly," said Lora.

"Sure it is," he agreed, "almost as ugly as living on coal miner's lungs or factory women's backs. Dear Lora, no taking in life is beautiful."

"It is undignified "

"Only to those who borrow their standards."

She shook her head vaguely; such things didn't matter, you talked of them only to be saying something. When Roy was born, she remembered, she had decided that the most undigni- fied process in the world was giving birth to a baby. What were you going to say for dignity after that?

As the weeks passed Max grew more and more insistent; Albert no longer loved her, he declared; obviously she did not love him; he, Max, could be and would be patient, but why not open the gate of his paradise? Lora, smiling and frowning by turns, kept him delicately suspended on the thread of her inde- cision. She liked him, but she mistrusted his smooth ready speech and more particularly his total lack of moral attitude. Steve had been brutally selfish; Albert, by his own admission, was constitutionally volatile; but neither, ignoring the moral verities, had deliberately insulted them. But no, she finally felt, that wasn't it either, it was just something indefinable in the way Max talked....

One rainy day in December, after a long afternoon with her in the little flat, he gave up. He went to the closet and put on his coat and then returned and stood in front of her with his hat in his hand.

"I annoy you, dear Lora," he said. "I am a nuisance to you and to myself. You were nearer to me that first day in the Square, when you let me hold your hand. You are more beautiful than ever—oh, so beautiful—but you are farther away. It is something I cannot conquer with my devotion and my desire —something I can't help—my race perhaps, or my modest stature, something you're not even aware of...."

"That's it!" Lora suddenly exclaimed. She laughed.

He looked at her, his polite brows lifted.

"It's because you're a Jew. How funny! Isn't it ridiculous? I've always been a little afraid of you, a little doubtful, and I didn't know why. That's it, because—"

She stopped; Max had gone to the door and opened it and was passing through without a word.

"Don't go, Max!" she said, but the door closed behind him, and his rapid steps sounded from the hall.

She ran to the door and opened it. He was just starting down the stairs.

"You're a fool," she said. "Go if you want to, but you're a fool."

He stopped and looked back at her down the length of the dim hall. His tone was suave and emotionless.

"What's the use, since it is, as I suggested, something I can't help—"

"You know very well you're a fool. We can't talk out here—come—"

"What's the use?"

"Come."

He turned and walked slowly towards her; she preceded him into the room and after he had entered closed the door.

"Aren't you ashamed of yourself?" she demanded.

"I'm ashamed that I came back."

"Silly! Would I have said it if there had been any hurt in it? Knowing it took it away—at once—like that!" She waved her hand. "I know what it is, it's the old peddler with a beard who used to come to our house long ago, many years ago, when I was a little girl—that's why it's funny. If you don't see it's funny!"

"It isn't funny, dear Lora."

"Oh, yes, it is! I can't say I'm sorry I hurt you because I didn't really—you had no right to be hurt—but you will forgive me—"

He still stood holding his hat, looking at her.

"I suppose it would be the same," he observed, "if I loved a Lesbian and she told me she despised me because I'm a man. That wouldn't be funny. I can't help being a man."

Lora shook her head.

"There's something wrong with that; I know; what if she wasn't really a Lesbian, and what if she didn't despise you? Anyway—it's late and I have to feed the baby and you must go. But before you go—"

She walked up to him, quite close, and stood there against him, her hands at her sides, smiling into his face.

"I'd love to be kissed by a Jew," she said.

He caught his breath. "You're playing with me."

"I'd love to be kissed by a Jew," she repeated.

"Any Jew presumably?"

"Please."

"This is not...dear Lora..."

"Please."

Then his arms were around her and his lips were on hers. She pressed tight against him so that her swelling breasts could feel his firmness, and he could feel them; her arms remained at her sides but her whole body was against him, not wanton, not aggressive, but lyrical and warm and ready. He kept her mouth a long while, and then buried his face on her shoulder and gasped for breath, his arms still holding her tight.

"Dear Lora...dear Lora..."

"Yes. Yes."

She raised her hand to pat his head and smooth his hair. At the touch he trembled, then raised his head and sought her lips again, but she put her hand on his mouth and he kissed the palm, over and over.

"Beautiful...oh, beautiful...." he murmured.

"You must go now."

"Let me stay. I can't leave now. I wouldn't know where to go. Let me stay and cook dinner—you can't go out in this rain—"

"Albert is coming."

"Don't make me go, dear Lora. How does it concern him that I have kissed you? Let me stay."

She shrugged her shoulders.

"I haven't two babies, I have four," she said.

When Albert arrived a little later he found Max in the kitchen furiously stirring a bowl of eggs and bread crumbs, and Lora seated across the table from him peeling potatoes.

That night Lora lay alone in bed, stretched comfortably under the warm blankets, looking through the open window at the street light glowing through the winter mist. Max had left early; at eleven Albert had got up from his chair, yawned, and announced that he was off for a party uptown. She was glad to be alone; after a last look at the children she got into bed at once but did not close her eyes. This is getting chronic, she thought, I'd better find out what it is I'm trying to do. She was committed to Max, that was sure. Why? His lips had felt soft and moist, not at all disagreeable, but certainly not exciting. His embrace was not as urgent as Albert's once had been—but that was actually a relief, let that dead lion sleep. Yet she had been excited. He had felt good against her breasts; she had pressed them against him exultantly, until they hurt; she had wished savagely that they might hurt till she fainted of it. Fearing to alarm him then, she had drawn back, pushing the thought away, patting his head and smoothing his hair as a mother might have done.

Beautiful, oh, beautiful, he had said. He meant her face, of course, and her hair, he was always talking about her hair and wanting to touch it. Well, she was beautiful. There was nothing more beautiful than her full breasts, just before she gave them to the baby, when she sat before her mirror with her dress open nearly to her waist, with their great drooping curves, drooping with weary grace like the branches of a peach tree loaded with ripe heavy fruit. Max of course did not mean that; think of Steve! Strange that men could be so blind to the only beauty that mattered. Probably Max wouldn't want a baby at all. Ha, wouldn't he though! Beautiful, oh, beautiful, he had said. How would he be, how would he feel? Suave and polite. That was one time that apparently manners didn't count, but in reality they did; politeness was just as pleasant then as any other time. My loins are two spent tigers drowsing in the sun, Albert had said that day, stretched six feet two on his back beside her, and she had smiled to herself, thinking of the new strength in her own loins to support the new life. That had been the last time with Albert, three months before Helen was born—to her great relief, for her indifference had almost become an active repugnance; and by the time it was over he had gone afield.

But, she thought impatiently, the question is what is it I'm trying to do? She couldn't go on having babies forever; this would be three, and certainly that was enough. If she weren't careful she'd be in a hole she couldn't get out of; what if Max became indifferent, as Albert had; what indeed if like Steve he made no bones about it, simply put on his hat and went away? Left alone with three infants would be no joke. She was headed for disaster then. Bah, she thought, there are no disasters left. Disaster, my god, that's funny. Disaster....

She shivered a little, turned on her side, pulled the covers tighter around her shoulders, and closed her eyes. By an old trick, born long ago of necessity, she suddenly was not there, she was far off in a sunny meadow of clover, running slim and youthful to greet a crowd of women, a great throng of them, all smiling and reassuring and beckoning as they approached through the clover blossoms from all sides, calling her name. They were her mothers....

She slept.

A week later, following a discussion and agreement with Max the preceding day, she announced their plans to Albert. It was late at night; he had not come home for dinner and she had waited up for him, out of respect for his distaste for morning discussions. Albert sat on the edge of the bed taking off his socks; he placed each sock precisely on top of its shoe with the garter neatly tucked inside, an infallible sign that he had drunk a little more than usual.

"You're crazy," he observed, with his bare foot carefully shoving the shoes and their cargo under the bed.

"I think you're lucky," she replied. "All your paternal duties ended, a free man, just think of it!"

"When does this happy hegira occur?"

"Friday."

He frowned. "Today is Tuesday. Are you in love with him?"

"No, today is Wednesday."

"You're crazy, it's Tuesday."

"All right. Anyway, it's to be Friday."

"Of course you'll want the furniture."

"No, only the cribs and our clothes and us. Max has bought furniture."

"The hell he has. The carriage."

"We're buying a new one."

"The hell you are!" He got up and stuck his hands in his pockets and started towards her, then suddenly sat down again. "Listen, Lora mia, this is a blow. You thought I would be pleased? Like hell I'm pleased! I'm furious. I'm Helen's father, you know. She's my daughter. I suppose you think I want that little squirt going around buying things for my daughter? You're crazy. I brought him here too; brought him into my own house, let him cook his damned scallopini in my own kitchen— Oh, that doesn't matter, I'm talking like a jackass, but you might have told me…I positively will not permit any man to buy a new baby carriage for my daughter.…"

"All right, we'll take the old one."

"Yes, and that damn wheel will break again and she'll fall out and smash her nose."

"Why don't you get her a new one yourself? For Christmas."

"Good god!" He got to his feet and this time kept them, staring at her, moving from the rug onto the cold wooden floor, in his bare feet, a thing he hated, without noticing. "By god I forgot! Christmas! We were going to have a tree, with lights, and popcorn and bags of candy—when is Christmas, you might as well tell me, when is Christmas? Let's see, today's the sixteenth, today's Tuesday—

"It's a week from Friday."

It took him a quarter of an hour to get Christmas talked out; he was overwhelmed by the thought that his daughter was to be torn from him just a week before the great Children's Festival. No man with any self-respect would submit to it. The word self-respect opened up new fields; obviously, he said, Max didn't have any. He should have come first to him, Albert, since his daughter was concerned, and arrive at an understanding. Not that any understanding under the circumstances would have been possible. Max was in fact an idiot, what with two children neither of them his own, bearing different names even…

"Their name is Winter. Both of them," Lora declared quietly.

"Like hell it is. Helen Scher. You agreed to it."

"Temporarily. Albert darling, don't fuss any more. You know you don't really care. Be reasonable. Names don't matter. You can come to see her as often as you like and call her Helen Scher or Helen of Troy or whatever you want. Remember, the rent hasn't been paid yet for November, and I made the coat Roy is wearing out of your old dressing-gown. Be reasonable."

Unbuttoning his shirt, he turned and grinned at her. "Lora mia, do you know what I really think? I think poor Max. Poor little Max. *Caveat emptor.* He thinks he's getting a gazelle, a trembling panting gazelle in heat, and when he finds out it's only a milch cow…."

"He does say I'm beautiful," said Lora, amused.

"So you are, Lora mia. As lovely as a eunuch's dream. I shall never forget the day I saw you standing white and straight in front of that purple curtain. I said to myself, with that massive central mountain once more properly subsided into a gently sloping mound, there stands Venus. Albert, my son, look no further; and calmly and patiently I awaited parturition and happiness."

Lora, offended at last by the coarseness of his "massive mountain," did not reply, and when he went on did not listen. A few minutes later they were in bed, side by side, with an inter-communication of warmth completely impersonal and dispassionate; their feet touched and then separated, with no gesture, without lingering and without haste. As Lora turned over on her side, with her back to him, she said:

"Why don't you help us with a Christmas tree anyway? Max would be glad to have you. It might be fun."

"All right," came his mumble through the darkness. "Damn silly custom though. We'll see."

VI

On Max, as it turned out, Albert's commiseration was wasted. With the two children, whatever their names might be, he assumed at once all the concern and responsibilities of a happy father. Often, downtown, he had eaten lunch with Lora and spent many afternoons with her, but after the establishment of the household in Seventy-first Street she never saw him after eleven in the morning or before seven in the evening. He must broaden his contacts and scare up all the business he could, he said; Lora's wardrobe was deplorable, the furniture he had bought so hurriedly was unsatisfactory, and there was nothing Roy and Helen did not need and should not have. Lora was touched and amused by the sight of the twenty-six-year-old boy taking so enthusiastically upon himself the obligations whose proper roost was not only upon other trees but even in another forest; but Max didn't need her pity either. When occasionally she remonstrated he would reply, "I know what I'm doing, dear Lora. As young as I am, I live my ideal; that is beautiful, almost as beautiful as you are." But he was not always so serious about it; sometimes he even burlesqued his own gaiety, as when one evening, taking a bracelet from his pocket, a circlet of amethysts set in dull white gold, he held it dangling before her and, with lifted shoulders and eyebrows and palms turned upward, "Jewelry from contented Jews," he said.

He would gladly have spent all his evenings at the apartment, but though Lora too would have been willing he wouldn't hear of it. She must have diversion. Both a nurse and a maid he insisted on, and he arranged with the nurse to remain three evenings a week while he took Lora to a play or a concert, and a party now and then. Occasionally they even had dinner guests, Anne Seaver perhaps, or acquaintances of Lora's from downtown or, more rarely, friends of Max's; often Albert Scher. Lora enjoyed those evenings; it was pleasant and restful to sit at the end of the long table, with its smooth white cloth and shining silver and glass and the maid carrying dishes of steaming meat and vegetables and cool red and green salad, the children safely asleep behind the closed door, and Max saying with pride, "No, Lora can't take any wine, not till the baby's weaned; pass your glass, Mrs. Seaver." It was rabbinical wine, quite good, and Lora regretted it a little; she hadn't had a drink for four years, what with pre-natal and lactal periods overlapping as spring and summer, with autumn and winter entirely out of it. The plays and concerts she attended chiefly for Max's sake; for the most part they bored her; she had never cared for the theatre, and music meant nothing to her but the mildly diverting pastime of trying to decide where it would go next. Except one night years before, when Steve Adams took her to a concert and the orchestra played a Brahms symphony…but that she had forgotten, that she would never remember. She had hated the name of Brahms ever since, and for a long while she had carefully kept herself away from music. If the grave of the past could not be entirely obliterated, at least the marked trails that led to it could be avoided.

One evening at a dance recital at Carnegie Hall, in the lobby during intermission, a man spoke to her—a tall middle-aged impeccable man with grey eyes. Then the man's glance fell on Max at her side, and he nodded again, "Hello, Kadish. Lolita's a sort of a bore, Miss Winter, don't you think?" He was off again.

"I don't remember that man, who is he?" she asked Max.

"Kane. Lewis Kane. He's probably been around with Albert; he buys etchings. Downtown lawyer."

"I don't remember him. Is he one of your contacts?"

"Well…he's a customer of the house. Nice fellow."

At the end of the recital Lewis Kane was again suddenly beside them, inviting them to supper. Max, plainly astonished, glanced at Lora; she said no, she was sorry, she mustn't keep the nurse up so late. Lewis Kane bowed himself away.

"We could have gone, Miss Ruggles is probably asleep," said Max in the taxi.

It was that same evening, a mild evening in April, after they had got home and sent the nurse off for the night, and gone to the kitchen for sandwiches and grape juice, that she said to him suddenly:

"Well, we've done it. I'm going to have a baby."

He dropped the breadknife and turned swiftly to look at her. "No!"

"Yes."

"Dear Lora. I can't believe it."

She put her hand on her dress, where Albert's massive mountain once had been. "It's here all right. Are you sorry?"

"I'm not sorry. I can't believe it. Does it hurt?"

She laughed. "Of course not. Oh, lord, there goes half the chicken on the floor. It will hurt before it's over, but I don't mind. I'd like to be sure you really aren't sorry."

"You know what I said." He had picked up the breadknife again, but now dropped it back on the table and went to her and gently grasped her arms from behind and smoothed them up and down. "I want whatever you want. I really don't care a damn, I argued against it at first for your sake. I don't want to hurt you, I don't want anything to hurt you…."

As they sat and ate their sandwiches and all the implications of this news began to find their places in his mind, he became more and more enthusiastic, more and more satisfied. "I begin to understand the patriarchs," he declared. "Doubtless I shall understand them better. But I could never be one. To me you could never be a means, dear Lora; you justify yourself; I welcome this only because you want it. How I shall feel after he comes I don't know—or she—"

He stopped, and suddenly exclaimed:

"When Momma hears of this! And Leah! Poor Momma. She'll hang me by the beard of Moses, she'll put a dybbuk in your soup—do you remember *The Dybbuk*?"

"I didn't care for it," said Lora. As a matter of fact, she had hated that play, and had left after the second act.

So much for that, she thought to herself that night in bed. He had really been very sweet about it. He would be. She wished he hadn't mentioned the dybbuk, and then laughed at herself for having any feeling about it. Such demons were invented to scare children. Enough things could happen, god knows, enough to make you hold your breath till you die, until there was no more breath, without dragging in nonsensical fairy tales. She remembered the white face of that girl in the play, the slender beautiful arms uplifted in terror, the shriek of fear....It was wicked to put such things on the stage, people were fools to make up lies like that....

"My baby, my little live baby," she whispered in the dark.

"What is it, dear?" Max murmured.

"Nothing. Prayers. I thought you were asleep."

"Prayers?"

"Nothing."

She stretched out her hand and patted his shoulder and then turned over, away from him.

As spring became summer and the weeks passed until half

her time was gone it was increasingly a surprise to her that she
did not resent Max. She didn't understand it and it amused her.
She would lie passive, aloof, her whole body relaxed and attending indifferently to its own affairs; that was to be expected;
but why did she not with repugnancy close her lids upon his hot
red face and staring devouring eyes, her ears to his gasping
breath and incoherent murmurings; why did her lips and skin
not shrink from his loose kisses and his clutching caressing
hands? Even as she felt them she would lie idly and wonder;
perhaps, she thought, it was because he demanded nothing of
her, because she felt in him no tinge of resentment against her
own passivity; he too was aloof, playing his own game as she
was playing hers, though he would have been astonished and
indignant if she had told him so. Once, as he dropped his head
on her shoulder and for a moment did not move, she smoothed
his hair and said quietly:

"It's a terrible waste, isn't it, Max?"

"My love," he murmured.

"I thought so," she smiled.

A little later, as he sat on the edge of the bed lighting their
cigarettes, he asked, "What was it you thought?"

"What?"

"You said you thought so."

"Oh. Nothing."

"No, tell me, what was it?"

"Nothing. I just thought you wouldn't hear me."

"I did hear you."

"You don't know now what I said."

"Sure I do, something about a waist, A terrible waist. I don't
know if you meant mine or yours. Yours isn't terrible. It's lovely,
it gets lovelier every day." He reached over and smoothed her
body, languidly and tenderly on the thin nightgown, not

without difficulty, for she was shaking with laughter at the inane and ridiculous pun.

"Go on and laugh," he said. "Half the time I don't know what you're about. I don't care. I know there's a lot of you I haven't got. Sometimes when you are in my arms I have a feeling it isn't you at all, and if your eyes are closed I ask you to open them and when you do it is less than ever you. Then I forget, I no longer care, I do not even feel you, I feel only myself. And when it is all over there you are back again, beautiful, more beautiful than ever, smiling into my face. Where do you go? Why are you not with me? It doesn't matter. I am happy."

"Maybe it's you who go."

"It doesn't matter."

He lifted her hand and covered her bare arm, systematically, with kisses to the shoulder.

When hot weather came he insisted on the seashore and they went for two months to a cottage on the south shore of Long Island. Endless afternoons Lora reclined in a chair under a huge umbrella, while Roy, now past his fourth birthday, played with other children in the sand, and Helen, just learning to walk, toddled herself from one sleep into another. Max would come out in the evening—business was slow, he said, with nearly everyone away from the city—Albert Scher spent a week with them, and Anne Seaver came for a Saturday and Sunday. It was at this time that Albert embraced his theory of esthetic education and put it into practice by drawing designs for Helen in the sand.

"Of course," he would say to Lora, standing mountainous in his bathing suit, his hair pale as bleached straw in the sun and the skin on his shoulders a fiery red, "she wouldn't understand if I tried to explain it. That must wait. For the present we merely put them before her in their simplest forms, a part of

the very earth she walks on—unconsciously they make their
picture in her mind."

"It wouldn't hurt to make them a little smaller," said Lora,
looking at the gigantic circle he had traced in the sand with
intricate radii and tangents in all directions. "She isn't six feet
two."

"Oh. By god, you're right." He turned to look, and instantly
shouted, "Hey, Roy, let that design alone! Hey! You vandal, get
off of that!"

In late September they returned to town, to the apartment
on Seventy-first Street, and there, ten weeks later, at noon of a
sunny crisp December day, the baby was born. The doctor had
advised a hospital, but Max was against it, insisting she would
be better cared for at home, and Lora was indifferent. At nine
in the evening she went to bed, the doctor came, and a nurse
was sent for. Max sat quietly in a chair in a corner of the room,
watching every movement they made.

"You'd better go somewhere," said the doctor. "Have you a
friend nearby? Go and get some sleep."

"I'll stay here."

"Then go in the other room. Go to bed. It's all right."

Max shook his head. "Let me alone." A groan came from
Lora's bed and he trembled all over. "I don't like this. Let me
alone."

He stayed. Once during the night he said to the nurse. "Good
god, it's silly. She's worth a thousand babies. I didn't want a
baby anyway."

"She was a baby herself once, Mr. Kadish."

"What's that got to do with it?"

In the morning, when the pains were more frequent and at
their worst, he held her hands for two hours; rather, he put his
own in hers and stood with his feet braced, bending over so she

could stay on her back, while her convulsive grip and tug crushed his knuckles and twisted the skin of his fingers. The doctor, returning, tried to get him away; he said, "This is none of your affair," and wouldn't budge. Towards noon Lora released him and pushed him off, with her hands and her eyes; he returned to his chair in the corner. When a little later he saw the nurse carrying something to the elaborately equipped table that had been set up on the other side of the room he didn't know it was all over; he got up to see what she was doing, and she said savagely, "It's a boy, and you get out of here. We're busy, get out, I tell you."

As he started toward the bed, where the doctor was, Lora said without opening her eyes, "It's fine, get out, Max. Please get out."

He turned and left without a word. In the dining room the maid met him with a tray of hot coffee and made him take a cup. "Miss Ruggles took the children to the park, it's a fine day for babies," she said. When an hour later the nurse went to tell him that the boy weighed eight pounds and that Lora was fast asleep she found him in the little bedroom in front, himself sound asleep on the floor beside Helen's crib.

The next morning he sat in a chair beside her bed and read stories aloud. He wanted to hold her hand, but she said no, it made her nervous. He was amazed at how well she looked, not wan, not exhausted even, her grey eyes quick and bright and strong, "I'm always that way," she said, "It's hard while it lasts, but it's wonderful." She laughed. "You look as if you'd done it yourself."

"I was a nuisance."

"Oh, no. You were very nice. Go on and read to me."

He chose the name Morris one evening a few weeks later as he sat and watched his son's bedtime meal. Lora didn't care, she said, names didn't make any difference; and Max replied that he didn't care much either, only if it was all the same to her they might as well call him Morris, the name of his younger brother who had died in childhood, years before. "I loved him more than I've ever loved anyone except you," he said. "It would please me to call him Morris, if you don't object."

Lora nodded, closing the front of her dress and starting to hook it. To free her hands Max took the baby, deftly and properly, and held it in his arms, looking down at it.

"By the way," he said, "shouldn't we have him christened or something?"

Lora glanced at him. "By a rabbi?"

"Lord, no. I don't know."

"He's already christened," she said. "By his father and mother. That's enough. You can sprinkle him if you want to."

So Max, grinning, handed the baby to her and went to the kitchen and brought a bowl of water, dipped his fingers and sprinkled a few drops on the little fat red face.

"By authority of the goddess Lora, divine in Beauty and Grace, I christen thee Morris," he said solemnly.

Lora, smiling, was wiping off the drops of water with her handkerchief.

By the time Morris was two months old Max had become completely a father. He was fond, solicitous, and inquisitive; he insisted on a weekly visit from the doctor; he tried to insist on a weekly test of Lora's milk, but she laughed him out of it. This was a new experience for her, and she was alternately annoyed and amused. What an idea, for anyone to pretend to an equal— superior even—concern about her baby! He was polite about it, of course, but what nerve! As it went on, a faint alarm stirred within her, and she determined to put an end to it. He was a fine sweet boy and she was really very fond of him, but he mustn't be permitted to get ideas fixed in his head....

As it turned out, no action was ever required; for on a miserable raw wet day in March, the day that he had prepared to celebrate as marking the completion of his son's third month, Max went to bed with a cold which within twenty-four hours the doctor pronounced pneumonia, and in less than a week he was dead.

The first day Lora got a cot and rigged it up for herself in the living room, with the baby's crib beside it, and arranged their own room, with the big bed and the sunny windows, for Max. She spent very little time on her cot, for at first he insisted on her presence, he would take medicine or food from no one but her, and by the hour he would lie and stare at her without saying a word; if she left the room he would rise up and call for her, and try to get out of bed, and when she returned would have nothing to say but her name. It got him like lightning. When the delirium came he could be quieted only by her, and on the fourth and fifth nights she had her cot moved in beside his bed and lay there in the dim exasperating light, with the nurse upright on a chair against the wall; when he moved and began to murmur or cry out Lora, at once on her feet bending over him, would touch him, grasp his arms, and talk to him. She wondered that he did not once speak of Morris.

When the delirium left he was so weak that he could not lift his hand; he could not even smile, though Lora saw that he tried to as she leaned over to wipe his brow or arrange his pillow. It was his heart that did it; no good, the doctor said. He did once insist on talking and managed it with a great effort, while Lora was alone with him, holding his hand. She could see the effort in his eyes.

"Dear Lora," he said.

"Sh, be quiet, dear," she whispered.

"Thank god for this," he said. "I thank god for it. I was just fooling myself. I would have hated to go on fooling myself all my life. Momma and Leah will say you killed me. Don't believe them. They're terrible hateful people. They're right though. You killed me, dear Lora."

She drew back as if he had struck her, took her hands away, then for a moment controlled herself.

"Max darling, that's a wicked lie," she said.

But abruptly she got to her feet and left the room; in the living room she stood, quivering with a remembered terror, her face white. Again she controlled herself. He's sick, he's going to die, he doesn't know what he's saying, she forced herself to think; and swiftly she got Morris, sleeping, from his crib and went back to the sick man's room. The nurse had returned from the kitchen and was bending over Max with her finger on his pulse. Lora advanced to the bedside with Morris in her arms.

"Max dear," she said softly, "here's your baby."

But he did not hear, for he was dead; Lora saw it on the nurse's face. She said nothing; she stood a moment, then went back to the living room and put Morris back in his crib; he had not awakened.

VII

By May she was broke. She took a necklace out of the brass box which she kept in a locked bureau drawer; she knew that it had cost Max four hundred dollars and that its current retail price was at least a thousand. The pawnshop on Columbus Avenue offered her a loan of three hundred, or three seventy-five outright. She put it back in her purse and went to a jeweler's shop on Broadway; his offer, cash, was even less. The next afternoon she took it downtown and Max's firm paid her five hundred and fifty dollars for it. "It's a high price," said the ugly and kindly old Jew, smiling at her like a grandfather, "but Max was a good boy and we like to do all we can...."

If Lewis Kane had telephoned in May instead of seven months later when the brass box was all but empty, he might not have fared so well. Lora was pretty well done with men, she thought, there was something wrong with all of them. Women were worse. This time I mean it, she said. Anne Seaver, informed by Albert of Max's death, had been sympathetic and helpful; but Anne herself was so lugubrious at bottom, even when she laughed her short sharp laugh with her white teeth showing, that a day or two of her was enough. She had tried to keep Lora away from the funeral, but Lora wouldn't hear of it. The day after Max's death the Kadish tribe—mother and sister, uncles and aunts and cousins—had presented a demand for his body, and Lora had consented without a struggle. "Max himself would be the least concerned, he would be the first to say it isn't worth fighting about," she told Albert Scher, who was for grimly withstanding the Oriental hordes, as he called them. But Lora insisted on attending the funeral, and she went with

Anne and Albert on either side of her and Morris in her arms; she insisted on that too. It was there that she first saw Leah; she did not really see Mrs. Kadish, who was swathed in veils with only her eyes showing.

It was a month later that the bell rang one afternoon and Lora, opening the door, saw Leah standing before her, her black eyes glowing with desperate resolve.

"I want to see Maxie's baby," she said.

"You're Leah."

"Yes."

"Well. Come in."

That first day she wouldn't sit down; she stood by the crib and looked at him, and when he awoke and Lora picked him up she turned without a word and departed. In a week she was back again; by June she was there nearly every day. Lora didn't mind; it was a nuisance, but also a convenience, especially after she let the nurse go and had the maid only four hours a day. She had begun to draw in her ropes, wondering what she was coming to. Max had once said something about insurance, but she couldn't remember what it was, and there was nothing among his papers regarding it. Albert consulted a lawyer friend and the lawyer, so he reported, "communicated on several occasions with the mother and sister of the deceased," but nothing came of it.

Albert indeed was a source of astonishment the first months following Max's death; voluntarily and for no discoverable reason he seemed to be reassuming a share of the burden of which he had so providentially been freed. Lora was surprised and touched, but skeptical, and a little wary. Often he came for dinner and stayed the evening; or he would come in the early afternoon and spend hours on the floor with Helen and Roy in endless impromptu games or with blocks or picture-books. Helen, he declared, was responding splendidly to his experiment; her esthetic sense was obviously far finer than Roy's, who would probably end in a stockbroker's office. He devised various tests and kept records of the results; for example, Helen, on three different occasions placed within reach of a chair on which had been deposited, side by side, a daffodil and a can opener, each time grabbed the daffodil and made off with it; Roy, under similar conditions, took the can opener twice and the third time ignored both of them. Another test was snapshots. Six of them were placed in a row on a chair and Helen instructed to choose one; she selected one of Lora standing beside a rhododendron bush in Central Park. It was replaced; and in his turn Roy, with a brief glance down the line, took an automobile, a big handsome car which Lora had snapped beside the curb one day to use up a roll of film. Could anything be plainer, Albert demanded. Wasn't it obvious that Helen saw the composition and the line, whereas Roy saw nothing, he merely reacted to an acquisitive instinct?

"It's much too simple," said Lora. "What about me for instance? I'd take this one."

She picked up a group, taken by her only a couple of weeks before Max's death, in the park; the ground was covered with snow, Max stood with the baby in his arms, Albert was beside him with Helen and Roy perched on his shoulders. It had turned out so well that she had had an enlargement made and sent it to her parents, with a note on the back explaining identities and relationships.

"Sure you'd take that one," Albert laughed. "If you ever had an esthetic impulse it died the day Roy was born. Maybe before that, I don't know what may have happened to you in some savage province B.C. Before Conception, that means. It also means Birth Control, though I blush to mention it in your presence. I know what it was, out beyond the mountains, beyond all the mountains—in Cedar Rapids, Iowa, for instance, that's a romantic spot—you were raped by the devil and begat an Imp of Fecundity, only you forgot to let him out. He's still in there, running the show—"

"You're a fool, and you talk too much," Lora said; and gathered up the snapshots and returned them to the drawer.

All this time, probably unknown to himself, he had a surprise in store for her; it kept itself in reserve another month or so, and then, on an afternoon in May, the very afternoon she took the necklace downtown and returned with a check for five hundred and fifty dollars in her purse, it burst forth. On her return she found Albert seated on the stoop, his hat pulled over his eyes, half asleep in the sun.

"Where the hell is everybody?" he demanded. Lora explained that Leah had gone to the park with the children and that she had been downtown on an errand. He had tried the park, but hadn't found them, he said, out of sorts; then went upstairs with her and helped wash the dishes from lunch. Afterwards, in the living room, he said he guessed he would go, no telling when Leah and the children would return; and then, suddenly and without warning, Lora found herself in his arms, his lips violently upon hers, his hands resuming long-relinquished privileges. Taken completely by surprise, for an instant bewildered, she merely submitted; tardily she got her hands against his shoulders and pushed, throwing back her head, but he was a giant against her little efforts and at once had her lips again and lifted her in his arms. She ceased struggling, aware of his fumbling at the fastening of her dress, then feeling herself carried to the couch against the wall, where he put her down, following her without freeing her lips. "The fool, the damn fool," she was thinking; and finally, getting an arm free she reached up, grabbed a handful of his hair and pulled as hard as she could. He let out a yell and released her; she hung on, still pulling; he seized her wrist and jerked it away, then got to his feet and stood there, panting, looking down at her. She twisted around and sat on the edge of the couch, panting too.

"Well, for god's sake," he said quietly. "For god's sake, Lora mia, explain that if you can. You damn near pulled my hair out, and I damn near pulled your dress off. You don't deserve that, you're by no means good enough for it. Jackass—ho, ho, what a jackass!"

She did not reply, and abruptly he turned, and was gone. She heard him getting his hat in the hall, and an instant later the door slammed.

"As long as you admit I don't deserve it," she said aloud; and feeling something in her hand, looked at it and found a strand of fine blond hair twisted between her fingers. That's a pity, she thought.

It was a month or more before he showed up again.

That night in bed she amused herself matching the afternoon's episode with the Albert of four years back. He had always been direct, but directness like everything else is a matter of degree; he had always been stupid too, but never so stupid as this. Once she had been very fond of him; still was, for that matter, for she would never forget his blunt and unassuming kindness during a whole year, a year and more, before there was any hint of a reward. Nor would she soon forget the uncomfortable and all but hopeless situation out of which he had yanked her.

Five years ago, she thought; yes, all of that, for Roy would soon be five. Just think of it, so short a time ago there had been no Morris, no Helen, no Roy! Now Roy could read, Helen could talk, Morris would soon have a tooth. But that was a fix for you, five years ago. Steve had gone for good, with so natural and unembarrassed a brutality that she had felt no resentment or indignation, leaving her lying on a couch in the living-dining-bedroom of a tiny furnished flat on which the rent would be due in three days, with—to his knowledge—something under three dollars in her purse and seven months of his child in her womb. Anne Whitman—poor Anne she had thought even then—waiting at the door below for him to come down with his bags, had gone with him.

Anne had sought her out two weeks later—to apologize! She had gone first, she said, to the flat; the janitor told her that Miss Winter had gone, and after various inquiries she finally got an address from the girl at the drugstore on the corner. She explained this somewhat breathlessly after climbing three flights of stairs to the little furnished room on Fifteenth Street to which Lora had moved two days after Steve's departure—the rent was only six dollars a week, whereas the flat had been three times that, and light and linen, clean each week, were furnished. They called it linen, a technical term, to be broadly interpreted.

There were two chairs in the room, one made entirely of wood, the other with a seat of green imitation leather. When Anne entered Lora was seated on the latter, sewing linings in coats. There were two piles of coats on the narrow bed, one with linings already in, the other without; the ready linings were at one end, and the wooden chair served as a sewing-table. Standing, Anne explained how she got there, stammering with embarrassment; then Lora moved the wooden chair over for her to sit on.

"It took a lot of courage to come, didn't it?" Lora observed. "You needn't have bothered. I have nothing against you."

Anne had had to come, she said. It had taken courage all

right. If Lora didn't have anything against her she was an angel; she must have, she couldn't help it. "I hate myself, I can't expect you to forgive me," Anne said. "I would have done anything, that's all there is to it. I'd do anything for him, and he loves me, he does truly love me. You do believe he loves me, don't you, Lora?"

Lora pitied her a little. "It doesn't matter," she said. "Yes, he loves you. He was through with me anyway."

Anne nodded eagerly. "That's it. He told me so a long while ago, two months ago, in March it was, you remember the night you wouldn't go to dinner with us and we went to a party at Joe Curtis's? I told him it wasn't any use, he'd have to stick to you, he really ought to marry you I said, and he was wild, he swore you'd played a trick on him and were trying to force him into it and he wouldn't stand for it. I didn't believe that, of course I told him I didn't believe it. We were in that little alcove at Joe's, and he put his arms around me...."

"It doesn't matter," said Lora, who had resumed her sewing, wishing the little idiot would go.

"Anyway," said Anne, and stopped. "I don't know how to say it," she continued, "but anyway it's about money. I know you haven't got any, and here—" she was fumbling in her purse— "here's twenty dollars—of course it isn't much—" She laid two ten-dollar bills on the corner of the bed; one of them slid to the floor and she picked it up and put it back. Lora looked at her, at the money, and back at her again.

"Steve didn't send that," Lora said.

"I get a little from my father," said Anne. "Please don't be angry. Steve doesn't realize, it isn't that he doesn't care, he just doesn't realize…"

"I need it all right." Lora picked up the bills, folded them, and placed them on Anne's lap. "Steve's out of it, I wouldn't even take the trouble to call him names. The only thing I'm concerned about is the baby. I need money all right, but I'd rather not take yours." She grinned. "You'll need it too, see if you don't. Not for a baby maybe. Perhaps you'll need it to get Steve out of jail, you'd better hang onto it."

"Jail!" Anne stared at her.

"Don't be frightened; nothing will happen probably. He got himself exempted by calling himself married, maybe he said I was pregnant too, I don't know. I don't blame him; I wouldn't want to go to war either."

Anne had jumped to her feet, fright and terror in her eyes. "I didn't know—good god, they might shoot him—they might take him—if you don't tell—Oh, Lora, for god's sake don't tell—"

"It isn't that, why should I tell, but there must be people who know about it."

Lora was sorry she had mentioned it, there had been no gratification in it anyway; and now she had a terrified and imploring Anne on her hands, begging her not to tell, begging her to do something—tell everybody they were married, for instance—anything to save Steve, careless and imprudent but well-meaning Steve. Finally with a flood of promises and re-assurances Lora got rid of her—got her out of the room and the door shut, and heard her footsteps clumsily negotiating the dark narrow uncarpeted stairs. Then she restored the wooden chair to its office of sewing-table and picked up another coat. Stupid fool I was, she thought, to say anything about it.

Stupid too to have refused the money. Why shouldn't she take it? Twenty dollars—that was four dollars more than she had got for the watch she sold yesterday—the watch Pete Halliday had given her. Almost would she have preferred to cut off her hair and sell it, the hair Pete had braided—not that, enough of that. She bit off a thread, compressed her lips, and started the other edge. She should have taken Anne's money, why not? Idiotic stupid pride—if she wasn't above that she might as well give up. Nothing in god's world mattered but the baby, she was going to have that baby—ha, wasn't she though! But it was about time she used her intelligence, everything she did was stupid. These coat-linings—she couldn't possibly do more than fifteen a day—at eight cents that was a dollar twenty—the rent alone was nearly a dollar. Imbecile. Instead of jumping at this the minute that little tailor suggested it she should have waited, looked around for something worthwhile. She was handicapped by her condition, of course; she couldn't get a job in a store or an office with her front bulging out magnificently like a dahlia and ready to burst; anyway, she simply had to lie down once in a while. If she could have stood it the baby couldn't, she felt sure of that. If she could only see it! It was dumb to fix it so it couldn't be seen; there ought to be an opening somewhere so you could look in, so you could touch it even; what if one of its legs got twisted or its arm doubled under? Lord, it would be ugly, an awful-looking thing probably, but how she would love to see it! You could see it move too, it certainly did move, no doubt about that.

She took another thread. Damn the coat-linings; even if you worked like the very devil each one must take at least thirty minutes; she wished she had her watch so she could time herself. Or the alarm clock from the flat; that was stupid too, not to have brought anything that had belonged to Steve. Pride, ha! Pride was well above the subsistence level.

But something, Anne's visit perhaps, or the natural progression of her own intelligence and will, had cleared her head a little. This was not only stupid, it was dangerous. If she didn't look out, she reflected, she'd be having her baby in a charity ward or on the sidewalk, and she did not propose to do either. To hell with the coat-linings; she wasn't such a boob, she'd find something. When the boy came at six o'clock she gave him the finished coats and told him not to bring any more.

The next morning, a warm June day, she put on the thin dark grey coat, which didn't look bad at all with the buttons moved over, and started out. The man at the drugstore liked her, he might have something—what about making pills for instance, somebody had to make them. No, he was sorry, nothing. Mr. Pitkin, at the office where she had worked the summer before, was genial but had no suggestions to offer; he cracked a joke or two and tendered a ten-dollar bill which she took calmly with a smile of thanks. By noon she had about exhausted her list of possibilities, and she was dead tired; she had been unable to keep her breakfast. She stumbled into a bookshop and sank into a chair, but after a few minutes saw that that wouldn't do; obviously she wasn't welcome, and anyway she couldn't hold her head up. So she got back to her room, somehow climbed the stairs, and tumbled onto the bed without taking off her coat. She was furious; I'm nothing but a damn weakling, she thought, it makes me sick, some girls work hard right up to the very day. That gave her a start—could she have counted wrong? She lay on her back with her eyes closed, touching her fingers one by one, naming the months aloud. No, she was right, it wouldn't be for five weeks yet, maybe more.

It was the woman at the tea-room who told her the next day about Palichak. She had been told by Joe Curtis, who of course would know. It appeared a remote chance to Lora, but by that time she was desperate, so she trudged down to Macdougal Alley and rang the bell at Number Seven. Palichak himself, short and dark and massive, let her in; inside were a couple of girls drinking cocktails and a man with a beard at the piano.

"I came to see you because I'm pregnant," said Lora. "Mrs. Crosby at the tea-room said you wanted a model."

"I beg your pardon," he said, his thick accent almost unintelligible.

"*Enceinte, mon vieux*," called the man with the beard. "*Beremenna*."

Palichak took her in with a swift inclusive glance. "Of course, how very nice," he bowed. "You would like to work?"

"I don't know," Lora hesitated. "I came to see, I don't know anything about this."

"Ah. If you would be so kind—*par ici*—you take your clothes off—" He led her to the rear of the room, where an enormous metal screen enclosed a corner.

Behind it Lora removed her coat and hat and placed them on a chair. Then her dress, and her shoes and stockings. Then she stopped. What did he mean anyway? She called out:

"All my clothes?"

"Of course, Madame."

A minute later she called:

"All right, I'm ready."

He appeared at the edge of the screen, turning it back a little. "Good. Come where I can see you."

She didn't mind the men, but she wished the girls weren't there. Oh, well, to the devil with them. She stepped out, away from the screen, into the window's direct light. She looked boldly at the girls and saw only mild curiosity, then admiration in their eyes; the man with the beard had turned on the stool, with his elbow on the keyboard and his chin in his hand, his other hand dancing on the treble, his eyes carefully appraising her; Palichak stood away, gazing at her with a frown. Suddenly his teeth gleamed in a smile and he clapped his hands.

"Hair!" he exclaimed. "Hair too! What do you think, yes?"

"She's perfect," said one of the girls.

"Wonderful, marvelous," said the other.

"*Laissez tomber les cheveux*," demanded Palichak.

"Let your hair down," the man with the beard translated.

She pulled out the pins and shook her head, and the red-brown curtain fell below her waist, covering her shoulders and back; a strand hung sinuous through the valley between her breasts. She stood natural and straight, creamy-white curves and columns glowing with life even in the shadows, unmindful of them, entirely at ease to their businesslike appraisal.

"She will do, eh?" Palichak beamed.

The man with the beard left the piano and strolled towards her.

"You know what this is," he said. "Pally is doing some murals for the Institute Building at Detroit, and he wants a model for Fertility. He wouldn't explain, he can't talk you know. Thought you might fear it was for a barroom idyll."

She returned to the screen and dressed herself, overhearing meanwhile their unanimous agreement on her perfections. When she came out again Palichak hurried over.

"You can begin tomorrow?"

"How much do I get?" she demanded.

"Three dollars is usual."

"Three dollars a day!"

The man with the beard spoke up. "Three dollars an hour. Some days one hour, some two, some three if you can stand it. You may rest of course."

Lora hesitated, looking from one to the other.

"I'll have to have five," she said.

Palichak glared at her, and let out a flood of Russian. The man with the beard shook his head at him and grinned.

"It's extortion," he said, "but of course you'll get it."

"I can't help it, I need the money," said Lora.

That evening she ate at Mrs. Crosby's tea-room, a dollar and a quarter. I can't do this every day, she thought, but I can afford to celebrate.

It was upstairs at Number Seven that Palichak worked. Lora stood on a velvet mat on a little wooden platform, her right arm upraised with the hand back of her head, her hair flowing loosely over her left shoulder, and a filmy strip of silk gauze draped from her right shoulder to her left thigh and thence to the platform. Behind her, from ceiling to floor, were the rich folds of a purple curtain. Palichak never talked. He frowned sometimes and swore often, always in Russian, and did not address her except to announce a rest period. He was considerate about resting, except occasionally he would forget, and then when Lora could stand it no longer she would drop her arm, he would frown and then grin at her, and she would step down. They were nearly always alone, but now and then someone would drop in for a moment. The most frequent visitor was the man with the beard, who would enter without knocking, look critically at the picture, glance at Lora with a nod, settle himself in the big leather chair near the window, and remain there an hour or more without speaking.

One day he brought a stranger with him, a tall blond blue-eyed man in his early thirties, with his suit unpressed and his necktie under his right ear.

"You know Scher," said the man with the beard. "Albert Scher of the *Star*."

Palichak nodded, not offering to shake hands, and went on working. The blond man looked at the picture and said nothing. Then he looked at Lora, and he looked so long and his blue eyes seemed so friendly that, feeling she must do something, she winked at him.

"Venus *vulgaris*, you ought to be ashamed of yourself," he said, and rejoined the man with the beard.

A week later she was dining with Albert Scher at the Brevoort. He was careful to explain that this would probably prove to be unique, not by any means a precedent. "I eat here," he said, "every time I find a woman more beautiful than any woman I have ever seen. If possible, with the woman, but it doesn't often turn out that way. Though I should say you aren't even a woman, you're just a girl—how old are you?"

Lora, tasting for the first time the devilish and irresistible savour of clams à l'ancienne, said simply, "Twenty-one."

"You're not married."

"No."

"I knew that. I wanted to see if you'd be embarrassed. A girl pregnant at twenty-one who doesn't blush when asked if she's married is either dumb or divine. Which?"

"Right now I'm just hungry. I think you're trying to shock me, Mr. Scher. I don't mind."

"Shock you, after the way you winked at me the other day?"

"Oh, you understood that."

"Not at the time. Since then I've found out about you. You're alone, and broke, and on the verge of a tribute to embryology, which is quite apparent. If I were capable of sustained indignation I'd seek out the fond father and knock his block off. I'm told his name is Steve Adams. He ought to be in France anyway; that's all wars are good for, they kill off a few like him."

Lora looked at him, and took an olive.

"Me, you're thinking," he grinned. "They won't have me. My eyes are in wrong side up. That's how I got a job as art critic on a newspaper. Thank god for that—the eyes I mean. I was born in Austria; my father got naturalized."

"Oh. Naturally you'd be pro-German."

"Pro-nothing," he snorted. "Pro-intelligence, so I'd be in a minority no matter where I was."

Lora glanced at him; would she want to fight, she wondered,

if she were a man? She thought not. Her baby might be a man....

After dinner he wanted to take her home in a taxi, but she said no, they should walk the ten blocks, they must avoid bad precedents. "Unless I'll embarrass you; people look at me."

"Embarrass, hell—but I can't walk slow," he declared; lifted his hat, bowed, and was gone, leaving her on the sidewalk. She leisurely made her way home, loving the warm summer air, reluctant to return to the little furnished room. It would be fun to have a baby outdoors, she thought, on the grass in the sun, beside a little stream perhaps—you could wash it in the stream if it wasn't too cold—with the crickets hopping around wondering what was going on. Probably women used to do that before there were houses....

When in the middle of July Palichak was finally through with her she had saved nearly a hundred dollars; this she kept always on her person, in a little bag sewed to a string around her waist. She didn't seek another job; she expected and hoped there wouldn't be time. She had seen Albert Scher only once since the dinner; he had come to the room one evening, sat and talked for an hour, and departed. There should be a doctor, he had said, he would arrange it, and the next day one had come; but Lora, informed of his terms, outrageous she thought, had sent him off and made arrangements with a midwife instead, a kindly, middle-aged, not-too-clean Italian woman who talked of the prospective event as if it were no more than a tooth-pulling, and who advised Lora to ride a lot on street-cars. "It don't cost much," she said, "and the bumps bring it on. Busses are better because they bump more, but they cost a dime and there's no use spending the extra money." Lora smiled and sat in Washington Square as a compromise.

It began late one night, after she had been in bed several hours. That's funny, she said to herself, I thought it always started after you had moved around or stooped over or something. But this must be it. Oh, lord—this must be it. It felt just like that, exactly like that, the other time....

She clamped her jaws together. "I will not think of the other time," she said aloud to the darkness. "I will not, I *will* not. I will think of this time, this wonderful lovely time—oh lord, my god—there it's over....I think...."

She lay a minute or two, waiting, then, when it did not return, got up and turned on the light, put on her bathrobe, got a nickel from her purse, and made her way down the three flights of stairs to where the slot telephone hung on the wall at the rear of the hall. A door opened and a face appeared; then it opened full and a woman in a torn white cotton nightgown came rapidly to her. "You poor thing—you should of yelled—I told you to yell, didn't I—you go right back—here, give it to me."

"I'm all right," Lora said.

"Go on back—what's the number?"

"Really I'm all right, Mrs. Pegg."

But the woman pushed her off down the hall. "Go back I tell you, go to bed, do I want to be getting Tom up to carry you upstairs...."

Lora gave her the number and climbed back up the three flights. In bed again, she was suddenly alone and afraid; she felt no pain or movement whatever, and all at once she knew, the conviction took her by the throat, that the baby was dead. She became instantly rigid from head to foot, and stopped breathing, choked with terror. She tried to scream Mrs. Pegg's name, but no sound came. Slowly her hand, under the sheet, made its way down her body and on her abdomen stopped, pressing at first lightly, then strong and stronger; all was still. "By god, I'll get it out," she said aloud in a calm voice, "I'll cut myself open and get it out and look at it." She jerked herself upright, then fell back again on the pillow, doubled herself up with her knees almost touching her chin, and began to scream as loud as she could:

"Mrs. Pegg Mrs. Pegg Mrs. Pegg!"

At once rapid footsteps were on the stairs, and the door opened.

"Shut up, it won't kill you," the landlady snapped. "She'll be here in a minute."

Lora sat up and stared at her.

"You're a nice one," she said, "it's dead."

"What's dead? Lay down, lay out straight. It will be dead if you don't behave yourself. Lay down and shut up. You'll wake the whole house."

A bell sounded from below and Mrs. Pegg hurried out. Lora lay back and closed her eyes, and almost at once it came again. It began in the inmost center of her, then spread swiftly throughout her body, to the utmost extremities, so that her toes stretched and tightened and then drew themselves in and her fingers gripped the edges of the mattress with each little muscle fierce and fighting to help. She pulled up her knees, then straightened out again, and repeated it many times, pulling at the mattress each time, not hearing her groans or caring about them. She was aware that the door had opened again, and she heard a new strong voice:

"Don't relax, dearie, push it out, that's right."

But it was slowing down, fading away from her, and she let go of the mattress and turning her head saw the dark-skinned wrinkled midwife, bareheaded, in a black dress with a long yellow scarf around her shoulders, taking things out of an old suitcase and an enormous paper bag and laying them on the chairs.

The midwife pulled down the sheet and felt her and looked at her; her hands were deft and swift and gentle.

"It's dead, isn't it?" Lora said wearily.

The other's black eyes darted at her. "So that's what you want, is it? What makes you think it's dead? What did you do, what makes you think it's dead?"

"You're a fool," said Lora sharply. "I didn't do anything. It doesn't move. If it's dead I'm going to die too."

Chuckling, the midwife took a towel from a nail on the wall and wiped the sweat from Lora's face and brow. "There's nobody dead in this room yet," she said cheerfully. "You'll have enough to keep you busy this night dearie without worrying about things that's none of your business." She straightened up, and said suddenly, "I thought you said this was your first one."

"It is."

The midwife chuckled again. "Then I'm a virgin and God help me if my Luigi could hear that."

"It's my first one I tell you."

"All right, all right, dearie."

She turned and busied herself with the articles she had arranged on the chairs. Mrs. Pegg appeared with two wash basins, a pitcher and some old towels, and the information that there would soon be plenty of hot water in the bathroom; she had turned on the heater in the basement. Would she be wanted any more? No, the other said, she wouldn't need any help; she had once handled triplets all alone, with a sore back too, and they were all alive to this day.

Mrs. Pegg's footsteps could still be heard descending the stairs when Lora said suddenly, sharply:

"Ah, look out, look out."

The midwife glanced at her face. "It's coming, dearie? Don't let up on it now—here hold on to this—that's right, my little one—push it out, it comes quicker that way, an hour maybe, soon now—push it out."

But nine hours passed before it would push out. Lora had long since ceased to care about anything, anything in the world, except to have it end. At times she imagined the midwife was torturing her; at others she pleaded with her to do more, do something, do anything. Gradually the night's stillness surrendered to the city's million morning sounds, infrequent at first—the clatter of a milkwagon or a taxi's horn—then two or three together, and more, until it swelled into another day's bedlam. Along with that the window which Lora faced became again alive; when the blind was raised it was already dawn; steadily the light increased so that soon the midwife turned off the electric bulb that hung from the ceiling by a cord; and then the sun was blazing in and the pulse of the July heat throbbed again. The midwife pulled the blind down. She had put on an apron, her sleeves were rolled above her elbows, her coarse grey-streaked hair was tumbling over her left ear, and now and then she yawned wide and long. Lora, in those intervals when she could think, decided that a week must have passed, a month, a year. It seemed impossible that it had ever begun or that it would ever end. It was easy to see what was going to happen—it would keep up a little while longer, and then she would die without knowing it. How many more times would she have to do that? Five more, ten more? Ten more would do it perhaps. She couldn't do ten more, nor five either; not even one, no by god not one, not one, not one....

It was nearly noon when, lying with closed eyes, dead at last, she became aware of a noise beside her, and slowly and wearily lifting her lids, saw the midwife standing there expertly balancing in one hand a red and squirming baby.

"You're lucky, dearie, it's a boy," said the midwife. "No wonder he nearly split you open, he's as fat as a priest."

Lora tried to smile.

"It's wiggling," she said, "look at it wiggle."

VIII

Roy was eighteen months old, big and healthy and already argumentative, before Lora paid the debt she owed Albert Scher.

By that time the debt was a large one, though doubtless he did not consider it a debt at all. When the baby was only a week old he had appeared one evening at the room, astonished to find that it was all over. He had expected, he said, to be on hand, and was furious to learn that the doctor had been replaced by a midwife. Midwives were not worth a damn, they were dirty and superstitious, and might easily ruin a baby's entire life by giving it an ugly and erroneous first impression. Lora replied that doctors were swindlers and pigs, and anyway look at the baby— nothing wrong with that baby. Doctors were expensive, Albert agreed, that's what he had come for; and pulled from his pocket a roll of crumpled bills and proceeded to count it out upon the bed.

"Hundred and sixty-two dollars," he announced. "Oh, it's not mine, I never had that much money in my life. I described your classic plight to some of my friends and they passed the hat. Not a jitney from me, I couldn't afford it. This was to be for the doctor; now what?"

"It won't be wasted," said Lora. "If I tried to thank you I'd cry. I cried yesterday because Mrs. Pegg brought me some soup. I hope I soon get over it."

But that was a small part of the debt; it was he who solved the problem of a job for her. She had tried to think of something that would permit her to have the baby with her, at least something that would not keep her away all day, but besides office or counter work there seemed to be nothing she could do. Thanks to the generosity of Albert's friends there was no immediate hurry, but she wanted to keep something in reserve. What if the baby got sick? Worse, what if she did? For the first time she began in dead earnest to appraise her situation and calculate the possibilities, and decided in the end that she was in a hell of a fix. Luck would see her through, nothing else. To pretend that hard work, any work that she could do or would be permitted to do, could bring ease or security or even a pleasant though hazardous journey along the road she was started on, was pure buncombe.

The immediate luck came through Albert, who turned up one day with the news that a friend of his would like to have her for a series of posters for Daintico Dental Cream. At least he would like to see her. Only, Albert said, she must first get some new clothes. Lora refused point-blank to squander her cherished capital on such a risk, but finally he persuaded her; and on a September afternoon, leaving the baby with Mrs. Pegg, she went in her new dark green tight-fitting suit, deep brown hat and alligator-skin shoes, to an elaborate studio in the Fifties. A smooth little man, polite and effusive, with a pale miniature moustache and no eyebrows at all, accepted her for the job at once on generous terms. She would be an inspiration, he said; and would be needed only two hours a day.

It was that same afternoon on her way home that she sent a telegram to her father and mother. Since the baby's coming she had written them three letters, the first since she had left them, but sent none. For one thing, she had feared they might somehow trace her address through a letter, and for another she didn't like what she had written. Re-read the next day, they sounded like bragging, and she didn't want to brag; strength doesn't brag, and they should, indeed they should, feel her strength! But this afternoon, passing a telegraph office, on the impulse she entered and sent a wire to Mr. and Mrs. Leroy Winter.

Hurrah nine pound baby boy born July twentieth named Leroy mother and child doing nicely father not to be found.

The girl at the desk counted the words and surveyed her with cold hesitation, wondering, perhaps, if this should not be refused on the ground of obscenity; but finally mumbled, sixty-nine cents. She added mechanically, "Your address at the bottom in case of reply."

"It isn't necessary," said Lora, paid and departed.

The man with no eyebrows she called, in her mind and to Albert, Daintico. His name was Holcomb Burleigh. The third day she went there he asked her to dine with him; she declined, saying that she never went out evenings, she had to stay with her baby.

"I know, Scher told me," he said. "You're a brave little woman, Miss Winter. A noble woman."

"Sure," Lora said.

A week later he asked her again; arrangements could be made about the baby, he suggested. No, Lora said, she wouldn't like to do that. Lunch then. Goodness, no, lunch was impossible, she always went out with the baby at noon and stayed three hours; that was more impossible than evening even, for then he was usually asleep. Daintico blinked at her and appeared to give it up.

But two months later he presented her with a problem. In the meantime she had had other jobs which Albert found for her—a life class that met once a week, a man who did North Africa and Hawaii for a travel bureau, a young woman who painted her in pink and purple vertical lines and called it simply and unassailably, Study. She was sufficiently good-looking, especially her fine brow and eyes and the clear living quality of her skin, but it was her glorious wealth of hair and the rarity of her type that brought her, finally, more offers than she could accept. Soon Albert's offices were no longer needed; she could choose and reject; and when he brought her another summons from Daintico she hesitated, then decided her first client should not be abandoned.

He used her for an outing series for a fashionable sports apparel shop. This, she thought, was ridiculous, it should have been a bobbed-hair flapper; what was the matter with him? She found out one day towards the end, she was to return only once more, when he took her hand suddenly, kissed it, and with a quiet and remarkable dignity asked her to marry him.

The next day, seated on a bench in Washington Square with Roy's carriage beside her, wrapped in a thick wool coat with a fur collar against the December wind, she told Albert about it. He often joined her there, usually briefly, sometimes sitting with her for an hour or more. Now and then he even pushed the carriage as they encircled the Square, amusing Lora with his unconscious defiant glare at the casual glances of passersby.

"You misunderstood him," Albert declared. "If Burleigh ever marries he'll have to be kidnapped. He was reciting poetry."

"He made it fairly clear," said Lora. "He said he would ask me only to exchange Miss Winter for Mrs. Burleigh and let time defeat him or make him the happiest of men."

"I told you it was poetry," He glanced at her, frowning. "I might have known it would be something like this. A cottage at Great Neck, a new carriage of art wicker for the baby and a nurse with sterile rubber gloves, even a chauffeur perhaps if all goes well....Ha! To this, Venus has come." He got to his feet, thrust his ungloved hands into his overcoat pockets, and stood looking down at her. "Listen, Lora mia." That was the first time he called her that. "The baby could be put down to accident and ignorance; I forgive it. It is at any rate an inescapable prostitution, impossible to approve but necessary to condone. But to prostitute that divine body to a clipped lawn and a solarium is an intolerable affront to beauty. You'll rot; the first of each month, promptly, he'll pay the rent and the grocer's bill, and each Saturday night, promptly too, you'll pay your share of it. To escape that repulsive routine is the first necessity of a decayed and degenerated race. It began fifty thousand years ago when some hairy fool, sick perhaps from over-eating, first discovered that instincts were negotiable. Now we have nymphomaniacs and Lesbians, neurotics and prostitutes, wives and husbands, but Venus and Adonis are dead. Spermatozoa, once laughing children at play innocent even of curiosity, are skinny underpaid old men carrying indecipherable messages from one sickroom to another. The day you marry Holcomb Burleigh I'm going to wear a black band around my sleeve and get drunk."

"That's too bad, we'd like to have you at the wedding."

"Go to hell."

"What are spermatozoa?"

"You're too young to be told such things."

"I'll ask Roy." She leaned over the side of the carriage, where he lay with wide-open roving eyes, smiling as he saw her face above him. "Baby, tell me, honey, what are spermatozoa?" She went on without looking up, "Of course you know I told him I wouldn't marry him."

"Ha! You'll marry him."

She shook her head, making sure the blanket was well tucked

in around the edges. "I'm cold, I've got to move around." She stood, shivering a little. "I wouldn't marry him if he were as handsome as you and as rich as Rockefeller. I wouldn't marry anybody."

"If you mean that, Lora mia, I'll make the band a flaming red and wear it every day."

"Well, I mean it. Come on, let's walk."

She never saw Daintico again, nor heard from him.

With the passing months she wondered mildly about Albert. What was it that moved him, selfish as he was, to devote so many of his hours to her? He said he loved to look at her, that it cooled his eyes to let them serenely enjoy her living loveliness, aloof alike from passion and from puzzles of technique. Having no such high opinion of her comeliness, she doubted this esthetic detachment, but she had to confess that he carried it off. As she knew, there was an apartment on Bank Street and a studio in Patchin Place where he was a privileged and favored visitor; a thousand morsels of Village gossip floated to her as she stood, draped or naked, on rugs or platforms, wondering whether Eileen had found the baby's rattle or deciding what to take in for dinner—for long since she had moved into a large room downstairs, with a bath partitioned off in one corner and a sink and gas-plate in another. With hot soup and some chops and potatoes and a salad, she loved to sit in the big soft chair and eat leisurely, Roy in his crib not ten feet away against the wall, within her view, his eyes shaded by a scarf draped over the side of the crib, with a magazine or novel on the table beside her plate. It amused her sometimes to feed him and eat her own meal simultaneously; the double sensation brought a confusion of pleasure and each stimulated the other. "Wait a minute," she would say, "the salad comes next, can't you wait a minute, pig? Not there, you ninny, this one is the salad."

She had never seen the studio, nor the apartment, nor the tenant of either, but she had heard all about them. One, Marie Stoeffer, tall and dark and not too young, was a secretary in an office downtown; the other, Anita Chavez, also dark but not so tall and much younger, modelled furs at Russeks. What she chiefly overheard regarding them was the argument, often repeated, now desultory, now furious, as to whether either knew of the other's existence. Obviously not, one side declared, since the fiery Anita if she knew would stick daggers both in Albert and in her rival, and the dignified Marie, if she even suspected, would put a new lock on her door.

At about this point Lora would decide to try hamburger and onions for dinner, and not have any salad.

It was in midsummer that she received an unheralded visit from Anne Whitman. Coming home early one afternoon from a job uptown, Eileen, on the sidewalk as usual with Roy in his carriage, greeted her with the announcement that she had a caller. Mrs. Pegg, on her way to the meat market, had stopped and told her, she said; a young woman had come and, being told of Lora's absence, had prevailed on Mrs. Pegg to let her in to wait. Lora asked Eileen to keep Roy out a little longer and, entering her room, found Anne lying on the bed with her eyes closed.

Lora guessed the story before she heard it, but it was none the less painful. At first Anne wouldn't talk; she said merely that she didn't know where Steve was, and that she had come to find out if Lora had seen him or heard from him. Then she sat on the edge of the bed and stared as Lora changed her dress, her hands folded in her lap, motionless.

"I'm going to kill myself," she said finally.

"Not for Steve Adams, he's not worth it," said Lora.

Anne went on, "I started to yesterday, and what stopped me

was the thought that maybe he was with you and I could see him. So I went to the tea-room and Mrs. Crosby told me you were still here. You've got a new room, it's very nice. You don't know where he is?"

"I haven't seen him since the day he went off with you."

"Oh. You haven't. He left me a week ago. Twice before he left me and I found him again and he took me back. He said he pitied me."

"That's funny. Steve's supply of pity—"

"Now I can't find him." Anne got up and started to walk towards Lora, then went back and sat down again. "First he went away, uptown, I found him up there with a woman as old as you and me put together, and then in May he went out to Pennsylvania and got a job with the Pittsburgh office of that same oil company. He was out there alone; anyway I didn't see anybody. God knows where he is now; down at the Federal Oil Company they won't tell me anything, they say they don't know."

She stopped, her eyes levelled on Lora, and said with sudden shrill sharpness:

"I think you're lying. You've seen him."

"Well, I haven't."

"He used to talk about you and call you names and wonder about the baby."

"How did he know there was one?"

"He didn't. I don't know." Anne got up, took a step, and stood there drooping, all will visibly gone from her body, her face, her spirit. "You've got to tell me where he is, Lo, somebody has got to tell me, I've done everything I can. I am going to kill myself, really I am."

"You're not pregnant are you?"

"No. I thought it was better to be careful, after the way he acted with you...."

"Have you got any money?"

"Yes." Anne's shoulders lifted a fraction of an inch and dropped again. "I get money from home."

Lora regarded her a moment in silence. She sighed, shook herself a little, went to the front window and called out to Eileen to bring the baby in, and then turned again to Anne:

"You'd better lie down a while. Later we'll have something to eat and talk things over."

For a month after that she had Anne on her hands. Lora's old room upstairs was taken for her. She asked that she be permitted to take Eileen's place in caring for the baby during Lora's absences, but Lora firmly said no; and she gave Eileen private instructions never to leave Roy alone. She thought Anne was half crazy; there was no other way to account for her idiotic mooning over Steve Adams—over any man, for that matter, but particularly Steve. Of him nothing could be learned, he seemed this time to be gone for good, until one day Lora, nagged into it by Anne and sure that nothing would come of it, wrote a letter to the Federal Oil Company representing herself as Steve's sister. Within a week a reply came stating that Stephen R. Adams had on July twenty-seventh been transferred to the Shanghai sales office. His mail would be forwarded. The next day, without warning or farewell, Anne disappeared. When Lora got home in the afternoon she was gone.

The little fool has actually made for China, Lora thought, and was convinced of it when no word came from her for months. Autumn arrived; the trees in the Square dropped their scrawny and grimy leaves; snow had fallen and the winter holidays come and gone, when one morning Lora found in the mail an engraved notice which stated that on January eleventh Miss Anne Whitman had been married to Mr. Ernest Joseph Seaver.

Lora never learned the inside of that. Not long after the notice arrived there came a note from Anne inviting her to tea at an address in Brooklyn. She was minded not to take the trouble to go, but for once curiosity got the better of her; and there was Anne in a lovely yellow crepe gown, with a turquoise necklace and a permanent wave, smiling hostess in a large and luxurious living room to a group of chatty ladies none of whom Lora had ever seen before. She had no opportunity with Anne alone; and departed, furious, when it became apparent that there would be none. A month later Anne came to see her, but had little to tell about herself. She had known Ernest Seaver many years, she said, from childhood, in fact; they had been beaux at high school, upstate. He was one of those who get as a reward for heroic patience the cracked and empty shells from which bolder men have removed the kernels; or as Anne put it, "He used to say he'd wait, I'd take him some day; he's really very sweet, Lo." She had not rushed off to China, Lora gathered, but precisely where she had gone that summer day did not appear. Home probably, Oneida or Elmira or wherever it was. Steve was mentioned only once and then not by name; when Roy awoke and stirred in his crib Anne got up and went over to look at him and after a moment turned and said abruptly, in a voice so painfully tightened into casualness that Lora winced:

"You haven't heard from him."

Lora shook her head, too exasperated to speak, at a suffering so purposeless and so ineffectual. Killing yourself would be better than that, she thought.

As spring approached and it again became possible to spend whole mornings or afternoons outdoors with Roy without half freezing, she began to feel a touch of the restlessness that she remembered so well from that other life which seemed from this distance a dream. She shied violently from the comparison, but that did not remove the unrest. It was an annoyance, for it seemed to her to be clearly unreasonable. She had Roy, wasn't that enough? He was so sturdy and healthy and smiling that people were constantly stopping to look at him, make faces at him, make noises with their tongue or lips. Surely she could ask nothing better than this. Well…yes. That would be all right, her work was pleasant enough, by no means burdensome, sufficiently well paid. Not too secure though. Fads in models change; that man with a white beard who had been in such demand a year ago was now going around begging. Oh, well, there would always be something to do….

That was it, then, to bring Roy up, feed him, clothe him, watch him grow—soon he would be talking, he was already a year and eight months. That would be fun. She would teach him to say, Steve Adams is a dirty bum. Not that it mattered about Steve, she was nursing no grudge, but it would be fun to hear Roy say it, not knowing who he was talking about. What should she tell him about his father? That didn't matter, either, to her, but he would want to know who his father was; all children did, as if it made any difference. The war would do. Your father was shot in the war, my son, fighting for his country. Ha, thousands of children would be told that whose fathers would really, at that very moment….Enough of fathers, the less said about them the better. If she had a clever tongue like Albert….

Where was Albert this afternoon, by the way? She hadn't seen him for three days. Had he deserted Venus? Not likely; obviously he still liked to be with her; he was so transparent. Probably he was busy finding a successor to Marie, who had recently married and gone to France on her honeymoon.

She would like to go to France—that was an idea! She had over three hundred dollars saved in the bank, more than enough. There were lots of artists there too, thousands of them, and it wouldn't matter whether she spoke French or not. But Roy would make it difficult. What if something went wrong, that would be a fine fix, broke and without resource in a distant and foreign country, with a sick baby perhaps and unable even to understand what the doctor said. It was bad enough when you could understand them; no matter what they said you always felt they were entirely too intimate with death to be trustworthy. Like last summer when Roy had the colic and Doctor Berry called it some long name, rubbing his hands, as much as to say, ha, I know that fellow, we've had some great old times together.

No, France was out of it. Pretty much everything was out of it, except just this, just today and tomorrow and next week, with Roy not really a baby any more. She wouldn't teach him to call her Mamma or Mother, he should call her Lora. Why? No particular reason; she liked it better. Her own mother's name was Evelyn. It suited her all right, soft and mushy, plenty of tears but no....Oh well. That was done, none of that. Certainly Roy should call her Lora.

She smiled at herself. Here she was, finding out all over again that nothing ever turns out the way you expect it to. At least not the way you picture it. That spring and summer three years ago she used to think, walking home alone from the office or sitting at the switchboard waiting for the buzzer, just wait till she had a baby! She could feel the muscles in her arms fierce around it; she never tired, after a thousand repetitions, of the imagined warmth of its confident sweet-smelling little body. As a matter of fact, she might as well admit it...but no, it wasn't exactly a bore. But the fierceness soon disappeared or else it just simply wasn't there. It wasn't that she minded washing out diapers or getting up in the night or sitting on the floor rolling a ball back and forth instead of reading or mending her clothes; certainly it wasn't that she had any regrets....

It did seem though that it was a bit dull. Nothing desperate of course, she could go along all right, and god knows it was better than if, for instance, she had married Daintico and he were always hanging around. Married, no getting away from it. As a husband perhaps, but that was the joke of it, you could get rid of him as a husband if you wanted to, but as a father he was permanent. How could you make that seem sensible? When she had asked the lawyer he had talked a lot of nonsense. It wasn't just because a man helped make the baby, for unless he was a husband he had no rights at all, which was as it should be. No wonder men wanted to get married....

She didn't know a single man, she decided, not one, who was at all fit to be a father. A permanent father. Try to think of one of them that way and you could see how silly it was. Palichak. Mr. Pitkin. Daintico. Albert. Doctor Berry. Any one of them might in a pinch serve for any other imaginable purpose, but as fathers they were all equally unthinkable. Lovers? At that word something stirred within her, unbearable; a deep and bitter pain that exploded into a cloud of vapor which smothered her brain and concealed the source of thought, so that all that was left of everything was a numb resentment, a vast and intoler-able discomfort. She forced her way through it with all the scorn of her will. Lovers hell, she thought, what of it, don't be an ass, anyone would do for that.

The word attacked her again, one evening not long after, under somewhat different circumstances. Up to a certain point it was much like a hundred other evenings that had preceded it. Albert had come in an hour or so after dinner and found her sitting with her legs curled under her in a big chair, her only big chair, brushing her hair preparatory to putting it up for the night, eating peanut brittle and reading a magazine. As dressing-gown she wore a white robe which had originally served as her drapery in a frontispiece for a new edition of Baudelaire. A screen papered in black and silver, with a hole in one corner, bought at an auction on University Place, sheltered Roy's crib in the corner, and a little heap of coals glowed in the grate, for though it was nearly May the night was quite cool and there was no heat.

She finished her hair, then made some coffee and brought out crackers and cheese. Albert was all in, he said; he had spent the afternoon at the Independents' and had only one thing left to decide, whether to sit in the bathtub and slash his wrists or get a job in the subway. He lay on his back on the floor in front of Lora's chair with a cracker in one hand and a piece of cheese in the other, now and then rising on his elbow to take a sip of coffee, demanding of her for god's sake never to pose again; join him instead, he begged, in a campaign to blow up all paint and canvas factories.

"They'd still have paper and charcoal," Lora said.

"And ink and tempera and chalk and graphite and bug juice and the blood of plants," he groaned. "It's impossible to believe that two things, one as lovely as you and the other as ugly as art, can exist in the same world."

"You'll be sorry for that in the morning."

He grinned. "Half of it maybe. Only half. The other half stays good sober or drunk, morning or night. Even El Greco never made you up."

"That's nice." She smiled back at him. "I never saw an El Greco, but that doesn't matter, I know you're crazy about him." She drained her coffee cup, then, reaching for a cigarette and a match, said suddenly, "You'd better take a good look, for this is your last chance."

He sat up. "What do you mean? You're not going away?"

She shook her head no, smiling.

"Getting married!"

Another shake.

He lay down again. "I know what it is, you're going to paint. I knew you would, everybody does sooner or later. What the hell, I don't have to look at your pictures, you can turn them to the wall when I come around and I'll never know. If you have a show you can write my piece about it."

"Really, I'm serious. I can't see you anymore. I'm afraid to."

"Afraid of me? Come now, you've withstood my charms nearly two years."

"Oh, it isn't that. You've been careful not to make it difficult. It's Miss Chavez."

He pulled himself up with a jerk, sitting straight, pushing cigarette smoke out of his nose and mouth with the words:

"That little devil! Oh ho! I'll strangle her with the mantilla the greatest bullfighter in Mexico gave her the day she broke his heart, the little liar. She came to see you, eh? What did she say?"

"No, I haven't seen her."

"How is it her then?"

I must be careful, thought Lora, or this won't come out right at all.

"It's nothing very definite," she said, "only I've heard things. I hear a lot of talk you know. Apparently Miss Chavez thinks she has discovered that your interest in me is not purely esthetic. She talks too much, I don't like it."

"By god, I shall surely strangle her. Who does she talk to?"

"Oh, I don't know. Everybody." Lora waved her hand vaguely. "I could stand the talk I suppose, but it seems she's threatening all sorts of things. Anyway, as you said once, who wants their name signed to a picture they didn't paint?"

"Blah," said Albert scornfully. "You don't know Anita. She's as harmless as a garter snake. Of course she always talks, but confound it all, when did she start on you? You are my vestal virgin, my Brünnhilde surrounded by a protecting flame, my Eloise inviolate through an unfortunate physiological accident transformed by a perversion into diseased poetry; and she's got to let you alone or I'll strangle her."

"Oh," said Lora, looking at him straight, "I didn't know there was anything wrong with you."

He stared at her and then laughed, bellowing, plumping back on the floor and up again. He didn't stop laughing.

"Well, I didn't," she declared stoutly. "Be quiet, you'll wake the baby." She got up and went to the screen and disappeared behind it. Her voice could be heard, low and soothing. Soon she came out again. "You did wake him," she said. "You'd better go if you're going to roar like a bull."

"I'll be good," Albert promised. "But my god that was funny. You're as literal as an academician. The only thing wrong with me, Lora mia, is that there's nothing wrong with me. In a world of sick men the healthy are perverse. But Anita. Don't worry about Anita; I'll fix her. Don't for god's sake cast me off; you, the sacred grove where I rest my feet. The true madonna, the hope of the world. I'm going to learn to paint, and do you and Roy, naked in the sun, and call it triumphantly Virgin and Bastard. I hope they'll let me take it to prison with me, and you must come now and then and let me talk to you."

"You're an awful fool," said Lora. "So is Miss Chavez maybe; all the more reason why you'll have to find another sacred grove to rest your feet in. I don't intend to be made uncomfortable for a sin I've not committed."

"And one you're not interested in."

"I didn't say that."

"Right. Carefully you didn't say it. You did also, however, mention a picture you hadn't painted. And that I've been careful not to make it difficult. Are you doing this deliberately?"

"I don't know what you mean."

"Ha, you're not so dumb." He sat, still on the floor, with his knees crossed and his arms folded, directly in front of her chair, looking up at her; and she felt a quickening in her heart, a faint pleasant alarm through her body and limbs, as she saw his eyes fastened on her with no admiration, no fondness even.

"You're not so dumb," he repeated. "But for the sake of clearness let's put it this way. What would be your reaction if I were to announce that I intend to sleep here tonight, in that rather narrow bed, with you?"

"Announce? To Mrs. Pegg? To Miss Chavez? To the newspapers?"

"Don't quibble. What about it? You don't need to look triumphant, I know my voice is trembling. What about it?"

"I'm not triumphant."

"What about it?"

"Well...it would have one advantage, it would save Miss Chavez from being a liar, wouldn't it?"

"Many advantages. It would extinguish the flame that surrounds you."

Lora smiled at him. She had an impulse to touch him too, but kept her hands in her lap. His arms were still folded.

"You're pretty funny," she said. "You propose—this, like—this—without ever having wanted to kiss me—"

"I haven't wanted to kiss you." His voice trembled in earnest now; he got to his knees, close to her, and put his hands on the arms of her chair; she no longer enjoyed his eyes, but was held by them. "For god's sake, Lora mia, pay no attention to what I say. From this moment. Until peace comes again. But understand distinctly that I know it is you who did it, though god knows I don't know why. Ah, I have never touched you before —there—there—good god to be drowned with you—I never expected this...."

IX

Helen was six months old before she was named. She was born in the flat on Eleventh Street, to which Albert had taken his pregnant Brünnhilde in the fall following what he had one day labelled the immaculate seduction scene. The first week or so after she came he called his daughter nothing at all; of a morning, sometimes early, usually late, he would leap out of bed, get dressed in five minutes and leave for the little restaurant down the street to get his rolls and coffee. He would find a moment though to stop at the crib, pull down the blanket and take a look. "At last I know what obscenity is," he would say; or perhaps, "No wonder they invented maternal love, it would be either that or manslaughter."

This baby had been easy, almost too easy, Lora thought; the third day she had got her own breakfast and lunch, and now from the little kitchen she would call indifferently:

"Don't pretend, Albert dear; if she's as bad as that why do you take the trouble to look at her? Remember what you told me, one should have the courage of one's emotions."

And he would call back:

"Don't get analytical, Lora mia, it's not your line. Where the hell is my necktie? As a physical fact I'm a father; as a further physical fact this thing in here is a complicated worm. You might at least buy it a wig. So long—I'm off."

A month later he was calling it Paula; after Saint Paul, he explained, a tribute from fornication to its first great antagonist. Others would make rival claims, he said, Buddha for instance; but Buddha was no antagonist of anything, merely he was lazy, he wanted a good excuse to go off and sit down somewhere.

But Lora objected. She didn't like Paula; it sounded too much like a boy with curls. Almost anything else.

"All right," Albert grinned, "then Fornica. Not so bad. Fornica Winter Scher. Fornica darling. Fornica Scher."

"Winter."

"Why not keep the Scher? It's usual. You'll get along lots better in this world if you respect the conventions."

"You're an awful fool. I'll name her myself."

Anne Seaver, over from Brooklyn one day, called her Baba, and that stuck for several months, until Albert finally declared he could no longer bear it because it made him think of Sir Joshua Reynolds; this went unexplained. Besides, Baba was extraordinary.

"The trick in naming children," he said, "is to avoid all distinctive flavor. Sink them at once into the universal mire and they're much less apt to get disturbing ideas. The ideal way would be to call all boys Tom and all girls Helen; indeed, when certain present tendencies reach their destined goal even that distinction will disappear and everybody can be called Sam. We shall discount the inevitable and call her Sam."

"We shall not. I hate girls having boys' names."

"At least halfway then; Helen."

Lora sighed; at last that was over. She might have known better in the first place than to let him get started on it.

She had admitted to herself long since that Albert was rather beyond her. That first night he had slept in her room she had decided that he was like all other men, calculable to the extent of his desires, but then another complication arose: what was that extent? He really did seem to have some sort of desire beyond the food he ate and the love he took and the fun of making himself felt on other people. He put up that claim; she got those phrases from him. What was that desire, she asked him once, during those first two months when they spent every night together in the narrow bed that made them sleep stretched out close, their bodies touching at each slight movement. The desire to die intact, he replied; and then said he was too sleepy to talk about it and it didn't matter anyway.

When he learned she was pregnant—she waited three months to tell him—he insisted that she stop work at once. She might as well, he declared, for pretty soon she would have to, no one would want her. She protested that she had got her first job, with Palichak, less than two months before Roy was born, but he dismissed that as a special case. What the deuce, he said, he might or might not be able to support the child of his loins after it was born, but he certainly would manage to get it that far.

"You didn't want it," said Lora.

"Perfectly indifferent," he declared. "I did think I was taking precautions, but only because it is old-fashioned not to. I don't mind a bit, so long as you understand my attitude."

It was a little after that that he took the flat on Eleventh Street; he had a little furniture of his own, and Lora took the few pieces she had bought: the crib and the carriage, of course, and the easy chair and the screen with a hole in it. They bought a new bed, a big wide one with coiled springs and a new mattress. Lora said nothing of the money she had in the savings bank—a new crib was going to be needed, and lots of other things. She was ready also to yield to his insistence on a doctor instead of a midwife, though she doubted if it would make any difference; it was in there, and it had to come out, and that was all there was to it.

Distinctly she did not want Albert any more. She still liked to hear him talk and have him around, and it was convenient that he was often ready to take Roy somewhere or stay with him when she needed to go shopping, but she wished they had separate beds. She didn't mind him really; she just didn't want him. The chief trouble was the necessity of concealing her indifference and coldness, for she felt she owed that to him. Not wanting to hurt his feelings, she used the old gestures and phrases and accepted the old refinements and ingenuities, and it was really quite a bore. At length she decided that he must be the most insensitive of men; otherwise, in spite of her pretenses, he would have felt her detachment. But no, his groping hand still trembled and he still gasped, afterwards, flung away from her and his voice thick with satisfaction, "Let there be peace."

But one night in her sixth month with his child she heard suddenly out of the dark, long after she thought he had gone to sleep:

"Listen, Lora mia, I'm going to speak and you are not to answer. I know Venus is dead. You've been very sweet about it. But it gets too painful; we might as well give it up. I said to myself, by god, she shall shudder once, she shall push my hand away, she shall turn her back on me, at the very least I shall feel her flesh minutely withdraw in spite of the will of her muscles. But you're too much for me; I realize it at last, you're pure prostitute, the only one possibly in existence, and I had to find you. I'm very fond of you, Lora mia, let's forget our little tournament and go to sleep."

"Albert, you don't—"

"You're not to answer."

"You don't realize when a woman is pregnant—"

"Blah. Superstition. I'm serious, really. You are not to answer. I beg you, spare me that."

He found her hand under the covers, took it to his lips and

kissed it; then, with a grunt, turned on his side with his back to her. Well, she thought, I might have known I wasn't fooling him; and turned on her own side away from him, and they both slept.

Difficulties about money did not begin until Helen was several months old. That was summer; Roy's third birthday was in July, and when Lora went to the grocer's or the meat market he would trot along beside the carriage with one hand on its rim and in the other a bag of fruit or vegetables. He paid little attention to the baby except when an opportunity for action presented itself; he loved to hold the towel in readiness when it was having its daily bath, and out shopping, when Lora entered a store he would stay on the sidewalk with the carriage, to keep off dogs and other dangerous animals, he explained. He had already been to the zoo several times with Albert, and stood ready, he announced, to repel anything from a beaver to a giraffe.

It was around this time that Lora asked Albert one day if he would go with her to a photographer and have his picture taken with the children. He regarded her in amazement, actually speechless, unable to believe his ears.

"Not me, just you and the babies," she explained.

"My god," he cried, "and I thought I knew you clear to the bottom! You can't mean this, it must be the heat. Flatly, no. I'll stand on my head, I'll roll a hoop in Washington Square, but I'm damned if I'll have my picture taken with two infants."

"Please, I don't often ask you—"

"Not a chance."

She levelled her eyes on him:

"You must, Albert. I want to send it to my father and mother."

She had never before mentioned their existence. He looked at her a moment and then said, "I see. They do have fathers, don't they?" Suddenly he grinned, "When were we married, Lora mia? Judging from Roy, it must have been about a year before I first saw you, *Venus gravida,* against the purple curtain—"

"All right, forget it," she said shortly.

"But you do intend to exhibit a husband?"

"Of course not; you don't know what you're talking about. Let it go, forget it."

"By no means; you excite my curiosity. I'll do it if not gladly at least hopefully; if I submit to this degradation maybe some day you'll tell me all about it."

But she never did, though she got the picture; three different poses, of which she chose one with Helen seated on Albert's knee and Roy leaning against the arm of his chair. The photographer was almost incapacitated with bewilderment at her refusal —mother, obviously, he saw—to make the group complete.

At that several weeks passed before she actually did get it, for lack of money to pay for it. Gradually money was becoming her one important concern; all her savings were gone, and Albert's weekly seventy dollars was developing an elusive quality which he could not comprehend and she could not control. He dined in the flat only once or twice a week; more than half of his nights were spent elsewhere; that's all right, it's none of my business, she thought, but what am I going to do? She could, she supposed, go back to the studios, it would be possible to get someone like Eileen to look after the children, but she had been away from it a long time and she had never really liked it. Almost certainly, though, it would before long have become unavoidable if one autumn day Albert had not happened upon Max Kadish in an uptown gallery and brought him home to where Lora sat placid and smiling with Helen at her breast.

Even at times when the rent was long past due and Mr.

Halpern at the grocery store had begun to take on a doubtful and reluctant air, she was not genuinely concerned. This mildly puzzled her; was it because she had Roy and Helen, she wondered; but no, that should work the other way—she had good cause to be worried with two small children to care for and Albert already more than halfway out of the straitjacket she had made for him. I'm getting old and sensible, she thought; it's about time; nothing is worth worrying about; something always happens. Look at the day Steve left; that was difficult enough, desperate even, but how nicely it all came out! Or the day, nearly five years ago, she first arrived in New York....

But that was different. That wasn't really a question of money, though she hadn't had much. She remembered the exact amount: seventy-two dollars and forty cents; she had counted it on the train after it had passed the station at One Hundred and Twenty-fifth Street. Forty-three cents really, but she had spent the pennies for an evening paper at Grand Central and had decided that it shouldn't be figured as part of her New York capital. She had calculated that at eighteen dollars a week she had enough for four weeks, and certainly it shouldn't take a whole month to find some way of making a living.

But that hadn't really been a question of money. In the first place she had been ill, frightfully ill. During the five-hour ride to Chicago she had had no thought of that; she had felt it but not thought about it, keeping herself back in the darkest corner of the car she could find with her coat collar turned up and her tam o' shanter pulled clear down to her eyes, afraid to look up, terrified lest at any moment she might feel a hand on her arm and hear a familiar voice or the tone of authority. Only one thought was in her mind: she would not go back. Everything else was excluded from consciousness to keep her will clear and strong on that: no matter what happened, no matter who found her or what they said or did, she would not under any circumstances whatever go back. She wouldn't tell why not, she would never tell anyone that, but rather than go back she would throw herself off the train.

When the train finally stopped at the Chicago terminal and she arose to file out with the other passengers, her knees trembled so she could not stand without holding to the back of the seat. She knew that the chief danger was here. If they had wired or telephoned there would be policemen outside, and they would spot her at once. They had no right, but they wouldn't listen to her. She was of age, wasn't she? Was she? She was twenty. Was it eighteen or twenty-one? She wished she knew. Directly in front of her was a middle-aged well-dressed woman with greying hair; Lora seized her arm and when the woman turned, startled, shot at her in a breath, "Listen, I've got to know quick, when is a girl of age, eighteen or twenty-one—" The woman jerked away and made no reply whatever.

I'm making a fool of myself, go to hell, Lora thought, and climbed down the steps of the car to the platform. At the gate at the platform's end was a waiting throng; she saw uniforms, she thought, but walked straight through with her chin up and was not stopped. In the station she conquered the impulse to break into a run; and a few moments later, safely in the taxicab, she first became aware that she was in fact ill, almost to the point of collapse. It was a terrifying and overwhelming wave of physical despair, worse than any pain; her nerves and muscles and veins were giving way, impersonally and inevitably, like a beam subjected to a load beyond the maximum calculations of the engineers. She might die, that was all right. But also she might not die; the cab driver might find her helpless and insensible there on the seat, and somehow they'd find out who she was and send her back. Was there anything in her purse that

would tell them? She would throw it out of the window, at
once, while she could still move. Then what, with her money
gone? Give him the address of the apartment, where Cecelia
was? Ha, she was not such a fool. She bent over double, with
her head touching her knees, by instinct or pure luck, for that
brought a sharp stabbing pain that roused her and made her
gasp. When the taxi reached its destination and the driver
opened the door she was sitting up straight with her clenched
fists in her lap. She got her purse open and handed him some
bills.

"Will you get me a ticket to New York on the next train," she
said.

He kept his squinting knowing eyes on her.

"The next one's more than an hour," he said. "Seven-twenty.
It's no good. The fast ones are all gone."

"And a lower berth," she said. "I don't feel very well. I want a
lower berth."

He made no reply, but turned and disappeared into the station. A few minutes later he came out again and handed her the
tickets and change; she put them carefully in her purse and
closed it.

"Can I wait here till it goes?" she said.

"Sure, in the waiting room. They got seats, and there's a
place you can lay down."

"I mean here in the cab."

"Sure, if you pay for it. There won't be no heat though with
the engine off."

"How much?"

"Three dollars."

She decided it was worth it; she couldn't risk the waiting
room. Twice during the hour and a half she felt herself going
again; each time she tried the trick of doubling over with her

head on her knees, and was convulsed back into life. When the driver finally opened the door she let him help her out and held his arm through the station and down the platform clear to the steps of the pullman. There he turned her over to the porter, squinted at her, "Good luck, lady," and went off shaking his head. The porter asked her doubtfully if she wanted the berth made up at once; she nodded and sank into a seat at the end of the car. A little later he came for her and helped her down the aisle; she was dimly aware that the train had begun to move and that other passengers were staring at her. Sprawled out in the berth, face down, with all her clothes on, she heard a man's voice, in a moment of extreme clearness that came just before consciousness departed, asking the porter if a glass of brandy might not be helpful to the lady in lower six. But some time later, she did not know when, only it seemed like the middle of the night, she came to again, half freezing. She got her dress and shoes and stockings off, and the porter brought extra blankets. Interminably she lay under them numb as ice, not suffering for she was not feeling anything; but at length she got frightened and called the porter again and told him desperately that of course he did not have a hot water bag. He disappeared and soon returned with one so hot she could not touch it, wrapped in a towel. As its warmth called her blood back to duty her body, relinquishing by slow degrees its tenseness, ached and throbbed in protest; for hours, it seemed to her, it fought against renascence, then gradually it surrendered, relaxed completely, and she slept.

Late the next afternoon—early evening, rather, for the eager January darkness had fallen three hours before—she stood in the middle of the vast hall of Grand Central Station. There were no seats. A porter directed her to the waiting room, and there she sank into a vacant corner of a bench and turned to the

list of furnished rooms in the newspaper she had just bought.
She had resolved not to waste money on a hotel even for one
night. Not many rooms were listed, and she decided she hadn't
got the right paper; in Chicago, she remembered, it was the
Globe. However, one of these would probably do; too bad she
knew nothing about neighborhoods. Didn't railroad stations in
big cities have bureaus of information where you could ask
questions like that? She twisted around on the bench to look
for signs, then suddenly came back again straight front and sat
quite still.

If it hurt her like that again she would scream or faint.

She decided all at once, calmly, that a furnished room was
out of the question. So was a hotel. She was damn good and
sick and there was no use being stupid about it. For a single
instant she was overwhelmed by the flash of an amazing suspicion: was there another one inside of her? Or maybe it had
never really come out, maybe she had been wrong all the way
through....

No, this was different, totally different. If she didn't watch
out she'd get hysterical and be no better than a lunatic. This
was different; she was just sick. She sat a long while, consid-
ering, laboriously calculating this chance and that; then she
opened her purse and removed each object from it, one by one,
inspecting each in its turn and making a pile of them on the
bench beside her. When she was through and the purse was
empty she returned to it all but three things: a letter in an
envelope, a printed card, and a little silver-backed mirror with
initials engraved on it, LW. These she grasped in one hand,
placed the purse securely under one arm, and walked down the
aisle until she found a refuse can over against the wall. In it,
into the midst of a pile of old newspapers and orange-skins, she
deposited the envelope and card and mirror. Then she stopped

a passing porter and asked to be directed to the bureau of information.

One of the men at the little circular desk in the middle of the vast hall looked up at her wearily.

"I'm sick and I've got to go to a hospital," she said. "What do I do?"

He looked slightly wearier. "Travellers' Aid second room through there," he said, pointing. Then he straightened up and called past her shoulder, "Hey, take this lady to Travellers' Aid."

The redcap preceded her, walking so fast she almost lost him in the crowd. At the desk in the second room he touched his cap and left her. A man and woman were behind the desk, talking.

"I want to go to a hospital," Lora said.

The woman looked at her. "What's the trouble?"

"I'm sick and I haven't any money."

"You're sick all right," said the man.

"A charity ward is pretty bad," said the woman. "Haven't you any friends or relatives in the city? Do you know what it is that's wrong?"

"Please don't make me talk," Lora pleaded. "Just send me to the nearest hospital. I have no friends."

"I can't do that till I know what's wrong with you. Were you on a train?"

"Yes. I had a miscarriage on a train. Please hurry. Please let me sit down. The charity ward's all right."

"Have you got enough money to pay for a taxi?"

"Yes. Please hurry."

The man had come through the desk gate and was standing beside her. "I'll run her up to Presbyterian," he said.

"I'll have to phone first," said the woman.

"You can phone after we're gone. If you phone now they'll say take her to Bellevue. She don't want to go to Bellevue."

"Ha, I know, it doesn't matter about the old ugly ones," said the woman.

"Please," Lora said.

The man took her arm. "This way, the taxis are this way," he said.

She was in the hospital three weeks. It was an acute inflammation, they told her, and that was all she ever learned about it, for she didn't want to ask questions. Nor would she answer any: at first she refused even to give her name, then when they insisted on that and other details she invented one, Mary Scott she told them, but that was as far as she would go. Her home? Was she married? What train had she been on? Who was to be notified in case of emergency? Not bothering to argue, she merely smiled and shook her head until officially they gave it up. Thus without identity, invulnerable to official curiosity, she became mysterious: obviously either criminal or sublime. The nurses glanced at her speculatively as they passed, and the internes on their rounds lingered at her bedside. There she was, a perverse fish on a bank, flopped by her own will out of the soothing oblivious stream of history; it was at once offensive and fascinating. There were no more princesses, but she might be almost anything else. The petty and desperate insistence of society that no one under any circumstances shall lose his tag kept her on the defense up to the very minute she walked out of the hospital doors.

Even Dr. Nielsen, who saw her every day for the first week because her condition required it, and thereafter because she had aroused his interest, joined mildly in the hunt. "Come," he said, "we know you haven't told the truth. You couldn't have had a miscarriage on the train. I'm discreet and it needn't go on the records; you'd better tell me. In fact, Hornsby suggests that the circumstances require a report to the police. I'm not trying to frighten you; I talked him out of it."

"Thank you, thank you so much," Lora smiled. But she told Dr. Nielsen no more of her past than any of the others.

It was he who solved her immediate and pressing problem, when she was well enough to leave, by getting a job for her through a friend of his who was a high official in the export sales department of the Federal Oil Company. Later, presumably, through that friend, if he was still curious, he learned at least her true name, for she decided to use it on the application form that was given her to fill out; but she never saw Dr. Nielsen again. From her brief local eminence as an insolent rebel against the demands of social responsibility, she was swallowed into the churning amorphous mass of a metropolitan digestive apparatus that assimilates daily much tougher and more unlikely material than a redheaded good-looking girl.

From nine till twelve-thirty and from one-thirty till five she sat at a telephone switchboard, and twice each month received the sum of fifty-five dollars. That was on account of the war, the other girls told her; three years before it would have been only forty. She had a room on West Thirty-fourth Street, a neat clean little room with a view of the river from the window. She ate breakfast there, an apple and a roll and milk; lunch was provided for its employees by the company, at cost they said with dignity; and for dinner she went usually to a little place not far from her room where they had good soup and plenty of bread and butter.

Five evenings a week she went to a business school. Dr. Nielsen's friend, Mr. Pitkin, the high official, had said that if she learned stenography he would see that she was given a chance to get ahead; that offered the best opportunity, he explained. His secretary, who had been a stenographer only twelve years, got twenty-eight hundred a year. Good god, twelve years, Lora thought. Twelve years! Incredible; even more incredible that the secretary, a plump efficient person with intelligent brown eyes, looked contented, lively, and not at all decrepit. In twelve years, Lora reflected, she would be thirty-two. Well. At any rate she might as well learn it; she had to acquire some sort of competence beyond sticking brass pegs in little holes.

She did not at all know, that spring and summer, what she was looking forward to. But forward she must and would look, there was to be no glancing backward, no examination of that scar. Sometimes at night before she went to sleep it would be suddenly upon her like a flood, overwhelming her; her father's presence and voice, her mother's pallor and tears, Pete Halliday's irresistible smile, all in a jumble, defying chronology, merging into a thick vapor of misery that for the moment overpowered her brain and stifled her. She would not fight it, feeling it was useless. She would lie on her back in the dark, perfectly still, her arms straight at her sides, thinking, it will go away, it might as well go away, for I'm not afraid of it and I'm not going to think about it. Some day someone is going to pay for it, that's all. You'll see.

Pete was dead probably. She had heard nothing, but he had been in the war over a year—angrily she stopped herself, What did it matter whether Pete was dead or not? No more of that.

Jostled by a passerby on the sidewalk one August evening, walking home from the office, to her astonishment she became suddenly aware that the daydream she had been bumped out of was a baby cradled in her arms. For ten blocks she had been carrying a baby, now in her arms, now inside of her, now beside her in bed nestling against her. Tommyrot! she exploded. Imbecile! That's a swell idea, that is. Oh, grand. You damn fool. But before she got home the baby was back again, and this time she merely smiled at herself. Why not, if it's fun, she thought. Sure it's silly, but anything to amuse a poor girl alone in a great city. After that she accepted it whenever it came, and it came more and more often; rarely did she walk home without it. Idle at the switchboard she would sometimes be startled by the buzzer out of that dream; once at school in the evening the instructor asked her a question three times before she heard it.

Partly it was the evenings at school that kept her from seeing more of the other girls outside of the office, but even when some of them arranged a Saturday night movie party or a Sunday trip to the seashore she usually did not care to go. They decided she was snooty, but she was scarcely aware of it, and certainly was unconcerned. She liked to sew, and made most of her clothes; the movies bored her. Her chief diversions were sewing and reading and automobile riding; the last she loved, but she got more invitations than she cared to accept. She went now and then on a Sunday trip with a handsome youth who was Mr. Pitkin's assistant, once or twice with a man named Gilstairs, an office manager from the floor below, and somewhat oftener with Steve Adams, one of the field men who had been called in from Canada a year after the war started and was now at the desk of one of the department heads who had enlisted. Around thirty, erect and slender, not much taller than Lora, personable and well-featured save for a nose slightly too flat and muddy brown eyes that never quite opened, he continuously smoked cigarettes and carried in his watch case a photograph of his mother taken many years before; this he had shown to Lora at their second meeting.

There was something about Steve she did not entirely like, something in him that seemed to be saying, be careful, don't hurt me or I'll run. That was the impression she got, though she didn't put it into words; what she knew was that she was always a little ill at ease with him. On the other hand there was something pleasing in his quiet manner, his courtesy in little things, his disinclination to take anything for granted, so that she enjoyed

being with him more than with Gilstairs, for instance, who
apparently proceeded on the theory that a slight initial propul-
sion is all that is required for the development of an emotional
avalanche. Although this did not frighten Lora it annoyed her;
after two experiments she let him apply his theory elsewhere.

What was Steve afraid of, she wondered. He wasn't exactly
shy, she couldn't call him timid, but when she was with him she
was always aware of a sense of fragility, of a necessity to avoid
with more than ordinary care the danger of intrusion into for-
bidden places. There was nothing concrete about it; his warn-
ings were conveyed so subtly that it was impossible to put your
finger on one and say, why did he do that? In fact, as Lora grew
to know him better she became fairly persuaded that it was all
her imagination.

He offered no caresses or solicitations, but as time went on
he showed a growing tendency to talk intimately about himself.
Lora, he said, was the only girl he had ever known with whom
he felt he could talk freely. He stated categorically that he was
sexually a virgin, using that word, virgin, which Lora thought
absurd and amusing. He had often thought of marriage, but
there had been two obstacles: first, no girl had ever sufficiently
attracted him; and second, his mother. Was she so opposed to
it, Lora asked, because his pause seemed to invite a question.
Oh, no, by no means, not at all, he replied; but it had always
seemed to him that one of the most important functions of a
mother was to set a standard by which other girls and women
could be measured, and he had the fortune, good or bad, to
have thus acquired a standard that was all but unattainable. His
mother had faults of course, for instance she was a little too tolerant of masculine peccadilloes among friends and acquaintances, but doubtless without a slight blemish here and there
she would have been unendurable in her perfection. His father

was dead, Lora somehow supposed, but it appeared not; he was in fact very much alive, a professor in a technical college who had made quite a name for himself in a minor sort of way. Brothers or sisters? No. None. He returned to marriage. It was really terrifying, he said, to think of marriage. Not on account of the involvement of sex, not at all; though he had never experienced it he had no reason to suppose that he was any different from other men in that respect, and he had yet to learn that any healthy man had died of it; no, the trouble with marriage was its finality; in spite of divorce laws it was in its nature irrevocable. Lora asked what about children, and he looked at her as if he had never heard of such a thing; she had a queer feeling that he was going to begin talking about storks. But it appeared that in connection with this subject children simply had never occurred to him; he seemed quite startled and upset, as if an Einstein had introduced a new and disturbing element into his most searching and abstruse calculations.

He returned to the topic on various occasions. He often referred, as to something which others might deprecate but which he was prepared to defend and justify, to his own lack of experience with sex; and one day he said to her point-blank:

"Of course I don't suppose you've had any either."

At last he's asked it, Lora thought; he's been wanting to know that for three months.

"Yes," she replied calmly and readily, "I have."

"Oh," was all he said. She could see his suddenly flushed face in the bright glare of a streetlight beside which they had stopped; they were on their way home from a Sunday at one of the Long Island beaches and were now in a solid endless line of traffic near the approach to Queensboro Bridge. The smell and noise and confusion engulfed them.

After a while he spoke again:

"I mean really. You know, really."

"I know. Yes, I have."

"Often?"

She laughed at him, without replying.

"Of course it's none of my business," he said after a silence. "But I've told you all about myself, you know it's not just curiosity. No one has more respect for women than I have. You might think I might respect you less, but I certainly would not. I don't put myself up to judge anybody, especially if I don't know all the circumstances. My mother taught me that, she's more tolerant than I am even. I don't respect you a bit less."

After another long silence, a little island of silence in the midst of the bridge's uproar, he asked suddenly:

"Was it one of the fellows at the office?"

This is beginning to get irritating, thought Lora, this is plenty for one day. "No, it wasn't," she said shortly. "And if you don't mind I'd rather talk of something else."

"All right." After another pause he resumed, as they swung into Sixtieth Street, "I do want to be sure though that you don't misunderstand my—my motives. With me it isn't a matter of respect at all, it's just ignorance. There doesn't seem to me to be anything—well—unclean about it. I won't talk about it any more."

A few days later, at lunch—for he had recently acquired the habit of asking her several times a week to lunch with him—he announced that the relation of lover and mistress appeared to him the ideal solution of the problem of sex. It certainly was capable of being a perfectly honorable relation, the French had proved that, he asserted; and added with a smile that while he was in no position to set himself up as an authority still he had thought about it a lot and it seemed to him amply demonstrable. The main thing was mutual respect, the circumstances had to be such that there could be no question about that. Didn't Lora agree with him? Of course. Probably half the girls in the office were no better than they should be—that is, he explained hastily, from the conventional viewpoint. And the men, not one of them was pure, absolutely not one. You could tell from the way they talked. As for the physical experience, that was to be expected, even a reputable doctor would admit that the physical experience was healthy and natural and in a way inevitable; but the way they talked was disgusting. Of course they didn't all have mistresses; the married ones had wives, which was just as good for those who were built that way; and many of the others were engaged in a sort of haphazard prowling and ambushing which to him seemed inhuman and indefensible.

At the end, after he had paid the check, not looking at Lora but busy ostentatiously with counting his change and getting it put away, he asked her to dine with him the following evening. She replied that he knew very well she couldn't; what about her school?

"Saturday then," he said, still not looking at her.

"I don't know," she said doubtfully. "I'd counted on sewing; I've been out so much recently I've nothing fit to wear. I think I'd better not."

"I'd love to buy you a dress," he declared.

She stared at him, and he blushed to his ears, but he said manfully:

"Please come Saturday."

"Maybe," she said. "I'll let you know tomorrow."

X

There was a little entrance hall, a kitchen and bath, a medium-sized living- and eating-room with two windows both at one end, and a small bedroom with one window in the rear and one on the side court. The place had been recently remodelled and was bright with new plaster and fittings, but the furniture was dismal, nondescript, and—not to be offensive about it—inharmonious. The curtains particularly were soiled and bedraggled, and one of the first things Lora did after she moved in was to take them down and send them to the laundry. Whereupon the colors in the borders ran so outrageously that they were worse if anything than before, and she had to get new ones after all. On a Saturday afternoon Steve went with her to a department store to help select the material; he fancied his taste in such matters.

This was in November, more than two months after their first dinner together—a dinner which Lora never remembered without a quiet inward smile and a chuckle of incredulity at the verisimilitude of memory. She had supposed when she left the office with him that Saturday afternoon that they would drive somewhere in his car and later eat at some outlying roadhouse or at one of the well-known uptown places—for she knew that Steve had an extraordinary salary out of all proportion to his age—among the girls at the office it was commonly reported to be a hundred dollars a week or more. But instead he had driven around the park for an hour or so, apparently preoccupied, talking very little, and then headed downtown, down Seventh Avenue, halting the car finally in front of a dingy red brick building in a part of town she had never seen before. The sign at the nearby corner said Bank Street.

Steve was fumbling with a bunch of keys, locking the car. Without looking up he explained that he had given up his place in Brooklyn and had taken some rooms here, a little apartment in fact—and he had thought it might be nice—he hoped she wouldn't mind....

Lora saw that he was stammering, almost incoherent with excitement; his hand trembled so he couldn't get the key in the hole.

The ride had made her hungry. "What about dinner?" she asked.

"It's coming—that is—I'm having it sent in. From Chaffard's, in a taxi." He looked at his watch. "Seven o'clock, I told them. It's six-thirty. We could have a cocktail...."

Lora looked at him, the man of action, and considered. He has no more idea what he's doing than the man in the moon, she thought; and she pitied him and felt suddenly tender toward him with all her twenty years.

"What's the matter, won't it lock?" she asked.

"Yes. It's all right now."

He made the cocktails in the kitchen. After she had taken off her hat and jacket and looked at her hair in the mirror on the wall of the front room, and powdered her nose, she went to the kitchen and watched him, sitting on the wooden chair in the corner. She saw that the refrigerator was stocked with ice, and oranges and grapes and a melon; on another shelf was bacon, milk, butter and cheese; and in a cupboard at one side was a conglomerate array, everything from salt and pepper to two tins of caviar. She observed that he must have been living here quite a while, but he said no, he had moved in only the day before.

She liked the bitter cocktails, and they drank the shaker empty, sitting on the couch in the front room. It wasn't a couch precisely; it was low and very wide, with neither head nor foot, with a soft dark blue coverlet. Steve gulped the cocktails down, but said little, and seemed immensely relieved when the doorbell rang to announce the arrival of the dinner. They both helped the waiter arrange it on the oblong table against the wall: salami and olives and anchovies, a whole roast chicken smoothly brown and glistening, peas in tambour shells, stringy crisp potatoes, an enormous fruit salad, and two bottles of wine.

"It's enough for a whole family," Lora said. "And two bottles! We'll both be drunk."

"It's quite mild, just something to wash it down," said Steve.

The cocktails seemed to have dissolved his excitement; he carved the chicken neatly and expertly, explaining that he had performed that duty at home for years. "Father doesn't carve well," he said, "he maintains that after he gets the legs cut off he can't tell which is front and which is back." Later, when their plates had been once emptied and refilled and the first bottle was nearly gone, he got started on the war. He had about decided to enlist, he said, and now with the draft on he wished he had; certainly it was more honorable to go voluntarily than to be forced into it. Not that he approved of war, no man of sense did, but one had to accept the liabilities of citizenship along with its benefits. His mother didn't want him to go. Only yesterday he had had a letter from her, saying that the only thing worse than having her son murdered would be to have him a murderer. Of course she didn't mean that literally, it was just her way of putting things.

He got up to take the empty wine bottle to the kitchen and open the second one, and came back and refilled their glasses.

"I mustn't drink any more," Lora protested. "My head is like a merry-go-round already."

"It's quite mild, quite mild," he insisted. His eyes, shining, seemed a little uncertain of their focus. "Oh, I forgot, I ought to make coffee. Should we have coffee?"

"I don't care. If you want it."

Standing, he served the salad, spilling a little over the side of the dish and letting it lie there on the tablecloth.

Lora ate her salad carefully and to the end; it tasted fresh and good after all the meat and vegetables she had eaten. She knew she was not drunk, for she heard all that Steve said and was able to decide what she agreed with and what she didn't. He was talking about the war again. That was nonsense; why did he have the war on his mind? Pete had gone to war. And got killed maybe. All right, what if he had, to hell with him, not a pretty sentiment, but to hell with him; if he hadn't gone to war he'd have gone somewhere else, and left her like that. Not that it was Pete's fault, she had nothing against Pete—no, if you were going to talk about fault she would have something to say that wouldn't be forgotten very soon. She wouldn't think about that though—she had sworn she would not and she never would. It would have been a year old now—no, it would be—it would be—she couldn't figure it. Who was that? Oh, it was Steve; what did he mean asking her what was the matter with her? Well…would you believe it, he was right, she was crying, there were tears in her eyes, she could feel them….

She wiped her eyes with her napkin, laughed aloud into Steve's face, got up and pushed her chair back, and walked across to the couch. Stretching herself out, she put her hands up behind her head and through half shut eyes looked at Steve as he got up from his chair and came towards her.

"No one but a pig would eat as much as that," she said. "I'm ashamed of myself. I think I'll go to sleep while you do the dishes."

He stood beside the couch looking down at her.

"Of course you know—" he said, and stopped. He said it again, and stopped again: "Of course you know—"

She felt removed and skeptical, and her head hurt.

"Of course I know what?"

He opened his mouth but said nothing, and then he sat down on the couch, clumsily bumping against her thigh; she didn't move. His eyes were bloodshot and he kept looking at her armpits, as she lay with her hands back of her head. Let him, she thought defiantly, I can't help it if this dress shows spots.

"You know I'm a virgin," he said.

She laughed directly into his face, as she had before she left the table, but his expression did not change.

"So am I," she laughed.

He stared at her, and burst out, "But you said—"

"I was just talking. You had no right to ask."

"I don't believe it. I tell you I don't believe it." His voice trembled and his hands wavered towards her and then dropped again. "If you deceived me—if you made me think—oh, my god—"

And all at once he fell forward beside her on the couch, clutching her dress in his fingers, burying his face next to her body, trembling all over so violently that the couch shook under them; his shoulders went up and down in spasmodic jerks, and unseemly muffled noises came from his buried face. Good heavens, he's crying, Lora thought, now if that isn't funny I'd like to know what is. That's funny, his head and shoulder bumping against me like that, up and down, just listen to him, he sounds terrible. His head was rubbing against her breast, and all at once it ceased to be the head of a crying man, a strange object to be commented on and thought about, and became something directly personal to her; her breast, beginning to enjoy it, swelled toward the pressure with its own welcome, and was encouraged by her hand, which came down and buried its fingers in the hair of his head, holding him against her. "Oh, my god, oh, my god," he was saying over and over, like a phonograph record with its spiral impeded, unable to leave its groove. Within her was a deep displeasure and a profound irritation, at the very moment that her other hand was working at the fastening of her dress, to uncover the breast to him. Neither the displeasure nor the hand's betrayal was present in her consciousness; indeed, consciousness had given up the affair altogether, saying in effect, as defeated and embarrassed it turned its back on the painful scene, "Very well, have it your way, but I'm off, I don't intend to get involved in this sort of thing. See you later."

So it came to pass that the venerable and somewhat withered bloom of Steve's virginity had its petals scattered to a September zephyr. Lora did not stay the night. She slept, but later awoke into darkness and, slipping quietly out of bed and groping her way to the kitchen, saw by her watch that it was half-past two. If she stayed there, she reflected, she would lose all day Sunday, and she simply must get that tan dress fixed and her stockings darned. Ten minutes later, dressed but drowsy, she let herself out quietly without disturbing Steve's gentle and regular snores. Outside his car was standing at the curb and she felt something should be done about it—wouldn't it be stolen or confiscated or something? At least she would turn on the lights, she knew that was required, but she couldn't find the switch and so gave it up and went on home.

But most of her Sunday was lost after all. She slept till noon, then, uncommonly hungry, went out for breakfast; and when she returned found Steve sitting on the stoop waiting for her. He saw her halfway down the block and sprang to his feet and hurried to meet her; his eyes avoided hers, he extended his hand and then drew it back, and finally for greeting awkwardly kissed her cheek. He reproached her for leaving him; they could have had a wonderful breakfast together, he said; what did she mean by going off that way? He had expected to cook breakfast for her and had made special preparations for it.

"You expected?" Lora smiled at him.

He flushed suddenly and violently, then took hold of her arm and looked boldly into her eyes. "I guess you know I did," he asserted. "Anyway we can go for a ride, a long ride, and have dinner together." He was squeezing her arm. "Did anyone ever call you Lo? I was thinking this morning, I'd like to call you Lo."

So the dress and stockings went unmended.

Every evening after that he begged her to go home with him. He wanted her to give up school so they could go to shows and take evening rides and have more time together. "I suppose I seem silly to you," he would say, "you're so sensible about it, because you're experienced of course. I didn't know how ignorant I was—gosh I was an ass, wasn't I?" He laughed at the ass he had been. "Going around talking about mistresses —and now I really have one, I keep saying it to myself when I'm alone, I really have a mistress, Lo is my sweet mistress—I love calling you Lo because no one else ever did. One day Father said to me—it was when I was home for Christmas three years ago, I was working up in Canada then—he saw a photograph in my suitcase, just a girl I'd taken to a party some- where, I'd forgotten I had it even—and he said, Since you say you have no sweetheart I suppose that's your mistress. I felt myself blushing all over and I was so mad I couldn't speak. That was the first time, the only time in fact, he ever said anything of that sort to me. I had a notion to tell Mother about it, but I didn't. Anyway, I remember that night I couldn't sleep, I kept fancying myself saying, Father permit me to introduce my mistress, and imagining what he would do. I was an awful ass."

Lora succeeded in preserving her evenings for school, and she spent not more than two or three nights a week in the apartment on Bank Street, but he had his way in another matter. There was no opposing his determination to buy things for her—clothes particularly, but also bracelets, trinkets, flowers, perfumes, bags. The bracelets and earrings were of necessity silver or glass, but were tastefully chosen; he insisted on accompanying her to select dresses and hats; and underwear and nightgowns he bought himself, bringing them to her folded in their boxes, removing them from the rustle of the tissue-paper and holding them up by fragile shoulder-straps for her inspection. On another point he was less successful: his attempts to persuade her to give up both her school and her job and install herself and her belongings in Bank Street. He grew more and more determined about it; it was obviously the thing to do, he said, no man of spirit would want his mistress to work in an office any more than he would his wife, not so much, in fact; but Lora wouldn't even consider it. She didn't argue about it; she would let him go on and then smile and merely say, "There's no hurry; we'll see." She was of course awaiting an eventuality the possibility of which seemed, amazingly, never to occur to him; deciding that either he was trusting implicitly to her superior experience or that he did actually believe in storks, she continued patiently to wait.

When in the middle of October it became evident that nature's routine had suffered no interruption she frowned with puzzled resentment; what sort of cheat was this? Too, she was momentarily alarmed, for her own experience was after all superior to Steve's only as thick twilight is superior to darkness; but common sense soon told her that the hazards of life are not confined to a dandelion seed fallen upon a stone, and when four more weeks had passed, then five and six, six whole weeks, and the interruption had assuredly occurred, she began to weigh Steve's proposal seriously. When in the course of the next day or two he renewed it, she replied promptly:

"All right, I will, if you're sure you want me to."

"You will!" he cried, blushing with pleasure. "This very evening—well, tomorrow then. Tomorrow?"

"I ought to give them a week's notice at the office."

"Nonsense. They've got a hundred telephone girls scattered around, what's the difference. Tomorrow? Please."

The moving was simple; two trips did it, with a big brown suitcase he bought for her and one of his own. The first morning he kissed her goodbye and departed for the office, leaving her confronted by a whole day to be disposed of by choice instead of necessity, she sat at the oblong table on which they had eaten their first dinner nearly three months before, sipping coffee which didn't want to go down and feeling doubtful and ill at ease. She had done it, that was all right, but it wasn't so simple as you might think. She couldn't expect long to conceal the fact that every morning she was sick, and Steve would naturally want to know what the trouble was and she would have to tell him something. Almost anything would probably serve, with him; and for that matter why shouldn't she tell him the truth? She didn't want to, that was all, she didn't like the idea. Well, she could say, you're going to be a father; but that sounded ridiculous; there was something outlandish about it. Or she could say, I'm going to have a baby; but why should she? It was none of his business.

As it turned out she used neither of those phrases; the communication was made impromptu one evening late in December, a day or two after Christmas. Throughout dinner, which she had cooked at the apartment, he seemed nervous and preoccupied, talking but little; and finally, swallowing his last mouthful of salad, he unburdened his mind. He began by glancing across at her and saying with an extravagant effort to be casual:

"Has anyone been here asking about me?"

What is it now, she thought. She replied, "No, who would be asking about you?"

"Oh—I just wondered." He emptied his wine glass. "You're sure no one has been here?"

"No. Unless they came while I was out."

"Sure. Of course. I suppose if you weren't home they might ask the janitor." He flushed, and then the flush went away and he frowned. "See here, Lo, I hope you won't mind. I told them I was married—I put myself down that way. The draft board, you know. After all, what's the difference, I'm supporting you just the same, I can't see that it makes any difference. It's wrong to make a man go to war that feels about it the way I do. The trouble is I don't know whether they investigate these things or not, but there have been rumors lately, I've been worried—I thought I'd better tell you because if they come around asking questions and you didn't know about it naturally you wouldn't know what to say and then I would be in for it. I don't know how much they go into it—just age and a few things like that I suppose—I'm thirty-one, thirty-one last May—and they'd ask if you were my wife and if you just said yes that would be all there'd be to it."

"Well, that's easy," Lora said.

"You're sure you won't mind?"

"Lord, no, why should I? I don't know anything about the war and I don't care anything."

"That's just the way I feel." He reached across the table and patted her hand. "You're fine, Lo. Fine all the way through. I never had more respect for you than I have this minute. Anyway, as I said before, I'm supporting you and providing for you, what's the difference whether we're married or not?"

"Yes, you're supporting two of us."

"Oh, well, as for that, that hardly counts, I'd have to support myself in any event—"

"Two others, I mean. Two besides yourself. I'm pregnant."

"You're what?" he exclaimed in astonishment.

Heaven help me, thought Lora, I'll bet he doesn't know what it means. "I'm pregnant," she repeated, carefully getting out all the consonants and raising her voice a little. It is hard to pronounce, she thought.

"But how—I don't see—good god it isn't possible." From the expression on his face it might have been thought she had told him she had a shameful disease. He looked pale, incredulous, permanently stupefied. "You must be mistaken—how do you know—really you must be mistaken...."

Lora shook her head. "I know all right."

"But I don't see—I thought it was necessary—" He was speechless. Then, "It's my damn ignorance, that's what it is!" he exploded furiously. "Good god, what a mess! I don't even know what to do. I suppose you do—you ought to know—it takes a doctor of course—that's the only way out I suppose, I don't know—it certainly is a fine mess, it certainly is—"

"I don't think it's such a mess," Lora said scornfully.

"Oh, you don't? You don't, eh? Do you happen to know that abortion is a crime? Well, it is. I've heard the fellows talk about it—my god, I never thought I'd be tangled up in it. It's a crime, don't you know that? Women die of it too. It's dangerous any way you look at it; it's sickening."

"I won't die of it."

"You might as well as the next one."

"Well, I won't. I'm not going to have an abortion, I'm going to have a baby."

That made it worse than ever. His stupefaction returned, his jaw hung open, he glared at her in the effort to comprehend this new threat in all its enormity. Finally, so pale now that faint purple tracings showed on his forehead, stunned out of his fury into the chill of fear, he stammered at her:

"I see—that's it—that's the trick, is it—you think I'll have to marry you—that's it—"

Lora wanted to throw something at him. It was unbelievable, she thought, that any man could be so great an idiot. Such a talent for asininity transcended all ignorance; you couldn't even laugh at it; it befuddled you and made you think you were standing on your head. She made him sit down again, for he had got to his feet and stepped back as if to retreat from imminent and deadly peril; she made him sit down, held him there with her eyes, and explained carefully and lucidly that, first, she did not want an abortion, second, she did not want to be married, third, she would be at pains to inform any inquirers that she was his lawful wife, and fourth, she would leave, or he could leave without interference from her, at any time that such a course seemed to either of them desirable. No repetition of these assurances could remove all his suspicion; plainly he was still harassed by the possibility of deception and disaster; but at length he grew much easier. There did remain the fact, as he himself remarked, that it was easy enough for her to talk of non-interference with his freedom when she knew very well that he was practically chained to her by the necessity of maintaining his claim, as good as publicly made, to the responsibilities of a husband; but to this she replied that an explanation could be found for that if necessary, and anyway such things were almost certainly not investigated—if all those details had to be checked up for everyone who registered it would take a whole army just for that. This seemed to satisfy him; he admitted its reasonableness; but his brow remained clouded, hours later even, after he had got his pipe lit, turned on the reading-lamp, adjusted the easy chair by the table, and sat down with a book.

That night she left the inner room to him, making up a bed for herself on the wide low couch in the living room. It was soft and comfortable, but it was a cold night even for December and there were not enough blankets, so she used their over-coats and a rug from the bedroom floor. This arrangement he tacitly accepted; as she was spreading the sheets on the couch she saw him watching her over the top of his book and thought he was about to remark on it, but he said nothing.

The following afternoon he arrived home a little later than usual, carrying an enormous bundle; it proved to contain two pairs of thick warm blankets and some sheets and pillowcases. "The landlord really should furnish extra bedding, what would you do if you had guests," he observed; and Lora nodded, and thanked him. The new blankets were much softer and finer than the others; she started to use them in the bedroom, but he insisted that she keep them on the couch for herself. "I'm something of a Spartan that way," he declared, "I'm not at all particular just so I don't freeze."

The blankets were his last gift, and that was almost his last speech—at any rate the last which contained any friendly im-plications. More than four months were to pass before his final flight, months during which Lora often felt that if she were called upon for one more sacrifice—of pride, or convenience, or more especially of the skin of her defense against the scratches and lacerations of his suddenly hostile and alien claws—one more sacrifice for the sake of a breath of a hope which she scarcely dared believe in—she would—she would—well, she would do something. Only there was nothing to do; she was trapped. So without any outward sign she accepted the rather difficult conditions which followed upon Steve's emancipation from his novitiate. His gifts ceased abruptly; within a month he had stopped entirely coming to the flat for dinner, though he still slept there. For a while he continued to give her money, a little now and then, but it was not long before that too stopped. She tried running a bill at the delicatessen shop, but at the end of the week he refused flatly to pay it, standing at the door with his hat on, on his way to the office, looking her straight in the eye and reminding her that she had said he was free to leave whenever he wished. "If I was gone I wouldn't be paying your bills, would I?" he demanded, which of course was unanswerable. Lora, not bothering even to observe that the delicatessen account included the morning coffee and cream which he helped to consume, let him go without a reply, and then systematically and thoroughly went over everything in the house. When she got through she had a pile on the living-room table of varied and miscellaneous objects: an etching he had once bought for her, two little figures of carved ivory, a fur neckpiece, three pairs of gloves she had never worn, bracelets, earrings, finger rings, a fountain pen, fifteen or twenty books, a tiny gold compact. Then she stood and considered: what to do with them? She bethought herself of two girls in the flat on the ground floor whom she'd grown to know fairly well; one was Janet Poole, who did designs for wallpaper, and the other Anne Whitman, a slim pale quiet girl, younger than Janet, who was studying at a music school. She went down and rang the bell; Anne opened the door and invited her in.

"I can only stay a minute," said Lora, "I just came down to ask you a favor. I have some things I'd like to leave with you, only I'm afraid it will be a bother, I'll have to be coming in from time to time, it's nothing that will take up any space to speak of, just a few small things...."

It sounds idiotic, Lora thought, I should have made up some kind of plausible excuse. Obviously Anne didn't understand the unusual request, she looked puzzled; but she was very nice about it, it wouldn't be any bother at all, she said, they had plenty of room. So Lora made three trips up and down the stairs with the new suitcase Steve had given her, on the last trip leaving the suitcase itself, in a closet in the girls' bedroom. Anne helped her, declaring that Lora mustn't overdo; she had known of Lora's pregnancy for a month or more and was quite excited about it, asking all sorts of questions.

Three days later, a Sunday, Lora, happening to look out of the living-room window around midday, saw Steve's roadster, in which she had in days gone by had so many pleasant rides, standing at the curb below. The day was sunny and extraordinarily mild for February, and the top was down; thus her view was unobstructed of Anne Whitman on the roadster's seat, in a fur cap and coat, with Steve beside her warming up the engine. Lora drew slightly back from the window and watched them until the car jerked forward and rolled off down the street; then with a grimace she said aloud, "Damn the luck anyway," and turned and went directly downstairs and rang the bell at the ground floor flat. Luck was with her here at least; Janet was at home, in a pink negligee and fur-lined slippers. Half an hour later everything which had three days previously been so laboriously carried down had been equally laboriously lugged back up. Janet thinks I'm crazy, maybe I am, Lora reflected as she put the things away in the two lower drawers of the bureau. Would Steve's emancipated ideas extend to the appropriation of the gifts of his former tenderness? She would have to chance it.

She lived on the proceeds of her cache for nearly three months. None of the objects had great value, but she squeezed all she could out of them, and on two or three occasions good fortune attended her; the fur neckpiece, for instance, brought a generous thirty dollars from Mrs. Crosby at the tea-room, who also took the books, the etching and the fountain pen. Lora was niggardly with everything but food; she did the laundry herself, in the tub in the kitchen, and with remarkable ingenuity made over her old dresses to accommodate the swelling amplitude that had already set in and would soon be discernible even to a casual eye. She was relieved of the expense of Steve's coffee and cream, for he began to take his breakfast out, leaving, usually without a word, as soon as he was dressed in the morning; often, indeed, he did not come to the flat at all, and when he did come it was commonly long after Lora had gone to bed. They seldom spoke to each other, and Lora avoided occasions for speech as much as possible, for when he addressed her his tone was so laden with resentment, with contempt and hatred even, that she shrank in pure physical repugnance. This attitude of his had come on gradually, growing steadily and as from one day to another imperceptibly, like a poisonous fungus on a tree, and she did not at all understand it. She did not hate him; why should he hate her? One morning as he was tying his shoe with his foot upon a chair in the living room, he expressed the opinion, apropos of nothing, that she was a whore; the word came out of him tight and intense and he repeated it and was incited by it to further observations. Lora made no reply. She found it painful but only because it was ugly; he was an ugly noise, that was all. Once or twice, minded to leave, she vetoed it at once; no, as long as he paid the rent she would stay. Too late; it was too far along for avoidable risks; for some time, trembling, breathless with apprehension, exultant, in an ecstasy of hope, she had been aware of the pushing within her; and now, when she lay quite still in a certain position with the palm of her hand on a certain spot, she could actually feel it, the little devil seemed actually trying to make a break for it....No you don't, she would admonish it, no you don't, you'll just have to be patient a little while and so will I....

At the very moment that Steve called her a whore she had her hand there, for since he had stopped breakfasting in the flat she often stayed in bed till after he had gone. Usually she did not feel well when she awoke in the morning; to move at all was an effort and this disinclination was increased by the certainty that if she did get up and squeeze oranges and make coffee it was heads or tails whether they would be wasted. But it would be only a few minutes before she would frown at this weakness, sit up for a moment or two until the worst of the dizziness passed away, get up and get dressed and start the day's activities. She made a point of getting out for a walk at least twice a day; towards noon she would go to the market on Hudson Street and make her modest household purchases, and after lunch it would be Washington Square or perhaps across to the river and back. When the springtime brought warmer days she found an isolated corner on one of the piers near Fourteenth Street where she could sit in the sun and watch the tugs and ferryboats and an occasional great liner gliding by. This ought to be good for it, she thought, the sun and the beautiful river and all the movement of the boats with the smoke curling up. Then, after leisurely making her way through the narrow streets back to the flat, never failing to be amused at her absurdly timid care at street crossings or when the sidewalks were wet, she would languidly, slow-motion, remove her hat and coat and hang them in the closet, and stretch herself out on the couch; and wait. That was all she did: wait. There was no virtue left in the world but patience, and no interest but expectation. It was May; her cache was empty, her money nearly gone, and Steve no longer bothered even to call her a whore. Somewhere within her was the conviction that she was acting like a stupid fool, but smothering and effacing it was a much livelier and more intimate conviction that action must wait upon emergency and that emergency, however desperate, must inevitably carry its solution along with it, like a kite its tail. Consolingly but dangerously she believed in life, much as a metaphysician believes in truth or a husband in chastity.

She was lying on the couch late of a May afternoon when the door opened and Steve entered. This was extraordinary; not for many weeks had he appeared at such an hour. He extended no greeting, but proceeded directly to the bedroom, and Lora lay and listened to the noises he made in there, interpreting them, at first indifferently and half unconsciously, then with an access of awareness and interest. The scraping and subsequent plop was certainly his suitcase being drawn from under the bed and being planted on a chair; the other suitcase followed. She smiled to herself: not hers; it had more than a week back been transferred permanently to other hands. Drawers were opened and closed; collars rattled; a trip to the bathroom was made; now, she thought, only one toothbrush is left on that rack, and his bathrobe is no longer hanging so you can't close the door. He had not been about it long, not more than ten minutes altogether, when the sound came of a suitcase closing, followed by a click; then another. At the approach of his footsteps, heavy with the weight of the bags, entering the room where she lay, she opened her eyes.

She didn't know why she spoke, except that it seemed insane, not human, for him to go off like that without a word and for her to lie silent watching him go. All she said was:

"You might as well say goodbye."

Nearly to the door he turned and looked at her, his shoulders pulled down by the heavy bags.

"I'm leaving an overcoat and two suits; I haven't room for them," he said. "I'll send someone for them tomorrow. Why should I say goodbye? I don't want to say anything to you, goodbye or anything else."

His tone was incredible; Lora shivered at it, struck by an odd uncomfortable fancy: it was as if a man done to death, rotting in his coffin, should suddenly, at sight of his murderer, open his mouth to let the fumes of his defeated hate mingle with the other unpleasant odors suitable to the circumstances. She shivered and said nothing, though an instant before it had occurred to her to say this at least, "I have three dollars and the rent will be due day after tomorrow." Surely she could say that much; but it remained uncertain whether she would actually have got it out before he disappeared, for just as he put down one of the suitcases to reach for the knob the doorbell rang sharply, startling them both. He pulled the door open, and a girl stepped in; it was Janet Poole from the flat below. She stood there glaring at Steve, small and dark, sharp-featured, her little black eyes pinning him to his spot.

"You're a lousy bastard," she said with certitude.

"Get out of my way," Steve said, picking up the other suitcase.

"Good god," she went on, "if they squirted skunk-juice all over you it would be a big improvement." She turned to Lora. "Do you know what? Anne's down at the door waiting for him; they're going off. I don't know which is worse, leaving you like this or taking that poor kid—it'll be something to think about while I knit. From this day on I'm either a Lesbian or a nun, I don't care which; if you ever catch me with a man again you can geld me without even a local; I'll watch it with pleasure."

Steve was trying to push past her but, hampered by the suitcases, couldn't make it.

"If I don't spit on you," she continued, feet spread out, refusing to budge, "it's only because I'm a little particular about my excretions. What am I doing? Relieving my mind. I've been trying to hammer sense into her, and it's no use. She must have necrophilia."

Lora was thinking, all I need to do is tell her how Steve got exempted from the draft. Ha, wouldn't she jump on that though! All right, I'll tell her, why shouldn't I? Then I wouldn't have to worry; it would take him about one minute to get the suitcases unpacked and his bathrobe back on the door. He must be crazy, he knows very well I could do that just with one word to her, or anyone, and it would be all up.

She said nothing. Janet Poole was still paying her respects to Steve in her colorful and expressive idiom, until all at once he charged, head-on, with the suitcases held in front of him for battering-rams, knocking her into the hall with some violence, but without apparent injury, for she continued to relieve her mind. Lora could hear him lumbering downstairs, with Janet's unceasing fire following him from the landing. Then there was a pause, during which all other sounds were lost beneath Janet's voice now raised to a shout, and finally there came from below the slam and rattle of the outer door closing, and all was suddenly silent.

Janet appeared in the open door.

"Shall I stay?" she asked abruptly.

Lora shook her head. "Please not now."

"All right. See you later."

She reached in to close the door, and then was gone.

XI

Lora, lying on the couch in precisely the same position as when Steve had entered a brief fifteen minutes earlier, heard faintly through the closed door the quick nervous rhythm of Janet's footsteps descending the stairs. Then her ears, despoiled of that diversion, caught at other sounds: other tenants' voices that came from the court through the open window in the bedroom, the pattering of an animal's feet—she had never known whether it was a cat or a small dog—on the floor above which topped her ceiling, the rumble of a distant elevated train, the confused medley from the street. For a while nothing was alive but her ears; she had no thoughts or feelings, not even the feeling of herself as a phenomenon; she was neither conscious nor unconscious.

Then she stirred and turned over on her side, and the sounds all at once ceased to exist; her brain awoke. "How do you do," she said aloud, "you've done it this time, haven't you, darling." A thought darted at her: how about Steve's overcoat and two suits? He wore good clothes; the tailor at the corner could probably get a good price for them. Or what about his false information to the draft board? Weren't rewards offered for things like that? Momentarily the idea diverted her, and she smiled into space; then, frowning, she turned to serious considerations. She might get a loan from Janet Poole, or Mrs. Crosby at the tea-room, or even Mr. Pitkin. She pictured herself making the request, and her frown deepened; she would almost rather steal than borrow; however, it was just as well to have the possibilities in mind in case of desperate emergency. Surely there were other means.

Again she spoke aloud, more for the companionship of her own voice than anything else. "Money is the root of all evil," she said clearly and distinctly. Ha, it hasn't any roots, she thought, it's like that plant in the picture in geography in school which went crawling around through trees without any roots of its own. It was in school too that she had written the sentence, money is the root of all evil, in a clear round hand which, according to the teacher, however legible she might painfully make it, never did sufficiently slant.

I still write that way, she thought, only I almost never write.

The chief difference between her school days and the present, she reflected, was that then other people had always been on hand to point out her mistakes, whereas now she had to find them out for herself. Childhood, so it seemed, had been nothing but an endless process of fresh discoveries of the remarkable and often bewildering boundaries of the permissible. The hardest part of it had been the unbelievable confusion: a thing perfectly all right in one place was utterly wrong in another; actions strictly prohibited in school were overlooked, even encouraged, at home. It changed with people, too; one teacher would smile indulgently at something which another severely reprimanded. And as for time, that was the most confusing of all; you never knew today whether yesterday's rules still held, you simply had to try it out and see; whereas on Tuesday Mother snatched the scissors out of your hand the minute you picked them up, on Wednesday she sat and placidly read a book while you clipped all the arms and legs off your paper dolls. In the end you felt despairingly that the jungle of complications was much too vast and intricate for any exploration you might attempt; you gave up all idea of rules and fastened a wary eye on each situation as it presented itself. That simplified the problem enormously; if Mother's face looked like this, for instance, you let the scissors alone; if like that, you used them for any reasonable purpose that occurred to you. Obviously, the point was Mother's face, not the scissors at all.

You were aware though that this was true only relatively; the purpose must be reasonable; you could not cut the borders off of window curtains, or leaves out of books, anywhere at any time observed of anyone. You could not use pee as an intransitive verb, meaning go-go, except slyly with other children, who did not count anyway, being in the same precarious and anomalous situation as yourself; and since go-go was at an early age discarded as infantile, you were left without any verb at all for that particular function and were driven to the expedient of expressing the need for its performance by a series of facial and bodily contortions which seemed to you grotesque and shameful, so that you always felt yourself blushing; though your elders appeared to find them vastly amusing, since invariably they laughed and giggled when they saw you. One result of this was that now and then your underthings got wet; on those occasions the only desire left to you was that the crust of the earth should open under your feet and swallow you into the oblivion of hell.

Certain admonitions from certain people were as inevitable as Mother's goodnight kiss or oatmeal at breakfast. From Miss Wright, "Take your pencil out of your mouth"; from Mother, "Don't annoy your father, dear"; from Sam who tended the furnace, "Get on out of here now"; from Father, "Pull your skirt down."

The last was the best remembered of all; she would never forget it; it made her uncomfortable and resentful even now to recall her father's "Pull your skirt down." When had she heard it first? No telling, that was lost somewhere back in the origins of things; nor could she remember specifically its farewell performance, after she had graduated into high school and begun to have beaux, had become a young lady in fact; but in between those two forgotten occasions, the first and the last, it had persisted throughout, with or without reason.

Come to think of it, that *was* her father, "Pull your skirt down." That was him. Most other memories of him, from childhood and early youth, were fleshless and bloodless, mere punctuations of time, with no significance beyond the chronological. Her first remembered reaction to that command, as a plump freckled youngster of five or six, had been simple and instant obedience. She had pulled her skirt down, though there had been very little to pull. By the time it had undergone a dozen repetitions she had, unconsciously of course, added it to the category of rules headed: Father Specialties, No Exceptions. It first became annoying on account of its indiscriminate use, a purely logical indignation against the requirement that something be pulled down which was already down as far as it would pull. The day came when the command was uttered and her hand did not move; after a brief interval it was repeated, in a tone that surprised and shocked her into a sudden violent tug.

"If you don't care about decency, I do," said her father.

She was at that time twelve or thirteen. The plumpness was all gone, and the freckles had disappeared; her hair had already begun to assume the dark rich tone which later became her chief attraction. He, her father, standing near the door putting on his overcoat, looked as to her he had always looked, large, well-built, handsome, not so old as other girls' fathers but infinitely more terrifying. She liked to watch his mouth when he talked or laughed; his red lips and gums and white teeth made fascinating combinations. At one time, when she was almost too young to remember, he had worn a short moustache, but it had been gone now for some years; of mornings in the bathroom she was often permitted, when necessity required it, to wash her hands and face at the tub faucet while he shaved at the bowl, and on these occasions she consumed a lot of precious time with her surreptitious delighted glances at his distortions and grimaces in the mirror, with the thick creamy lather making his white teeth seem by comparison a sickly yellow, and his skin, as the razor-strokes uncovered it, a fiery pink.

"Come come, you'll be late for school," he would say. "I'm not making faces to amuse you."

There were at that time many things about many people which she did not begin to understand, but she understood her father and mother least of all. Why did it make him angry when her mother said, "Don't annoy your father, dear," and why in face of that invariable result did her mother keep on saying it? Why was he always in such a hurry when he told Mother good-bye in the morning, though often, on leaving the house, he would linger in the front yard, leisurely smelling the flowers, pruning with his pocketknife a shrub or rosebush here and there? Why did her mother always cry when he called her "my pale love" in that funny tone? The definitions of "pale" and "love" in the dictionary seemed to offer no basis for tears. Why did he dislike boys so much, and chase them off, even the nicest ones when they were doing no harm? Above all, why did he kick the cat? Four times he did that: the little black and white cat, when Lora was five or six; two years later the same cat, this time blinding it and injuring its jaw so that it had to be killed; somewhat later Brownie, no harm done; and the last time when Lora was in her early teens, a big male Maltese which afterwards limped around for a month or so and then suddenly disappeared.

In addition to these more or less frequently recurring enigmas and innumerable others like them, an isolated and unique one now and again offered itself. For a late example, why did he all at once stop kissing her, his daughter, goodnight? He made no announcement and offered no explanation; he simply stopped. This was at about the time when she was becoming for other males objectively kissable: sixteen, in her second year at high school, her hair up. For that matter she had always been pleasing to look at, even during her freckle period; a lovely child, everyone called her, then a lovely enchanting girl, which indeed she was, with her amber-grey rather solemn eyes, smooth fair skin, mouth a little too large and, closed, a little too straight, but, in articulation or smiling, flexible and sympathetic and capable of charming curves and twists. What startled was her hair; at first sight the contrast seemed freakish, put on a bit; but the harmony was there and soon made itself felt. She lost her girlish angularity earlier than the rule; at sixteen the final full-nesses were already shaping her calves and arms and shoulders, and her breasts could no longer be called hints or promises nor her chest boyish—obviously something was preparing there beyond a meager and superfluous decoration, plain to see when she drew her shoulders back to stretch and the silk of her blouse tried in vain to make a level plane from her throat to her middle.

She was minded, as a matter of research, to ask other girls in her class if their fathers still kissed them goodnight, but never got around to it.

She felt indeed that there was something peculiar about her father and she didn't want to discuss him with anyone; least of all with her mother. He was not untouchable exactly, nor was he terrifying to her anymore; certainly she was not consciously afraid of him; and yet fear was in it somehow, though it was not fear of his authority or of anything he was likely to say or do to her. The feeling was with her constantly in his presence, and made her a little uncomfortable; she was always self-conscious with him, she couldn't help it. Sometimes she was reminded, without knowing why, of an experience some years before, at the circus, when she had seen a man enter a cage and stand there smiling, surrounded by a dozen snarling and crouching tigers; it was the first time she had seen such a thing, and she had been rigid with fear, forgetting to breathe so long that finally she had to gasp for it. Why her feeling regarding her father should remind her of that was inexplicable; nothing resembling a threatening tiger, let alone a dozen, was discernible; certainly her poor mother was no tiger. Her poor mother! Whose tears became more frequent with each passing year, and who, with her comely daughter almost grown, had apparently only one piece of advice left for her, often repeated: "Never give your heart to a man, my child, never." Weeping, she would add, "You're too young to understand, but you're not too young to be told." To Lora that sounded like poppycock; her poor mother was unhappy, that was plain, and it was equally plain that her father was too. That was a pity, she thought; and that was as far as she got.

But when young men began to call at the Winter home it was not her mother, but her father, who acted—as it was described in Lora's circle—goofy. He would sit in the living room where they sat, though he ordinarily read in the dining room because he thought the light was better. If he spent the evening downtown at a lodge meeting and on returning home found a young man—no matter who, for there were many—on the premises, Lora could see that he was furious, though he said nothing. He would certainly have kicked the cat, she thought, if there had been one. The difficulty was that he said nothing. If Lora asked whether she was to be permitted to have friends he would reply, certainly, of course, why not; and then proceeded to make all their lives miserable if a friend appeared. It was an attitude invulnerable because unexpressed; there was no word or action that permitted of challenge or even discussion; had Lora requested to be left alone in the living room when she had callers he would immediately have acquiesced and then have conveyed on every occasion, by word and tone and gesture too subtle to be seized on, that the arrangement was an outrage. He no longer told her to pull her skirt down or made observations regarding his devotion to decency; in much more concealed and effective ways did he gradually induce a highly charged atmosphere which in time brought upon his wife a condition of chronic pallid tight-lipped silence and began to make a noticeable impression even upon Lora's young and hardy nerves. On one occasion at the end of her eighteenth year, returning in mid-evening from an automobile ride with Speedy Clarke, who was halfback on the high school team, being accompanied to the porch by her escort in spite of an obvious reluctance which had descended upon him when they turned into the Winter driveway, they found the scene suddenly flooded with light from the bulb on the porch ceiling; and almost instantly the front door opened and Mr. Winter emerged. "Good evening," he said, looking at Speedy Clarke, and that burly athlete blushed, stammered incoherently, and fled. On the spur of the moment, standing there on the porch, Lora said:

"Why do you dislike him, Father?"

Mr. Winter seemed astonished. He didn't dislike him, he said; quite the contrary, he was obviously a nice young fellow.

"Then why do you look at him like that?"

"I wasn't aware that I looked at him like anything in particular." He was frowning. "It's customary, I believe, to look at people when you greet them."

Lora took a sudden resolution. "Look here," she said, "if I do anything you disapprove of why don't you say so? You act as if

you didn't want me to have any friends at all." As she spoke she
became aware that the front door had not been entirely closed,
and that from within her mother had approached and now
stood with her face wedged into the narrow opening, silently
regarding them on the porch, but she went on breathlessly,
"You must know how you look at them, they all hate to come
here. If you don't want me to have anybody come to see me
why don't you tell me so?"

Her father's expression did not change; he continued to
frown. He spoke quietly. "This is somewhat unusual, isn't it,
reproaching your father like this? Especially since it is entirely
uncalled for. To answer your question: even if I wanted no one
to come to see you I see no reason why I should tell you so; you
are old enough to have a right to your own whims and opinions.
Anyway I don't at all object to your having friends; not at all;
nothing could be more natural. As to the way I look at them, I
don't know what you mean; I look as I look, that's all."

"They're all afraid of you, you know they are."

"I hardly think it is your place to tell me what I know."

But she kept to the main issue, refusing to be sidetracked.
She insisted, "All I want is, tell me what to do. If I'm to see
people only at other places, all right, that's all right. Pretty soon
they'll refuse to come here anyway."

"I repeat, I have no idea what you're talking about."

And all at once she hated him, despised his monstrous and
meaningless pretense, despised it all the more for her bewildered inability to understand it. He must be, no doubt of it, he
must be, in some obscure and limited manner, insane; yes, to
put it plainly, he was crazy. She was frightened and profoundly
repelled, and at the same time she wanted to laugh and dismiss
it with a shrug of the shoulders; it was all so trivial, so absurdly
childish, getting—all three of them—mixed up in these idiotic

twistings and turnings about something which was of no real importance. What did she care whether Speedy Clarke, or anyone else, was permitted to come on that porch? It was fit only to be laughed at, she saying to her father, "You quit making faces at my friends," and he replying, "I'm not making faces," like two babies in the kindergarten and not very intelligent ones at that. Her father at least was old enough to know better.

Nevertheless she hated him, and for the first time the hatred was in her voice as she flung at him:

"All right, if you won't say what you think, but you might as well know right now you're not going to do to me what you've done to Mother. I won't stand for it."

There was an immediate reply, but it came in a thin tense voice from the crack in the door:

"Leave me out of it, child, just leave me out of it. You go right on, I'll take care of myself."

She's afraid of her life, Lora thought, she's scared stiff. Her father turned to observe disdainfully towards the crack, "Oh, you're there, are you," but the face had disappeared. Then he turned back to Lora, and she saw that his face had suddenly gone red and his hands were trembling.

"What have I done to your mother?" he demanded.

Lora did not answer. She knew what it meant when he looked like that, though she had seen it but seldom; and without stopping for consideration, either of valor or of policy, she fled. She darted past him toward the door which still stood a little open, burst through it, and was halfway up the stairs on the way to her room before he could have had time to move. Inside her room, she closed the door and locked it; then deciding that to be an unnecessarily theatrical gesture, she turned the key back again, but left the door closed. She observed that she was panting much more than was justified by a bound up the stairs on her strong youthful legs.

Sitting at her dressing-table and starting to do her hair, she was conscious of neither anger nor hatred; of no emotion whatever in fact except a feeling of emptiness and sour dissatisfaction. She wished vaguely that she had stayed for the explosion, something positive and definite at least might have come of it; but she knew it was well that she hadn't; he might have kicked her; not to be funny about it, he might really have done something terrible. She heard her mother's light hesitating footsteps on the stairs, and some ten minutes later her father's heavier confident ones; neither approached her door; she heard each time the door of their room open and close. This night she was struck with fresh and increased horror on consideration of a fact which had seemed to her incongruous and grotesque for as long as she could remember: the fact that her father and mother slept in the same bed. However incredible—in view of their waking relations—it was unquestionably so; in childhood she had on various occasions actually seen it; and to this day circumstantial evidence proved that the strange practice persisted, unless she was to suppose that one of them slept on a chair. Maybe they took turns. Maybe Father perched on the footboard. She giggled to herself, her nerves still on edge a little, opened the windows, turned out the lights, and bounced into bed.

That was all. Nothing happened. In June she finished high school, and having decided against college and being impelled toward no particular vocation, found herself without any functional activity save the desultory continuation of her piano lessons. There was nothing for her to do at home; her mother always said that there was scarcely enough to keep herself and the maid occupied. Mr. Winter, holding that automobiles were dangerous, refused to buy one, though he could easily have afforded it, since the business of his hardware store, wholesale and retail, continually prospered—and though Lora had long since learned to drive the cars of her friends. She was not at all bored; she played golf and tennis, danced, rode horseback now and then at the home of a friend a few miles out of town, took her piano lessons, went to the movies once a week, played bridge occasionally, and as opportunity offered permitted kisses to any one of a dozen young men—boys rather—in the circle of her orbit.

The kisses she found anywhere from distasteful to keenly pleasurable, according to the circumstances. There was not much savour in them, she thought; it surprised her and made her uncomfortable to observe the condition to which certain of her best friends could be reduced by an indulgence which to herself was no more than one item of the diverting routine of friendly intercourse with people she liked. She was of course aware, in a general sort of way, that in this department of social activity one thing had been known to lead to another and that carried to extremities it was even possible that disaster might ensue. She had experienced the assault of the hand on the knee, under the skirt even, the touch of the center lip, the clumsy trembling fingers seeking the neck-fastening—all the traditional half-daring half-pathetic little gestures of the male king groping doggedly for his destiny. They neither repelled her nor excited her nor amused her; she was as indifferent as it is possible to be in a situation which calls for action; with admirable lack of concern she succeeded in conveying the information that this laboratory was closed to experiment. Once, dared by Cecelia Harper, she did slap the face of an enterprising youth with such force that his head banged against a sharp edge of the car window and brought blood—which she compassionately wiped away with her handkerchief and then permitted him to keep the bit of linen and lace as a souvenir. He placed it, red with his blood, in the breast pocket of his vest, declaring that it should repose there forever.

It was this same Cecelia Harper who was eventually responsible, indirectly, for her final passage at arms with her father. It came in early autumn, just two months before her nineteenth birthday. For a week or more Lora's head buzzed with her friend's proposal; it was this proposal, in fact, which first made her sharply aware that life did present concrete problems which called for practical solutions, and that those solutions could not be arrived at without deliberate and intricate calculation. So at least it seemed to her; and for more than a week her head was filled with all the implications and counter-implications of Cecelia's proposal, its probabilities and perils and advantages, until her brain swam and it became evident that it was impossible to reach any sensible conclusion whatever. That very evening she discovered to her astonishment that she had in fact decided the matter definitely and purposefully; what made her aware of it was this, that she found herself standing, straight and determined, by the long table in the living room, directly facing her father who sat with a cigar and a book, and saying to him:

"She's going in two weeks, October twentieth. That's two weeks from tomorrow. Of course in addition to my living expenses I'd have to have enough to pay for my lessons, but there are hundreds of teachers there, any of them better than I could get here, Mr. Vickers says so himself."

She was thinking to herself, good lord I'm off, I'm actually doing it. Her father said nothing, he merely sat and looked at her as she rattled on, explaining that an old friend of Cecelia's mother who lived there would see that they were properly settled in a proper neighborhood, a small furnished apartment probably, since that way two could live almost as cheaply as one. It sounded odd, even questionable, she admitted, but really it wasn't at all; in Chicago such an arrangement was perfectly natural; why, Clem Baxter said there were at least a hundred thousand young women in Chicago, students and business women, living just that way. Still her father did not seem ready to speak, so she continued at random, in spite of her determination confused by his silence, speaking not much to the point, of Cecelia's plans and ambitions, of her own delight at this opportunity to make something of herself, of the innumerable cultural advantages offered by a great center of commerce and the arts such as Chicago.

Finally her father opened his lips; but all he said was, in a dry restrained tone:

"So you want to go."

Lora nodded.

"You want to leave your father and mother."

Now listen to that, she thought, isn't that awful. She said, "I'd have to leave someday I suppose."

"Yes. Of course. You want to leave now."

"It's not leaving exactly—not as if I were going to be married for instance. Goodness, it's only five hours away—I can come for visits—"

She was interrupted. Her father suddenly leaned forward in his chair and said sharply:

"You're lying to me."

"Lying! Why—what—"

"Why did you mention marriage?"

"I don't know—I just happened—"

"Oh, you just happened. Just a slip of the tongue. That's quite likely. Look, you know, you think I haven't noticed anything?

The way you've been going, you're never at home anymore, there's no use going into details, but I've had my eyes open. I suppose I'm scaring you away by looking at you; why don't you tell me that? I have honestly and conscientiously tried to be the best kind of a father to you. The best I know how. So it's not as if you were going to be married—it isn't, eh? Why did you say that? I want to know why you said that."

"I don't know—I just said it—"

She stopped. She saw that her father's mouth was shut tight, and a tiny pink spot had appeared in the middle of each cheek. He looked at his cigar and saw that it had gone out and suddenly hurled it across the room toward the fireplace.

"You can't go," he said in a new voice.

I've handled this stupidly, Lora thought, surely it could have been done without getting him like this. Her own lips tightened as his had done.

"Why not?" she demanded.

"Because I say so. You can't go."

"What if I go anyway?"

The pink spots were larger, and his hand in his lap was trembling; the fingers of the other were pressed around the arm of his chair. Then suddenly, as if by magic, the pink spots disappeared, leaving his face and brow quite pale; Lora stared at the phenomenon, fascinated; she had never seen it happen before.

"You wouldn't do that," he said; it was a plea. "You know you wouldn't do that. Listen, Lora, there are lots of things you don't understand. The business, for instance, it hasn't been doing so well. You have no idea how the mail-order houses are cutting into us. That's just one difficulty; it's a long story. Have you figured up how much this plan of yours would cost? The lessons themselves would be a big expense, nothing like Vickers; those fellows up there pile it on; they have to. Rents are way up in the clouds—everything you do, every time you turn around; you've never been in a big city and I have. I don't say I couldn't find the money, but it would be difficult, it would be a big drain. At any rate, just at present—later, perhaps, say a year or two from now, it might be quite different. That's the truth of the matter."

Lora was speechless. She knew nothing of all this save that it was totally unexpected. But she had a feeling about it, and she was now so aroused that nothing but feelings counted; accordingly she looked straight at her father's shockingly pale face, and said clearly and deliberately:

"I don't believe that. Not a word of it."

That brought the pink spots back! He was out of his chair on the instant, towering above her, glaring down at her, his fists upraised, trembling from head to foot. He was speaking too, shouting rather, but Lora did not get the words. Ha, she was thinking, now I'll find out what would have happened if I'd held my ground that time on the porch. She didn't budge; and the result was that she soon found herself alone on the field; for abruptly her father turned, his fists still upraised, his face purple, shaking as if in an ague, and rushed from the room. From the house also; for Lora heard the front door open and bang to, and even the pounding of his footsteps on the porch.

Not till those sounds had gone did she realize how rigid she was, how she had fastened herself to that spot, head up, hands clenched at her sides. She let the muscles go, hunched her shoulders up and released them again, and turned and made her way upstairs to her mother's room. Her mother had heard it all, it appeared, from the stairs, through the open hall door. She was already weeping, and as Lora patted her arm and told her not to worry the flow increased. She implored Lora not to go, declaring that it would be unbearable to be left alone with him; she couldn't stand it. To avoid being betrayed into a promise Lora made her escape as soon as she could, to her own room, where she threw herself on the bed to get her mind straight.

Of course, she reflected, there was no use tearing her hair out. All girls had trouble with their fathers, good lord she knew that well enough—look at Bess Updegraff for instance, who had to be home at ten o'clock absolutely, no exceptions if the house burned down. Still Bess knew what to expect at least, whereas she, Lora, never knew anything; her father was just plain crazy and besides he was a damn liar. That wasn't true about the business. How did she know? No matter, it wasn't true. And her mother was a pill, no good to herself or anyone else. Afraid to ask him to pass the butter at the table. It was painful and shameful, enough to give you the creeps. As for herself, she would show him. She felt a lump as big as a potato at the entrance of her throat as she made the resolution that she would show him. She would go. She would live somehow—not with Cecelia probably, for Cece would have plenty of money, but she would live. There were just two things she could do, play the piano and drive a car; neither seemed to offer great possibilities, but there were plenty of girls as stupid as her who weren't starving.

A long while later—she thought it must have been hours, but the clock on her dressing-table said only eleven—she undressed and went to bed. Her father had not returned. She determined to work out her plans to the last detail; she would not close her eyes until everything was arranged and settled in her mind; but as it happened her head had rested on the pillow scarcely long enough to hollow out its nest so that the tip of her nose touched the smooth white muslin, before she was sound asleep.

In the morning she awoke to the sound of her name. She heard it twice before she got her eyes open; then, blinking, she saw the early October sun slanting through the open window, the curtains shivering in the chill breeze; and, all at once, became aware that her father was standing at the foot of her bed with his eyes on her. "Hello," she said, sleepily astonished, for she could not remember when he had last thus entered her room, it had been so long ago. There was something distinctly strange about his face, she thought confusedly, but decided that impression was caused by the window and sunlight at his back which made it impossible for her to see clearly. He did look peculiar, though. He uttered a few brief sentences, in a dry quiet tone, and then turned and abruptly departed without waiting for a reply.

She sat up in bed and stared in amazement at the door through which he had disappeared, now fully awake. Good lord, had she dreamed it? No; he really had been there, and he really had said that having carefully considered the project of which she had spoken the evening before he had come to the conclusion that it was desirable and wise, and that she could count on his support, financial of course, and moral if need be.

"See that, he's crazy any way you look at it," said Lora to the sunbeam, shaking her hair back out of her eyes. She wished the light had been the other way so she could have seen his face.

XII

"Come on," said Pete, "immerse yourself, for god's sake give these miserable plebeian waters a treat; let them taste divinity."

"I can't, really I can't," Lora protested.

"What do you mean you can't?"

"Well then—I don't want to."

"I know what it is," he declared, "but it's superstition. Its birth was doubtless similar to that of a million other fond lunatic beliefs of old homo. This one is older than most—a billion years probably. When some strange four- or six-legged creature first discovered it could live out of water it began to think up excuses for not going back in. It's bad for the fur, it takes the gloss off, was probably one of the first. We never shake off a habit; we haven't got rid of that one yet, though its utility vanished before homo began. Look at you, convinced that the internal flow prescribes a dry exterior, afraid I'll bet even to take a sponge bath until nature's dam has closed the gates again...."

"It's not that," Lora smiled. "I just don't want to."

"But you love it. I like to see you too, you swim like a dolphin—though I've never seen one."

"Not today."

She was minded to tell him. Already it was obvious that it could not have been kept forever a secret—this incident alone proved it. For that matter why had she not done so at once? She would be proud to tell him! But she had been silent. She sat now laughing at him as he plunged again into the water of the lake, staying under for thirty feet or more, then coming to the surface and lying flat on his back, wiggling his toes at her. And the next day but one he would be gone. As he turned over on his belly and with slow steady strokes headed for the center of the lake she lay back on the pebbly sand, drowsy in the hot July sunshine, drowsy too with sadness.

The middle of July. June, May, April, March—she had known him only four months, then. Just think of that—over nineteen years up to the day she met Pete Halliday, and only four months since! That was nonsense, no matter how many calendars verified it.

Even the very first meeting had been memorable. She and Cecelia had gone to an evening party at the home of Mrs. Ranley, the old friend of Cecelia's mother who had helped them get settled in Chicago, and as usual had been somewhat bored. There was no dancing at Mrs. Ranley's gatherings—the nearest thing to it was when someone played Tales of the Vienna Woods or the Hungarian Rhapsody on the victrola, and even this was frowned upon in the next room where the bridge tables were. There had been the usual crowd, mostly middle-aged business and professional men and their wives, a daughter or son here and there, a few friends, both sexes, of Grace Ranley, whose mother believed in a pleasant mingling of the generations—because, Cece Harper declared pointedly, she herself, a widow, liked to have young men about. At any rate, there they all were, as usual, and as usual Lora had begun to look for Cece at an early hour to persuade her to go home, when she found herself suddenly confronted, and her progress blocked, by a tall white-faced bony young man whom she had never seen before. Looking up, for he was a good nine inches above her level, she found his deep-set restless brown eyes regarding her approvingly. As she looked the eyes smiled.

"It must be that this is what I was dragged here for," he said.

"Oh," said Lora.

"I have always had a theory," he continued—the "always" somewhat rhetorical, since he could not have been more than twenty-one or two at the most—"that dark hair renders grey eyes insipid. Here in the midst of this den of pseudogentility—"

"Mine are yellow."

"They might be in a different light. I speak subjectively. Come." He put his hand on her arm, gently but not at all timidly, and started to turn, turning her with him, toward the large inner room she thought.

She stood fast. "I don't play bridge. I'm going home."

"Bridge, my god!" He threw up his hands, releasing her arm to do so. "We're going somewhere to talk about eyes. I'll go home with you if that's feasible. Better yet, I know a place down in the Loop—"

"I don't know you."

"Easy. Pete Halliday. You're Lora Winter."

"How did you know that?"

"Easy again. It was Stubby Mallinson that dragged me here. Directly I saw you I demanded details. Come, let's get out of this."

She shook her head. "I'm here with a friend—I was just looking for her to get her to go home—really I must go—I'm awfully tired and I have to get up in the morning—I'm a working girl."

"What do you work at?"

"I run the telephone switchboard in a candy factory."

"Preposterous! You shouldn't submit to it!"

"No, it's fun," Lora declared. "I don't mind it, except that I have to get up at seven o'clock. That's pretty bad. But if I didn't do that I'd stay in bed till noon, and that's worse. I'm lazy."

"I'll take you home."

"It isn't necessary. Cece—my friend—will come. You can help me find her."

He went with her through the various rooms, but Cecelia was not to be found. At length, about ready to give it up and trying the porch as a last resort, they discovered her there on a rug in a corner with six or eight others, laughing and giggling, huddled together to keep warm in the cold and darkness. Cecelia didn't want to go home, she said, she was having a good time, she was going to stay.

"All right, I'll go along," said Lora.

"Alone?"

"Mr. Halliday will take me."

She hadn't intended to say that; she wasn't at all sure she liked Mr. Halliday; but it was out before she knew it. They went back in to get their wraps.

As they reached the sidewalk and turned north toward the nearest traffic street, Pete Halliday suddenly asked, "Have you got money for a taxi? If not we'll take a car."

"Yes. I've plenty. But I'd just as soon take a car—"

"By no means." He drew her hand through his arm. "I hate the damn cars." After a moment he went on, "To avoid confusion you should know at once that the one thing I never have is money. It is simply astonishing how little money I have."

"You live, apparently."

"I doubt it. I must owe enormous sums, and yet that doesn't seem plausible, for no living soul would lend me a cent. It's a mystery."

At the corner, after waiting a little, they hailed a taxi. It's nice, Lora thought as he helped her in, that I can do this, since he hates cars so.

He sprawled in a corner as they rattled along, with his legs extended and his feet up on the little folding seat in front.

"This is the way to travel," he declared. "This or walk. Communal vehicles are abominable. Here's an experiment: look at the faces you see on the street, preferably a street not too crowded, so that there's no bumping at least. Examine them and note them; they're not beautiful, god knows, but in many there is still a gleam of spirit, you suspect the presence of life. Then look at them on a street-car or elevated train; even that tiny gleam is gone, they're beyond hope, you imagine you're in a catacombs where they bury them sitting or standing to save space. Why? They've lost the last vestige of their freedom of movement. Walking, even on a crowded street, you're more or less your own man, you can stop and turn as you please and the worst that can happen is that you knock some-body down, not of necessity a calamity. This taxicab will go wherever we tell it to, we can change our minds at any instant; it would even turn directly around if we said so and dash off in the opposite direction. Whereas a street-car is an inhuman and uncontrollable juggernaut, a blind senseless force of nature, yes nature, created originally by man and now in obscene dis-dain thumbing its nose at him. There goes a car bound for the Stanton Avenue terminal; it is beyond any human power to turn it from its course or halt it in its obstinate career; it's as inevitable as an avalanche."

"The motorman—"

"Bah, I was speaking of passengers, but let even the motor-man try it. Jail or the insane asylum; the mere fact that he thought of such a thing would prove that he was crazy. The division superintendent? They'd fire him. The general man-ager? The same; there'd be a meeting of outraged and horrified directors at midnight. Even the owner himself couldn't do it; they'd take his franchise away from him. No, by god, in spite of anything living man can do that street-car is going to the

Stanton Avenue terminal. That's why it makes me ill to ride on them; I get a headache, I grow dizzy, and I can't breathe."

"Not really?"

"No. Of course not. As a matter of fact I've never been on one; but I've reached my conclusions. You will pay for this taxi, but I couldn't very well expect you to pay for one to take me home, so I shall walk. It's no hardship, I've nothing else to do."

So there was no talk of eyes after all; apparently he had forgotten all about it. He rambled on about communal vehicles and their share in the destruction of the human spirit—airplanes and airships would, he thought, in time prove to be the most loathsome of all—until the taxi pulled up at the curb in front of her address. He got out and helped her out, and Lora paid the driver. She was a little embarrassed, which was most unusual, indeed unprecedented, for her. She wasn't accustomed to paying for a man. Should she invite him up? Should she offer him money to ride home? How far had he to go? Without a hat, he stood there with the March wind blowing long strands of his hair across his forehead and over his eyes, stooped a little, peering at her in the dim light.

"I can walk six miles an hour," he announced. "That is prodigious, but it's true. I'm going to come and see you some time and make sure about the eyes."

"Yes. Do. I'd be glad."

"Fine! Goodnight."

"Goodnight."

He turned and was gone, in great strides, but before she had had time to enter the vestibule he stopped abruptly, ten paces off, and called to her:

"I shall be damned uncomfortable the next day or two, thinking of you at the telephone switchboard of a candy factory! Preposterous!"

He turned again and was off for good.

A strange roaring sort of young man, Lora thought, as she got ready for bed. Overpowering and confusing, like a waterfall when you stand too close to it. If she had invited him up and he had come what would have happened? Would he have been like Stubby Mallinson, trying to paw you like a bear before you had time to get your hat off, or like Mr. Graham—who owned the candy factory—sitting up straight with his hands folded in his lap, constantly wetting his lips under his little grey moustache so that the bright red tip of his tongue went in and out until, fascinated, you dragged your eyes away? Neither one; none of them. He would have been different. What made his face so white? She decided to stay awake until Cece came and ask her if she knew anything about him, but when the door softly opened an hour later she was sound asleep.

She thought of him through the next day as she sat at the switchboard, yawning and wishing the buzzers would sound often enough to keep her awake. She had decided the first week that this job was far too monotonous, but there seemed to be no alternative. At least it was better than the piano lessons, which she had given up after a brief month's trial. That had been late in November, and for a few weeks thereafter, until the time came for her and Cecelia to go home for Christmas, she had done nothing but loaf. At home she had not mentioned the abandonment of the lessons, and Cecelia had been sworn to secrecy. Returning to Chicago the third day of the new year, and letting it be known through Cecelia and Mrs. Ranley that she was seeking an occupation, she had been invited by Mr. Graham—timidly, by way of Mrs. Ranley again—to join the staff of the most sanitary candy factory east of the Mississippi. When she found that joining the staff, translated into concrete and specific terms, meant sitting on a stool nine hours a day connecting Mr. Warton with Miss Goff, or getting Michigan 3208 extension 41 for Mr. Graham, she felt mildly that she had been cheated; but after all she was only nineteen, totally without training or experience, and it was a clean agreeable quiet place to work, if only Miss Goff would quit sneezing her glasses off her thin sharp nose.

Each week, promptly on Tuesday morning, she received a check from her father, and each time she removed it from the envelope she felt guilty and uneasy; this was her first major deception. But she could not bring herself to tell him that the piano lessons were no more—not that she was afraid of him exactly, she had pretty well shown that she had a mind of her own—it was merely that she felt it undesirable and impolitic to reopen a painful question. Thus it was impossible to inform him that the remittance need no longer include the sum required for Mr. Burchellini's fee; so each week after the check was cashed she carefully put away a twenty-dollar bill at the bottom of the drawer where she kept her handkerchiefs and stockings. Some day she could return it to him; that would be a pleasant surprise, she thought, and nothing to turn up his nose at, either; it was amazing how fast it piled up.

Joining the staff at the candy factory had somewhat disarranged the domestic scene. Whereas Lora now had to arise at seven and therefore needed to be in bed by ten-thirty or eleven, Cecelia did not have to appear at the School of Design before noon and could stay in bed till eleven if she wanted to. This had its drawbacks; they could no longer have pleasant leisurely breakfasts together by the sunny south window, talking over new acquaintances, mimicking Mrs. Ranley, recalling personalities and episodes and scandals from home, laughing at nothing and at each other. Lora missed this; so did Cecelia, who declared it was idiotic for Lora to waste her time sitting at a silly switchboard, actually getting up at seven o'clock six days a week for *that;* if she was really convinced she couldn't do the piano—though for her part Cecelia thought she played very well indeed, take the Melody in F, for instance—she should try design, or modelling perhaps, if not sculpture then at least pottery—something worthwhile and creative. Unquestionably Lora had talent, she said—look at the decorations she had made for the high school pageant—everyone had been charmed by them. Which reminded her, why not try the stage? That was interesting and exciting and offered splendid opportunities for self-expression; she would like to take a go at it herself if she weren't so buried in her career as an artist. Not that actresses weren't artists too in a way....

Lora smiled and said nothing; her disagreement with this analysis was expressed only tacitly, in action. There were other disagreements—as to whether both windows should be left open on winter nights, for example—in which she was more vocal; but that and all others were friendly and without acrimony. The first that really produced heat was started by Cecelia's objections to Pete Halliday.

She was as tolerant as the next one, she asserted, but Pete Halliday was a little too much. She didn't know what Stubby Mallinson could have been thinking of to take him to the Ranleys'. All the boys agreed, even Stubby, that he was the most notorious character at the university; the only reason he hadn't been kicked out was that he was so clever they couldn't prove anything on him. It appeared that he would now be permitted to remain until June and get his diploma, that was true; it was also true that in the classes he condescended to attend he was insufferably brilliant; but he was a liar and a thief and a sneak. He was suspected on good grounds of things like stealing over-coats and selling them, things too petty and disgusting to talk about. When some of the boys made certain arrangements regarding examination questions he squealed on them. He exhibited a compromising letter which he had received from the wife of one of the professors, and then left it where the professor was sure to find it. Proof? No, he always arranged it so there should be no proof. He stole an automobile which belonged to one of the students and ran it off a pier into Lake Michigan....

"I know," said Lora, "he told me about it. He said the student said all poetry should have a moral purpose. Anyway he said it didn't do any good because he found out later that the insurance company paid for it."

"Why shouldn't poetry have a moral purpose?"

"I don't know, I never read poetry. Neither do you."

"I might. That doesn't help matters anyhow. You know very well he's not a decent person. You're just being contrary; you're just doing this out of spite."

"I don't see that it spites anyone."

"All right; you'll be sorry."

It was around midnight, and they were getting ready for bed. Pete Halliday had left only ten minutes before; it had been his third or fourth visit; Cecelia had returned from the theatre just before his departure. She sat now on the edge of the bed massaging her scalp with her fingers, with her blond bobbed hair flying first this way then that; all of her fair white body was exposed save where the flimsy silk underwear, the straps slipped from the shoulders, had fallen about her middle; one stocking was off and the other was in loose folds about the knee. Lora, in a long yellow nightgown, to her ankles, her feet bare, with a toothbrush in her hand headed for the bathroom, stopped to fasten her regard on her friend with her eyebrows down.

"Look here, Cece," she said, "you can be nasty about Pete if

you want to. Your dumb friends, too. You might as well shut
up."

"If it's a question of being dumb—" the other began; but
Lora had gone into the bathroom, so she raised her voice:
"What do you mean my dumb friends? They're yours as much
as mine."

There was no answer save the sound of the running faucet
and the swish of the toothbrush. Cecelia hauled off the other
stocking with a tug and threw it at a chair.

That was the beginning of April, and Lora had entered upon
a new experience. She had sat at a restaurant table and seen
Pete Halliday's hand resting on the cloth before her, within
reach; and later, alone in her room, had shivered with pleasure
at the thought of that hand touching her. She did not like the
feeling and assuredly did not invite it, but try as she might to
replace it with more comfortable reflections, such as the birthday
present soon to be sent to her mother or Grace Ranley's recipe
for fudge, there the hand was back again, on her shoulder or
arm—even, if not caught in time, on her leg or her breast—the
skin shrinking and tingling with horrified delight, her throat
obstructed so that she had to gulp two or three times to get her
breath normal again. It created in her a curious sort of panic,
more confused than frightened; she simply didn't understand
it. Its threat was much more profound than anything she had
guessed the existence of. Factually she was anything but ignorant;
two of her school friends had already become mothers before
she left home; another had been disgraced and the details were
known to her; while she had never actually seen a man naked
she knew the geography of the male form as well as she did that
of Illinois, her native state; and she knew that girls trembled
and lost their heads—lucky if that was all—under certain trying
conditions. She herself had momentarily trembled now and then,

having indeed on one occasion been sufficiently aroused so that by way of reaction she almost cracked the young man's head in two. But this was so different that it was not the same thing at all. Pete Halliday had not once offered to touch her; she had no reason to suppose that the idea had ever occurred to him; and yet she would sit at night on the little chair at the dressing-table she shared with Cecelia, her hair down over her shoulders like a rich dark shawl, the brush forgotten and idle in her hand, lost in a vague but overwhelming expectancy that seemed to begin in her stomach and spread irresistibly—destroying even the wish to resist—throughout every drop of her blood and every ounce of her flesh. It came with greatest force just then and there, with the hairbrush in her hand, for he had used that brush himself one evening on his own tangled hair, having walked four miles in Chicago's March wind with no hat.

"It won't help any," he had declared, jabbing the bristles violently into the disorderly mass. "Anyway it's better not; when it once gets good and matted it can't blow around so much."

"Let me do it," Lora offered. He grinned and sat down.

With the aid of a comb she finally got the tangles out and achieved a semblance of order. She detected a salty odor, she thought, and wondered if the ocean smelled like that. She kept her hands indifferent and perfectly steady; it was an effort, but a choking feeling in her throat made her aware how perilously near she was to betraying herself. Until that moment, indeed, until she felt herself almost overpowered by the salty odor from his hair, there had been no real alarm. She had to be careful about her face too, for he could see her in the mirror.

"It's too dry, may I wet it?" she said.

"And me with no hat, and going out into that wind? Delilah with her scissors wanted only castration, you would take life itself. I prefer tonsorial chaos to pneumonia."

"Does castration mean cutting off hair?"

"Symbolically, yes." He grinned at her reflection in the mirror. "It makes the hair fall out, they say."

"I don't know much about words. I wish I did."

"You don't need to. You know something much more important than words. Words are no good."

She wanted to ask what it was that she knew more important than words, but was afraid further to trust her voice. As she placed the comb and brush on the dressing-table she saw some of his hairs, lighter in color than her own, clinging to the bristles. Cecelia will notice that, she thought, and picked the comb and brush up again and put them away in a drawer.

It was somewhat later, early in April, a week or so after Cecelia's final valiant effort to rescue her friend from the clutches of a blackguard, that Lora for the first time extracted a crisp twenty from the hoard in the handkerchief drawer. The occasion was this: Cecelia had departed on Saturday morning for a weekend visit to friends in Eastview, and Pete and Lora had arranged to dine downtown and afterwards go to the theatre. She had already given him money to get the tickets, but was doubtful whether she had enough left for the dinner. The event proved that the precaution was well taken, for what with an elaborate meal at Dillon's, a taxi to the theatre, a rarebit with beer afterwards, and a taxi out to the apartment, the remains of the twenty were hardly more than chicken feed. That was how Pete phrased it, as he searched his pockets for bits of change to hand to her—for it had become the custom for him to assume the functions of chancellor of the exchequer and return the residue at the end of the evening. Sometimes this was done on the sidewalk, when it was late and Lora had to work the next day; on other occasions, as the present one, the transfer was made after they had mounted to the apartment and Pete had got comfortably into his favorite chair.

"We ought to figure it up," he declared. "How do we know but that I've a five—a ten even, though that transcends all likelihood—stuck away in my vest or in this little trick pocket in my pants that I pretend I can't get my fingers into? It would be just like me. I seem to have a faint memory of folding up a five separately and tucking it away somewhere, while we were in the restaurant I think. You didn't happen to see me?"

Lora was seated cross-legged on a cushion on the floor, in front of him, not far away, watching the smoke curl upward from the tip of her cigarette.

"Yes," she said, without looking at him, "it's in that little pocket in your trousers."

He threw back his head and burst into a roar of laughter.

"You're not so smart," she went on, "I knew you knew I saw you. You were trying to see if I'd lie about it."

"How much have you got there?" he demanded.

She fingered over the little pile beside her on the carpet—three silver dollars and several smaller pieces.

"Four dollars and forty cents."

"A goodly sum." He made his voice deep, down in his throat. "Almost precisely a day of your wages. I shudder—absolutely and visibly shudder—to reflect that that miserable little heap of metal represents nine hours, nine glorious miraculous hours, of the coursing of your sweet young juices and the disintegration of your lovely flesh. There it lies, look at it, four dollars and forty cents."

"My flesh isn't disintegrating."

"Oho, it isn't, eh? Immortal? You've learned the secret...."

"No, I'm too young. I won't begin to disintegrate for ten years at least."

"You began the day you were born. However, let that pass. The point is, you're a slave. Not to the switchboard or the little worm that owns it, but to yourself. For illustration, that five dollars I may have thoughtlessly tucked away; why do you let me keep it?"

"I don't."

"Demand it then."

Lora stretched out her hand and said commandingly:

"Give it to me."

He grinned at her, not mockingly or in refusal, not with any content whatever; he simply grinned. She got onto her knees so as to reach further; her hand was nearly touching him.

"Give it to me," she repeated.

Still grinning, and leaning back so as to release the pressure of his belt, he got his fingers into the little waistline pocket of his trousers and pulled out a small folded wad, no bigger than a postage stamp. He unfolded it and smoothed it out.

"Good guess, it's a five all right. Do you mean it?"

"Yes."

He placed it, flat, on her outstretched palm. Her fingers closed around it and she dropped back from her knees onto the cushion. Then her fingers opened again, letting the crumpled bill flutter to the carpet, and her head bent suddenly forward, lower and lower, and her hands came up to cover her face, spreading themselves protectingly over her face that did not want him to see.

"I warn you, it mustn't be left there," she heard his voice. "Either you take it or you don't. Slave or master, either will work; in between those two honesties are all the lies and pretenses in the world. You take it, that's fine, your pretty little ankles are still free to dance and kick all they want to—or give it back to me, frankly I prefer that, I happen to need it, and then we'll know where we stand. But for god's sake don't leave it between us on the floor, that's humanism, the cooperative society, the triumph of liberal progress, the only real hell, the

Great Universal Smirk. What if I grab it and run? It's quite possible, for I shall want to eat tomorrow. Then you are in a mess,
the painful position, not at all uncommon, of wanting what you
didn't take and taking what you didn't want, and after all left
with nothing...."

Lora's hands suddenly came down and her face shot up; it
was flushed and marks showed where her fingers had pressed,
but there was no trace of tears.

"Oh, shut up!" she flung at him.

She reached out with her foot, got the toe of her slipper
behind the folds of the five-dollar bill and shoved it across the
carpet towards him until it touched his shoe.

"I don't want it, it isn't worth the fuss," she said. "It's all right
as far as I'm concerned if you take money from me, I don't
mind, but you might have the decency not to talk about it."

He reached down for the bill, smoothed and folded it as
before, and returned it to his pocket. Lora watched him.

"I wonder," he remarked, "whether you have any idea what
you mean when you say decency."

"Maybe I mean decency. It's a plain word."

"Not at all plain. Did you ever hear of sex? If I take money
from a man without intending to repay it, it may not even be
dishonest; many men have done it whose statues are in our
public parks and buildings. But if I take it from a woman we
don't stop at dishonest; it becomes, as we say, positively indecent. Now why? Obviously because man wants a woman's body,
particularly that portion of it which he customarily uses, constantly available at a minimum cost of time and effort; the simplest way out of that is to own a woman. But if he owns her he
must feed her; more, he can't expect to be permitted to own
and feed one unless other men will do the same. In defense of
this manufactured right—masquerading as a duty—he is led

inevitably to the corollary: any man who instead of owning and feeding a woman permits himself to be fed by one is unmanly. Indecent. See how smoothly it works? Imagine the system functioning on an isolated island where there are only ten men and ten women and you'll see how dangerous the exception would be to the institution. But here's where the real joke comes in: women, completely bamboozled by man's superior capacity to twist words, have become more ardent supporters of his system than man himself. It was you, a woman, and by no means an inferior specimen, quite the contrary, who just now spoke of decency. You ought to be ashamed of yourself."

"It's very complicated," said Lora. She was thinking: anyway I'm not an inferior specimen, that's something, that's exciting, that is.

"So if I take money from you, and even go to the unheard of extreme of talking about it," he went on, "it's really a compliment. At least it's a compliment to your sex, for to be perfectly honest about it I was never able to comprehend how it was possible for a man to want to own and feed a woman till I met you."

"Oh," said Lora.

"I don't mean the underlying economic and biological motives, I understand them of course; I mean the individual man and the individual woman. It has always seemed to me that a man who willingly—nay, eagerly—jumped into that pot was an emotional lunatic. I see now that it's possible. Not that I'd do it, but it's conceivable. I can easily believe that a man might regard you as something much more serious than a brief and pleasant episode. The first evening I saw you, out at that bridge den, I thought to myself, ha, here's a nice little posy for the buttonhole, and then after I got you into a taxi all I did was give you a sermon on street-cars."

He stopped to light a cigarette. Lora was silent, and when he offered one to her she shook her head. Now, she supposed, thus interrupted, he would jump back to economic and biological motives. But after he had taken a puff or two, inhaled, and expelled the grey smoke through his mouth and nose simultaneously, what he said was:

"You know, I've got a confession to make that I'm ashamed of. I'd like to give you something.

"It's the first time I've ever felt that way," he went on, as she said nothing. "I've given people things, but only as a gesture of contempt or indifference. This is different, and I don't like it. Just last evening I caught myself looking in the window of a confectioner's shop thinking it would be nice to take you a box of candy. Then I remembered you work in a candy factory, so flowers or a book would be better."

"I would have loved flowers."

"Sure you would. Why not? Anybody would. You notice I didn't get them, but even that doesn't make me entirely easy, for I was influenced by the consideration that the money in my pocket had come from you and that it would be idiotic to present you with flowers bought with your own money. That is, not your own, but it had been. By god, if I catch myself going around like a brainless ass giving flowers to girls—"

"I'm not girls."

"Aha!" She was startled, he leaped to his feet so suddenly and unexpectedly. "That's what I've been looking for! That's the signal, is it? No, you don't, it won't work! I've still got my head on my shoulders, thank god! What signal? The signal for going home—you ought to see it. The signal for walking the sight of you out of my eyes! The wind will blow it out!"

Lora sat on her cushion, not moving. But he was going, no doubt about it; already he was halfway across the room; in another instant his hand would be on the doorknob.

"Pete!" she cried, scrambling to her feet.

He glared at her with his deep-set eyes.

"Look here," he said, "you'd better let me go. I'm no good for you. You're no maid of pleasure, nor wife on half rations either. That shouldn't make any difference, not to me, but it does. What you want is a husband and a little house at Oak Park with a garage and peony bushes. I have other plans. Good night."

Lora felt that she would never swallow again. Could she speak?

"Don't go," she said.

"Good night, I tell you."

"No. Don't go."

He took his hand from the doorknob and turned towards her, his broad shoulders and his head bent a little forward as he peered at her across the room.

"If I stay, I stay." He laughed, a short roar of a laugh. "I'll bet you have no idea what that means."

This to Lora, who that very afternoon, after Cecelia's departure for her weekend at Eastview, had made the bed up with smooth clean sheets, though they were ordinarily changed on Monday! As she did that there had been nothing definite in her head, there had been no room for anything definite, it had been so filled with a wild and sweet bewilderment. Her hands, smoothing out the sheets, had not needed to know where their orders came from; nor did her tongue now, as she gave Pete look for look and said quietly:

"Come and sit down again."

XIII

A little more than a month later, around the middle of May, Lora went to see a doctor. It was not easy to select one; there was nobody she dared ask, not even Pete, she thought. Finally, one evening on her way home from work, after having funked it for nearly two weeks, she stopped at a house three blocks down the street from the apartment which bore a sign in neat black and gold: Adrian Stephenson, M.D. She walked up and down on the sidewalk, passing the entrance half a dozen times, before she could screw her courage to the point of mounting the steps and ringing the bell.

She was shocked and indignant at the casualness of Dr. Stephenson's manner. He was a ruddy bulky man, his hair almost white and his dark eyes almost concealed under the drapery of his brows, with a tenor voice and an engaging homely urbanity; and he asked her if she had had a cold recently and whether her bowels were regular. He also inquired regarding morning nausea and a score of other phenomena. There was no examination; he didn't even take her pulse. When he asked if she was married the only answer he got was Lora's quick flush that included even her ears.

"Nothing to brag about," he said finally, looking at his watch. "Anybody might skip a period any time. Cold, or excitement, or a little congestion. Nature has her little pranks. Watch yourself and don't do anything foolish and take one of these pills three times a day for four days and if necessary come back here four weeks from today at ten o'clock in the morning."

"I can't; I work."

"All right, seven o'clock then."

She paid him three dollars, and left, walking slowly and reluctantly down the street toward the apartment. Cecelia would be there, and she didn't want to talk to her or listen to her. She wanted less, just now, to go to the room where Pete would be. She had overcome her dread and consulted the oracle, not without a vast swallowing of qualms and panic hesitations—and here she was, no better off than before. Another whole month of this business? Not even sure of what to hope for. That doctor was an ignorant old fool; surely there was some way of telling. Oh, she thought, and all her heart was in it—Oh, if she could only talk it over with Cecelia! But she pressed her lips tightly together and shook her head.

Four weeks later it was settled; Dr. Stephenson confessed that it would be most extraordinary for nature to carry a prank to this extreme, with all the corroborating symptoms. Yes, no doubt of it, another miracle had been performed, as he playfully put it. Then, as Lora sat and stared helplessly at him, he volunteered an offer to act as guide and counsellor during the pre-natal period, and got out of a drawer of his desk a card on which to record her name and address and other pertinent information. Lora stood up abruptly and shook her head.

"Thanks, no, it isn't necessary. I shall probably be going home—that is—I don't know what I'm going to do exactly—"

He insisted on the name and address with such emphasis that after she got out to the sidewalk again she kept looking back over her shoulder, wondering if she were being followed. Then she felt the absurdity of it and resolutely kept her face straight ahead until she reached her own address; but there the impulse again overcame her, she couldn't resist a swift anxious glance to the left as she entered the vestibule.

What made it worse—or better, she didn't know which—was

Pete Halliday's announcement, made a few days earlier, of his intention to join the Canadian army at the end of June, immediately after commencement. In less than a month, then, Pete would be gone. He could say that, or she could say it, aloud even, to herself, but it didn't mean much of anything in the face of her present devouring delight at feeling herself in his arms, feeling his caresses and kisses, above all feeling herself dropping with him into that whirling pool of madness where the senses ceased to exist and everything, life itself, fainted away into an ecstasy of groans and writhings and convulsions. She loved that. "I love it, you don't know how I love it," she would say to him, crouching over him, running the fingers of both hands through his hair, tousling him beyond remedy. She loved every bit of it, from the moment when they met at the corner of Stanton Avenue and he would grin at her and squeeze her arm—even that thrilled her so that she trembled all over—to the end, the next mornings when she would climb softly out of bed so as not to disturb his sleep, dress hurriedly and trot down to the street-car on the way to her job at the switchboard. He had rented a room on Cameron Street, only a dozen blocks or so from the apartment, and nearly every night she was there with him; the exceptions were of his choosing, left to her there would have been none. Dining at a little Italian restaurant down the street and then going usually directly to the room—a program that was varied only now and then by a theatre or a movie or a walk to the lake front and back—he would want to smoke and talk, or read aloud perhaps, but she would have none of it. With a thousand tricks and traps she would tease him out of it, and in the end he would respond with an energy and insane ardor that sometimes genuinely frightened her, though she would have bit off her tongue rather than confess it. Then he would dress again, usually leaving off the necktie, sometimes even the coat, when the warm May evenings came, and go to fetch a pitcher of beer from the corner saloon; and she would listen to him contentedly for hours, no matter what flights he attempted, until the time arrived to go to bed in earnest. Not that he was then permitted to go quietly to sleep; she had first to sit on his stomach, tie ribbons in his hair, make sure if he had any new moles, find out how hard a pinch he could take without squealing; and this led not infrequently to further and more exhausting delights, so that sometimes when the alarm sounded in the morning she felt that she would give all the wealth of a million worlds just to lie there one more hour. Pete never heard the alarm at all.

How glad she was now for the pile of crisp twenties in the handkerchief drawer! It held out bravely; for while all girlish caution and reserve of her body had expired in one swift leaping flame, other cautions not only remained, they took on a new shrewdness and ingenuity. For one thing she kept her job. When Pete asked her why—for he had soon perforce learned that the switchboard was not her only source of income—she would pull his nose and tell him it was none of his business. (Rarely was she so far away from him that she couldn't pull his nose without moving anything but her arm.) Declaring that the little Italian restaurant was just as good, she would no longer go to Dillon's because it was too expensive; she limited the movies to once a week, and all but abolished the theatre entirely. Pete would make faces and roar against her tyranny but offered no serious objection. She had the good sense never to suggest the ignominy and outrage of riding on a street-car; it was always either taxi or walk, and always he would just as soon walk if time did not press and there was any chance of her keeping up. She developed a gait that was very effective, a sort of compromise between a walk and a lope, and dared him to lose her.

After her second visit to the doctor she grew more sedate. He could either walk more slowly, she said, or go on alone; for her part she was tired of galloping frantically at his heels until her breath gave out. "What's the matter?" he demanded, "I thought you liked it." For reply she would grab his coat and pull him back, and he would slacken his pace for a few blocks, then gradually and unconsciously work back into his stride until she pulled him up again.

The two last Sundays in June they took trips to the lake shore, north of the city, a short journey by train to a spot where two or three dilapidated huts stood isolated on a sandy strip of beach. The huts were abandoned and Pete said he had never seen any sign of life around them; he had discovered the place by accident, the preceding summer on a walking trip. They took their lunch and ate on the sand in the sun, and Lora found that and the swimming delightful; but what she liked most about it was the hour after lunch in his arms on the sand with the sun insolently staring at them, and the cool breeze on her naked thighs as she would lie afterwards not bothering to put her skirt down, learning to breathe again. The breeze caressed her skin as she lay with her head on his shoulder, his arm encircling her and her own arm lying dead across him; his eyes would be open gazing at the sky above, while hers would open and close indifferently and indolently, and she would wonder what he was thinking about without daring or caring enough to ask. Or he would perchance talk, as he did when once the breeze deposited on his cheek a gossamer thread of white, lighter than a feather, with a tiny brown speck at one end. She picked it up and laid it on his lips, and he gave a puff and off it went again.

"Seed on the wind," he said, gazing after it. "That one's out of luck, destined for powder in the sand. Or who can tell, if the breeze stiffens a bit it may be lifted far across the lake and finally come to rest against a dirty board fence in a vacant lot in Gary. Ha, it will exclaim triumphantly, I guess this shows what a determined seed can do. Never say die."

After a while they undressed again and plunged back into the water, laughing and shouting and leaping, and swam out to the little island and clambered up onto its ledge of rock.

But the second time she got a scare. On the train on the way back she was suddenly taken by a cramp in her abdomen that made her bend over double and bite her lip to keep from crying out. Pete, seated beside her, put his hand on her shoulder and leaned down to look at her face.

"My god, you're as white as a sheet," he said, startled, "we'd better get off at the next stop and do something."

"It's nothing," she gasped, "I'll be all right in a minute."

And in fact she was. Before they reached Chicago the pain was entirely gone, and she decided that it was merely that she had gone in the cold water too soon after eating. But she had been thoroughly frightened, and for days afterwards, when alone, she would put her hand on her belly and rub it softly, with a thoughtful and questioning look in her eyes.

Then something else came to drive that out of her head: the day of Pete's departure for Canada was definitely set, July twelfth. He was really going. Originally he had meant to leave sooner, almost immediately after commencement, but there had been no specific date for it. Now it was different, you could count it up—just six more days! July twelfth. Five days after that, according to the doctor, she would know about the other business beyond all peradventure—though for that matter she knew that already, it was accepted. With Pete gone too—well, she thought, this is going to be altogether a little more than I bargained for—I don't know, I really don't know....

The Sunday before his departure they went again to the

beach with the abandoned huts. Lora, afraid to go in, sat on the sand and watched him swimming, floating, diving, hurling taunts at her for clinging to an outworn superstition. The sun made her drowsy and sluggish so that even the thought, this is the last time we shall come here, induced only a dull and vague sadness, nearer to pleasure than to pain. When they left though she cast a lingering glance backward at the spot on the sand in front of one of the huts where she had lain in his arms, under the staring sun; and on the train on their way home she broke a long silence—Pete hated to talk on trains—by suddenly laying a hand on his arm and saying to him:

"I wasn't going to tell you, but I've just got to. I'm going to have a baby."

He replied at once, "I know it."

She was amazed. "You know it!"

"Sure," he said. "I knew it a week ago. Your breasts show it. It's hard to see, but I was curious, and I looked at them carefully with my scientific eye. I've seen them that way before, had it all carefully explained—I tell you, education owes a lot to exhibitionism. There have been other indications, of course, the boomerang tendency of your breakfasts, the hiatus in your tidal schedules...."

"Oh," said Lora. Her voice wanted to tremble, and that made her furious. But it was simply impossible to say anything else; all she could do was repeat it, "Oh."

"I thought if you didn't mention it there was no occasion for me to," Pete explained. "I can't do anything anyway; what it takes is money. It can be done as cheap as fifty dollars, but you get a much better job for a hundred. Do you know a doctor?"

Lora did not reply. He looked at her, squirmed around in his seat a little, and went on:

"Look here, it's my fault, and I'm sorry. I knew you didn't

know anything and I should have been more careful. It's a damn nuisance, and I'm sorry. This is life, isn't it lovely? Isn't it sweet the way they've got it fixed up? I said it was my fault—well, it isn't. That's a lot of bunk. What if you want a baby—how do I know you don't? Maybe you do. All right, try and get it and see what happens. What if you don't want one, and precautions, just once, fail? Just as bad—worse even. It's one of the major jests."

"Yes," said Lora. "Of course that doesn't help—"

He pulled a card out of his pocket, wrote a name and address on it, and handed it to her.

"That man will do it, he's comparatively unobjectionable," he said. "Mention my name if you want to, he knows me. And don't be frightened, there's nothing to it if it's done right. It is said that this particular light of the medical profession cleans up forty thousand a year at this chore; he handles most of the university trade."

Later that evening, at the room after dinner, Lora told him that she intended to have a baby. She returned the card to him, and he tore it up and threw it in the wastebasket. She wanted him to know, she said; not that it would make any difference in anything, but he was going away and probably she would never see him again and she wanted him to know. When she had said that she saw him bend forward a little, peering at her, with the characteristic stoop to his broad shoulders.

"And you not yet twenty," he said. "Good god, it's criminal."

"It's all right," she said. She added, "I'll be twenty before it's born."

He threw up his hands. "And I was about to get sympathetic. You are what is called in superstitious circles a brave little woman, meaning that the cells of a certain portion of your post-Rolandic area are below normal in sensitivity." He grinned, a twisted grin that distorted his whole face. "By that prosaic fact you escape all the acute and subtle tortures. You've no idea what you're missing. Lucky girl."

"You're being smart," said Lora, "and I don't want you that way this last night. Don't."

"There's tomorrow."

"That will be goodbye. It won't count. I don't want to think of tomorrow."

When she got to the office, the next morning she told Miss Goff that she would not be able to be there the following day. It would be her first absence in the six months since she had started to work. Miss Goff made some remark about the annoyance and inconvenience of unexpected absences, whereupon Lora replied that it would perhaps be just as well to make this one permanent. At this Miss Goff took alarm; oh, no, she said, she hadn't meant to offend, Mr. Graham would be terribly put out if Lora should leave, he thought very highly of her....

So the next morning Lora lay luxuriously in bed till nine. From seven-thirty on she was wide awake, but there at any rate she was, with Pete asleep beside her. At nine she arose and dressed and proceeded to prepare the farewell breakfast, all of Pete's favorite dishes: a melange of grapefruit and fresh pineapple, Irish bacon, an omelet with anchovies and fresh tomatoes, fried potatoes, preserved watermelon rind, and strong coffee with thick cream. It took longer than she had calculated, nearly an hour, and at the end she hurried a little, for his train was to leave at noon. Pete ate in his shirt sleeves, without a necktie; Lora, already fully clothed, bobbed up and down continually taking this away and bringing that. After breakfast she helped him finish packing; and then after putting on her hat and taking a last look in the closet and under the bed to be sure he wasn't leaving anything, offered him her parting gift.

Pete looked at the offering in her hand, then at her face, and shook his head.

"I don't need it," he said, "I've got enough."

"Please, I have plenty," she said. "I want you to."

But he refused. "I don't know much about the Canadian army," he said, "but I imagine one gets fed. I'm not being sacrificial, I've simply got enough, mostly from you of course. You need it more than I do. How much have you got there?"

"It's a hundred dollars."

"A goodly sum." He grinned. "Remember when I said that before? Sure you do.—All right, I'm off. What's the idea of the hat?"

"I'm seeing you off to the war."

His hands went up. "Good god, no! I couldn't stand it. You on the platform with your handkerchief, and me leaning out of the car window and waving. I beg you not."

She was seized with panic. What, this was the very last minute then!

"I won't do that," she said. "I won't get out of the taxi. Just let me ride down to the station with you. I won't get out."

That he agreed to. They got the bags to the street and found a taxi, and after Pete had run back to the room for a book he had forgotten he helped her in and got in after her. She sat up straight on her side, her hands folded in her lap, and he after his custom sprawled in the other corner, his legs stretched out with his feet resting on the bags. The taxi sped along, and neither spoke. Lora thought she had never seen a cab go so fast; they were already more than halfway, almost to State Street. Pete broke the silence.

"I never bought you those flowers," he said suddenly.

"No," said Lora.

"Well, it's too late now. That's the closest I've ever been to a sentimental jag. I even decided it should be roses."

Silence again. She was wondering whether he would kiss her goodbye, and whether she wanted him to. The idea bewildered and embarrassed her, for they had never kissed except in passion. He wouldn't, she decided; and on that instant felt his hand on hers. His fingers rather; he had reached over and with his fingers was awkwardly stroking the back of her hand as it lay on her lap. Her head dropped, and she could see the moving uncertain clumsy fingers; she wanted to look at him but couldn't; and all at once she knew she was going to cry. She could feel it in her throat and high up on her cheeks, inside, and back of her eyeballs, inside of her head. At the same time she was overwhelmed by the conviction that to cry now, in front of him, these last two minutes, would be a calamity and an everlasting shame. Damn him, oh damn him, for touching her hand like that! *That* he had no right to do. Then she was aware that she had violently jerked her own hand away, he had retrieved his own, and the crisis was past.

The taxi had stopped in front of the railway station; the driver had opened the door; porters were standing there expectantly. Pete got out and lifted out the bags, waving the porters off, then he turned back and stuck his head in the door.

"You're going right back home? To the room, I mean?"

Lora nodded. Home, yes.

"All right. Don't believe anything anyone tells you and for god's sake keep off of street-cars. When you read of a Canadian soldier shooting his colonel in the back because he was too stupid to live, that will be me."

He flipped his hand at her and turned and picked up the bags.

"The soldier, I mean!" he called, grinning, and strode off toward the entrance to the station.

Lora gave the address to the driver. All the way home she sat up straight, her hands with the fingers intertwined pulled against her abdomen. He hadn't kissed her; she might have known he wouldn't; and that was as it should be. Pete was Pete. He wasn't a lover going off to war, or a man running away from a girl with his baby in her; he wasn't anything like that, he was Pete.

The room was a mess. Dirty dishes were everywhere, the bed was chaos, there were glaring vacancies where Pete's things had lain and hung, a piece of thick fried cold greasy bacon was square in the middle of the floor. Lora did not even pick up the piece of bacon; she sat on the edge of the bed with her hat in her hand surveying the dismal scene. She would get her things out of here tomorrow, she decided; today even, for it wouldn't be much of a job, most of her belongings were still at the apartment the rent of which she had continued to share with Cecelia. Explanations were due there too and could no longer be postponed; Cecelia was going to be a problem. Other problems too—plenty of them! What a mess. The room, that is. The first thing to do was to clean this up and get out of here—forget it ever was, for assuredly it would never be again. Sighing, she put the hat down on the bed and got to her feet, and as she did so her eye was caught by an object lying on her pillow. She went closer to look, and found it was two objects: a wrist watch with a leather strap, and a piece of paper with writing on it.

The watch she recognized at once; it was one that she and Pete had seen some weeks before in a jeweler's window, and she had admired it; had said, in fact, that it was just the sort of watch she was going to have someday. The writing on the paper was in Pete's irregular hand:

To a brave little woman—ha ha—with most sincere wishes for an early miscarriage—or, if she prefers, a painless parturition—Pete.

Well, she thought, I suppose he must have put that there when he came back in to get that book. It's the very same watch....

She sat down again on the edge of the bed, and cried at last.

XIV

Lora kept her job till the middle of October. She did not give it up then because of physical discomfort or inconvenience, for she experienced very little of either. Indeed she felt uncommonly well; her face was blooming with health, her eyes shone fresh and clear, and the feel of her muscles took on a new and sharper pleasure. For the first time she was fully aware of the sweetness of her body, and she loved all its trivial and commonplace joys: the joy of sitting down, of getting up again, of feeling her strong young legs swing, at their leisure, as she walked along the street in her own rhythm, of moving her pretty white arm, now down pressing, now up with a free swing, as she brushed her hair at night.

She quit her job because Miss Goff began to look at her. Not at her face, either, nor at her feet, but at a point midway between. Partly it was merely an annoyance, resulting from her own self-consciousness as much as from the other's impertinence; but it was also a real danger, for Miss Goff might say something to Mr. Graham, and Mr. Graham to Mrs. Ranley, and Mrs. Ranley was an old friend of Cecelia's mother, down home.... So on a crisp autumn morning Lora went to Mr. Graham's private office and told him that after the following Saturday she would not return. He timidly and nervously pulled at his little grey moustache and expressed his regrets and his best wishes for a happy and successful career, offering no objection after he had learned that she intended to resume her piano lessons. Which of course she didn't.

Cecelia knew. Around the middle of July, only a week after

Pete's departure, she had gone home for a brief summer visit; and Lora, after long consideration of all the chances and probabilities, had gone with her. On the train on the way down the need for an ally and confidant had become suddenly overwhelming. Cecelia had of course been aware for some time of the nature of her relations with Pete; it had been the cause of many strained and uncomfortable silences and two or three hot debates between them; now she learned that one of the direst of her various dire predictions had come true. She claimed to have already discovered it for herself, but Lora doubted that, for she herself had difficulty detecting any objective difference even when she was naked. At any rate, Cecelia knew it now, and for the last three hours of the trip, as the train sped through the lazy fat summer fields and the factories and houses of villages and towns, she offered a voluble mixture of sympathy, advice, compassion, suggestion, and vows of loyalty and silence. She had taken it for granted, she said, that Lora would resort to abortion; her voice was shrill and her eyes gleamed with excitement as she said abortion. But she was even more excited by the news that Lora meant to go through with it. This was where the suggestions mainly entered; she offered a dozen different plans in astonishing elaboration of detail, and was willing to help with any of them. She would not breathe a word, not a word to a living soul.

Lora pressed her hand. "If you love me, Cece."

"I won't, don't you worry. I can keep my mouth shut."

Apparently she did, for Lora detected no whisper during their two weeks' stay. Her mother, paler and more tearful than ever, obviously saw nothing to arouse her suspicions, and her father was scarcely curious enough to ask about her progress with the piano lessons. He was more aloof than ever; it appeared to have become habitual with him to spend practically all of his evenings away from home, at the lodge perhaps, or the movies, or the library—Mrs. Winter professed to know nothing about it and he vouchsafed nothing. Only on the train on the way back to Chicago did Lora realize how little she had seen of him.

After she quit her job, in October, she was amazed at the rapidity of the flight of time. She had supposed that with nothing to do the days would hang heavy on her hands, and she was afraid of them; she didn't at all relish the prospect of so much time to sit and think when thinking offered no solution to the questions she had to answer. Insofar as she decided anything at all, she decided that the questions would have to answer themselves. Fate, or Pete, or the will of heaven, no matter what, had put the seed of a baby in her, and in the course of time it would be ready to come out. So much for that. Cecelia's complicated plans seemed to her ridiculous and fantastic. None of them altered in the slightest degree the essential fact that the baby was there, and would soon be here. What to do then, when it actually was here, a living breathing kicking baby out of her own insides—well, that question too would apparently have to answer itself; certainly there seemed to be no answer handy at the moment. There was indeed one practical preparation that might be made, and Lora did not overlook it. It made her feel silly, and it seemed grotesquely unreal, but she visited the infants' wear departments of the large uptown stores and acquired a complete wardrobe. Some few garments she made herself, sewing them delicately and laboriously by hand.

Cecelia was both moved and amused. "I've never understood how you can do that until you know how big it's going to be," she declared.

"Oh, they're all about the same size," said Lora, as one who should know.

To her surprise the time flew by. She seemed never to have

got much of anything done—a little sewing, a walk down to the park and back, a trip uptown with Cecelia, a book read—in particular one called *Before the Baby Comes* which Cecelia brought her one day after having lectured her for not getting advice from a doctor—and the only tasks that immediately confronted her were inconsequential, just as good for tomorrow as for today—but it was amazing how quickly each Sunday came with Monday hardly out of sight yet and the new one waiting only upon the morrow's awakening. She had quit her job four weeks ago—no, five—no, great heavens, six! She must count up again. It would be soon now, so soon it was no longer months, only weeks, and before she knew it would be days.

The calendar computation was verified by the evidence of her body. It was no longer merely swelling, it was positively a balloon; as Cecelia said, she stuck out like a sheet on a clothesline with the wind puffing it out until you expected it to pop. Of an evening Lora would lie on the couch, reading, and all of a sudden would call out, "Quick, Cece, come!" Cecelia would bounce out of her chair and run over and put her hand flat on the balloon, her eyes gleaming expectantly, and after a moment would say in a voice trembling with excitement, "I felt it! Just as plain! My god, it's *strong!*"

"Sure," Lora would nod complacently.

For one thing she was grateful: her body no longer yearned for Pete. The first month after his departure had been misery, plain physical misery. It might be felt at any time of day, on her stool at the switchboard, at home in the evening trying to read, at the movies, where she went frequently in desperation, but it was worst at night in bed. Whether with Cecelia or alone—on those occasions when Cecelia had at bedtime not yet returned from a party or the theatre—made no difference; she would squirm and turn and toss endlessly, she simply couldn't help it.

Her loins and limbs and all the inside of her were miserable
with loneliness; time and again she would get into a half sleep
only to awake with a groan and a start and feel the restlessness
and woe swell again throughout her body until she wanted to
scream. She dreamt of him by day and night, but never did she
see his face or hear his voice; never indeed did she see him
properly at all, but felt him with an acute and startling vivid-
ness. She talked in her sleep, Cecelia said; during all this
period Cecelia had a good deal to say. Often after Lora had
tossed and turned sleeplessly for an hour or more Cecelia's tart
voice would snap in the darkness:

"Your little playmate certainly taught you bad habits. For
god's sake, can't you be still?"

Habits, ha, little she knows about it, Lora would think, not
bothering to reply. Sometimes she would crawl out of bed and
go to the front room and smoke cigarettes until Cecelia had
had time to go to sleep.

But all that was now, thank heaven, a memory; either her body
had become reconciled to that sudden and violent deprivation,
or, more likely, it was too busy with a new job which required all
its resources and faculties. She thought of Pete many times a
day; always at night when she wound the wristwatch, and often
when she walked alone over routes they had taken together or
when she saw newspaper headlines about the war, but the sharp
edges of her loneliness had rubbed smooth. Sometimes on going
to bed at night, after kicking off her slippers, all ready to crawl in,
she would whisper to herself a line from a poem, an Indian poem
translated by Byron, Pete had read to her once:

Oh my lonely, lonely, lonely pillow

But that was literature, and she knew it; within three minutes she would be sound asleep.

The Saturday before Christmas Cecelia went home for the holidays. This raised a difficult problem, how to account for Lora's failure to go too, Cecelia offered to forego her own visit, but Lora wouldn't hear of it; no, she said, it would look even queerer if neither of them went. She would write to her parents and tell them—well, tell them what? That she had decided to visit a friend somewhere. What friend, and where? Very well, she would merely tell them that Mr. Burchellini had said that her lessons and practice should not suffer any interruption; the present was a critical time in her development and she should not miss even a single day. But though she started the letter three times she found she could not write it. It was too barefaced a lie and involved too many details; she simply couldn't make it sound right. In the end it was agreed that Cecelia should go on Saturday as planned, and on the evening of her arrival, without delay, should call on Mr. and Mrs. Winter and explain the situation to them; she could say that Mr. Burchellini had made his stern decision at the last minute. That would look more plausible, they agreed.

"Your father's so goofy, if he suspects anything he might get on the first train and come up here," Cecelia warned her.

She could take a room somewhere for the period of the holidays, but that might only make matters worse; if a letter or telegram arrived at the apartment she should be there to answer it at once. It would be better to stay.

"Promise you'll be back sure the day after New Year's," Lora implored, the morning Cecelia left.

"You bet I will, I wouldn't miss it for anything. If anything happens too soon don't forget the doctor's phone number is on the pad on the bureau, and send me a telegram and I'll come at once. If you have it while I'm away I'll never forgive you."

"Don't worry, I won't if I can help it," Lora promised. She let

Cecelia go to the station alone, for *Before the Baby Comes* said that all rapid and violent movements should be avoided, and she didn't want to risk the jolting of a taxicab.

The next day was Sunday, and she lay abed till late—a habit carried over from the switchboard days. The apartment seemed silent and very empty with Cecelia gone, and in spite of herself she was tormented by a vague feeling of restlessness and un-easiness. In the bath she did not as usual find a leisurely delight in letting the tepid water from the shower trickle over her smooth shoulders and arms and the round magnificent protru-sion of her middle, turning into little rivulets down her legs; she was irritated by a baseless and unreasonable impulse to hurry through with it and get her clothes on. After breakfast she tried both sewing and reading, but couldn't get settled to either one; a walk was out of the question, for outdoors the first real blizzard of the season was howling down the street and around the corners, with great gusts of snow and sleet, straight from the bleak northwest, serving notice on anyone who ven-tured to peek out that this was a day for those who had walls and roofs to use them and not try any funny business. Sometime after noon Lora was seated by a window surveying the turbu-lent scene with an idle and indifferent gaze, with a closed book in her lap, thinking that it was about time to prepare something for lunch, when the doorbell rang.

It rang objectively the way it always rang, whether for the iceman or for Stubby Mallinson or for Cecelia when she had forgotten her keys, but Lora was so startled that she jumped to her feet like a shot, letting the book fall to the floor. She stood there trembling all over. That was no iceman or Stubby Mallinson or Cecelia; she knew it.

It's him, she said to herself. He caught the eight o'clock morning train, and that's him. He bullied Cecelia, and she told him.

She stood without breathing. All at once the bell rang again, and she quivered as though the wire had been connected directly to her and had sent a shock throughout her body. She decided that the only thing to do was to open the door. It was useless and senseless not to; somehow, sometime, he would get in; he would get in all right if it took a year; open the door and get it over with. But she did not move, until suddenly her legs gave way under her and she sank back into the chair. She sat there gazing at the little button on the wall with which the lower door was opened, and as she did so the bell rang once more; this time it had no effect, she continued to gaze unmoving at the button. After another and longer interval the bell rang again, and this time it seemed it never would end; it clanged, insistent, loudly peremptory, until she thought she couldn't stand it another second; finally it stopped, and the ensuing silence was more terrible than the clangor had been. Still she sat motionless for a long time, every nerve on edge against another assault, but it didn't come. Many minutes passed; that was all, apparently, for that time.

Fool, she thought, I should have gone to the window and looked out to make sure. It might have been almost anyone....

Oh, no, it might not. Oh, no. She was just a plain ordinary coward. She had been too scared even to think, she told herself; still was, for that matter. Absolutely scared stiff. Brave little woman....But what can you expect? After all it wasn't so simple; one could hardly call it simple. Damn Cece anyway, damn her little soul—but no, that wasn't fair, not at all fair. She would hate to have had the job of standing up to her father and going through with a straight hard lie. Poor Cece. Where was he now? Had he gone? Was he standing below in the vestibule this minute, waiting? Down there so close he could hear her if she yelled out of the window or if she opened the hall door and called down to him, just one flight. Well. He couldn't stay there forever.

At any rate she must eat. She went to the kitchen and made some toast and fried a piece of ham. The eggs should be coddled, the chapter on diet said, so she heated a pot of water to the boiling point and then turned out the gas, put the eggs in with a spoon, and replaced the lid. She had just taken them out and got them opened and scraped into a cup, and dropped a piece of butter on top, when the telephone began to ring. It startled her a little, but her hand was perfectly steady as she picked up a spoon and stirred the butter into the steaming egg meat so it would melt quickly. The phone rang on; she took the toast from the oven and arranged everything on the tray and carried it in to the table in the front room. "Not at home," she said aloud to the corner of the mantel where the telephone stood; and sat down to eat. She ate slowly and methodically, and finished every crumb.

If her restlessness of the morning had made sewing or reading difficult, they were now impossible. But the deuce of it was that nothing was possible. It was out of the question to attempt to fly; it was impossible to remain. She had decided to let the unanswerable questions answer themselves; they were setting about it with a vengeance. She was cornered. Cornered? By what? Her mind slipped away from that question; but back in it somewhere, not permitted to get into words, was a conviction that if her father got his hands on her he would kill her. There was no justification in history for that conviction; after all it is a considerable step from kicking a cat to assaulting murderously your only child; but that belief and dread were in her. She had not known how profound and intense a fear of her father had been buried in her heart; even now it did not come clear and full into her consciousness, but it was close, right at the door, ringing a bell of alarm and warning, just as he had brought her out of her chair, trembling to her feet, with the jangle of the bell screwed there on the wall.

When the bell on the wall finally rang again the early winter dusk had come. Inside the apartment it was so dark that the outlines of the furniture could barely be discerned, but Lora did not turn on the light. The luncheon tray still rested on the table, and she still sat in her chair beside it, waiting. All afternoon she had sat there. She had taken no measures and made no decisions, but she knew what had to be done—or rather, what had to be borne. It was a blessing, she thought, that Pete had gone beyond all hope, for if he had been within reach the temptation to fly to him would have been irresistible, and it was just as well not to know what might have come of that. Assuredly anything is preferable to death, granted that the alternative leaves it thinkable to go on living; but that's just the trouble, it may merely remove death a bit in time and space while it renders it more painful and hideous in quality.

When the bell rang again at the end of twilight she went at once to the button and pressed it several times, then switched on the light and opened the hall door. She recognized his footsteps on the stairs. He appeared on the landing and came down the hall to where she waited at the open door and stood there looking at her, offering no greeting, his hands in the pockets of his heavy woolen ulster, which was turned up and buttoned around his throat and covered with snow.

"Hello, this is a surprise," Lora had said as he reached the top of the stairs, and now she spoke again:

"You'd better shake your hat and coat, they're covered."

He took them off and shook them thoroughly, and preceded her through the door. She followed him into the front room, where he threw his hat and coat on a chair and turned to look at her; she stood almost in the center of the room, with the light from the ceiling fixture shining directly on her; impudently she stood straight in the fullest light.

"Where were you at two o'clock?" said her father.

"I was here. I've been here all day."

"You didn't answer the bell. Who was with you?"

Her heart jumped a beat. I see, that's it, she thought, I never thought of that. She shook her head:

"No one."

"Is anyone here now?"

"Of course not."

She was looking straight into his eyes, and his gaze met hers. Neither wavered. But suddenly his eyes slanted off downwards, and slowly descending their focus became successively her nose, then her chin, her throat, the pass between her breasts, her abdomen, the apex of her thighs. It was a complete and deliberate violation, and she stood without moving a muscle and watched him do it, knowing only that she should not so stand and submit, she should strike him dead, at the least tear out his shameless eyes and leave the glaring empty sockets as testimony of his punishment. There was a crooked twist to his mouth, and it reminded her of the way Pete looked the day she told him about the baby. That was an insane idea, she thought; certainly there was no resemblance between her father and Pete Halliday, inside or out. Let him look, let him get his eyes full. That was what she had stood under the light for.

"Who was it?" he said.

She shook her head.

"Who is he?"

Well, she thought, what's the use, I can settle that.

"He's gone away. To the war. He's been gone a long while."

His mouth twisted up again, but he said nothing.

"Cecelia told you all about it I suppose."

This he disregarded. He stuck his hands in his trouser pockets, took a long breath, and said calmly:

"We're going home on the six-twenty. That's an hour; you've got twenty minutes to get ready."

"There isn't any six-twenty."

"There is the way we're going."

Lora didn't move. "But why go home? I don't see—"

"Good god," he burst out, "you don't mean to say you're going to argue about it!" At once calm again, he added, "Your mother is at home waiting for you."

For a long instant she hung on the edge of final and desperate rebellion. This sudden and unexpected proposal bewildered her. Why home; what could be his idea in that? Certainly it sounded harmless enough, but she was suspicious of it. Indeed, now that she saw his face, his unreal composure, his eyes that were hiding behind a film she could not penetrate, she realized that anything he proposed or did would be suspicious, and she wished with all her heart that she had had the courage to act on her impulse of yesterday, after Cecelia's departure, to pack up and go—lose herself a thousand miles away. Then suddenly all that seemed tommyrot, mere weak hysteria; after all, what else would a father do but take his daughter home, that was natural enough. She remembered her room there, large and airy and comfortable, with windows on the south and east so that the morning sun always came in to greet her, with two big easy chairs and the shelves of books on either side of the fireplace, where she could have a blaze whenever she wanted it, the winter wind whistling around the corner and through the trees, or, in summer, the breeze rustling their leafy branches so close to the open window that they seemed about to come in and dance around the room; and the wide soft bed, all her own, so wide it didn't matter which direction she lay there was plenty of room, and so soft—oh, that was the bed, for any purpose whatever....

She let her father take her home. He sat on a chair waiting while she packed a suitcase and a bag. After ten minutes had passed he kept looking at his watch and calling to her to hurry, so that she forgot several items which she thought of afterwards on the train; but two things she did not forget: the miniature wardrobe she had assembled during the preceding two months and the contents of the handkerchief drawer. Since Pete's departure it had again grown to respectable proportions, but it was all in twenties, so she could stuff it into her stocking just above the knee. She made sure it was safe; that was her only insurance against fate.

They went to a railroad station she did not know. At first sight it seemed unfamiliar, and she gazed around at the row of ticket windows and the arrangement of benches in the waiting room to make sure. Immediately she was seized with panic; she stopped dead and refused to move a step. Her father yelled to the porter, who halted to wait for them, and then turned to her and explained. This train did not go home, but was on another line which stopped at Overton. At Overton they would hire a car to drive them home, forty miles over a state road. Did Lora want to arrive at their home station and descend from the train with everyone there from taxi drivers to the ticket agent recognizing her and looking at her? He explained this patiently, and she was touched by the evidence of his thoughtfulness and ingenuity. It seemed a bit over-subtle even for him, but of course he was right; she would have hated that. She walked beside him down the long platform, and they had barely found their seats in the parlor car when the train jerked forward and rolled slowly out of the shed.

They got to Overton after midnight, an hour late on account of the snowstorm. But their real tussle with the storm then began, during the forty-mile drive northwest, directly in the teeth of the blizzard. They had difficulty finding anyone who would undertake it, and finally persuaded a man who owned a little garage on the edge of town and whose only available vehicle was an open touring-car. He put up curtains, but the wind tore them open before they had gone a mile; and a few miles further on they got stuck in a drift. That was what he had put in the shovels for. Ten minutes' furious work by the two men, while Lora sat huddled in robes and blankets on the rear seat, got them underway again. Four times more the performance was repeated before they got through, and in between these episodes they shoved the wheels stubbornly forward in low or second gear, with a wind of hurricane force, cruelly cold, blinding and stinging them with the icy particles of sleet and snow it drove before it. Once the driver had to fight his way through the drifts to a farmhouse and bring the farmer with a team of horses to pull them back on the road, or at least where the road was supposed to be. This was mad, Lora thought. Plain crazy. They should have stayed at a hotel in Overton. But the driver, a wiry little man with a strong foreign accent and bushy eyebrows which now were shelves of frozen snow, evidently didn't mind it at all; he would laugh in gay excitement and shout encouragements to the car as it plunged and struggled forward. Lora was certain her feet were frozen.

As they turned into the driveway of their home her father looked at his watch by the dashboard light and announced that it was four o'clock. He paid off the driver, repeating his advice against attempting a return trip until the day came. He wouldn't, the driver said; he knew a place to go where he could get just what he needed, inside and out. Then Lora wriggled out of her nest of blankets and robes, and her father picked her up in his arms and carried her through the drifts that had piled up to the very door. As they went in a blast of wind and snow whirled in too. The living room was warm, all the lights were on, and logs were blazing in the fireplace; and Mrs. Winter was there, arising from a chair in front of the fire as they entered. More slight and fragile than ever, her eyes red with weeping, a brown shawl around her shoulders, she came a step or two toward them, then stood still, swaying a little it seemed with the dancing light of the fire behind her. Lora knew she had to put her arms around her and kiss her, and she didn't want to. She was filled that instant with a deep and overwhelming regret that she had let herself be brought home. Home indeed. This her mother! This weak ineffectual ghost—when what she needed was strength against her own weakness. That man would destroy them both yet—her mother was gone already beyond all hope of salvage; and here was she herself back again, and though she was by no means beyond hope she felt herself quivering with a distrust and revulsion that went clear to the center of her bones. Drowsy with cold and exhaustion, the warmth of the room was arousing her blood, awakening her momentarily into a curious trance of excitement and terror; everything was unreal and threatening and dangerous. She should not have come, she should never have let him bring her here.

Her arms were around her mother's shoulders when her father's voice sounded, dry and hostile:

"I told you not to keep the lights on."

This struck Lora as outrageously petty and unreasonable, and the remembered tone made her furious. She turned and flung at him:

"Oh, shut up. Just once shut up."

In a vague gesture, presumably comforting, the palm of Mrs.

Winter's hand was rubbing up and down the sleeve of her daughter's dress.

"I pulled the shades down tight," she said.

Mr. Winter paid no attention to Lora's outburst. "That would help a lot," he said sarcastically. "From now on do what I tell you, understand that. Come on to bed. I've got to be out at eight." His voice rose a little, thin and strained. "Lora, you go to bed and stay there. Understand that. Stay there."

On his way to the hall he pressed the wall switch, and mother and daughter, following him, guided themselves by the dancing firelight.

The following afternoon Lora found that she was a prisoner. She was not under any circumstances to go downstairs, she was not to show herself at the window, and the door of her room was to be kept always closed; she was to open it to go down the hall to the bathroom only with circumspection after making sure there was no one about. Her meals would be brought up to her. These rules were imparted to her by her mother, who repeated them as if she were reciting a lesson. To Lora, strengthened and refreshed by ten hours' sleep and a good meal, the arrangement seemed fantastic. She argued with her mother about it. Sooner or later people would know; things like that were always found out. Martha, the maid, would learn, and of course would talk. Cecelia already knew, and apparently had already talked. But this Mrs. Winter denied. Under a storm of questions and demands Cecelia had stuck to her story and refused to admit anything. His intuition, or maybe the devil, had sent him to Chicago. Cecelia could be trusted. Martha too. Martha loved Lora too well to give her away; she would be as tight as a clam.

Mrs. Winter sat in a rocker beside the bed and went on for an hour; Lora could not remember when her mother had

talked as much in a month as she did that afternoon. She
seemed more excited than distressed at her daughter's predica-
ment; she insisted on knowing all the details, the man's name,
the occasion, what he looked like.

"You're lucky he went away," she said, her eyes, usually so
dull and red, shining as Lora had never seen them before. "Yes
you are, you're lucky. I know what I'm talking about—whatever
else he might have done it would be worse than going away."
She sighed, a trembling miniature sigh, as if that was all she
could risk without danger of dissolution. "I know I've never
been a good mother. I've never been a good anything. I never
have been since my wedding day. That night he looked at me
with a look in his eyes I've never forgot, and if I'd known then
what it meant I'd have gone straight and jumped in the river.
There was a lovely river right by the house. You wouldn't
remember it, we left that place when you were still a baby."

Her eyes glittered.

"There's a lot you don't know. I was three months gone on my
wedding day; that's why he married me, I told him he had to.
And then after you came he pretended to believe you weren't
his daughter. He never believed that at all, but he claimed to.
How do I know he never believed it? Lots of ways. One thing,
he stopped kissing you when you began to fill out. I used to
watch every day, I used to notice how funny he acted, and sure
enough one day it was too much for him. That night in bed I
laughed at him and told him I guessed he might as well give up;
it was plain he knew where you came from. In bed was always
the only time I could talk to him, it's still that way, I'm not
afraid then, I say anything I want to and that's when I get even
with him. Lying down that way is the time to deal with a man.
Often it was too much for him, he couldn't stand it, he'd get up
and walk up and down, raving in his quiet voice so you and

Martha couldn't hear him—he always had a horror of you hearing us—and sometimes he'd go off downstairs no matter what time of night it was and I'd go to sleep. But he has never once admitted that he knows he's your father. I could never drive him to that, but he knows it all right. He even used to claim he knew who it was—made it up to torment me. At first I didn't have any sense about it. I would beg him with tears in my eyes to believe me. Oh, I didn't know him then. You were just a tiny baby, and with you right there in the room watching us I would get on my knees to him and beg him."

Lora, astonished and fascinated, lay and listened to this recital of her origin and early history. Her mother talked on and on in a ceaseless flood, protesting, accusing, justifying, revealing the details of the homely and vulgar tragedy that had ended by her grasping the occasion of her daughter's pregnancy for sharing the tortures she had kept concealed for twenty years. Lora understood that, and she understood too why her sympathy for her mother had always been smothered within her, never emerging into expression, never truly finding itself in her heart. She could not have explained it, but she felt that she understood it. As her mother's story went on Lora heard less and less of it; her mind was filling with the clear and strong conviction that she was going to have all she could do to manage her own affairs so as to avoid disaster; these people were dangerous; whatever prudence and good will were found to lift her out of her difficulty she would have to furnish herself or discover elsewhere, not here.

Except money. That was the real point: money. She felt this all the more strongly on account of an unpleasant discovery she had made a few hours earlier. Undressing the night before, cold and sleepy and exhausted, she had placed her roll of twenties carelessly on top of the bureau, and on arising shortly after noon and going to get her hairbrush had noticed that the roll was no longer there. She looked in all the drawers, on the floor, in her bag and suitcase, everywhere; it was gone. Later she asked her mother, who said she knew nothing of it. Martha was out of the question. Had her father come in her room before he left that morning? Her mother didn't know. It was quite possible. It was certain.

Her father knew that too, that the real point was money. He would. Of course the twenties were rightfully his, but that only made it worse. She was in a tight place. He had locked her door more effectually than he could have done with any key.

Her mother's mouth, once opened, seemed likely never again to close. Towards twilight that first afternoon she went to her neglected household duties downstairs, but the next day she resumed; obviously she was cleaning out a pool that had lain stagnant for two decades. For three weeks, daily, she poured into her daughter's ears all her accumulation of venom and despair. In the end Lora heard nothing; it became just a meaningless disagreeable noise whose only significance consisted in its interruption to her own thoughts. Her mother demanded a judgment in terms, but Lora could not furnish it; not bothering to evade, she merely shook her head and was silent. She had a feeling that not only was a judgment impossible, but also that neither her father nor her mother desired one. Her mother sought an ally, that was all; and no thank you, she had her own battle to win and could not afford to identify it with a cause already lost before she was born.

For three weeks she kept to her room. After the first day or two Martha brought up her meals. Martha didn't say much, refusing to answer the simplest questions; she had instructions not to talk, she said; plainly she was frightened and apprehensive. But good heavens, Lora protested, there was no reason why she shouldn't talk to her, it was too ridiculous, she wasn't a mysterious captive in a dungeon. Martha merely sighed and shook her head. In the morning Mrs. Winter would come in for a brief visit, and always soon after lunch she would appear again, establish herself in the rocker near the window, and knit and talk until long after the early winter dusk had compelled them to draw the shades and turn on the light. It appeared that Mrs. Ivers, who had come from Toronto not so long ago, had persuaded a group of ladies to knit socks for Canadian soldiers, and it amused Lora to consider that the very pair now growing so rapidly in her mother's deft fingers might be destined for Pete Halliday's feet. She doubted though if they were big enough; Pete had enormous feet.

She hated being confined to her room. Besides, *Before the Baby Comes* said that gentle but regular exercise should be continued right up to the last. Uneasily she submitted. She didn't like it. If secrecy was what he wanted why drag her down here from Chicago? It was idiotic to think it could really be kept a secret. For her part she was willing to let the whole town know it, and take the consequences. She wasn't going to stay here anyway; she had gone once and she would go again, just as soon as she could manage it. How, was another question, to be answered when the time came. For the present there was nothing for it but to let her father have his way, even to acquiescence in his elaborate and melodramatic precautions.

She was beginning to feel that her father might have been able to find something to say for himself. As for her mother, let who could unravel that tangle; but for her part what had she to complain of? After all, here she was, well cared for, warmed, sheltered, clothed, fed—which Pete said was all that life consisted of. And love, he had added, with his mouth twisted. Assuredly she had never been loved by anyone, except possibly

Cecelia; or if to love meant what she had felt for Pete, with the remnants of it still closing her eyes and accelerating her breath now and then like the fragrance from an empty scent bottle, she knew what to expect from that quarter. Nothing. That was done.

She was grateful to her father. In contrast to the sudden and prolonged volubility of her mother, he said nothing. Each evening he appeared in the room for a few minutes after dinner, inquired if she wanted anything, made sure that the shades were tight against the windows, remarked on the weather or the book she was reading, and departed. One evening he told her that Cecelia had returned to Chicago, and that before she left he had informed her of Lora's whereabouts and received again her promise of secrecy. It was thoughtful of him, Lora considered, to relieve her mind about Cece.

But mostly during those three weeks her mind was not on Cece or the memory of Pete or her father and mother. Even the farcical captivity and its restrictions and regulations were of no importance compared with her own intimate physical problem and its delightful and terrifying promise. There were so many different ways to think about it! The bodily pain and danger, the thought of which sometimes frightened her terribly and at others merely filled her with a calm assurance and fortitude; the speculation as to whether it would be a boy or a girl— she couldn't definitely decide which she wanted; the picture of herself afterwards, after the first two or three days were over, lying in the wide soft bed with her own baby in her arms; the dressing and feeding and washing, which took all one's time, positively every minute of the day; all these contemplations and images and a hundred others busied and thrilled her endlessly. She tried hard to realize—not just to say it, but actually to realize it—that a live baby with arms and legs and eyes and ears was really inside of her; it was enormously difficult no

matter how she concentrated on it. Not that it was possible to
doubt it either; it kicked and stirred and shivered too hard and
too often for any doubt; sometimes it seemed as if it actually
intended to turn a complete somersault, and she would hold
her breath until it quieted down again. Once it went two whole
days without a sign of life, and fear crept into her heart; then all
at once, just after she had gone to bed, it kicked so hard she
laughed aloud and scolded it for trying to make a break before
the time came.

One thing worried her. She decided to ask her mother about
it, but somehow the question didn't come out, though the
intention carried over for several days. When her father came
in the following evening she waited till he had finished his customary tour of the windows and then as he stopped in front of
her chair asked him abruptly:

"What doctor are you going to have?"

His eyes dropped.

"I've attended to it," he said.

"Not Doctor Graves?"

"You don't like him?"

"No."

"All right. There are plenty of doctors."

He turned as if to go. Lora said hurriedly to his back:

"A book I read says there should be an examination before-
hand."

He turned at the door, frowning.

"You'll have to leave those things to me. You can safely suppose that I know what I'm doing."

He was gone.

It was three days later, in the middle of the afternoon, that
the first pain came. Lora had both read and heard descriptions
of it, and had resolved to force herself to take it calmly. But at

the first onset her determination was swept aside in an irresistible wave of terror. She stayed in her chair though, grasping
its arms and holding her lips tight against the impulse to cry
out; then when it was over she went shakily to the head of the
stairs and called her mother, who came running and told her to
undress and get into bed. Then Mrs. Winter went out again,
and downstairs. Lora opened the door a crack and heard her at
the telephone, but it was too far away to get what she said.
Before she was ready in her nightgown her mother returned, a
little flurried and excited, but with a new air of competent
command.

"There's no hurry," she said. "Don't be frightened. It may be
an hour or more before another one comes."

"Did you phone the doctor?"

"I phoned, yes. Don't wear that gown, you'll ruin it. Here,
wait, I'll get you one."

"What doctor?"

"You can ask him. He's coming."

"Which one?"

"Your father, I mean."

It proved to be many times worse than any picture her imagination had drawn. As the book had said was customary, the
pains were at first infrequent, only five or six of them in the
first two hours, but after that the intervals were shorter, until
finally it became, as it seemed to her, an unbroken and intoler-
able agony. Her father, who had arrived shortly after her mother
had telephoned, had said at first that there was no hurry about
the doctor; somewhat later, as she lay gasping trying to arouse
her strength for the next one, she overheard talk between them
which confirmed her suspicion that no doctor had been sum-
moned. A wave of fear and fury swept over her; she sat up in
bed and started to shout at them, not knowing what she was

saying; they both ran over and pushed her back onto the pillow; she felt another convulsion gathering itself together down in the center of her, and braced herself and held her breath to meet it. She would deal with them after it passed. But then she was so exhausted that everything seemed hopeless and futile; she looked at them and thought of things to say, tried to invent a formula for imposing her will on them, but it floated off out of her grasp, no words would come. It wasn't important enough; nothing was important but to get rid of the terrible and inexorable pressure that was tearing her body in two and ripping her bones open. She saw her mother's face leaning over her.

"I had…no idea…" she said. "How much longer do you suppose…."

"It will be all right," her mother said. "You're having a hard time. Do you know it's nearly midnight? Try not to groan so loud."

Every now and then she was aware that her mother was fooling with her down there, putting something in apparently, or taking something out, she didn't know which. It appeared to help; she believed that it helped until the next time came, and then it seemed worse than ever. Once they got her onto her knees, with her head forward and down and her legs spread apart; her mother argued with her insistently that that was the natural way, quicker and better than lying on her back. At first it did seem so, but then all at once it felt as if her legs were being grasped, one on either side, and torn violently asunder; seized with panic she flopped onto her back and wouldn't let them touch her. It was plain by that time that it wasn't going to come out at all; this was a part of their scheme; she was done for.

Even then the end was still far off. When it came her mind was numb. She was aware of everything, but the thread of her consciousness was so frayed and attenuated that her awareness was like a vague and feeble dream. She knew that something unprecedented was happening, something that had never happened before; she felt her mother's hands, quick and strong; and all at once she realized that the terrible expectancy, the desperate gathering of forces from muscles and veins and nerves and bones from which all force had disappeared never to return, was gone. The world had come to an end at last. She wanted to open her eyes, but could not. She heard footsteps— that would be her father—and a door open and close. Her mother was still doing something with her. What for? It was all over....

She opened her eyes. "It came," she said.

"Yes. Lie quiet. You're not through yet."

"It came. Where is it?"

"Getting fixed. Lie quiet."

"Fixed?"

"Of course. Fixed and washed."

She closed her eyes. It was not long before other pains came, but they didn't amount to much. She helped them indifferently, not caring and scarcely feeling them. After a long time she opened her eyes again. Her mother was kneeling on the floor, busy with what seemed to be a pile of newspapers. Her father was not in the room.

"Where is it?" she said.

Her mother looked up. "It's all right. Go to sleep. You must go to sleep."

I will not, Lora thought, and then knew nothing more.

When she awoke the shades were up and the pale January sunshine was streaming in at the east windows. She looked idly about. The room had been tidied up. It looked remarkably tidy, in fact; even the chair on which she laid her things when she undressed at night was empty; there were no books or magazines on the little table beside her bed. Most curious of all, and she decided that was why she felt so queer and stuffy, the windows were not open—only a crack of a few inches in the one next to the bureau—and the room was quite warm and there was an odd smell in the air. Her head felt dizzy.

Suddenly she threw the covers back and sat up straight and looked sharply around. She got out of bed and for an instant stood there beside it, swaying a little on her feet, then made for the door and down the hall to the head of the stairs.

"Mother!" she called, and repeated it at once more loudly, "Mother!"

Her mother appeared at the foot of the stairs, and started up towards her. She came quickly, and grasped Lora's arm.

"Get back in bed," she said. "You're crazy, don't you know you're sick?" She led her down the hall and into the bedroom. "Come on, back in bed this second. I'll bring your breakfast. I was only gone a minute or two, and of course you had to wake up while I was away. No, wait, I'll change the sheets while you're out. Here, put this around you and sit here. I'll shut the window."

Lora took the shawl and stood with it in her hand. "Where is it?" she said.

"Where's what? It's all right. Don't bother me with questions, wait till I get your bed fixed and bring your breakfast." She was a miniature cyclone, dragging off the old sheets, flapping out the clean ones, running from one side of the bed to the other. "I haven't had a minute's sleep, not a minute. Neither has he. And Martha got here late—she was at her sister's last night—and I had everything to do myself—it's past ten o'clock and she's just started on the breakfast dishes—"

Lora took her by the arm and turned her around.

"Where is it?"

Her mother became perfectly still in her grasp as an animal will, feeling itself caught. She made no reply.

"What have you done with it?"

Her mother's eyes met hers, and she stepped back from them.

"It's dead. You've got to know. It's dead."

Lora stared at her. She stared back, and added:

"It was born dead."

Lora took two steps to the bed and sat down on its edge. "No," she said. "No, it wasn't."

"It was born dead," her mother repeated. "That's why you had such a hard time. It was terrible. I ought to know, I took it myself."

Lora continued to stare at her. Finally she said, "That's a lie. It wasn't dead. I heard it. I knew you were no good. Oh, god, I've known all my life you were no good." Her fists were clenched tight, separately, in her lap.

"It's not the first time a baby was born dead," said her mother. "I know it's terrible. It's hard. Look here, you say I'm no good. I've told you, haven't I? I'm not as big a coward as he is. I've stood up to you and told you. He went early, so he wouldn't be here when you woke up, I know. He went as soon as it was daylight, leaving me to tell you. I know I'm no good, but look at him." A laugh rattled out of her. "You're none too lucky in your mother, but your father, your own father—"

"Where is it?" Lora demanded.

"What? It's dead I tell you."

"Yes, I mean where is it." She unclenched her hands and stood up, steadying herself by the bedpost. "I want to see it."

"It's gone."

"It can't be. I want to see it. Listen, Mother, please, can't you see I've got to see it?"

At that her mother flopped on her knees by the bed and

began to cry. Her thin shoulders rose and fell, her head rolled back and forth on her folded arms, and she sobbed as Lora had never heard her before. Lora stood a moment, then sat down on the bed again. After a while words began to come in the interstices of her mother's sobs, with her head still buried in her arms. Of course Lora wanted to see her baby, she said. Of course she did. She couldn't. It was really gone. He had taken it. He had taken it right away and gone out of the house with it and stayed a long while; he had stayed two hours or more. When he came back he wouldn't say anything except that he had attended to it. Then he ate breakfast, a big breakfast, four eggs she had never known him to eat before, and pretty soon, after daylight came, he went again, leaving her, Lora's mother, to tell her. Lora was suffering of course, but so was she; she had suffered for twenty years and there would never be an end of it.

Lora reached down and gripped her mother's shoulders and pulled her up to look at her.

"Was it dead?" she demanded.

Her mother nodded. "It's dead."

"Was it dead when he took it?"

That question was never answered. Not then or ever. Mrs. Winter got to her feet and stumbled out of the room, sobbing afresh, and down the stairs. Lora sat on the edge of the bed staring at the open door. She got up and pushed the door shut, then returned and sat down again. She felt cold and faint and the objects in the room were staggering crazily in front of her eyes. She fell back onto the bed and pulled the covers up, turned over on her face and lay there without moving.

When Martha came in with her breakfast tray half an hour later she refused to move or make any reply to the maid's greeting, until, frightened, Martha approached and touched her shoulder; then she turned her head a little.

"Let me alone, I'm all right."

"You've got to eat, Miss Lora. You ought to eat while it's hot."

"All right. Let me alone."

At the sound of the door closing behind Martha she suddenly turned over and sat up. The dizziness was all gone. It was all quite clear; it would be the simplest thing in the world. Her father's loaded revolver was of course in the drawer of the desk in his bedroom, where it had been kept as long as she could remember; as a child she had often opened the drawer a crack and shudderingly peeked at it, not daring to touch it. To get it now, unseen, would be easy, with Martha and her mother both downstairs. Then under her pillow. In the evening he would come to her room as usual, right after dinner. Maybe he wouldn't. Tomorrow evening then, or the next, or the next; he would come; she could wait. The revolver held six bullets, and all it needed was to pull the trigger. She would wait till he was quite close, the closer the better, even so she could touch him with it. Then she would get back into bed and lie there peacefully, and when people came she wouldn't bother to say a word. She would never say anything to anybody again. If Pete came she wouldn't speak to him even; she'd just twist up her mouth the way he did and he would hump up his shoulders and peer at her and she would know it was all right.

At the same time, without words, her mind was making its practical decisions. To carry them out she needed all the strength she could muster; the fragrance of the coffee floating over from the tray started that. She could see the little clock on the bureau but wasn't sure it had been wound, so she got out of bed and went to get her wristwatch which she had wound herself when she undressed the afternoon before. Not twenty-four hours ago; that was hard to believe. Somewhat less in fact, for the watch said twenty past twelve. She had a full hour; the afternoon train was at one-thirty. She put on her dressing-gown and carried the tray to the bed, and efficiently and deliberately went through the fruit and toast and eggs and coffee to the last drop and crumb. All the time she felt herself tremulous inside, but her hands were perfectly steady; the swallowing was difficult and required some determination. Then she put the tray back on the table and went to the head of the stairs and called her mother, and at once heard her pattering footsteps.

Mrs. Winter entered the room hesitantly, stopping just inside the door, and looking at Lora and the empty tray tried to smile. Lora gazed at her in contemptuous astonishment. It was incredible, but there was no doubt about it; pathetically and idiotically she was trying to disarm her daughter with a smile.

"How much money have you got?" Lora said.

The attempted smile disappeared for faint amazement.

"Why—I don't know—"

"I need all I can get. I'm going away. I have to leave in half an hour, to take the one-thirty train. Have you got as much as a hundred dollars?"

Her mother's mouth opened, and closed again. Opened by Lora's words, and closed by the look on Lora's face.

"You can't go like this," she said. "It will kill you."

"Please," Lora said. "Listen, if you ever did anything....Go and see how much money you've got. In that jar in the attic, I know."

Her mother looked startled. "How did you know—"

"I know lots of things. Hurry up."

"Child, you can't go—"

Lora interrupted her, suddenly blazing:

"Can't you see it's silly to talk?"

Her mother turned and went without a word, and Lora took off her dressing-gown and nightgown and started to dress. She wouldn't stop to pack a bag; she wanted nothing from there; she would like to leave that house naked if it could be done. Anyway, she didn't want to be encumbered with a bag—and she might never need one. She hated everything in that room; she loathed the smell of it. God, what an unspeakable and unforgivable fool—but she shook her head and set her teeth together against that useless indulgence. Later would do for that.

Her mother came in panting a little, her eyes gleaming. She had a little over a hundred dollars, and she had got twenty more from Martha. Lora took it, a large roll of ones and fives and tens, and stuffed it into her purse. That was it. Money. Then she sent her mother down to phone for a taxicab.

When she got downstairs, steadying herself by the rail on one side and her mother on the other, Martha was there, crying as though her heart would break. She threw her arms around Lora and implored her not to go; she would die, she was sure to die. Mrs. Winter, her thin little body erect and only her glittering eyes betraying her excitement, said nothing. Once more upstairs she had tried to protest; now she was silent, but kissed her daughter on the cheek and buttoned her coat collar for her.

"Don't come out, I'll get to the taxi all right," Lora said.

But they both went with her through the snow-covered yard, down the walk to the curb, and stood there gazing after her till the cab turned the corner two blocks away. She saw them through the cab window, but somewhat dimly, for she was beginning to feel cold and faint again. She kept saying to herself, if once I get on the train I'm all right.

It was not so bad. The ticket-seller recognized her and was obviously surprised. Perhaps others did; she looked at no one.

In a few minutes the train arrived and she went to the platform and got on, pulling herself up by clinging to the iron railings. There was an empty seat not far from the door and she sank into the corner of it and let her head go back. Her feet were terribly cold, there was an aching hurt inside of her, and her head was whirling madly, but as the train jerked forward she turned a little to look out of the window.

XV

If Lora's mind had been consecrated to the preservation of enigmas a considerable portion of her waking thoughts, as well as her dreams, from her twentieth to her thirtieth year, might easily have been devoted to the several questionable aspects of her management of life during that period which began when Pete Halliday accosted her at Mrs. Ranley's party, and ended when she sank into a seat in the day coach of the Chicago express. But in the first place she never at any time had the slightest idea that life was susceptible, in any broad sense, to management; and in the second place enigmas bored her. With her the fact that a question was complicated and difficult was proof that it deserved only to be ignored; and if the question were posed by the past instead of the present or the immediate future it wasn't worthwhile even to listen to it. So in the hospital bed in New York she not only made no attempt to retrace to their sources the threads of accident and design that had led her into catastrophe, but even devised no solution of her present difficulties until one was offered to her through the interest of Doctor Nielsen; the day she looked out of the window and saw Anne Whitman and Steve Adams drive off in his roadster she went downstairs to get the things she had so carefully deposited in Anne's room only three days earlier, and then calmly arranged herself for her afternoon nap; the broken baby-carriage wheel, which Albert Scher, his pockets inside out, despairingly and clumsily repaired with picture wire, produced in her one sole reaction, an added caution in avoiding bumps and negotiating curbs; when Max Kadish died she let his family take his body without a struggle, not enough interested in Albert's feeling of outrage to try to comprehend it; and when Lewis Kane insisted that the four-page contract be signed before they proceeded to the execution of their project she would have affixed her name without reading more than a paragraph or two if he had not made her go through it from beginning to end. She kept the copy he gave her though, in a wooden box which contained an assortment of trinkets, some sketches Albert had made of her, a poem Max had written, and her snapshots.

She had been called a whore twice: once by Steve Adams and once by Max's sister Leah. That created no problem whatever. She knew what a whore was of course: a woman who lets a man go to bed with her for money—just as a rug is a piece of carpet you put on the floor without tacking it down, or a doctor is a man who treats people when they're sick. That she should have been called a whore neither offended nor amused her; it was simply nonsense. She had entirely forgotten that Albert Scher had once called her a prostitute, but then she seldom bothered to remember what Albert said on any subject. She had a suspicion that he remembered mighty little of it himself.

She was surprised that Albert and Lewis Kane became good friends and apparently had a good opinion of each other. This happened after she and the children had moved to the country, to the house on the edge of the village of Maidstone which Lewis paid for, with the title in her name.

She never felt that she understood what people were trying to do or why they were doing it, but Lewis Kane especially was a puzzle. He would prepare an elaborate contract, with intricate provisions against every imaginable circumstance, regarding a child not yet born, not conceived even; and on the other hand he would pay thousands of dollars for a house, with lawns and

gardens and a garage, a meadow and a grove of birch trees, and
put it in her name apparently without a thought. She could
mortgage it or sell it or give it away, anything she wanted to.
That seemed to her stupid; when one day she told him so he
merely smiled and said she couldn't do any of those things.

"Why not?" she demanded. "I own it."

"Try it."

"Oh. I see. You've done something legal."

"Not at all. Just try it. Tomorrow morning, say."

"But I don't want to tomorrow morning. There's no reason."

"That's just the point. How can you do anything there's no
reason for? That's why I say you couldn't do it."

She still thought it was stupid.

The house stood at the top of a gentle rise, where the road
west out of Maidstone lifts itself in readiness for the long descent
into the valley where the main line of the railroad runs. On a
clear day she could see the hills bordering the Hudson to the
west, and toward the north a corner of one of the reservoirs,
lined with evergreens, was in plain view. The grove sheltered
both the garden and the house from the winter winds, and a
high hedge served as a screen from the road in front. But from
the windows of her room on the second floor Lora could see
the cars go by, over the top of the hedge. On that floor were
four bedrooms, not counting the maid's; the room downstairs
that had been intended for a bedroom she had arranged as a
playroom for the children. Stan, whose last name Lora knew
but could not pronounce, a black-eyed Pole with a little tuft of
black hair in the middle of his chin, who did the outdoor work
and tended the furnace and could drive the car when necessary, lived on the other side of the village with his wife and
seven or eight children. When Lora asked him one day if he
didn't think that was too many he shrugged his shoulders,

screwed up one eye, and said impassively, "It don't matter what I think, she's as full as a frog."

He's a sensible man, Lora thought, I must ask him to bring his boys with him some day to play with Roy. A week or so later they came, three of them, straight and slim with flashing black eyes. Not more than ten minutes had passed before Lora heard a frightful uproar in the back and ran out to find two of the visitors rolling on the grass locked in a deadly embrace, screaming and jabbing at each other. Roy's velocipede lay on its side nearby, and Roy himself was standing calmly with his hands in his pockets, watching the battle with detached interest. He explained that they were trying to decide who should have the first ride on the velocipede. The third visitor, the biggest and handsomest, was jumping up and down shouting encouragement to both combatants, while their father was methodically raking the grass not far off without bothering to look at them. The experiment was not repeated.

So far as Maidstone was concerned, Lora was a widow; her name was Mrs. Lora Winter. But for the insistence of Lewis Kane she would not have bothered with the transformation of the Miss into the Mrs., but seeing that obviously it would simplify matters she did not oppose it. The first autumn, when Roy started to school, he came home one day in October and demanded to be told the name, occupation, and date and place of demise of his father. Lora supposed it was a question of official records; but no, he explained that the other boys were all talking about their fathers and he wanted to talk about his; besides, they asked questions.

"It's none of their business, your father is dead," said Lora.

Roy stood, keeping his eyes on her, without speaking. She went over to him and put her hand on his head and turned his face up.

"You don't tell me any big lies, do you?" she said.

His head wiggled from side to side under her hand.

"All right, I don't tell you any either. I can't tell you about your father now, but someday we'll have a long talk about it, so if the boys ask questions just tell them to mind their own business. Fathers don't matter a bit. They're just a nuisance."

That had faint repercussions, the first one coming the following Sunday, when Albert Scher arrived for his customary visit and Roy informed him briefly and categorically that he was a nuisance. When Albert laughed and demanded specifications Roy merely said, "You're Panther's father, so you're a nuisance."

In time things got somewhat complicated. As the children grew into the confused and shifting comprehensions of childhood it became difficult to explain how it happened that whereas Roy's and Morris's fathers were dead everywhere, Panther's and Julian's fathers were dead only under certain circumstances. At school all fathers were dead—not only that, they were all somehow the same person. At home Panther's and Julian's fathers were alive, and they were different people; in fact, they were Albert and Lewis. Then at home did Roy's and Morris's fathers, though they remained dead, become different people too? The confusion of course extended to the children's playmates, the other boys and girls of the village, and from them into the homes, so that it ended by becoming Maidstone's favorite puzzle, and finally got so inextricably tangled that no amount of research could ever have straightened it out again. So far as the children's acceptance in their community was concerned all the deliberation and shrewdness in the world could not have managed it better, for Lora was accused of so many things that not a tenth of them could possibly have been true; and Roy and Panther were clever enough not to waste any time in discovering their superiority when it came to a discussion of fathers.

To Lora it was a matter of indifference. The first year or so there was the baby. She discovered it was vastly easier to manage a baby properly in the country than it was in town. But not necessarily more pleasant; now and then, with little Julian in his carriage on the lawn or along the paths of the grove, she would remember the days of the others, in Washington Square or the park or along the piers, with all the people to watch, all the movement and excitement of the great city at her elbow, and a faint regret would flow peacefully across her mind. But this, she knew, was better. With four young children, one still a baby, she was sufficiently occupied so that the stimulation of the city was better at a distance; and if it did now and then get on her nerves a little to be so bound by the wall at the end of the grove and the abrupt termination of the village sidewalk there was always the car and the picnic hamper; the roads north to the foothills, west to the river, or east to the sound. In the summer, when there was no school, they would make these excursions two or three times a week.

After Julian's second birthday she went oftener to the city. There would be shopping to do, or a visit to Anne Seaver, or perhaps Albert would meet her for lunch and afterwards take her to some of the galleries or to a tea at some studio—once it was Palichak's, and she was pleased that he evidently remembered her so well. But mostly that bored her; on the train on the way home she would wonder idly why she had bothered to go. There was nothing in it. It passed the time. But time passed at home just as rapidly and pleasurably and with less fuss.

At the house in the country Albert Scher was apt to show up at any time. He might come as often as two or three times in a week and then not put in an appearance for a fortnight or a month even. He came frequently on Sunday, when he knew he would find Lewis Kane there.

Unfailingly Lewis arrived on Sunday, throughout the year, just in time for the midday dinner, which was at twelve-thirty precisely; Lillian never missed it more than five minutes either way, and Lewis was never late. He always had something for each of the children, and he was careful that Julian's gift should not be more desirable or costly than the others. Albert occasionally rode out with him, but ordinarily came on the train somewhat earlier and walked up from the station. All seven of them ate together, Julian and Morris and Panther on high chairs and Roy on a regular chair, so low his chin could have rested on the tabletop. Lora was well aware that Lewis behaved admirably; she knew, for instance, that he thought children should eat by themselves and should not speak when adults were talking, but he continued to accept the arrangement without a murmur and maintained an unruffled temper even when his twentieth attempt to get a sentence out was smothered in the general hilarity. He permitted himself to offer correction only when a personal issue arose between himself and one of them, and he never presumed to impose rules of conduct. This applied to Julian as strictly as to the others; it was of course as remarkable and admirable as to Lora it seemed, but she might have found it all provided for in paragraphs 14 and 15 of the contract which lay forgotten in the wooden box. Sunday evening there would be a light supper just before the children's bedtime, and when that was over Lewis would go to the kitchen and give Lillian a two-dollar bill—always laying it on the table and always saying, "For the extra trouble"—tell the children goodbye by patting them on the head, take Lora's hand and hold it a moment, and depart. Albert always rode back to town with him; only two or three times in four years did either ever spend the night, and then the couch in the living room was utilized. Lora wondered what they talked about during the ninety-minute ride. She knew they rarely saw each other in town, but she had a suspicion that Lewis was helping Albert in his newly projected venture as an art dealer.

After four years she remained aloof from Maidstone. There were agreeable casual contacts, but that was all. It was a bridge and golf community, but she hardly knew that much about it. During the first six months she had refused two or three invitations, giving the children and baby as an excuse, and had never returned the four or five calls she had received. This created a little atmosphere, but subsequent accidental encounters at the grocery or the drugstore, or on the sidewalk, had made it so obvious that she was totally unconcerned in the matter, one way or the other, that finally she was accepted on her own terms, and even, eventually, ceased to be a topic of general debate.

She had no arguments with life. At the age of thirty-three she remained as devoid of intellectual attitude as a cat, though she had by no means lacked exposure to that contagion—running all the way from the diluted second-hand humanism of her high school English teacher to the anarchic egoism of Pete Halliday and the unlabelled and confused vagaries of Albert Scher. It was not so much a failure in comprehension as it was a constitutional immunity. When on a Sunday afternoon Albert Scher—if in winter—sprawled on the living-room rug in front of the divan on which she and Lewis Kane were seated, or—in summer—lay on the soft grass under the big maple tree with his heels in the air, and demonstrated that the only progress possible to man was esthetic progress, she knew well enough what he was driving at, but she was as completely unconcerned as if he had been proving that apple sauce was made out of apples.

Or perhaps Albert would be expounding one of his various theories of art. Art, he would say, is merely one aspect of man's unremitting effort to triumph over nature. That's all right, Lewis would put in, if by triumph over you mean understand. Not at all, Albert would retort, not understand; conquer, defeat. For centuries man tried to put it over nature by showing that he could surpass her in the beauty of his creations. I'll show you how clumsy you are, he said to her, look, when did you ever make a woman or a tree or a blending of light and shade as lovely as that? But one day not so long ago it was decided that that game was played out. No more could be done, all the old tunes were stale, so he determined to turn his challenge upside down. You think you're beautiful, eh? he sneered. My god, let me show you, here's what you really look like; and he produced a million masterpieces of ugliness. Nature, of course, has remained stolidly unaffected in either case, but meanwhile man has his fun. It is an excellent arrangement that nature is provided with no technique for surrender, otherwise there would be nothing left to live for.

This too would leave Lora totally unconcerned, except that she would be faintly amused at Albert's idea of what it would take to make life not worth living. She knew well enough, she thought, what would make life not worth living for him: to suffer an amputation of either of two certain flexible members of his body, one of which was his tongue.

For herself the question did not arise. If contrary to all precedent she had elected to sport with an enigma that would have been the last one she would have chosen. She lived, after a fashion; that was her unconscious answer. There was nothing ecstatic about it, but neither was there any despair. She had sufficiently definite attitudes here and there, but they were unprovided with any intellectual foundation; it was merely that

regarding certain things she knew how she felt. She was disposed to be friendly toward all women, for instance, but the
ones she had known best—her mother, Anne, Leah—she despised for their weakness. Toward men her attitude was a mixture of fear, indifference and admiration—the proportion
which each ingredient contributed to the combination depended
on the man, but none was in any case wholly absent. Of these
and similar phenomena within herself she was completely
aware, and she enjoyed watching their development. When for
example one Sunday morning Lewis Kane telephoned that his
wife was seriously ill and that he would be unable to make his
usual visit, and Lora found herself contemplating the possibility of marriage with him in case he should become a wid-
ower, it amused her to uncover the reasons why it was more
nearly possible to consider him than any other man she knew as
a husband. First, she decided, money. Second, the comfortable
discipline of his emotions. Next, his practical competence.
Fourth—well, money again, probably. But with all those advantages she preferred the present arrangement, should the choice
present itself.

The problem remained academic, for Mrs. Kane speedily
recovered.

She had one habit that she did not like: she dreamed of God.
Or rather, of a god, for he did not at all resemble the insipid
bearded Jehovah of the brightly colored Sunday School picture
cards of her childhood. He was not young, nor yet old; of a
friendly yet forbidding countenance, with his body of unimagin-
able grace clothed in a loose white shirt and loose white trousers
which flapped about his legs in the breeze, he would suddenly
appear from nowhere and stride toward her, where she lay in
the center of a meadow surrounded by strange and lovely
flowers nodding on long and elegant stems. As he approached

her he would make a beckoning gesture with his hands, this way and then that, and hundreds of little figures—she could not call them dwarfs, for they did not look like men—would come bouncing up from all directions and begin plucking the flowers with their long stems and dropping them upon her. They would fall anywhere, on her legs, on her breasts, on her middle, even now and then on her face, and soon would pile up so that she could feel their weight. She would feel, without misgiving, that she was going to be suffocated—and would make no attempt to free herself from the increasing burden, though she could feel that she was being pressed into the carpet of the grass right against the ground and many of the sharp stems of the flowers were pricking her flesh. Still she would make no effort to move, until all at once, realizing that the face and figure of the god were now completely hid from her, and filled with a frantic desire to see him once more, she would impatiently push the blanket of flowers away, down from her face, and lift herself to look eagerly around....

She would be awake, in bed, in the night, sitting up or raised on her elbow, the covers pushed down, breathing quick and hard, feeling warm and disturbed and excited. Or half awake. After a moment her hand would reach up to grope for the light switch, and she would sit blinking in the sudden glare, getting back to reality by looking at the dressing-table, the chairs, the familiar pattern of the rug. Then she would go to the bathroom for a drink of cold water, and perhaps take a few puffs of a cigarette. After which she would sleep soundly till morning.

Sometimes she would not wake at all, but in the morning she would know the dream had come, for though she would not be able to remember any of the details there would be an unmistakable feeling about it. Her body knew. That feeling had a strange quality, an unnatural reconciliation of knowledge and disbelief, as though some new object had suddenly appeared in her room without having been brought there or having come.

She did not like the dream; there was something uncomfortable and a little disquieting about it; but neither did she greatly dislike it. She never recollected any other, but in time she grew to know the details of this one so well that it seemed almost like a part of her real existence. Sometimes she would try to remember when it had first come, but she could not even be sure whether it was before or since she had met Lewis Kane. The memory was lost.

She never mentioned it to anyone, not even to Albert Scher, one of whose favorite subjects was dreams.

In Albert she found a mild and comfortable enjoyment. He was good company. The same was true in less degree of Lewis; she was never wholly at ease with him; but now and then he aroused in her an interest and curiosity which Albert never awakened. Neither, however, cut into her very deeply; their visits to Maidstone were pleasant recurrent commas in the smooth phrases of her life; there were no sharp ejaculations or disturbing interrogations.

The infrequent major points of punctuation were furnished by the children. Roy came home late from the playground with a bloody nose. Panther contributed a sleepless and anxious week with diphtheria. Morris after three days' trial refused point-blank to go to school, the only reason he would give being that it made his legs hurt to sit down so long. Roy declared the true reason to be that he was jealous of Tony Rahlson, who, being a year older, was two classes ahead. That was not so, Morris protested vehemently; in the first place, he would soon be ahead of Tony anyway; secondly, the girl across the aisle made faces at him; and thirdly, it made his legs hurt. Lora let him stay out two days and then took him back and arranged with the teacher to seat him on the other side of the room. This solved the problem; he reported that his legs still hurt a little, so that he had to walk with a jerk—he showed Lora how this was, back and forth across the dining room—but that he was willing to put up with it for Lora's sake. She praised him for that, and he went out to play with Tony, Lora tactfully failing to remark that he was leaving his jerk behind.

This episode was in the autumn preceding Julian's fifth birthday, and Lora's thirty-third. It was still possible for Albert occasionally to call her Venus without sounding ridiculous, for the lines of her body were as clear and graceful as ever, and her face seemed unaware of time's chief function. She had never bobbed her hair; usually now she wore it coiled at the back of her head, brushed straight back from her brow over her scalp's well-modelled mound; when Albert tried to find a single grey hair to confront her with he had to confess defeat. The clear white skin still stretched with the most perfect smoothness over her cheeks and cheekbones, her chin and throat, even under her eyes and on her forehead; the amber-grey eyes held their steady unimpassioned light; the mouth, a little too large, maintained the line of its curve right to the tips of the corners, without a droop or any sign that the skin was finding it necessary to pull a bit here and there in the effort to adjust itself to unnecessary accumulations beneath. She had never cared for dancing, but now and then on a Sunday afternoon Albert would turn on the radio and insist on showing her a new stomp or drag he had picked up in Harlem; she would follow him properly almost at once, without thinking about it, close against him, letting her body move with his; Roy and Panther would imitate them, and Lewis Kane, half-reclining in a corner of the divan, would beat time with his foot and applaud them, with his eyes on Lora's still tranquil face flushed a little with exertion, or the flowing graceful response of her body. That was what was wrong with her, Albert would say impatiently, her body flowed, and you shouldn't flow with jazz; nor jerk either; what it required was a series of delicately broken motions, not legato, but each one beginning precisely where the last left off....

Don't tell me there's anything delicate about jazz, Lewis would object; and Lora, leaving them to have it out, would watch Roy and Panther and marvel at the tireless energy of their flying legs and supple little bodies.

Once, as they finished, she felt Albert's arm suddenly tighten around her, then his other arm, tighter still; pressed thus close against him, she felt his lips on hers. Too astonished to move, she suffered the kiss to the end of its brief but somewhat violent career; all at once, feeling herself released, she stepped back. Albert stood an instant, then, obviously needing something to do, went over and turned off the radio. A loud shrill laugh came from Morris, seated on the floor; Roy and Panther stood staring at their mother incredulously; Lewis Kane looked uncomfortable and cleared his throat three times in succession. Lora was furious that she felt herself coloring with embarrassment, and could think of nothing to say. Albert stood at the radio, grinning around at them.

"Good lord," he said at last, "I must have had a stroke or something."

"You're stupid," Lora said.

"Plunged straight into insanity by your resistible loveliness," he declared. He turned to Roy, "Listen, young man, beware of girls with smooth placid faces, high cheekbones and a wad of red hair—"

"Lora's hair isn't red," said Panther.

"The worst possible red," Albert insisted.

"Aw stuff," said Roy. "She's not a girl anyway, are you, Lora?"

"Don't mind him, he's just being silly," Lora smiled.

Lewis Kane said nothing, then or afterwards.

The episode meant nothing to Lora except as it concerned Lewis. She did not want him to have a false opinion of her relations with Albert Scher. It was a good thing, she remarked to herself after they had gone, that Albert hadn't repeated his performance six years ago and carried her to the divan and tried to tear her clothes off. He might; unquestionably he had a crazy streak.

The following Sunday Albert did not come. It was a brilliant sunny October day, with the sharp exhilarating air so clear that they could see the hills far away across the Hudson, and even make out the autumn colors of the forest on the ridge the other side of the broad valley. In the middle of the afternoon Julian was sent upstairs for his routine nap, and Lora instructed the other children to stay in the yard while she and Lewis went for a walk. "Remember, don't go away," she said, "we'll be back soon, and Lewis likes to have you here."

They went at a brisk pace across the meadows, up the rise to the edge of the woods, to where an old abandoned road once had entered. There they sat on a log, panting a little from the climb, and attacked a question that remained unsettled from a previous discussion: whether Julian should be sent to kindergarten. Lewis was inclined to favor it; Lora saw no advantage in it, since Julian played enough with other children anyway; she thought he would be better off at home for at least another year. Lewis didn't insist; he didn't claim any rights in the matter, he said. No doubt Lora's position was sound.

"All right, we'll wait a year," Lora said. She looked aside at him, and went on, "There's something else I wanted to speak about. I thought you might think there was something queer about the way Albert acted last week."

Lewis turned his head towards her and their eyes met. Neither held any suggestion of doubt or challenge; it was a simple meeting of glances, a greeting of understanding. Lewis smiled a little.

"You can depend on Albert to be queer," he said.

Lora nodded. "It was foolish to mention it, I suppose."

"Not at all. I'm glad you did." He pulled a cockle-burr from the knee of his trousers and flipped his fingers back and forth trying to get rid of it. "I have sometimes wondered," he went on, "what you and Albert are to each other. There's Panther, of course, but she is obviously yours, not his. That's true of all the children, even Julian, I've accepted that." Another cockle-burr. "Of course it's none of my business, but things often come into our minds without waiting for an invitation, and I've often wondered about Albert."

"Well," Lora said, "he's just Albert. To me as to you."

"So I gathered. But still…after all…."

She looked at him in surprise. Lewis searching for words!

"After all, you are a young attractive healthy woman, unencumbered by vows. And while you obviously hold men in contempt, there is evidence that you are willing to tolerate their performance of a necessary function."

Lora laughed. "Albert would like that. But where do you get the idea that I hold men in contempt?"

"Oh, it's obvious." He crossed one leg over the other and turned about on the log so as to face her more directly. "It shows in everything you do; but it's easy to get along with, it's so good-natured. It just happens never to have bothered me, because from the beginning I've had the good sense to know where your fences were. And I know my own limitations. There are various ways of getting things you want out of people. Look at Albert with the children for instance; they'd do anything for him just because he knows how to act with them and what to say to them. He makes a face at Julian, or a noise like a rooster, and Julian is his. I can't make faces and noises. I'm perfectly helpless with children and women too. So I bring them things Albert can't afford, and as a result they're just as anxious to see me as they are him. The same with women. I've got to buy what I want, and it's easy enough, as long as you don't forget that you can only buy what is for sale. That's why your contempt for men doesn't bother me; I don't get in its path. Aside from everything else, in a purely physical way you are the most exciting and desirable woman I've ever known. Everything about you is provocative and seductive, the full free lines of your body, the glance of your eyes, the way you walk, the positions you take when you lie on the grass, or dance, or sit and cross your legs, particularly your mouth with that look it has of always being just ready to open though it is forever closed….I like to observe those things, but I don't make the mistake of supposing that they have any significance for me. I know I've bought everything you have for sale so far as I'm concerned. What I've been curious about sometimes is whether it's for sale at all or not—to anyone, for any price. Impertinent, of course. That's why I wondered about Albert. Beyond him, I still wonder…."

"You needn't," Lora said.

"That's hard to believe, but I believe it."

"It's true."

"But why—" He stopped, frowning, then suddenly smiled. "You're probably making a mistake. You mustn't let a prejudice get between you and the possibilities you possess. I'm not arguing for myself; I know I'm out of it." The smile broadened. "I'm not arguing for Albert either; he's out of it too, I can see that. I guess I'm not arguing for anything, for I'm by no means anxious to jeopardize my present privileges. They are very dear to me—my greatest delight. You know that."

As sure as you're born, Lora thought, the poor dear is

making love to me. Probably he has wanted to for quite a while, and seeing Albert kiss me has brought it out. Well, why not? It would be a nuisance. How could we manage it anyhow, with the house full of children? He could stay and sleep on the divan downstairs, and come up to my room. Then he'd have to sneak out again; that sort of thing is a nuisance. What about right here, in the woods, on the leaves? No, not outdoors with him, in the daylight. In the house then, at night. Why not, if he really wants to so much?

She smiled, and murmured, "It might be possible to extend your privileges, if you think I'm making a mistake."

He seemed a little startled. "Well—you mustn't suppose— you mustn't misunderstand me, you know."

She smiled directly into his face and shook her head.

"I won't misunderstand you."

"We'll see." He stood up and shook himself and stamped his feet on the ground. "It's getting chilly, hadn't we better move? Shall we go into the woods, or start back?"

They decided they had better return, and headed down the hill. They were both stiff from sitting on the log, and jumped and ran to warm up. At that sort of thing Lewis was not precisely in his element; he came down hard, without bending his knees, jolting up and down, slipping and barely saving himself a dozen times. He did look ridiculous, Lora thought, but after all when a man is over fifty years old what can you expect. In another twenty years she might have a little trouble with that hill herself.

There was no extension of privileges that night, and no further mention of it. Lewis left as usual, immediately after supper, to drive back to town—alone, since Albert had not come—and Lora spent the evening helping Roy with his arithmetic, until the children's bedtime. Then she lit a blaze in her own room, in the fireplace which had been specially installed after Lewis had bought the house, arranged a chair and the reading-light, and settled down with a pile of magazines. This was the most luxurious hour of her day, with the children safely asleep, downstairs locked up for the night, and plenty of wood in the basket. She read a while, then sat and watched the fire. How pleasant it all was! There was going to be a little complication with Lewis apparently, but that was of no serious consequence. There was nothing at all objectionable or repugnant about him, and certainly his requirements would be moderate, you could trust him not to go to extremes. She was glad she had said what she did; she was perfectly willing—ha, there was an idea: did he mean to give Julian a brother or sister? But no, that couldn't be what he was driving at; if that was what he wanted he would have said so in so many words. Nevertheless, it remained an idea, whether he had had it or not. She smiled at the fire, pondering whether it would be worthwhile to start that business all over again....

It was four days later, the following Thursday, that she saw Lewis's coupé turn in at the driveway, and then, looking through the dining-room window, stood stupefied at the sight of Pete Halliday's white bony face and tangled brown hair as he descended at one side of the car while Lewis got out at the other.

XVI

Two hours after Lewis Kane left in his coupé that afternoon, with Pete Halliday incredibly seated beside him, having been informed by Panther that her mother had gone to Anne Leaver's to stay the night, Lora got ready to go down and help Lillian put the dinner on the table. She was more vexed with herself than she had ever been in her life. Funk was the word for it, she said to herself, plain unmitigated funk. What had done it was the preposterous combination of those two men; Pete, alone, however unexpected, would have been a manageable apparition. That explained it, but assuredly did not excuse it. In her shame and vexation she would have given anything for the chance to do it over again. She was reminded of an occasion many years before when she had ignored the prolonged ringing of a doorbell and let the telephone go unanswered; she had felt somewhat the same today as on that distant day, and that astonished her and added to her vexation. It was an insane idea, since the two situations were in no respect similar. However, she had then, as again today, been not only cowardly, but stupid. She could not forgive herself.

The opportunity of re-establishing her self-esteem came that very evening. At the dinner table she withdrew her instructions to Roy regarding the telephone; and the meal had not long been over—she was coming downstairs again after telling Julian and Morris goodnight—when it rang. It was Lewis, talking from New York, She would have liked to see his face while she was explaining to him that she had been at home all day and had been in the next room while Panther was delivering the message regarding Anne Seaver. She offered no apologies, and his only reply was that he wished to see her at once and would start for Maidstone immediately; she could expect him in an hour and a half. She asked him, would the other man be with him? Yes, he said, he would.

Well, Lora thought after she had hung up, he certainly is in a terrible hurry about something.

She was no longer in a funk, but was nevertheless too disturbed and restless to read or even to help Roy and Panther with their lessons. She sent them upstairs earlier than usual, so as to have them out of the way; when she explained that Lewis was returning with the strange man who had come that afternoon they accepted the premature banishment without a murmur. Their mother's remarkable conduct in the afternoon and something in her manner now evidently impressed the gravity of the situation upon them; Panther's goodnight kiss was unusually prolonged, and Roy before turning to go assured her solemnly:

"They won't hurt you."

"Hurt me!" Lora laughed. "It's Lewis, you silly."

"That other man looked funny," said Panther.

After they had gone, Lora, seated before the fire, waiting, found herself entertaining the echo of an old regret. She wished she had the wristwatch she had found on her pillow that day twelve years before. She had once spent a good deal of time, with the help of Max Kadish, trying to trace it, but it had long since been disposed of by the jeweler to whom she had sold it in the necessity created by Steve Adams's departure, and the man who had bought it from him could not be found. The one she now wore, given to her by Lewis on Julian's first anniversary, was an altogether different sort of affair—it was much smaller, with a platinum case, and was engraved with her initials. She had another one too, a large silver one, which she wore when working in the garden or generally out of doors. She had not thought of that old one for a long while, not for years; now she wished she had it, but frowned the wish away.

When finally around half-past nine she heard the car turn in at the driveway and pass the house on its way to the back yard, she did not move from her chair. She could not keep her heart from beating faster, but she could sit still. Her ears waited for the sound of the back door opening, but it did not come. Instead, after an interval there was the faint shuffle of footsteps on the flagstone terrace in front, and the doorbell rang. Ha, she thought, as she crossed to open the door, everything is to be proper tonight, one uses the front door and rings the bell; I should have had Lillian down, with a clean cap and apron, to let them in. Or Stan in a uniform—that would have been swell. She swung the door open.

Lewis stood back to let the other precede him. "Hello," Lora said, with a smile, without any pretense of surprise, and gave her hand to Pete. Then she took Lewis in completely with a glance, as he took her hand in turn. They left their overcoats, and Lewis his hat, in the vestibule, and followed her into the living room. She had resumed her chair, and as they entered she invited them to two other chairs nearby, facing the fire. Lewis took the one nearest her; Pete stood close to the fire, warming his hands.

"I suppose I ought to get some gloves," he said, "but I hate the damn things." His eyes were on Lora. "You must be your own daughter," he declared. "You can't be a day over nineteen. That was it, wasn't it? Nearly twenty; I remember you said you'd be twenty before—by a certain day."

"You haven't changed much yourself," said Lora. "Yes, you

have though, you're a good deal older, but you look just the same."

Lewis Kane had been silent since his first greeting. Now he looked at Lora and said briefly:

"You do know him then."

Lora took hold of herself. Had she already made a misstep? There was nothing to be afraid of, nothing she had any reason to conceal, and yet....With men it was best to let them do the talking. Both of these men could be depended on for that. What did they think they were going to do to her? Bah, of course she knew Pete Halliday, why shouldn't she say so? Did she know Pete Halliday!

She smiled not at Lewis, but at Pete.

"I think we've been introduced, haven't we?"

"Never to my knowledge," he replied promptly. "I forget who it was told me your name that night."

"Stubby Mallinson."

"Sure!" he grinned. "So it was. Thirteen years ago; I'll bet he's a stinking millionaire." He nodded affably at Lewis, "No offense."

"Not at all," said Lewis drily. He turned to Lora. "You haven't seen him for thirteen years?"

She nodded. "Thirteen...twelve..."

"I don't suppose he had already entered the profession of blackmailer?"

Pete intervened. "Come, no use forgetting our manners," he protested. "I'm here, ask me." He bowed ironically, with so perfect a reproduction of the well-remembered blending of clumsiness and grace that Lora caught her breath. "At the time of my previous acquaintanceship with Miss Winter I was a student of philosophy; and having just discovered that all optimism comes from arrested development and all pessimism from a belly-ache, I was in the act of joining the Canadian army on the off chance that I might get a crack at a few descendants of Kant or Hegel or— Oh, you know."

With a shrug of his shoulders Lewis turned to Lora:

"In a word, Mr. Halliday asks to be paid fifty thousand dollars to refrain from printing pictures of you and me and your children and your house and garden in a tabloid newspaper."

Lora stared at him, and at Pete, and back again at Lewis. In her breast relief was rising. She had no idea what she had feared, but if this was all….Well. He wanted money. Nothing startling about that.

Pete had hunched up his shoulders and spread out his hands as if to say, there, that's putting it neatly for you; but when he spoke it was to enter an objection:

"Really, that's a little too bald, don't you think ? Oversimplification, let's call it. I represent the press—"

"Bah!" Lewis interrupted scornfully. He went on to Lora. "Mr. Halliday calls himself a reporter. He came to my office on Monday morning and told me an ingenious and complicated story, consisting of lurid details of your past life, especially an intricate fairy tale regarding the past five years. He has an amusing theory, for instance, that one of your children is my son—oh, unquestionably he has imagination. I got rid of him; the whole thing was of course beneath discussion. That afternoon I called on the editor of the paper, with whom I am slightly acquainted; I was told that this investigation, as he called it, was entirely in Mr. Halliday's hands. I was also told that his paper was interested solely in the disclosure of facts; the editor was aghast when he learned of Mr. Halliday's offer to exchange silence for a sum of money. He declared indignantly that he would discharge Mr. Halliday at once, and it appears that this really was done a few hours later; apparently the offer of exchange was in fact Mr. Halliday's own personal idea, for the editor assured me that his paper would not dream of entering into a conspiracy to suppress news; it would not be ethical. He courteously insisted that the story must be printed. I was driven to a recourse I very much disliked; I saw the owner of the paper, an old friend of mine, and succeeded in persuading him to my point of view. It appeared to be satisfactorily settled. But no; Mr. Halliday returned to see me this morning. He resented having been discharged from his job, and was politely truculent. He made another threat, this time openly on his own responsibility; he stated that there are four tabloid papers in New York equally intent on giving their readers important and interesting news, and that no one man can muzzle all of them. He proposes to peddle his fairy tale unless he is paid not to. His figure remains the same; it had occurred to him to double it, he said, but modestly he refrained."

Pete bowed to Lora again. "You see, I'm not grasping."

"For my part," Lewis went on, "my inclination would be to turn him and his fairy tale over to the police. I think he's pulling a bluff and I'd like to call it. But the chief concern is you and the children. This man claims to have known you intimately a long time ago. He states that there has been an extended investigation, financed by his paper, and he recites a long rigmarole which he calls facts. Granting that they're lies, and are printed, and you sue for libel—even granting that you get a judgment—it would be quite a mess. It would be disgusting for you, and it might ruin the lives of your children. Obviously you had to be consulted. I could have paid this man without telling you anything about it, but I saw no means of providing against future additional demands; he might even be after you already; I didn't know. Since you know him you are probably aware that he has unlimited effrontery and no discoverable vestige of scruple or decency."

Lora was looking steadily at Pete, who had seated himself in the other chair and was gazing into the fire, apparently paying no attention to Lewis's recital. His face was as expressionless as it was possible for it to get, with the sharp straight thrust of its disdainful inquisitive nose and equally sharp chin, the restless deep-set brown eyes, the startlingly white skin, the mouth always ready to twist itself into the smile she remembered so well. When Lewis paused she was looking across him at Pete, and said abruptly:

"Once you told me what decency was. Remember?"

"Did I?" He darted a glance at her. "Probably."

"Yes. You knew all about it."

"I still do." He was looking again at the fire. "Decency, like all other moral concepts, is a weapon for the strong and a pitfall for the weak. It's a grand tool for those who know how to use it." He turned to Lewis. "Look here, don't let's get into a discussion of scruples and decency, or I'll make you look silly. Do you know the only reason I'll have any squeamishness about taking your damned money? Because I know how you got it. You're a successful corporation lawyer; don't you think I know what that means? I'm no Robin Hood either; that's another species of blah; not interested. You talk as if I were going to spread Lora and her children all over a dirty tabloid and expose them to the sneers and persecution of a herd of swine. Not at all; that would be vulgar and unlovely and I should hate it. All I'm going to do is transfer a wad of money from your pocket to mine; by any realistic standard where is the indecency in that? It's merely a matter of cash, which by the way you'll never miss, since by the operations of your own special banditry you'll make it up within a year. Extra, of course, over and above your normal depredations. So you take care of your own decency; I'll attend to mine. Don't worry about it."

Lewis's eyes were levelled on him. "I see. You admit it's a bluff then."

"Hell, no. I swear I don't see how you lawyers get along, you're so remarkably obtuse. Patiently I'll explain. The technique of this transaction is the immediate and open threat. That is obviously the whole technique of life, with variations; there's the delayed threat, the indirect threat, the removed threat, the covert threat—categories a mile long. The capitalist says to the laborer, work here and give me a big share of what you make, or you starve. Now it's manifestly indecent for one man to force another man to starve; then why isn't the capitalist indecent? Because he doesn't force the laborer to starve; he merely threatens to. Pushed, would he let him starve? Wouldn't he, though; it's been done on occasion. Pushed, would I in this instance carry out my threat? Sure, I'd have to, to preserve my integrity. But thank heaven, I won't have to; like the capitalist, I save myself from indecency by devising a threat that works. You'll pay, just as the laborer does."

"I may. And I may not." Lewis's eyes were still on him, speculatively. "I can see one thing, Mr. Halliday, I've done you an injustice. I thought you were a common blackmailer and thief. Quite the contrary, I see, you're a dreamer, a radical, a socialist, a philosopher bent on evening things up. That you should begin with yourself is doubtless merely a matter of convenience."

"Is that irony," Pete demanded, "or are you really as dumb as that? The socialist part, I mean. I see; irony; forgive me. The socialist, of course, imagines he can remove the threat from life. I entertain no such illusion, I merely perceive its omnipresence, and am acute enough not to be deceived by any of its disguises, even the most subtle and elaborate.—But I repeat, you'll pay; that is our present business."

"I may not," Lewis repeated. "The further I see into your intelligence, the more I'm inclined to tell you to go to the devil. You are fully aware of the danger you're running, but let me emphasize it a little. First, every word you uttered in my office Monday, and again this morning, was taken down by a stenographer. Oh, don't doubt it, I'll be glad to show you a transcript. I need not point out that Miss Winter is with us this evening. I accept your terms, let us say, I hand you money; and suddenly concealed witnesses appear and the money is taken from you and identified by marks; a simple and ordinary arrangement often used on blackmailers, invariably with success. All it requires is a little courage on the part of the victim. Do you think it entirely safe, in the present instance, to assume that the courage is lacking?"

Pete was laughing. He had thrown his head back to release the explosive roar which, Lora saw, was another phenomenon on which the years had left no mark. She could have shut her eyes and, hearing that laugh, have imagined herself back in that furnished room....

"First decency, then courage!" Pete exclaimed when his roar was finished. "A regular catalogue of virtue! And having been instructed in threats you think you'll try one of your own. Bah, get a better one."

"I don't bluff much myself," Lewis said quietly.

"No? Me, I never do. As for your courage—well, courage is merely the absence of fear, and you may as well know that there I'm your master. I'm not afraid of death or prison or ignominy or any torture you could devise. I do not even fear the loss of my reputation—for a most excellent reason. No, I'm sorry, your little threat is so puny that I regret having taken the trouble to laugh at it." Suddenly he frowned, and his mouth twisted. He went on in a different tone, "Look here, Mr. Kane, there's no use cutting any deeper. Let's get it over. You can't scare me out. To be frank, I don't know what the hell I'll do with fifty thousand dollars, but I'll take a chance on my ingenuity. You see, I didn't start this affair. The paper I worked for, like its competitors, has an informal intelligence service which is constantly on the lookout for items of news that will further its efforts to educate the masses in the various aspects of modern life. But for this laudable enterprise the people would remain grossly ignorant of many salient points in the careers of prizefighters, chorus girls, bankers, politicians and pimps. A few weeks ago I was admitted to a discussion of a new and especially juicy item just dug up by one of our research workers, and naturally I was peculiarly interested when I learned the name of the woman chiefly concerned. I came out here to the charming village of Maidstone and unobtrusively established the identity. Like all investigations of this nature, we did it thoroughly. We learned the names of the fathers of the four children. We got dates and addresses, with hardly a gap. We took pictures of everyone involved, without their knowledge in all cases but one; Mr. Scher nearly smashed a camera in Washington Square last week. We sent an agent to the woman's childhood home, where he secured items of great interest—among others the details of the father's suicide the day after his daughter departed, many years ago, under peculiar and suspicious circumstances. He found her childhood chum in Chicago and interviewed her—a Mrs. Ogilvy, formerly Miss Cecelia Harper—"

He stopped abruptly, looking at Lora, who had half risen from her chair and then dropped back into it. She was staring at Pete with her mouth open; her face looked vacant and stupid, not like herself at all. Lewis, following Pete's glance, was looking at her too.

"My father. You said…" she stammered.

"Sure. Shot himself the day after you left." He leaned forward to peer at her, looking suddenly astonished and incredulous. "Good god, don't tell me you didn't know! Preposterous! You must have known. As long ago as that.…"

Lora was leaning back in her chair again, her mouth closed, her lips pressed tight together. She shook her head with a faint sidewise movement, and kept on shaking it, saying nothing.

"That's about enough, don't you think?" said Lewis Kane.

Lora could see Pete grinning with his mouth crooked.

"My infallible luck," he said. "What do you mean it's about enough? I arranged it I suppose. Ha, there's only one time it's enough, when you quit breathing for good, then it's plenty. Mr. Leroy Winter had enough apparently, but you and Lora and me, hell, we've no end of fun to look forward to. It makes me maudlin just to think of it. To continue: you understand that all this was the enterprise of my paper, admittedly a public servant, not mine. It was entrusted to my charge at my own request —my first major operation, for I'm a comparatively new hand. So it was within my power to convey to you an offer of personal cooperation; and by the way, you would have done well to accept it offhand. That might easily have aroused my admiration and sympathy; they're on a hair-trigger as Lora will tell you; it would probably have saved you a lot of money. But you insulted my pride; you got me fired from my job; my dander rose; and there's nothing doing. You know my terms, and I'm ready to close."

Lewis had got up from his chair and was standing with his back to the fire, looking down at Lora. She did not return his gaze; she sat motionless with her eyes still on Pete.

"I'm sorry I brought him, Lora," he said. "Forgive me. I thought you should be consulted.…"

She turned her head to glance at him. "What?"

"I say, I thought you should be consulted."

She nodded. "I suppose so. What are you going to do?"

"That's what I'm asking you. What do you want me to do?"

"How can I decide?" she said. "I have no money to give him. I don't care anyway. What about you? I don't care."

He turned to Pete. "Of course fifty thousand dollars is out of the question. Even if I had it. I'll tell you what I'll do, I'll give you ten thousand in cash tomorrow morning if you can furnish satisfactory assurance that that will be the end of it."

"I said nothing doing."

"Take it or leave it."

"This is painful," Pete grimaced. "I loathe bargaining. You'll pay my price. But I don't see how I can furnish satisfactory assurance short of cutting off my head. You wouldn't take my word for it? No. We're in a fix. It looks as if you're going to pay fifty thousand dollars for practically nothing."

"Ten thousand *and* the assurance. That's up to you."

"I tell you I detest this!" Pete exploded. He got to his feet and stamped on the floor to shake his trouser legs down. "By god, I may have my faults, but I'm damned if I'll haggle. You know perfectly well you'll come to it. You wanted to consult Lora; all right, you've consulted her, let's get out of here. I can invent an assurance, and you can make up your mind to the amputation, on the way back."

Lora no longer heard them. It seemed to her petty and utterly inconsequential. The money was strictly Lewis's affair, she considered; after all, the danger was chiefly his; for herself and the children she could manage no matter what happened. The men's voices went on. She sat almost without consciousness. Her mind was not stunned, it was smothered rather, under a blanket of feeling which left it dull and dead and overwhelmed.

Pete was in it, and her father who had killed himself, and this house in her name out of which she might be driven if Lewis forced Pete to make good his threat, and Roy and Panther and Morris and Julian who would be driven with her....

Their voices annoyed her. Why didn't they go? Why had they come here to do their wrangling ? But no, that was as it should be, that she should learn about her father like this from Pete. There were things she wanted to ask him; how could she manage it? There was something else too, something was happening to her....

At length the two men reached their impasse, and were silent. Lora became aware that Lewis was speaking to her; Pete, he said, would go back by train, he had no desire for his company on the ride to town. Whereupon Pete shrugged his shoulders and went to the vestibule for his coat, and Lora saw that Lewis meant to stay behind. She was aroused then to speak. She could not talk now, she said, not tonight, if he didn't mind she would rather be alone. Not tonight. He might as well drive Pete to the railroad station.

Pete stuck his head in from the hall:

"Don't bother, I'd rather walk. I hate the damn train, but I prefer it to listening to a stuck pig squeal. I'll phone you tomorrow to arrange an appointment. You may have forty-eight hours to get the cash. Goodnight, Lora."

The outer door banged behind him. Lewis went to the hall and returned in a moment with his coat on and his hat in his hand.

"I should have come alone," he said. "But it seemed to be better—to tell the truth, from one or two things he said I thought it might help for him to see you. He's right, of course, I shall probably have to pay up—I'll sleep on it. I've got an idea—well, we'll see. I wish I knew more about him." He paused, and then went on, "About your father, that was unfortunate. I'm terribly sorry. I don't make an exhibit of my feelings, but I feel very badly about it. If there's anything I can do, anything you'd like to have me find out—a will, for instance, or anything of that sort—"

She shook her head. "Thank you, Lewis. A will? No."

"You knew he was dead of course?"

"No. I didn't know anything."

"You don't suppose this man had anything to do with it?"

"What? Oh. Pete? No, he didn't." She got up and stood straight, facing him. "If you don't mind, Lewis, this is the one thing in the world I'd rather not talk about."

"Yes. Of course." He hesitated. "I just thought if it would help any...well, I'm sorry." He went to the door, and there turned again: "Don't worry about this business, I'll attend to it. He'll have to be gagged somehow. It will be all right."

"I'm sure it will," said Lora.

When he had gone she dropped into her chair again, and heard his car backing out and swinging into the road. What she had to do, at once, was to get her mind straightened out and find out what was going on. That seemed to present considerable difficulty, for it wouldn't fasten on anything. After having successfully evaded complicated questions all her life, she suddenly found herself confronted by several all at once, each demanding immediate consideration, and she knew not where to begin or what direction to take. There was her father; or rather, there he wasn't. That fact was of profound significance... and yet...it was of no significance at all. But he had always been dead! It was incredible. All those years, with Steve and Albert and Max and Lewis...even at the very first, as she lay on the hospital bed in New York, gathering unconsciously her forces for a struggle that would last as long as her breath lasted, he

had been dead. Really dead. Gone. A ghost had lived in her...
all that had been a ghost. Her mind darted back over the years,
pouncing on this situation then that, feeling it and weighing it
in the light of this amazing disembodiment. What would she
have said here, how would she have acted there?

Rot, she said to herself of a sudden, impatiently; that was all
poppycock, it would have mattered not at all. More to the point
to consider what was going to happen now. But for some reason
that consideration couldn't be made to stick; it shied off from
her intention like a wise old crow from a gun under cover.
What was she going to do now? Well, nothing. What was there
to do? Lewis would attend to Pete, she felt sure of that, it
would be arranged somehow; there was nothing for her to
worry about. But she could not rid herself of the feeling that
she was immediately confronted by the necessity of making the
most important decision of her life; that this was indeed the
focus toward which all the radii of her character and of the past
years were pointed, and that the direction they would take
from this focal point into the future was put strictly up to her
and the decision must be hers. Regarding this feeling about the
future her common sense spoke as it did of her fancies about
her suddenly dead father and the past. Rot; poppycock; where
was the dilemma? For Lewis maybe it was difficult; poor dear
Lewis, he would hate to give in to Pete, he would hate to give in
to anybody, for he was accustomed to having his own way. Not
so long ago he had said that he had to buy everything he got;
well, it would be hard to pay the price this time, but he would
pay. For his reputation, for his son, possibly even for something
else—an extension of his privileges? Oh. That. No, decidedly
not. She was sorry she had offered him hope in that direction.
Decidedly not that....

The doorbell rang.

Startled, she glanced at her watch. She would have guessed that an hour or more had passed since Lewis had left, and was surprised to see that it had not been more than fifteen or twenty minutes; it was only a little past eleven. She went to the door and was minded to call out to ask who it was, but after a moment's hesitation she opened it, pulling it wide with a sweep of her arm; and when she saw Pete Halliday standing there on the stone terrace in the shaft of light that shot out at him through the door, she knew what it was she had to decide.

XVII

Inside, with the door closed, after throwing his coat on a chair, Pete asked abruptly:

"Did you expect me back?"

Lora shook her head. "Why should I?"

"Intuition," he grinned. "You might have, since there's no train for nearly an hour."

"You've been to the station and back?"

"Sure. When I walk fast I jerk a bit—souvenir of the war—but I can still get along."

"Well. You have thirty minutes to wait. You may as well come in and sit down."

He followed her into the living room, back to the chairs in front of the fire. She was thinking, I shouldn't have let him in, I've got to have more time, I won't say a word and just wait for him to go, it wasn't fair for him to come back like this....

"It's crazy not to wear gloves," Pete was saying. He stood close to the fire, warming his hands, exactly as he had done when he had entered with Lewis two hours before. "You can't walk satisfactorily with your hands in your pockets, and nowadays it takes a couple of miles or more to get my blood going enough to reach my fingers. Not age, surely; I'm not that far gone; I think it must be another trench memento. It thickened my brain and thinned my blood."

He paused, rubbing his hands, and Lora inquired politely how long he had been in France.

"Four months and eleven days after the armistice. Then I went back again. But I'm sorry I mentioned it. It's not fit to talk about."

"You came back here then?"

"Roundabout." He grinned. "Since I've unearthed the details of your history you think it only fair that I divulge my own, is that it? Nothing simpler. I spent a year in Paris—according to the official Canadian records, at the Sorbonne. I taught mathematics at a college in Ohio. I drove a moving-van in Cleveland. I worked on newspapers in Montreal, Saint Louis, Peoria and Chicago. Two years ago I came to New York. My career has just begun. That, you will notice, is one of the outstanding features of my career, its tendency to keep on beginning. It preserves my enthusiasm and prevents my getting into a rut."

"You've been in New York two years?"

He nodded. "So near and yet so far, is it not? That's what I was thinking here a little while ago, sitting here, while your boyfriend was trying to stick his tongue out and say boo."

"I didn't say that."

"No? How about thinking it?"

"I didn't think it either."

"Well, I did." He had taken the chair nearest her, the one Lewis had sat in earlier in the evening, and now he bent his head and drew his eyebrows down to peer at her. He said abruptly, "I see you've got a new watch."

She stirred a little and put her right hand over her left wrist, then at once removed it again.

"It isn't new."

"It's very pretty. Much nicer than those cumbersome things they used to make. I noticed it, earlier, as soon as I came in the room." He took his eyes away and directed them at the fire, and after a short silence he went on, "You know, giving you that damn watch was my one undiluted stupidity. I've never been able to forget it. It was a symbol, a token of a weakness I disown and the validity of which I deny. Thinking of the watch, naturally I thought of you, I thought of you wearing it—" He broke off shortly, and turned to her, "You did get it? You went back to the room...."

For reply she nodded. His eyes went back to the fire.

"Of course you would. I had no doubt of that. I used to say to myself, well, there was Lora. The pretty little piece who worked in a candy factory and never ran out of money. I used to sing here and there—you can imagine it, you've heard me sing: Lora and Petey were lovers, and oh, my, how she could love....Then I'd think of the watch, and I could see you finding it there on the pillow and putting it on....Bah. It made me sick. It interfered with my mitosis, it induced a suspension of function among my viscera." He turned to her and said abruptly, "Have you still got it?"

"No," she said, "I'm sorry—"

He said nothing. She went on, "I was in trouble, and I sold it. I was going to have a baby. It was a long time ago."

She knew perfectly well he would smile with his mouth crooked, but nevertheless she winced a little when she saw it.

"Afterwards, when I got money, I tried to get it back, but it was gone."

"Splendid!" Pete exclaimed. "You sold it to buy baby clothes. It wasn't anything to brag about, I suppose by now it's junk, but if not I'll bet I know who has it. It is being worn by a clergyman's wife who lives on Staten Island, and on Sundays when her husband's watch isn't running, as it usually isn't, she lets him take hers to the pulpit with him to time the services by. *That's* the watch I bought. Splendid! A worthy fate. It was amusing just now, when you got apologetic. Good lord, have you never heard of the maternal instinct? Its resourcefulness? Its fierce indomitable will? The desperate extremes it will go to? Why, to gain its ends, an instinct like that would sell a grandfather's clock, even Big Ben himself, let alone one little wristwatch. Which reminds me, on one occasion your instinct seems to have slipped up somewhere. A couple of hours ago you heard me speaking—on a matter of business—regarding some children and their fathers. Four children, and four fathers—probably a record. But why not five? This is just between you and me, it's not intended for the official dossier. Why not five? The eldest was born in the summer of nineteen-eighteen. There is in the dossier one little hint of the question I'm putting; the man who went west discovered echoes of some old murmurs about infanticide in the inquiry that followed your father's death; but of course I have other reasons for asking myself, why not five? It occurs to me that you might be willing to help me find the answer."

He stopped and waited, but Lora said nothing and would not look at him.

"Come," he persisted, "I don't claim any rights—even though I'm supposed to have an instinct of my own which should clamor for its destiny—but you'll admit that my curiosity is valid. I might fairly press for an answer, don't you think?"

Still she was silent. He was peering at her again.

"I do mean to have an answer," he insisted. "Do you remember that? The Sunday mornings you would get breakfast at the room, and I would bellow at you, do I get another piece of bacon or do I not, I mean to have an answer, my love. That's the present situation, I mean to have an answer, my love."

Lora opened her lips long enough to say, "You won't get one," and closed them again.

"But it did arrive," Pete said. "That seems to have been pretty well established by the testimony of the maid—Martha, wasn't it—at the inquest. Reinforced by the information furnished later by Mrs. Ogilvy, otherwise Cecelia, I never liked her. Your mother, by the way, nearly got herself into serious trouble; they couldn't pry her mouth open. She was a medieval heretic confronted by the black-robed Inquisition; she raised her eyes toward heaven, or lowered them toward hell—the details are meager—and refused to utter a word. The sympathy of the community saved her from the righteous rigor of the law. But Martha was frightened and spilled the beans. There was a search for you high and low; you were traced as far as Chicago, and that's where Cecelia came in, they suspected her of having hid you in a closet or under the bed. Acute fellows. What they were looking for was a baby, live if necessary but preferably dead, for that was what they had smelled. Pleasant inoffensive little game of hide and seek. They didn't find it. It's all forgotten now, of course, so you run no risk if you satisfy my curiosity."

"No," Lora said. She said again, "No. I won't talk about it. There was no baby."

"Oh, well." He shrugged his shoulders. "If you won't. Maybe you're a little vague about it yourself; apparently your father was a man of action."

"You sent a man out there?" said Lora.

"My paper did."

"Did he see my mother?"

"He sure did. Oh, it's all right so far, he said nothing about you, he had strict orders on that point. He saw your mother twice, but she wouldn't talk, at any rate not about this. Otherwise she was quite chatty."

"She still lives there?"

He nodded. "In a big brick house with three or four servants and a bald gentle husband."

Lora stared at him. "A husband!"

"Indeed, yes. You know, it's hard to believe all this is news to you. You're not putting it on? No, I suppose not. She has a husband all right, got him years ago, I don't know just when."

"What's his name?"

"I forget." He considered. "It wouldn't be Davis?"

Lora shook her head. Bald, she thought, and gentle. A newcomer, probably. Well! Her mother had a bald and gentle husband and a big brick house! She didn't like the idea at all, it didn't fit, and she resented it. She felt the irritation of the resentment within her, and that seemed absurd—good lord, wasn't her mother welcome to a husband if she wanted one? The balder and gentler the better. But the resentment remained, and induced a sort of confused pseudo-disbelief. If she got on a train and went back to that town tomorrow she could not even go to her father's house, there would be strangers in it; her father would be nowhere, actually not anywhere; and to find her mother she must ask, and could not even properly ask, not knowing her name. Certainly all this was true, but it could not at once be believed, and meanwhile must be resented. She thought the resentment was silly, but she did not try to banish it; indeed, she clung to it, and to all the shreds of emotion she could muster, regarding her mother and the absurd bald husband, regarding the house of her father and her father himself, now a ghost, a wraith that floated grotesquely from the hard reality of memory into the unsubstantial vapor of fact, and back into memory again.

She clung to these because she was afraid of what was trying to replace them. Her mind kept trying to escape, and fiercely she forced it back. What had flashed into it when she had opened the door and saw Pete there on the threshold, was now perfectly plain, and that was what she was desperately determined to conquer and suppress, at least until he had gone and she could consider it calmly, could shut herself up with it alone in her room and have it out. The urgency of it amazed her and filled her with panic; with him sitting there in the chair next to her, so close she could have reached out and touched him, she knew she dared not trust her thoughts for a single instant. She *must* touch him—heaven help her, father, the ghost of her father, and mother with a bald and gentle husband....She must let him know that she wanted to feel him...dead now, and always had been dead, and mother wouldn't let them pry her mouth open, he had said, and he had said why not five, he wanted to know about the baby he had put in her....He had put in her, god think of that, there he was, and all those nights, he was the one who knew how to do that...right now, right this instant...but she couldn't talk about that, she had told him so, she would not talk about that time when she had without any doubt been ready to get her father's revolver from the bedroom and shoot him with it and now he had shot himself....No use pretending about it, what she wanted, look at his legs stretched out like that, and the cuffs of his shirt were dirty, they always were, if he put on a clean shirt when he got up the cuffs would be soiled by the time he got his hair combed, if you could call it combing...she could comb his hair all right, all his hair, and she would, his head first, it was more exciting to lead up to it...but not now, refinements could come later...not now...for now, oh, now....

She sighed sharply and deeply and jerked herself up in her chair. Pete glanced at her. She could not have told what he had been saying. She looked at her watch and said brusquely:

"You'd better go or you'll miss the train."

"What?" he demanded. "Already?"

"You have only fifteen minutes."

"I hate to leave this fire. And this chair. And you."

"I'm afraid there's no help for it."

"The hell there ain't." He grinned at her. "You haven't got a bed for me?"

"Of course not. Don't be silly."

"Well, here I go." He didn't move. "Isn't there a later train? There must be. God, I hate trains. And the subway; if I knew how to make a bomb I'd blow it up. Particularly do I hate trains at night. You know that. Now if I could sleep here, on that couch for instance, and get up to a good breakfast of eggs and thick bacon, and take a train in the daylight, when you can at least see where you're going—"

She had got up from her chair. She interrupted decisively, "Come. Really. You'll miss it."

He didn't move. Without lifting his head his eyes went swiftly up her body and down again, and though she didn't see it she was aware of it. "I've another idea," he said. "Come and sit on my knee—straddle, you know—and I'll tell you the story about the princess who couldn't remember what to do with her fingers."

Lora stood perfectly still, but she knew she couldn't stay that way; if she stood a moment longer she would begin to tremble and he would see it. Besides, standing there in front of him it would be too easy…just a step, two steps, to him….She sat down in her own chair again, upright, with her backbone stiff….

"I don't like stories anymore," she said.

"Don't tell me." He grinned at her. "That was the first thing that struck me when I saw you. Not tonight, a month ago it was, when I came out to make sure it was you. I walked out from the village and found a convenient hole in the hedge to look through. Your eldest boy came along and gave me a start—as sure as I live, I thought, there's one of my cells running around on its own legs. That was before details and dates had been collected; I discovered my mistake later. Then I saw the girl and another boy or two in the back yard, around the corner of the house, and I said to myself, there can no longer be any doubt of it, I've absolutely been cuckolded. Then suddenly you appeared around the other corner of the house and there you were, on the terrace, with your hair blowing into your eyes. You had some shears and a basket in your hand and you came across the yard and stopped not far from my hole and began cutting flowers. I almost called to you, but remembered the ethics of my profession just in time. Furthermore, it wasn't you—that is, it wasn't the veteran mother of countless children by countless fathers—it was instead a charming and appetizing little girl whose neck I had wanted to wring for twelve years because I had once been ass enough to give her a wristwatch. By the way, it appeared to me that day, from a distance of fifteen feet, that you were wearing it."

"No."

"It wasn't the one you have on."

"No."

"I see, your gardening equipment I suppose. One for golfing, one for motoring—didn't I tell you once your appropriate scene was stucco and roses in Oak Park? Congratulations, you've made good. Better, even; the flora are up to standard, and as to two-legged fauna, you've more than your share. That being true, why, you ask, do I offer to tell you the story about the princess who couldn't remember what to do with her fingers? Why do I seek to disrupt an established and smoothly running schedule? Albert the artist, let us say, on Mondays, Wednesdays and Fridays, experiments in rhythm and composition; on Tuesdays, Thursdays and Saturdays Lewis the lawyer, man of affairs—shall we suspect here a sacrifice to Mammon?

Looking at him, I should say certainly a sacrifice. And on Sundays catch as catch can."

"That isn't true," Lora said. She sat still upright, her hands folded in her lap with the fingers intertwined, her eyes on his face. "I know what you're doing, you're trying to make me angry. You used to do that and it used to work. But I don't get angry anymore, and what you say isn't true, not a word of it."

"It was only a guess, I may have the days wrong."

"I tell you it isn't true!"

"What isn't?" He peered at her. "What isn't true?"

"What you said." She stopped, shutting her lips tight, then began again, "You know I can't talk. Listen, Pete. I don't want to talk. That isn't true, what you said—it isn't true with Albert or Lewis or anybody. It never has been, the way it was with you. Now I'm an awful fool, I shouldn't have talked at all, I shouldn't be telling you this, but I've never felt that way, not once, I've never done any of those things, I've never wanted to. I think I was crazy, with you. It was so long ago it seems like another person and I can't believe it, but I must have been crazy. Now… again…I knew it right away this afternoon when I saw you getting out of the car with Lewis…"

She felt herself trembling, and stopped.

"Crazy hell," Pete said. "Come over here."

She shook her head. He got up and stood beside her chair for a moment, then reached down and began removing the pins from her hair. A strand fell, then another, while she sat motionless.

"I like it better down," he said. "What's the matter with you? Talk about crazy, you're crazy if what you just said is true. Good god, are you a dried-up nun, to take it out in praying and pinching yourself? Ah, your throat is as smooth and white, your hair still talks to my fingers, and who would dream—let me see, let me see—who would dream that four pairs of lips had dined and breakfasted there?" He chuckled. "Infant lips, mind you—the others shall not be counted now. Just as it should be, precisely a handful, a warm round handful—that is unquestionably an improvement, formerly they were firmer and more discreet—this is better, riper—Oh, much riper and better. You would deny all this? And this, and this? Here—come—what—"

Suddenly and swiftly she slipped out from under his hands and his face, drawing herself down and forward, free of him, and the next instant was on her feet three paces away, facing him. She was breathing quickly, and the hand that was rearranging the front of her dress was visibly trembling.

"What the hell," he said, straightening up but making no move towards her.

"Not here," she said.

"All right. But you needn't get heroic about it. I wasn't contemplating rape."

"I'm not heroic. I had to do that."

"Well." He grinned, and bowed. "What next? Your room? That would be better, of course. Upstairs? I confess I'm a little impatient myself."

She shook her head. "Not here. Not tonight."

"Not tonight! You are crazy. Good god, are you holding out for a courtship?"

"I'm not holding out. Don't be smart, Pete. Don't you see—I want it to be better. The children are upstairs, and I don't—not here. You can rape me if you want to, that's exactly what you can do—do you remember how we did that? I'll come anywhere you say. In town, in New York. Not here."

"So you're putting me off. What for?"

"I'm putting myself off."

"Come to town with me now then. Is there a train?"

She shook her head. "There's a train, the last one, but I won't go now. I'll come tomorrow, any time you say."

"Let me sleep here, and we'll go in together in the morning."

Again she shook her head. "Please, Pete, don't. I've got to arrange things. I'll come, listen, there's a train that leaves here at two in the afternoon, gets to Grand Central a little after three. You meet me at the station, or tell me where to come if you'd rather. I'll stay all night if you want me to; I can arrange that. You must go now, please. Please go."

"These long engagements are dangerous, my love. By tomorrow I might forget all about it."

"No you won't."

"The hell I won't. You're right probably, but you're not so nice this way, you know too much."

He stood an instant, intently and silently regarding her, then turned abruptly and started for the vestibule, and she followed. "You wouldn't like my room," he went on, as he got into his coat, "it smells of garlic, I think they must have rubbed it into the walls. Besides, it's barely possible we might be interrupted. There seems to be a lot of extra keys."

"Oh. Well…somewhere else then…."

"No, it will be all right, we'll barricade the damn thing. But I'd better meet you at Grand Central. Around three, in the waiting room?"

He was on the terrace, and she was standing on the threshold of the open door. She nodded.

"Yes. A little after."

XVIII

Breakfast was over, and Lillian was clearing the table. Roy and Panther and Morris had departed for school. Ordinarily, at this juncture, Lora went upstairs to make the beds in her room and Morris's and Julian's, for Lillian couldn't do everything, and Lora preferred to take a share of the work for herself rather than bother with a second maid. Roy and Panther made up their own beds and tidied up their rooms before coming down to breakfast. After the bed-making and a few miscellaneous chores Lora would usually select one room, downstairs or up, for a thorough going-over; she had no schedule for this, but followed her fancy and the pressure of circumstances. The living room and the kitchen were the only ones left to Lillian. Lora didn't mind her household tasks; quite the contrary; she went about them rapidly and methodically and effectively and was always finished by the time the children arrived for lunch. Julian would usually help her with the beds, standing on one side and smoothing and straightening each cover as she manipulated it into place; sometimes she would flip a sheet right over his head, making a tent-pole of him, and he would shout with glee, jerking his arms frantically up and down; the sheet had become an ocean and he was making waves. Morris had taught him how.

But this morning Lora put Julian's sweater on him and sent him outdoors to Stan. She wanted to be alone; she didn't feel like making oceans out of sheets. Indeed there was a doubt whether she would ever feel like that again; it seemed to her improbable. But everything seemed improbable, the past as well as the present. During the night she had dreamed of her father lying on the floor with a hole in his head and blood coming out of it; her mother stood beside him with lowered head, and when Lora asked her why she didn't cry and her mother lifted her head Lora saw that she had no face to cry with. Nevertheless she knew it was her mother. The dream had been very vivid when she awoke; now it was receding into vagueness. She wished she had asked Pete whether her father had actually shot himself in the head.

She was going to Pete. Or was she? Yes. He could have had her last night if he had held her down a moment when she slipped out from under his hands, out of the chair. She had got away by a miracle, not wanting to get away at all; and then had surrendered. Not, not surrender, it was no triumph for him, it was what she wanted that mattered, and that was plain enough. She wanted to say again the strong short words he had taught her so long ago, she wanted to do all those things again, she wanted to feel him and make him feel her; it was an inescapable necessity. She whispered the words to herself, one after the other, all she could remember of them, but they weren't right that way, though they did quicken her blood a little and bring a flush to her face; with him, saying and doing them at once, there was something indescribably exciting about them, about all that business....

Arranging the things on Morris's little desk, she saw that her hands were unsteady. Good lord, she thought scornfully, you might think I was a schoolgirl bride, I can wait till I get there, can't I?

She must ask Pete about her father, to see if her dream was right. Anyway she wanted to know. Perhaps he couldn't tell her. She could write to Cecelia, or her mother...no, not her mother....

Pete was to telephone Lewis this morning, to make an appointment to arrange about the money. If the appointment was this afternoon or this evening—but it wouldn't be, for he was just as anxious as she was. She knew the signs in men much better than she had twelve years ago. Ha, that would be one for you! Pete would get the money from Lewis and carry her off with it; they would go somewhere, anywhere. Lewis would have plenty of sons on his hands then. Albert would probably take Panther....But that brought a smile. She could hardly imagine Albert taking Panther; or, if he did, poor Panther would have a time of it. Lewis would take all of them, draw up contracts, probably....

Nonsense. That she had a rendezvous with Pete was no excuse for going out of her mind. She had said she would stay all night. Well, she wouldn't. Not that it couldn't be done, Lillian could very well look after the children. Roy and Panther could for that matter. She could say to Roy, I'm going to stay in town all night, and probably neither of them would ask what for. If they did she would have to have something to say. Also she must tell them not to mention it to Lewis; but that wouldn't be safe, on account of Julian. Better to tell Lewis; but that meant lying to him, and it wouldn't be easy; with all his transparencies he was no fool. Once or twice she could get away with it perhaps, but was this a matter of once or twice? A Night of Love, that was a piece Panther played on the piano, and Albert made fun of it. Albert too would know about this, for it was folly to suppose that once or twice would do it. A Life of Love rather. A life of love, she was ready for it and had it coming to her. Pete didn't call it love, he wouldn't use that word. Lying afterwards on his back with a cigarette in his mouth and his hands behind his head, he would discuss it at length, using words she had never heard of, most of them invented on the spot she suspected, saying the most outrageous things, stopping only to inhale a puff of his cigarette or to burst into a roar of laughter at himself. She scarcely listened to any of it, lying in languor beside him, not caring. Not caring about her body either, naked if it so happened, naked and satisfied. They would do that again, not once or twice, but a thousand times, ten thousand… a life of love.…

Pull down your skirt, her father said. Dead and done with. Those letters she had sent, Mr. and Mrs. Leroy Winter, and the snapshots, and him dead all the time, and her mother perhaps showing the letters and pictures to her bald and gentle husband.…

She had lied to her father month after month about the money he sent for the piano lessons, and the money had gone to Pete. Now she was going to lie to Lewis. But that was impossible, and it was nonsense. Why lie to him, it was none of his business. She went to town to see Pete; that didn't concern Lewis or Albert either. The children? Well, really, that was too much, dragging the children into it; it was about time she found it out if she was nothing but a nursemaid. A dried-up nun, Pete had said. Ha, not yet, thank god. It was a long time since she had properly looked at herself, but the point was not without testimony. He would see how dried-up she was—she didn't need to look, she could feel.

Well well, he would say, lying on his back with a cigarette in his mouth, my seed on the wind again; we must confess, my love, that nature's breeze has the true and ultimate vigor; compared with that, man's puny petty perversions are an electric fan in a pullman car—they give you a headache, and cure it if you can. Seed on the wind. He would inhale the smoke deeply and blow it out in a long thin column, straight up towards the ceiling, and stretch himself and close his eyes. His seed. She did not want that. Definitely now she did not want that, from him or anyone, and she would see that nothing of that sort happened. Her body had done enough work for a while. Forever. She wished she knew more about it; there was no one she could ask. Undoubtedly Pete would know; it was something you got at a drugstore, and she would see that it was used whether he wanted to or not.

However, she would rather not trust Pete. It would be much better if she could find out about it herself. Probably the druggist at the little corner store on Eleventh Street, the one who had been so sympathetic long ago when Roy was coming, would tell her. She hadn't seen him for years, but he would remember her if he was still there. It would certainly be better not to trust Pete, on that point or any other. He wasn't a liar though; Lewis was wrong to think that if he paid him he couldn't rely on his word. She would as soon take Pete's word as Lewis's or anyone's. He wasn't a liar, he was just cautious. You could depend on him to do anything he said he would do, but that didn't help much, since he would never say. Oh, she wasn't taking anything for granted with him; once or twice might do it after all and off he would go; but meanwhile....

She was jerked back into the immediate present by the sound of the radio, suddenly turned on downstairs. Startled, she glanced at the clock on her dressing-table. Already past twelve, and the children home for lunch! Ha, if she missed that train! What was it Albert said, you never miss a train you want to catch? More of his nonsense—what if you fell down and broke your leg? Well, she wasn't going to miss this one....

Downstairs the children were waiting for her and ran to seat themselves at the table as soon as she appeared. There was hot bean soup and a huge tomato omelet and crackers and jam. Lillian hurried in and out, and all four talked at once. Panther insisted that Julian go and wash his hands; Lora nodded, and Julian went. Morris said that the brightest boy in his class always had dirty hands and if he washed them they got cracks and he would bleed till they were red all over, and then if he kept on washing them they would keep on bleeding and get all over his books and all over his clothes—Roy stopped him. He needed twenty cents, he said, to help pay for a class basketball. He had thought it over and decided that it could not properly be taken from his allowance. Why not, Panther wanted to know, since her contribution for victrola records had been taken from her allowance. This was different, he retorted, basketball was sport, not lessons; what about her tennis racket, for instance, had she paid for that? It wasn't that he didn't have the twenty cents or was unwilling to spend it; the point was whether it was fair. He had thought it over carefully and decided that it wasn't. Lora agreed to pay it, and appeased Panther with a wink which she understood: oh, these men, it's simpler to humor them than argue about it.

Nothing was left but crackers and jam when Lora suddenly announced:

"I'm going to town this afternoon and won't get home till after dinner. Lillian is left in charge; do you hear, Lillian? Panther will put Julian to bed and the rest of you will go as usual, and don't turn the clock back."

"We were going in tomorrow to get me an overcoat," Roy reminded her.

"Yes." She hesitated. "Next week will do; there's no hurry. I may stay overnight and come back out in the morning. Or afternoon even."

"Will you see Lewis?" Morris demanded.

"I don't know. Maybe."

"Tell him my wagon broke."

Roy and Panther were looking at her. She felt confused and embarrassed, and was furious at herself for it. Her own children, nothing but babies really—how silly! She pushed her chair back and got up.

"Can we go in the car tomorrow?" Roy asked.

"May," Panther corrected.

"No. Not till I get home. Run along now, you'll be late."

Upstairs again she dressed hurriedly but with particularity, choosing a tan wool dress, and a brown coat with fur collar which she had bought only recently. It was her favorite dress, and she had a felt hat of the same shade. Assuredly it was no dried-up nun who faced her in the mirror as she stood for final inspection. She had sent word to Stan to be ready with the car at a quarter to two, and now she could hear the low hum of the engine, warming up, from the back yard. She was taking no bag. First she had thought she would, and then, without deciding not to, she just didn't. She had two errands left downstairs: she got her checkbook from the desk in the living room and wrote a check for two hundred dollars and put it in her purse, and on the way out she stopped at the kitchen to give Lillian a few instructions. Stan had the car waiting on the driveway; as she got in she asked him to go first to the village bank. She didn't know exactly why she was taking so much money; you might think it was me Pete's holding up, she thought, as she took the bills from the teller and stuffed them in her purse. From the bank it was only a minute to the station.

On the train she remained uncertain; maybe all night; maybe not; it all depended. What kind of a room would Pete have? Well…not fastidious. And the extra keys he talked about….It would be better to take a room in a hotel. Since he had lost his job she could pay for it. She had never been in a hotel room, not once in her life, and she shrank a little from the idea, but it was exciting too. They could go to a hotel at once and go to bed, and later they could have dinner brought to them in the room without bothering to put their clothes on; things like that were done all the time in hotels, they thought nothing of it. In the morning they could have breakfast the same way, and afterwards dress and go out for a walk, in Central Park perhaps; then lunch at the Swiss restaurant on Forty-seventh Street, and after that back to the hotel for an hour or two before she caught a train home. That would get her back well before dinner....

It was a shame about Roy's overcoat. The preceding Saturday it had been given up on account of the rain, and here it was postponed again. She was reminded of a time many years ago when she had wanted a bright red jacket that was on display in a store window and her father had said it was too conspicuous and wouldn't get it for her. She had refused to eat any dinner that evening, but when Martha brought a plate of escalloped salmon to her room at bedtime she had given in and eaten every bite. The next day her mother had spelled conspicuous for her and she had looked it up in the dictionary....

If Lewis refused to pay Pete and if Pete carried out his threat she would be conspicuous enough. And the children. They would have to leave Maidstone. Roy and Panther would see the papers and learn all about it. Well—about what? She was their mother, wasn't that enough? It was enough for her. But Maidstone was a nice place, and that house was in her name....

In bed with Pete she could say to him, listen, you gave me a wristwatch once, give me something else. Lewis doesn't matter, but I do, don't I? Only she would have to be careful when and how she said it or it might merely make him contrary. Before would be a mistake. Just after would be better, when he was smoking a cigarette and felt like talking.

The train had left One Hundred and Twenty-fifth Street behind and was gliding through the long tunnel between the rows of steel pillars which supported the mansions of Park

Avenue towering above. About here Lora often amused herself by trying to guess when they were passing Sixty-ninth Street, where Lewis lived in a duplex apartment with his wife who had furnished him with two children of alien baritone parentage. She did so now. Poor dear Lewis, who wanted an extension of his privileges! A week ago she had accepted that; now it appeared an absurdity.

The trainmen called out Grand Central, and the train slowed down and stopped with a jerk. What if he isn't here, Lora thought as she moved with the crowd of passengers down the long platform and up the runway into the station itself. He had said he might forget; and, looking at the clock above the information desk and seeing that the train had arrived precisely on time, she found herself thinking, if he isn't here and doesn't come in ten minutes I'll be able to catch the three-fifteen home. At that she stopped dead in her tracks, amazed at the feeling of that thought, for it was a feeling of relief! She stopped and stood still, incredulous and bewildered, demanding of herself what she meant by that. Then with a shake of the head she went on, to the waiting room.

She walked clear around it, up one side and down the other. Pete wasn't there, but that wasn't surprising, since he had never made a point of punctuality. She stood a few moments in the main aisle, and was about to look for a seat on one of the benches when she saw him entering at the Forty-second Street door. Hatless, in a dark suit that showed some signs of wear and none of ever having been pressed, he caught sight of her at once and strode towards her with a suggestion of a jerk, not enough to be called a limp, in his right leg.

"I'm late."

"Just a minute or two."

She saw that people were looking at them, and put her hand

on his arm and moved towards the door. No wonder, she thought, he absolutely looked like a wild man, out like this, among other people. On the sidewalk, Pete motioned for a taxi.

"My room's on Eighteenth Street," he said. He gave the address to the driver.

She made no reply until after they had got in and the taxi had started. Drugstore, hotel—here I am, my god, here I am, was buzzing in her head.

"Let's not go straight to the room," she said.

"Got some errands?"

"Yes. Well…not errands. Would you mind if we drove in the park a while?"

"With that meter staring at me, and me out of a job, and your boyfriend telling me to go to hell?"

"I'll tend to the meter."

"Ah! Just like old times." He leaned forward and slid the window open to speak to the driver, and, coming to Fifth Avenue, the cab swung north. Pete sprawled in his corner and looked at Lora.

"What's the idea of the park?" he asked.

"I don't know."

He peered at her for a long time in silence, while the cab crept forward with the solid lines of traffic on the avenue.

"Look at me," he said finally.

She shook her head.

"Something's happened to you," he declared. "What's up?"

Now was the time, she thought, to suggest the hotel, and ask him to decide which one; being a newspaper man he would know all about it. But first the drugstore. Perhaps on that point he could be trusted after all; it would be a nuisance to go clear to Eleventh Street and back. Of course there were hotels down there.…

"Nothing," she said.

"Don't tell me." He was still peering at her. "You look like Antigone ascending out of hell."

"Nothing is up. I've come, haven't I?"

"Sure you've come. What for? What has happened since last night?"

"Nothing."

As she said it she knew it was false; and yet it was true. Nothing had happened; but something totally unexpected and disconcerting was happening now. She was angry with herself, and frightened, and would not believe it. She forced herself to look at Pete and smile.

"I was thinking it might be better to go to a hotel," she said. "Your room...you said..."

"Yes, go on."

"You know what you said."

"No, I forget, what did I say?"

"It doesn't matter." She was floundering. "Let's go to a hotel."

He burst into laughter. "Hell," he exploded, "let's go and jump in the river; that's what you sound like. We're not going to a hotel, we're going to the middle of Africa and live in a hut and eat coconuts, didn't you know that? No, there wouldn't be coconuts. We'll eat alligators. By god, you've lost your nerve; something's taken it out of you. Last night you wanted me; yesterday you wanted me, first thing—as a novelty, I thought, until you set me right."

"I still want you," she said desperately.

"Bah. You're pale with terror for fear I'll take you up. Don't worry, my love; keep your legs crossed and I'll try to control myself. But what the hell did you come for? Put on your swell rags and ride the damn train and stand around waiting for me—what was all that for?"

"I don't know," she said. I'm giving up, she thought, I'm done for good.

She looked at him and asked abruptly, almost angrily, "Why didn't you take me last night? You could have."

"I don't think so."

"Yes you could. If you'd held me in that chair one more second—"

"I don't believe it. Why do you think I let you go? You weren't having any just then, I saw that, and I swallowed your twaddle about the children and the sacred fireside. Listen." He grinned at her and she turned her face away; he looked remarkably unprepossessing, she thought, with his teeth yellow from smoking and his white unhealthy face with the cheekbones sticking out. For that, instantly, she despised herself. To look away from Pete because he wasn't handsome!

"Listen," he was saying, "you mustn't take it to heart. Everybody has to sell out sooner or later, and you've made a damn good bargain. It's a very pretty little house, and the rugs and chairs and things are very nice. You're a good honest woman too; when you got on that train today you really thought you wanted what you were coming after, I've no doubt of it."

"I know I did," Lora said. "I do. I've made no bargain."

"Oh, yes you have. A good one. I envy you. Look at me, I was trying my hand at a little bargaining myself, and it didn't work. Your boyfriend was too much for me."

"You said he told you to go to hell."

"So he did." Pete grinned. "I saw him this morning. He said I had stated that I wouldn't do anything vulgar and unlovely, and he was curious to find out if I meant it. That was worse than telling me to go to hell, it was shoving me in and putting the lid on. He's no fool at all. That's why he took me out to see you, he wanted to size me up; and here I am, hung out on a limb, with no one to blame but myself. I'm no fool either, I know what the trouble is, I won't follow the rules. I despise their damn rules and I never have followed them and never will. One rule is you've got to lie; I never told anyone a lie in my life. I use these crude terms in deference to the simplicity of your mental processes. Another is that when you take something you've got to pretend you're paying for it. Odious hypocrisy; to hell with it. What's the result? I'm lucky to have a shirt. In the end I'll probably either starve or blow my brains out. If they still had monasteries I'd take a crack at that—provided there were some women handy...."

"You never lied to me," Lora said. So that was what Lewis had done, she was thinking. Did Pete mean what he said? She tried to remember whether it was really true that he had never lied to her. They were in the park now; she looked out of the window at the trees and grass and thought how dingy and disreputable they were compared to those at Maidstone, around her house and up on the hilltop. Did Pete mean what he said? Not that it greatly mattered; if Lewis was to get additional favors he could afford to pay for them if he had to.

She was dimly aware that Pete was talking. The taxi sped smoothly around the curves of the park drives, and Pete talked on. Lora scarcely heard. She had a feeling that she was losing something, leaving something behind forever, and that Pete was taking it. That was what she had come to town for this day, to get it away from him, and now he wouldn't let her have it. He had pretended to see something in her face—oh, no, he hadn't. It had been in her face all right and in her mind too; the only question was why she had been fool enough to come at all and what difference did that make....

The sound of Pete's voice annoyed and exasperated her.

"I want to go back," she said abruptly.

He grinned. "To a hotel?"

"To Grand Central."

He looked at her, but she looked away. Ha, she thought savagely, he wasn't sure after all. She was, though; perfectly sure.

He pulled the window open to speak to the driver again, and at the next entrance the cab wheeled out into Fifth Avenue and turned downtown.

Pete did not start talking again. Out of the corner of her eye she could see him with his head back against the cushion, the breeze from the side window blowing his hair across his forehead and over his eyes; he paid no attention to it. She was reminded of another taxi ride they had taken together, that day in Chicago when she had insisted on going with him to the railroad station; now he was taking her. A minute ago his voice had annoyed her; now she wished he would talk. She wanted to talk to him, but couldn't. She was full of things that must be told, and yet there was nothing to say. There was in her a compulsion that she knew she could not break, but the result was clearly insanity; no one but a crazy person would act the way she was acting. A safe and peaceful sort of insanity, the kind that makes you do things at once incredible and inevitable. She thought of the night before and the morning; and there he was, but he didn't mean anything. Might she not touch him, put out her hand and touch his arm? Yes, she might, but definitely and finally she wouldn't.

They made better time going downtown, and at Fifty-second Street the taxi drew up at the curb.

"I'm getting out here," said Pete, gathering his legs together.

Lora was startled. All at once like this!

"I thought you were coming to the station," she said.

"What's the use? My favorite speakeasy is just around the corner. I'd just have to walk back."

"But...I wanted to talk to you."

"Then you've wasted a precious ten minutes."

"Really, Pete." She grabbed his coat sleeve and pulled him back into the seat. "I want to ask you about Lewis. He isn't going to pay you?"

"He says he'd rather not."

"And you aren't going to—"

She stopped.

Pete grinned. "I suspect," he said, "that we've reached the real business of this conference at last. I think I shall probably not disturb your sacred fireside. Tonight I'll get drunk and then I'll know more about it.—What's that?"

Lora had taken something from her purse and was holding it towards him, thrusting it at him.

"Please," she said. "I don't need it."

He took the roll of bills and flipped its edge.

"A goodly sum," he said, brows lifted. "You're sure you can spare it? I wouldn't deprive any of those multi-fathered children. As a matter of fact, I'm broke. By god, you did have something to say; I might have known it."

He stuffed the bills in his pocket and slid out of his seat towards the door.

"And Pete—" Lora began. He was on the sidewalk with his foot on the running-board.

"Well?"

"I'd hate to have you think what you said about reaching the real business of the day. I really did want to come to you, and I know one thing, I'll never forget you—never—I don't know why I've acted like this—you're the only man—"

"Balls, my love," he interrupted her, so loud that passersby at his elbow jumped; and slammed the door. "Grand Central," he called to the taxi driver, and strode into the crowd.

The taxi started forward. Lora settled back against the cushion, and took off her glove and placed the palm of her hand on the seat where it was still warm from Pete's body. She left it there a moment, then took it away and put her glove back on.

At Forty-ninth Street she looked at her watch and found that she just had time to catch the four-seventeen. At Forty-fifth Street she was thinking that the next day she could bring Roy to town and buy his overcoat.